SONG OF THE CENTURION

By

Steven A. McKay

Copyright © 2019

Book 2 in the

WARRIOR DRUID OF BRITAIN

CHRONICLES

All rights reserved. No part of this book may be reproduced, in whole or in part, without prior written permission from the copyright holder.

ALSO BY STEVEN A. MCKAY

The Forest Lord Series:

Wolf's Head
The Wolf and the Raven
Rise of the Wolf
Blood of the Wolf

Knight of the Cross
Friar Tuck and the Christmas Devil
The Rescue and Other Tales
The Abbey of Death

The Warrior Druid of Britain Chronicles:

The Druid

COMING OCTOBER 2019

Lucia (an AUDIBLE exclusive)

Acknowledgements

Thanks to my old mucker Reay McKay for help with the sailing/boat sections, and Dave Slaney for being a great guy! As always, cheers to my mum for beta reading and pointing out any glaring errors, and my editor Richenda who always amazes me with her insights. My wife, Yvonne, helped with the blurb this time around too. Cheers!

Places in Song of the Centurion

ALT CLOTA   Strathclyde

ARACHAR   Arrochar, Argyll & Bute

ARD DRISAIG   Ardrishaig, Argyll & Bute

AUCHALIC   Lower Auchalick, Argyll & Bute

BALMEANOC   fictional settlement near Dunadd, Argyll & Bute

CARDDEN ROS   Cardross, Argyll & Bute

CARNGHEAL   Cairnbaan, Argyll & Bute

CREONAN   Crinan, Argyll & Bute

DALRIADA   Argyll

DUN BUIC   Dumbuck/Milton, West Dunbartonshire

DUN BREATANN   Dumbarton, West Dunbartonshire

DUNADD   Hillfort in Argyll & Bute

GARRIANUM   Burgh Castle, Norfolk

HIBERNIA   Ireland

IOVA   Iona, Inner Hebrides

LOCH FADA   Loch Long, Argyll & Bute

LOCH LAOMAINN   Loch Lomond, W. Dunbartonshire

LUGUVALIUM   Carlisle, Cumbria

TAIRBERT   Tarbet, Argyll & Bute

*Dedicated to my in-laws, Ronnie and Marjorie.
Thank you for all your help over the years.*

CHAPTER ONE

Northern Britain, Autumn, AD 430

"Get down! Their slingers are attacking!"

There was a horrific rattling as dozens of stones battered against the walls and the defending Damnonii soldiers crouched low to avoid being struck. A slinger's missile could do severe damage if it hit someone in the right place, as a few of the men had discovered to their cost during the previous days.

"Now!" Gavo roared as the attack ended without injuring any of the defenders. "Give them some back!"

Instantly, his men stood up and launched a volley of their own fist-sized rocks down onto the enemy below. The captain grinned as cries of anger and pain filtered up to him. It was much easier to hit people when they were beneath you, especially when they didn't have walls to hide behind.

Not all the enemy slingers were crouching under their shields though, and a sharp-edged, flat rock careered past Gavo, hammering into the neck of a young soldier at his side. The warrior reeled back, a terrible gurgling sound coming from his ruined, bloody throat as he dropped onto the wooden platform they were standing on and Gavo knew the lad would be dead within moments.

Thank the gods though, the enemy were taking casualties of their own beneath the hail of Damnonii missiles, and the besieging army pulled back now, out of range, heralding another in a long line of stand-offs.

"That's it," Gavo shouted in fury. "Run, you bastards!"

Dun Breatann, ancient capital of Alt Clota, was under siege, and had been for almost a week, the Picts from the far north led by King Drest having finally grown tired of the attacks on their raiding parties by King Coroticus's soldiers.

For generations, livestock theft from neighbouring tribes was an accepted part of life – part of a young warrior's coming-of-age. Unwritten rules made it clear that any captured during such an action could be beaten, but then sent on their way home, to try again another day.

Now, though, Coroticus, outraged by his daughter Catia's recent abduction, was slaughtering every such raider he could find in his lands and displaying their severed heads as ghoulish trophies – warnings – on the towering rock of Dun Breatann. It wasn't just Pictish thieves suffering such violence either – Dalriadans, Selgovae and Votadini tribesmen had all been killed by the Damnonii king's forces. In response, Drest had formed an alliance with the other kings and led them here for vengeance.

To Queen Narina it was a ludicrous situation to be in – a war started over the execution of a few cattle thieves. Yet her husband had broken with tradition, despite her protestations, and now Alt Clota was paying the price. Standing high on the eastern peak of the fortress, she looked away from the guard captain, Gavo, commanding the defending warriors on the walls, and turned her attention to the tents, cooking-fires and massed, undisciplined, ranks of the enemy camping at the foot of her home.

Standing two hundred and forty feet high, and surrounded on three sides by the river Clota, Dun Breatann had never been taken by a besieging army. The queen shook her head sadly and turned to her maidservant, Enica, whose downcast expression mirrored her own.

"They're wasting their time," Enica muttered, shifting her gaze back to the tiny figures on the ground so far below them. "King Drest must have known that when he embarked on this foolish course."

Narina didn't answer for a while. She could see Drest's tent, grander and more colourful than the others surrounding it, and she wondered what was going through his mind at that moment.

"I don't think their siege is so foolish," the queen finally said. "Coroticus pushed them all too far and they're within their rights to strike back. Besides, they might say they're here to avenge their dead warriors, but there's more to it than that. Drest, and Loarn in particular, would like to make our lands their own. This is merely their first move towards that end."

"They'll never take this place though, my lady," Enica said and her voice was full of conviction. "We have fresh water from the spring that comes up between the two peaks and enough men to rebuff any attempts to scale the gatehouses. Food is plentiful too, since your husband stockpiled it when he heard of the approaching army."

Enica was correct in her assessment and Narina wondered if the woman surreptitiously listened at Coroticus's door when he met with his advisors. It wouldn't surprise her. Enica was a canny servant, which was why Narina liked her.

"They'll need to leave soon enough," the maid went on as if she'd spent many hours thinking this over.

"Their men will be needed at home to bring in the harvests and so on, yes, I know that," Narina nodded. "But what of our people whose homes Drest's soldiers destroyed? The people he killed on his way here, and those he'll no doubt kill on his way back north again?"

"At least he didn't destroy our crops," Enica said and Narina peered at her thoughtfully. There was no way the servant could have known that unless she had truly spent a long time listening to Coroticus's private councils or…Narina took in the woman's unlined, pretty face, full lips, and firm, shapely figure and resolved to find out if Enica had taken a lover amongst the king's advisors. That kind of information could come in very handy.

"No, he hasn't destroyed our crops," said the queen with a wave of her hand. "Yet. Probably because he hoped they would belong to him once he defeated us." The queen turned away from the depressing sight on the ground far below and walked slowly back towards the royal chambers. They were located within the building in the very centre of the rock, flanked by birch trees and the rising twin peaks, one of which was gently rounded while the other, the higher one, was narrow and so steep that it was a challenge for many people to climb. Indeed, it was so narrow no proper buildings could be erected upon it and, other than a single sentry watching the Clota for invading ships, only a giant raven could be seen there most days, its strange cry—almost like the bark of some weird dog—heard pealing out across the ancient rock.

The thought of that majestic bird, black with a white tuft on its neck, brought Bellicus to mind. The druid had somehow trained the raven to speak—it could say 'hello' and cough like a person thanks to Bel's tutelage—and she felt an ache in her heart just as she always did when the druid came to mind. Was he dead?

Was her beautiful, sweet daughter?

A feeling of anxiety swept through her and she almost stumbled like one of the many people who grew dizzy when looking down from the lofty summit of Dun Breatann. What if Bel returned today, with Catia? They would walk straight into Drest's besieging army and be torn to pieces!

Enica noticed her lady's discomfort and placed a steadying hand on her upper arm as Narina pulled herself together. Bellicus was no fool, and besides, he knew Drest well; there would be no danger there.

If only the giant warrior-druid *would* return. It had been such a long time since he left to hunt the princess's kidnappers, with no word coming to them from any who had seen him on the road, and it was hard not to give up hope.

Or go mad, rather like Coroticus seemed to have done in starting this insane war that no-one could ever truly win.

As they walked in through the iron-bound doors to the main hall the king peered up from where he was sitting, ale mug in hand but clear-eyed and, when he spoke Narina believed her assessment of him to be close to the mark.

"I'm going to lead the men out," Coroticus said decisively, jaw set in determination.

"What? You can't!" Narina shook her head in confusion. "There's no need: they'll leave soon enough. Even my servant, Enica, knows that. Why take a chance of losing to Drest?"

"You think I'd suffer defeat?" Coroticus's eyes flared and Narina remembered too late that she had to speak carefully around her husband these days, as any slight or question of his manhood could send him into a sullen silence or, worse, a rage. Slightly behind him stood Senecio, an older man from the southern lands who seemed to have wormed his way into the king's favour recently. Narina wondered if he'd had some druid training for he had, on occasion, a silver tongue and mannerisms similar to those versed in the old ways.

"Of course I don't," she replied, turning her attention back to her husband and trying to make it sound as if she had every confidence in him. "But many of our warriors would die for nothing."

Somewhat mollified he sat back in his chair and shrugged. "That's a warrior's fate, my dear. To die. And I'm fed up sitting here like a frightened woman while Drest pillages my lands."

Before Narina could say another word the sound of someone running up the stairs outside came to them and a young man wearing chainmail much too big for his spare frame looked in through the open door, breathing heavily after his climb from the bottom of the fortress.

"My lord king," he gasped but his youth allowed him to regain his breath much faster than Narina could have and he continued in a steadier tone. "Drest would speak with you."

"He's at the gates?"

"Aye, my lord," the youth confirmed. "The captain says Drest has brought the Dalriadan and Votadini leaders with him to see you as well. Their attack has halted, for now."

Coroticus upended the last of the beer into his mouth and stood up with a determined half-smile on his face.

"Be careful," Narina cautioned, grasping his arm gently as he followed the young guardsman out the door. "Don't let them get to you." She smiled and was pleased to see the expression mirrored in his eyes.

"Come down with me," he said. "I always value your counsel. Not you." He waved a dismissive hand towards Enica and Narina wondered if he too suspected the servant had been eavesdropping on him, for his gesture seemed loaded with some hidden meaning the queen couldn't quite fathom.

Leaving Enica standing with eyes downcast Narina followed Coroticus and the guard out of the building and down the narrow steps which had been carved from the living rock. A robin flitted along before them, eyeing them curiously, and Narina couldn't help but feel her spirits rise. Perhaps the red-breasted little bird was a good omen and Drest was here to parley before lifting the siege and heading home again…

Gavo noticed them as soon as they reached the bottom of the staircase and hurried over to meet the king, nodding respectfully towards Narina as they continued to walk towards the gatehouse while the young messenger drifted away back to his fellows lining the wooden outer walls.

"Are they all here?" Coroticus asked, looking at the captain.

Gavo nodded, calm and as immovable as the rock they stood upon. "Aye, my lord. Drest, Cunneda and Loarn Mac Eirc. They're waiting outside."

"Have they said anything? Tried to speak to you or the men?"

Gavo shrugged. "The usual nonsense, you know how it is. Telling us we can't win this war, that we should overthrow you and let Drest in because he's a better leader than you. As I say: the usual shit. Don't worry, the men didn't care to listen to it."

Narina could tell by the man's expression he was holding something back, but she didn't press him, knowing Gavo was loyal to her husband—more so than any other man in Dun Breatann. Whatever he was hiding was presumably for what he saw as a good reason. She looked at the warriors standing on the platform that ran the length of the wall and took in the looks from them.

No doubt a few of them had muttered agreement with the Pictish king's suggestions. If so, it was entirely prudent that Gavo should conceal the fact from the unpredictable Coroticus.

She followed her husband up the steps of the gatehouse, guard captain bringing up the rear. The building had been built after the old Roman designs, with ditches outside to make the walls higher than they were on the inside, while a roofed platform offered protection from missiles. Even if the enemy were, somehow, to break through or destroy the walls or gatehouse, the men of Dun Breatann would simply retreat up the stairs and mount a new defence at a second gate which could only be approached by that steep, narrow walkway.

No wonder no hostile army had ever managed to mount a successful attack on the fortress; its reputation as being impregnable was well-founded and Drest had to know that.

Narina's hopes of a parley and peaceful conclusion to the siege were tempered but not extinguished with the first word out of the Pictish ruler's mouth.

"Surrender."

Coroticus simply laughed down at the men gathered outside the gates.

"Surrender," Drest repeated, expression solemn. Nor was there any sign of amusement on his companion's faces. Loarn Mac Eirc of the Dalriadan's was tall and slim, with grey hair which he wore long at the back although it was completely bald on top. Cunneda, king of the Votadini, was also tall, but younger than Drest or Loarn, with a great bushy red beard and close-cropped hair. Both men gazed up at Coroticus with looks of irritation.

"Why would I surrender?" the ruler of Alt Clota demanded. "You will never take these walls as you'll soon find out. We have enough food to last for weeks and, unless you have ships as well as infantry, we can simply sail downriver to replenish our supplies any time we need to." He waved a hand dismissively. "Go home, Drest. You're wasting everyone's time here and your people will soon need to start gathering their crops in for the winter."

"Is that Narina I see behind you?" Cunneda of the Votadini asked. "As pretty as ever, eh? I've always fancied a go on her. Once we smash these gates open my wish will come true." He leered suggestively, stroking his red beard, and the dozen warriors who had escorted them laughed, adding crude comments of their own.

The queen made as if to step forward and address the Votadini king, but Coroticus held out his arm. These preliminary insults were nothing new – part and parcel of battle negotiations since time began. "Ignore him," the king muttered to Narina not unkindly. "No doubt there will be more to come. Empty words." He turned back to the enemy delegation and spat over the wall towards them. "Like I say," he shouted, "try and force your way in. My men will slaughter you like animals and then I'll ride to your fortress in Dun Edin, Cunneda, and see how *your* wife enjoys the attentions of my Damnonii warriors! She'll probably enjoy it more than being humped by you, with that pitiful excuse of a beard, you ugly whoreson."

Coroticus's men cheered and hooted with laughter, glad to see their king strike back with a barb of his own. Narina simply rolled her eyes at the posturing but she was glad her husband wasn't rising to the bait. Waiting until the besieging army returned to their homes was the sensible thing to do.

Her heart sank, though, and a cold chill swept through her as a new voice, rich and powerful, carried easily up to her from below.

"Where is the princess, Catia?"

Narina shoved Coroticus's restraining arm aside and pushed past him to look upon the speaker. It was many years since she'd last seen the man, but she knew him well enough: Qunavo, the

7

Pictish druid. The man who had trained Bellicus in the old ways on the sacred isle of Iova. He'd served the kings of the northern lands for decades and was loyal to Drest. With his flowing white beard, hooded robe and long staff he looked every inch the powerful druid, and he stared up at the lord of Dun Breatann now with a knowing expression on his seamed face.

Then there was a flicker of recognition on Qunavo's face, and even a slight nod of the head as if in greeting and Narina turned to see Senecio had followed them onto the battlements. The man had lived in Dun Breatann for a number of years now, working as a clerk or some other administrative role, but he seemed more visible these days. Always hanging about Coroticus. Taking advantage of the king's weak state of mind perhaps.

"What do you know about my daughter?" Coroticus demanded, oblivious to Narina's thoughts, his composure severely rattled at this unexpected mention of the abducted princess. "Do you have her? Did you pay those mercenaries to take her from me Drest, you bastard?"

The Pictish king shook his head but it was the druid who spoke again.

"We know nothing about your daughter's disappearance," Qunavo attested. "Other than the fact she was taken south. But you already know that, don't you? You sent my pupil, Bellicus, after her."

"Should have gone yourself," Cunneda shouted mockingly. "Sending someone else after your own flesh and blood while you cower here in your stronghold like a frightened woman. For shame Coroticus, I thought men of the Damnonii tribe were braver than that!"

Narina had felt like her legs would give way beneath her at the first mention of Catia's name but she had, by now, pulled herself together and she grasped her husband's arm, whispering calming words into his ear.

"Don't let them get to you, Coroticus. You know how this game works. This is just another ploy to anger you and make you act rashly. Ignore them and they'll have to go away."

The king, eyes blazing, seemed like he wouldn't listen to Narina's counsel but, after a moment he let out a heavy sigh and forced a smile that was more of a grimace onto his face. Narina relaxed and wished Drest and his lackeys would just piss off back to their own lands right now.

The Dalriadan king hadn't yet had his say though. Loarn mac Eirc tilted his head back to look up at Coroticus and, in clear but oddly accented Cumbric, told the Damnonii king what he wanted to do, sexually, to the missing princess.

It was too much for Narina who let out a tortured sob and felt her legs give way. Coroticus instinctively steadied her so she wouldn't hurt herself as she fell, but she knelt on the wooden platform, mercifully hidden from the enemies' watching eyes, crying for her stolen child whose fate was yet unknown.

Coroticus, shocked into silence, stared murderously at Loarn Mac Eirc for what seemed an age and then, through gritted teeth spoke in a soft voice that somehow reached the men outside.

"I will kill you for that," he promised the Dalriadan. "It's one thing to trade insults about a man's wife, but to say such a thing about his missing child is…" He trailed off, lost for words, before drawing his sword and pointing it at the older king. "I swear to Dis, god of the underworld – I will send you to him as an offering. I will slice out your cursed tongue and fill your empty mouth with your own balls before I cut off your limbs one by one and leave you to die in agony."

The onlooking warriors from both sides remained quiet as the powerful oath was cast and the druid Qunavo stepped a pace to the side, away from Loarn, as if he feared to be tainted by such a hate-filled vow. The Dalriadan king seemed completely unfazed by the change in atmosphere however, laughing up at Coroticus and rubbing his crotch suggestively.

"Will you surrender?" Drest demanded, clearly trying to move the negotiation past this dark interlude. "Or should I order the attack?"

Coroticus replied to the Pictish king but his eyes never left Loarn Mac Eirc as he did so. "Do your worst, Drest. When your men are dead, I'll march out and become High King of all the lands north of the Roman walls."

With that he turned away and knelt to take Narina in his arms. Neither moved for a long time, not caring who saw them in their sad embrace but, after a while the sound of the enemy warriors heading back to their own lines could be heard.

"They were right," the king murmured as silence fell all around them. Even Gavo, faithful captain of the guard, had retreated off the gatehouse platform, allowing the king and queen some small measure of privacy.

"About what?" Narina asked, her voice thin and filled with despair.

"I should have gone after Catia instead of sending Bellicus to do it."

Narina didn't reply. Not because she agreed with the statement – she didn't. She was simply too dazed to reassure her husband at that point.

"What are we going to do?" Coroticus wondered. It was a rhetorical question but Narina looked up at him from tear-reddened eyes and bared her teeth.

"What are we going to do?" she demanded, and the king was taken aback by the fury in her gaze. "When those bastards leave to go back to their own lands," she growled, "you will take the men northwest and fulfil your oath to Dis, do you hear me? I want to nail Loarn mac Eirc's head to the top of this damn gatehouse myself!"

CHAPTER TWO

"Are you my father?"

The question shocked Bellicus and it took all his druid training to hold the neutral expression on his face rather than turning to stare at the eight-year-old princess.

Bel hadn't expected Catia, who was riding now with the former centurion Duro, to ask him this and he mentally kicked himself for not foreseeing it. He had to say something in reply, or the girl would grow suspicious, so he glanced across at her with a baffled look, one eyebrow raised, a half-smile on his lips.

"Eh? What are you talking about, lass? Coroticus – King of Alt Clota – is your father, that's why you're a princess. Did the Saxons addle your brain when they abducted you?"

Again, the giant druid mentally berated himself, this time for asking such an insensitive question. Of course her brain had been affected by her harrowing ordeal – being kidnapped by a Saxon warband and dragged half the length of Britain before being almost sacrificed to the invaders' brutal gods would do that to a person.

Anyone would have found it hard to deal with, never mind a little girl.

She had been mostly silent ever since Bellicus and the centurion had rescued her from the clutches of the warlord Hengist and his *volva* – witch – Thorbjorg, and now she retreated back into herself, staring at the road ahead as the two horses carried their passengers north.

"Sorry, Catia," Bel said softly. "You've been through a lot, but we'll soon be home. We'll be in Luguvalium in a day or two – that's where Duro lives – and then it's not very far back to Dun Breatann. Coroticus and Queen Narina will be overjoyed to see you safe again."

She didn't reply other than to purse her lips and Bel looked at the centurion who was staring back at him thoughtfully. Thankfully Duro kept any questions to himself, for now, but the druid expected the man might want to know the truth of it once they stopped for the night and Catia fell asleep.

It was another fine, sunny day although a gentle breeze from the east was bringing puffy grey clouds that promised to lower the temperature. Beside them, the druid's powerful dog, Cai, loped along, keeping pace with them easily enough, muscles rippling in his legs, tongue lolling, ever-alert for signs of danger.

Bel was glad of the hound's presence, but he had started the journey to rescue the princess with two dogs. The older one, Eolas, was killed in a fight with the Saxons and the loss was still painfully fresh in the druid's mind. Still, Eolas's sacrifice hadn't been wasted – Catia might not be quite herself but she was at least physically unharmed.

The memory of that dark night at the stone circle known as the Giant's Dance would live in his mind forever. The laughing *volva* ritually slaughtering four unfortunate Briton slaves as eerie blue lights and weird sounds terrified the Saxon warriors, before, at last, Catia was on her knees, preparing to have her throat cut open with the witch's stone knife.

Bellicus looked over again at Catia and his heart ached to see the once-gregarious child now so withdrawn from the world around her.

All he could do was show her kindness and compassion.

And pray to Lug that she wouldn't bring up the question of her parenthood in front of Coroticus once they were home again…

"Shall we stop for something to eat?"

That at least brought a smile from the princess. During the weeks of her captivity the Saxons had fed her mainly dried beef and bread; another trial for her to endure along with the rest. Bellicus had made an effort, therefore, to vary their meals as far as was possible given their circumstances. There seemed little chance of the thwarted Saxons tracking them, so the druid was content to allow a fire for cooking when they stopped at night.

They hunted, or bartered for ingredients in settlements they passed, and Duro, who made his living as a baker in Luguvalium, was able to cook up tasty soups and pottage which Bel would season with the herbs and spices he carried in hidden pockets within his dark robe.

It was a wonderful sight to see the little girl tucking into a steaming bowl of mutton broth in the evenings but, for now, they dismounted and made do with bread and cheese. It wasn't the greatest meal, the late summer heat making the cheese soft and warm, but Catia wolfed it down with gusto and Bel was pleased that she at least hadn't lost her appetite.

That was surely a good sign.

Cai, his own meal of dried pig liver quickly finished, lay next to the girl, great head resting protectively against her leg, and she stroked his smooth coat as she ate in silence.

Bel was unsure of his own feelings. He'd always felt an affection for the princess but now, as he looked at her, he wondered how he should feel and, rarely for him, didn't really have an answer. He thought he could see similarities in their features, and mannerisms, and a swelling of pride built inside him that he'd fathered such a strong girl.

But he could never tell her the truth – Coroticus would surely kill the druid if word was ever to get out. Or would he? Bellicus hadn't known he was sleeping with Queen Narina on that night nine years ago, and the king was his friend. Maybe the man would accept the reality - embrace it - once he came to terms with the shock of it. After all, as Narina had said before Bel left to find the abducted girl, Coroticus had been unable to produce an heir to his throne.

At least this way, when the king died or stepped down, Catia would marry a suitable chieftain or his son, and the throne would remain within the family. That was better than the other possibility, of a civil war within Alt Clota as ambitious lordlings fought for power. What difference did it really make anyway? Coroticus and Catia had a bond as strong as any father and daughter, and nothing could take that away.

Bel felt a wave of jealousy wash over him then and it shocked him to his core. He wanted the queen, and he wanted to be a father to Catia.

He brushed the feeling aside—he'd never had such thoughts before, and he attributed it to the strangeness of their situation and all they'd been through in recent weeks. Certainly, he didn't covet Narina or aspire to supplant Coroticus, the idea was ludicrous.

"You know the Saxons will be coming after us?"

Catia's statement brought him back to reality with a jolt and, almost guiltily, looked across at her.

"Even if they do, they can't catch us on foot. You don't need to worry about them anymore, princess."

"If your horse is so swift, why did it take you so long to rescue me?"

There was no accusation in her question, much to Bel's relief, just genuine curiosity.

"I had no idea where they were going." He shrugged. "I had to depend on my own tracking abilities and, more often, Cai's nose. The Saxons knew exactly where they were heading so made better time than me, blundering about the place looking for signs of your passing, asking locals if they'd seen you. I also had troubles of my own on the journey that held me up." He shrugged again. "But this time things are different. We are mounted, and we know exactly where we're going."

"So do they," Catia replied. "And Horsa will not let us just ride off without trying to kill us." She looked away into the trees thoughtfully. "He's an animal. We should be ready for them if they find us."

Duro finished his meal and took their small trenchers to the shallow stream that flanked the road next to them. Its waters were low thanks to the dry summer the country had enjoyed that year, but he managed to get the crumbs and soggy flakes of cheese from the wooden receptacles.

"Can't do any harm to follow Catia's advice," he grunted, nodding reassuringly at the youngster who managed the ghost of a smile in return. "If the Saxons can find horses of their own they'll push them hard along this very road. I don't think any of them recognised me, so they won't make for Luguvalium, but this is the only main Roman road that leads to Dun Breatann around here."

"Very well," Bellicus said, getting to his feet and making his way across to Darac. "We'll keep our eyes open and ride harder. Not camp so close to the road each night either." He waved Catia across to him. "And you can ride with me. If Horsa or Hengist or any of them do appear, I want you with me."

"Are you saying I couldn't defend her?" Duro demanded, climbing onto his horse with an expression of mock outrage on his face.

"You can stop and defend her if you like," Bel laughed in reply. "I was just thinking Darac can run much faster than your old nag, so don't expect us to hang around at your side as you fight them off!"

The druid looked down at the girl in front of him and was glad to see his joke had reassured her. She'd seen Darac in full flow back in Dun Breatann, where the big black had been well known as the fastest horse in the land.

If it did come to flight, the Saxons wouldn't catch Darac.

He hoped.

CHAPTER THREE

Lossio let go of the bowstring and there was a satisfying crack as the arrow shot across the open meadow before hammering home in its target. The old legionary, trim and lean despite his fifty years, grinned in triumph as the rest of the hares scattered, leaving their companion to his fate.

"That'll make a nice stew for tonight's dinner," the hunter muttered as he left the concealment of the birch grove and ambled across to remove his missile from the small carcass. He placed the hare inside a sack and thought about trying to bring down something bigger but rejected the notion. The little hare, along with some cabbage and fresh bread, would be enough.

The thought of bread reminded him of his friend Duro. They had served together in the legions twenty years before and been neighbours here in Luguvalium ever since. But the baker had followed the giant druid on his quest to rescue the Alt Clotan princess and no-one had seen or heard from him since.

Lossio headed back towards the settlement, wondering when, or if, Duro would return. The baker would surely have a wonderful tale to tell over a few mugs of beer. The old legionary hoped to Mithras that his friend and the druid had somehow managed to save the young princess from whatever fate the Saxon scum planned for her. He hadn't seen the girl himself as he'd been off hunting that day too, but the whole incident was the talk of the place for weeks afterwards. Some of the local men had died as a result of Duro's actions in standing up to the Saxons, but Lossio felt his friend had been right to try and help the lass.

He'd have done the same if he'd have been there. In fact, he wished he *had* been there, to stand shoulder to shoulder with the centurion—they might have made a better job of stopping the invaders if he'd been with Duro for the fight.

The thoughts filled his head as he walked, so he was close to home before he even realised it and, when he spotted his own house, he pictured the hare, neatly skinned and cooked, its juices mixed with beer and oats, and his mouth began to water in anticipation. In fact, he could almost smell the cooking fires.

Then a scream pierced the air, followed almost immediately by a man's howl of agony, and Lossio forgot all about his feast. He wasn't imagining the stench of woodsmoke – houses were burning in Luguvalium, as evidenced by the black soot curling into the air not too far ahead.

"Shit." What should he do? Yes, he'd been a soldier of Rome, but never more than that. Unlike Duro, he wasn't good at making quick decisions. That was why Lossio had remained a lowly legionary while the younger man rapidly rose to the rank of centurion.

Another woman's scream was cut off by the sound of a fist meeting flesh and he ran to press himself against the rear of the nearest building, restringing his bow and nocking an arrow to it, in case whoever was setting the fires appeared from the street at the front. He listened intently, trying to make sense of what was happening. There were harsh, guttural voices, laughter interspersed with the tortured cries of that poor woman, and footsteps as a number of men passed his position and moved on, no doubt to perpetrate more wickedness.

Lossio lived alone, with no family to rescue from the attackers, but Luguvalium was his home, its inhabitants his friends. If Duro could steel himself to make a stand against invaders, so could he.

Slowly he edged his way around the side of his hiding place and peered out into the street. He knew instantly who the enemy were: Saxons. They were here again! One of them was on top of a young girl Lossio knew well. Just fourteen years old, poor Velbutena stared across the ground, her eyes meeting his pleadingly, and the old soldier couldn't help himself. He brought up the hunting bow, sighted along the arrow, and let fly.

Decades of practise made his aim steady and the missile plunged deeply into the Saxon rapist's face, smashing apart most of the nose and right eye socket, rocking the hairy head backwards and killing the man instantly.

His victim needed no help to remove the corpse, the ordeal giving her desperate strength, and she rolled the Saxon off and tried to stand. Her legs gave way beneath her though, and she crawled, sobbing, past a rapidly burning house, towards the prone figure of an older woman.

Lossio watched the girl collapse on top of her mother's unmoving body but he couldn't just stand there, waiting for more of the enemy to appear. He raised his eyes to the sky, prayed to Mithras for luck, and crept back behind the house that had hidden him before, moving along it in the direction of the town centre.

It sounded like some of the local men had finally realised what was happening and come out with weapons ready to stand against the sea-wolves. The sounds of fighting—clatters, clangs, shouts and cries of pain—rang out across the town as the old legionary headed towards it, a fresh arrow already fitted to his bowstring.

He slipped in between another pair of wooden buildings which brought him, judging from the noise, almost on top of the battle. Peering around the side of the wall he was stunned by what he saw. Without thinking, he loosed his arrow and watched it slam home, through the wolf-pelt on his targeted Saxon's back. The thick fur, no doubt combined with chainmail beneath, took the killing force from the arrow, but it knocked the Saxon off balance, allowing the local he'd been about to kill the chance to land a flurry of furious slashes.

Lossio didn't wait to find out what happened next. As the Saxon died, the former legionary sprinted away to the northwest where he knew bushes grew thickly enough for him to hide in.

He felt no shame in his flight. He had done what he could and two of the whoresons were dead thanks to him, but Luguvalium was doomed. He'd known it as soon as he saw the battle, if it could properly be called that. Only four of the townsmen remained alive, as at least double that number of Saxons closed in to finish the slaughter. Lossio couldn't have stopped that happening; if he'd waited any longer he'd simply have died along with the rest.

He circled around, through the woods that came right up to the edge of the town, and found the juniper bushes easily – they'd been growing in that same spot since he was a child and used them for games of hide and seek. They served a similar purpose for him now and he threw himself onto the ground, trying to wish himself invisible as he stared back towards doomed Luguvalium.

By luck or design, the Saxon warband had picked a good time to attack the place, as many of the young men were out in the fields, harvesting the wheat that would see the town through the winter. Lossio hoped someone had gone to raise the alarm and the workers would return quickly but, for now, he watched, stomach tightened into a knot, as the invading warriors finished off the last of the Britons opposing them and then…

"No!" Lossio couldn't help an oath escaping his lips as a huge limping Saxon, taller than the rest of them, led a middle-aged lady out from one of the houses. Behind him a pair of similarly murderous-looking warriors pushed and kicked Dumnocoveros, the settlement's headman, ahead of them until he finally collapsed, distraught, onto the ground beside the corpses of his slaughtered countrymen.

The woman was stronger than the old man though, and she twisted around to try and slap her tall captor, but the Saxon knocked her arm easily aside and punched her in the mouth. She fell with a cry onto the road and didn't try to get back up, doubtless too dazed from the tremendous blow.

Only then did Lossio begin to wonder if Duro's impetuous actions of weeks earlier had been wise.

"The old man here," one of the warriors kicked Dumnocoveros brutally in the ribs as he addressed the fallen woman, "says you're the fat baker's wife. Yes?"

The Saxon's accent was thick, but he spoke the Briton language well enough and Lossio wished he could force his legs to carry him somewhere far away from this, for he knew only too well what was going to happen next. He was rooted to the ground though, too horrified to move.

"Mithras, I beg you: don't let her suffer too much."

As the giant Saxon undid his breeches Lossio knew his prayer would go unheeded and he tried to shut his eyes and ears to what was happening before him.

* * *

"About time you showed up."

Bellicus's head spun to the right, to the bushes that grew beside the road, his sword flashing out of its scabbard before another moment passed. Even Cai hadn't noticed the newcomer in the shadowy foliage but the voice that addressed him was hardly threatening. Bel was somewhat on edge given their circumstances though, and ready to defend Catia from anyone that might seek to thwart their journey home.

"Oh, it's you." The druid smiled in recognition, but he didn't put his sword away just yet. "Lug's blessings on you, old one—"

"Never mind that," the woman grumbled irritably, looking up at Bel and then to Duro, a look of distaste on her face. "What took you so long to get here?"

"What's the hurry, Tancorix?" the centurion demanded, her tone and agitation permeating the atmosphere like the scent of rotten eggs. Or death. "Look, we rescued the little girl—remember, the one whose life you saved with your potion?"

"Aye, I guessed as much," the white-haired, bent old crone replied, nodding ruefully. "That'll be why the Saxons returned. They obviously recognised you, baker, and came looking for revenge, or to recapture her."

A shiver ran through Bellicus and he glanced at Duro, whose face had turned pale. "They're in Luguvalium? Now?"

Tancorix shrugged. "They attacked the place earlier and some of the children ran to my house in the forest. They told me what was happening, and I figured you would be along any time."

"I have to go," Duro said, his voice a hoarse whisper as he hastily lifted the unresisting Catia from the horse they shared and down to the ground next to the wise-woman. "Alatucca…"

At the mention of the centurion's wife Bellicus understood the man's need for haste and he nodded decisively. "Can you take care of the girl while we head for the town?" he asked Tancorix, as Duro glared impatiently at him then couldn't wait any longer and kicked his horse into a gallop towards Luguvalium.

"She'll be safe with me, druid," the wise-woman promised, but Bel had already urged Darac into a canter, Cai running with them, following the stricken Duro at a short distance, not wanting to charge blindly into a place where they knew a Saxon warband had been on the rampage just a short time before.

Was he making a mistake going with the baker to see what had befallen Alatucca? They'd only just rescued Catia and here was placing her into the care of a doddering old woman. He pushed the doubts aside—Tancorix was no fool, she'd survived on her own in the forest for decades. She'd take good care of Catia until…What?

If the Saxons were in Luguvalium what chance did he and Duro have against them?

It didn't matter—Duro was his friend. He had to help him.

The trees whipped past and the settlement soon came in sight, the black greasy smoke that rose above it confirming their worst fears. That much smoke didn't come from just one or two houses—much of the town must be burning.

Bellicus kicked Darac's flanks, pushing the big black faster for fear he'd lose sight of Duro who would surely ride directly to his own home, searching for Alatucca.

As he barrelled into the outskirts of the settlement frightened faces stared up at him. Locals.

There appeared to be no fighting now, although a number of bloody corpses dotted the ground – there had been a battle of sorts earlier, but the Saxons had either been defeated, or moved on before a force of Britons large enough to stand against them could be mustered. Bellicus wagered it was the latter and he muttered a prayer to Taranis to strike down the craven sea-wolves.

The town was a mess. At least a dozen buildings were burning, some of which had collapsed in upon themselves already, and the corpses of men, women, children, even dogs, lay in the road. The air was thick with black smoke and the tortured wailing of the survivors.

Darac dodged past a smouldering cart that was tethered to a pair of dead oxen and around a corner into a narrow side street where Bellicus saw Duro's horse standing outside a low building he took for the bakery. The guess was confirmed a moment later when the centurion, spatha in hand, hurtled out through the open doorway and, apparently forgetting his horse, sprinted up the road past Bellicus.

"Wait. Where are you going?" the druid demanded, trying to turn Darac without much success in the confined space.

"She's not in there," Duro shouted over his shoulder. "I'm going to the town centre to see if anyone knows where she is!"

At last, Bellicus made his mount turn and they sped after the receding figure of the centurion, Cai just behind, passing more distraught locals on the way as another possible source of trouble hit the druid. It wasn't just the Saxons who would be in the mood for killing.

"Duro, wait!" The druid's call went unheeded again, but he reached the town centre moments later and jumped down in a fluid motion from Darac's saddle, sword coming into his hand almost of its own volition. Then, with some sense of what the future might hold, he sheathed the sword again and reached up to unclip his staff from the horse's saddle instead.

There were no signs of continued fighting here, so his staff of office would surely be more use than the naked steel of a longsword.

Almost as tall as Bellicus's near seven-foot height, the length of ashwood was topped with a finely cast bronze eagle—the sight of it would command respect from almost any Briton but even if it didn't, it doubled as an effective, and quite deadly, weapon in the druid's expert hands.

"Easy boy," he murmured, stroking Cai's ears reassuringly. The dog had seen plenty of death in his time, but an atmosphere like this was enough to unnerve anyone, man or beast.

Although the battle was over, the centre of town was a scene of carnage. Bloody, brutalised corpses, mostly of men but some women too, lay scattered about the place and, much to Bel's chagrin, only a couple appeared to be Saxon. He looked around, a sick feeling in his stomach at what the raiders had done to the people of Luguvalium, and then his attention was drawn to the kneeling figure of Duro.

An anguished cry came from the centurion's lips and he collapsed onto the lifeless body of a woman. Bel had no doubt who she was: Alatucca.

He stepped wearily past corpses and stunned locals to stand over his bereft companion and another body caught his eye. A man in his early-fifties, wearing hunting clothes, it was Duro's former legionary friend, a man Bellicus had met on his previous visit to the town. Lossio, that was his name. His proximity to the murdered Alatucca suggested the old legionary had tried his best to stop the Saxons from doing whatever it was they'd been doing to her.

It was easy to guess what that had been.

The centurion hadn't even noticed Lossio yet, so lost was he in grieving for his dead wife, and neither did he notice the arrival of half-a-dozen more townsmen, led by a stocky man - presumably the blacksmith - wearing a bloodstained leather apron.

Bellicus guessed what was going to happen next and he stepped in front of the sobbing Duro, staff of office held in front of him in both hands, defensively, knowing his great size, and the muscular wardog beside him, would force the men to take a moment before they acted rashly.

"It's the baker," the blacksmith shouted, pointing his reddened hammer at Duro. "The bastard decided to show his face here again. Too damn late though, the Saxons have already finished their bloody work and moved on!"

"Aye, where have you been, you useless sack of crap?" another demanded, cheeks flushing red with anger.

"This is all your fault, you fat old arsehole!"

One of the small party made to run forward, with the clear intention of attacking Duro who still hadn't lifted his head from Alatucca's chest, but Bel stepped forward, blocking the man's way with his staff.

The townsman seemed to notice the giant druid for the first time and stopped in his tracks, looking up into Bellicus's eyes. A slight shake of the druid's head, and a low growl from deep in Cai's chest, was enough to send the would-be attacker back a few steps, to the safety of his friends, but he pointed a long, bloody knife at Duro. "My brother's dead because of the fat baker. He should never have started that fight with the Saxons. What was he trying to do anyway?"

"Rescue some foreign lass," the blacksmith shouted. "None of his, or our, business. And this is what we get for it. Half the place burnt to the ground and a dozen or more of our people raped and murdered!"

Bel could see the righteous fury in the men's faces – it burned like the fire he'd seen in the eyes of the Christian priests when they'd come to Dun Breatann to convert the people to their new religion. It was a fire born of conviction. This blacksmith and his friends believed Duro to be the cause of Luguvalium's misery and, unless the druid could stop them like he'd stopped those priests, they would string the centurion up right now from the nearest strong branch.

CHAPTER FOUR

"Duro isn't to blame for what happened here today," Bellicus said, voice low but powerful enough thanks to his years of specialist training that it penetrated even the grief-ravaged minds of the angry townsmen. "We all are."

"What does that mean?" the blacksmith demanded, eyes fixed on the sobbing man in the centurion uniform. "It's not my fault the Saxons came here looking for revenge."

"Aye," one of his companions agreed. "We just wanted to be left alone."

"And that's the problem," the druid nodded, looking down at the ground sadly. "We all just want to be left alone." He waited until there were murmurs of surprised agreement from the angry blacksmith and his friends then his head came up and his eyes blazed. "Left alone? *That* is why your town was targeted by the sea-wolves. They knew you people were an easy target after their last visit here, when only your fat baker was willing to stand against them."

"Why would we stop them?" the blacksmith demanded. "That lass was nothing to us—"

"That lass was a Briton, and you knew that!" Bellicus roared, the rage in his voice making more than one of the men facing him step back warily as a crowd of soot-blackened locals began to form around them. "If more of you were as brave as Duro there, the Saxons might have been cut down like the animals they've shown themselves to be here today. If you—" he pointed directly at the blacksmith whose eyes narrowed "—had used that hammer to help a little girl, well…" He trailed off shaking his head, looking around at the scattered bodies sorrowfully. "None of this would have happened."

The men were either mollified by the druid's words, or perhaps embarrassed. Shamed by his accusations maybe. Whatever it was, most of them just stood there, looking dumbly at the druid. One stepped forward threateningly, clearly hoping his companions would follow his lead, but none did and, when Cai bared his teeth and barked at him, he stopped instantly in his tracks.

"The Saxons didn't come here today because Duro stood up to them," Bellicus went on into the uneasy silence that followed. "They came here because none of the rest of you were willing to stand up to them. And that," he spread his massive arms wide, as if encompassing the whole of Britain, "is also why they have invaded our lands. It's time we all understood this—it is no longer enough to want to be left in peace, in the hope that these raiders will pass us by. They see us as weaklings, and they'll not rest until either they've subjugated every one of us, or we've stood before them like men and shown them what it means to face a warrior of the Britons."

He walked forward and placed a hand on the blacksmith's shoulder, looking earnestly into the man's damp, tired eyes. "Duro isn't to blame. He's suffered as much as any of you this day. Look – his wife has been murdered, and his old comrade from the legions as well."

Beside him he heard the centurion's sobs grow quiet, and then the familiar voice mumbled the name of his fallen friend in surprise and despair, as if noticing the mangled corpse beside him for the first time.

"Lossio?"

* * *

When all the fires had been doused and the task of finding shelter for those made homeless by the Saxons' destruction was well underway, Bellicus rode back towards the forest accompanied by Cai, and one of the local men to show him where Tancorix's house was.

Before they reached the place the wise-woman flagged them down. She'd been hidden in a tall bush and Bel wondered how the prominent thorns hadn't scratched her skin bloody.

"Are the sea-wolves gone?" she demanded.

"Aye," the druid confirmed. "Although they've left the town in a mess."

She shrugged. "That's what men in a group always do if there's no-one around to stop them."

Her words, and her glare, seemed to be accusing him personally but Bellicus had no time to discuss the strengths and weaknesses of the sexes.

"Where's the princess?"

A small head peered out from the same thorn bush that had concealed Tancorix and the old woman waved Catia out onto the path. Cai ambled over, tail wagging, and lifted his head to lick her face.

Bel jumped down from Darac's saddle and, smiling, bent to give her an awkward hug. The girl returned his smile, but he wondered if she was also eyeing him accusingly, as if wondering how, after rescuing her from the Saxons, he could then abandon her into the care of some withered crone.

He asked himself the same question. Would Coroticus have acted the same in such a situation? Or would he have remained with the girl instead of seeing to the safety of a companion? How was a father *supposed* to act?

He squeezed Catia's shoulder once more then drew himself up, eyes and ears scanning the trees around, ever alert for signs of danger. Such questions could be pondered another time, for now they had to get back to the relative safety of Luguvalium.

"Thank you for looking after her." He lifted the princess up onto Darac's back and placed a foot in the stirrup to follow. "We'll get back to the town. Are you coming?" He glanced across at his silent guide who sat atop a rather old horse, then back at the crone. "You can ride with the lad there."

Tancorix shook her head as if he was the biggest fool she'd ever come across and gestured once again towards the thorn bushes.

"And what about this lot? Are they all going to fit on the backs of your two horses?"

Bellicus pulled himself up into the saddle and fixed his gaze on the thorny bushes which he now saw had been cleverly grown and tended to form a narrow, hidden pathway that allowed Tancorix and her charges to pass through without being ripped to shreds. A boy of about seven years came out, wide-eyed and clearly terrified. Then another boy, holding the hand of what had to be his grandmother.

Before long twenty women and children had filled the small space, every face tear-streaked and shocked. The druid looked at them, taking in their downtrodden, beaten look then he spoke to Tancorix again.

"The Saxons are gone—the townsmen rode out to try and track them, to gain some small measure of justice if they could, but the bastards' trail leads back south. So there should be no danger here, but..." he swept his gaze across the sorry group of refugees. "Some of them look in no state to make the walk back to the town. Their flight here has clearly taken everything out of them."

Tancorix nodded. "I'll take them back to my safe place. You send men with wagons. I'll be waiting." Without another word she gestured towards the passage and, obediently—their silence a clear indication of their defeated, exhausted state—the women and children filed back into the undergrowth.

Bellicus watched them go, impressed by the way the foliage swallowed them up. This Tancorix was a formidable woman and a true gift from the gods to the people of Luguvalium.

"Let's move," the druid grunted, kicking his heels into Darac and cantering back along the path towards the town, which was easy to spot thanks to the pall of black smoke that still lingered above it.

When they returned, Bellicus sought out the blacksmith and asked him to organise some ox-drawn wagons to bring the refugees back to town. Bel suspected it would do the man good to be given an important task to oversee, and keep his mind from thoughts of vengeance against Duro. For his part, the blacksmith seemed happy enough to take on the job and Bellicus rode, in no great hurry, to the bakery, with Catia and Cai.

Alatucca had been carried there by the centurion -- Bellicus couldn't think of Duro as a baker now, even in the man's own shop – and she lay on top of the long table normally used to knead dough and prepare savouries for the oven. The room was filled with sacks of flour, baskets, trays, barrels and all the other mundane paraphernalia required to craft bread and cakes. In the centre of it all, Alatucca's slim, pale figure seemed hauntingly, heartbreakingly beautiful.

"Are you all right?"

Duro looked up almost sheepishly as the druid came in, bending so his head didn't hit the doorframe.

"Aye, my friend, I'll be fine." The baker glanced at his dead wife's pale face and sighed. "We'll meet again one day, and I'll apologise for…" The words trailed off as he looked at Catia and a maelstrom of emotions flitted across his face. Bellicus felt terribly sorry for the centurion – if he'd left the princess to her fate she'd have died horribly at the Saxons' hands and yet, that's exactly what had happened to his own wife.

"Where's Horsa?" Duro muttered. "And his warband. Do you think they'll return?" There was a hopeful note in his voice, as if he wanted the Saxons to come back so he could slaughter them all, even if it wouldn't restore Alatucca to life.

"No," Bellicus said. "They've gone back to Garrianum. They must have given up looking for us, and travel now to give Hengist the news. We'll not see them again any time soon."

"Why do the gods torture us so, Bel?" Duro whispered and his head dropped.

Cai sat down, looking perplexed, but Catia strode past Bellicus and put her arms around the sobbing baker. Her empathy initially seemed to magnify his sadness but, after a few heartbeats he put one arm around the girl and wiped his tear-streaked, grimy face, smiling at her.

"At least she didn't die for nothing. She wanted to help you just as much as I did, little Catia."

There was silence for a time, not an awkward silence, just sad and thoughtful, and then Bellicus spoke, a grim determination in his powerful voice.

"We need to smash the Saxons completely. Wipe every last one of them out, starting with Horsa and Hengist. If we don't, they'll overrun the entire country within a few years." He gripped the hilt of his sword and met Duro's gaze. "When I return to Dun Breatann I will advise King Coroticus to send men for Arthur's army. He'll put a stop to raids like the one your people suffered here today."

"We." Duro said, and Bel's eyebrows drew together in confusion.

"We what?"

"When *we* return to Dun Breatann," Duro growled. "I'm coming with you."

The druid didn't say anything, for there was no need. He'd be happy to have the centurion along and, given the way things stood here in Luguvalium, it was probably the best thing Duro could do. If it wasn't such a sad day, Bellicus would have grinned at the prospect of continuing his adventures with the former legionary. As it was, he simply nodded, and that was enough.

"First, though," Duro said, and his voice dropped to almost a whisper as he returned his gaze to Alatucca's bruised body. "I need to bury my wife."

CHAPTER FIVE

Bellicus, Catia at his side, watched the funeral ceremony take place and sighed. Sorrow and anger filled his heart as he looked upon the faces of those who had lost loved ones, many of whom would suffer even more than Duro. The centurion had lost his wife, a woman he had loved for many years, but he was able to look after himself and earn his keep within the village, should he have chosen to stay. But many of the bereft townsfolk were women who had lost their men, and even children whose parents had both been slaughtered by the Saxon raiders.

Life, hard enough already, would be almost unbearable for those people unless their compatriots rallied around and helped them rebuild their shattered existence. The druid's resolve to convince King Coroticus to send men who could aid in Arthur and Merlin's fight against the foreign invaders hardened as he looked around at the grief-stricken inhabitants of Luguvalium.

Almost twenty people had been killed in the attack – not including two of the enemy whose corpses had been dumped in the forest for the animals – so this funeral was lasting much longer than normal. A great mass grave had been dug in the cemetery which was a little way off from the main town itself. The bodies were washed and prepared, then carried to their final resting place with great reverence, and now the grieving friends and family stood next to their loved ones as the ceremony reached an end.

Bellicus watched proceedings with interest, seeing a mixture of the native Britons' ancient rituals, along with Roman, and Christian elements, that offered a glimpse of how future generations would view religion: as a synthesis of all these disparate beliefs. It seemed a good compromise to him, but he expected one of the factions – probably the Christians since their faith was young and aggressive – would seek to sweep away the others.

Unless the Saxons managed to conquer the entire island. In that case, their harsh gods would destroy the followers of Christ and bring yet another new belief system to these lands.

Was there any hope for the old gods of the Britons? The gods that Bellicus's brotherhood had venerated for untold centuries?

Unlike the Christians, the druids did not believe in just one god, or even one unified pantheon of divine beings as the Greeks had done. Instead, the Britons had a countless multitude of gods and goddesses, different ones in every town and village, even if they shared certain aspects and traits.

Such ideas were unimportant before the Christians came. The Romans were happy to adopt local gods into their own pantheon – Belenus, the sun god, was analogous to Apollo for example, while Sulis, goddess of healing, was, for the Romans, an aspect of the one they called Minerva. Even the Saxons, despite their murderous ways, appeared to follow similar gods – their Thor being so similar to Taranis that, to the druid, it was obvious there was some connection between them, lost so far back in the distant past that no-one could now remember it.

But the Christians were a different matter entirely. They had no place for any other god but their own, although Bellicus found that confusing in itself, since they appeared to venerate more than one god themselves! What were saints, if not other gods?

"Druid?"

Bellicus was brought back to the present by a strong yet respectful voice and he looked around to see the blacksmith, hand outstretched as if inviting him forward.

"Yes?"

The blacksmith, who had taken on the mantle of headman since the murder of old Dumnocoveros, repeated the question Bel had missed in his reverie.

"The ceremony is almost over. Would you care to say a few words to speed our dead on their way? We would be very grateful."

"Yes. Of course," the druid readily agreed, stepping across and up onto the wooden platform that had been occupied thus far by Tancorix, the wise-woman having presided over the ceremony as she had done on countless occasions over the years, although rarely for so many soul-travellers as this. She stepped aside to allow him up, her small frame completely dwarfed by his, and the gathered townspeople craned their necks upwards to look at this distinguished visitor.

Like the crone, Bellicus had presided over funerals in the past but he could see, and hear – the earlier loud wailing and chanting having faded now to low sobs and sniffs – that all this ceremony needed to be complete was a blessing.

"It is natural to feel grief for the loss of loved ones," he said. "Yet their souls have departed this earthly realm only for a short time: they will be reborn anew, and the cycle will begin again, as it always has and always will." There were nods at this from many of the crowd. "So, grieve not overmuch for your lost friends and family – you will meet them again on this earth one day. Instead, give thanks to have known such fine people, to have enjoyed their fellowship, even for a short time, and take strength from the knowledge that you will carry them forever within your hearts."

His words seemed to galvanise the townsfolk, jaws firming, small smiles forming where there had previously been twisted frowns, and thoughtful gazes replacing tears. Duro stood in the grave-pit next to Alatucca's body, nodding silently at his friend's comforting words. His wife, like all the other dead, was laid out with her head facing to the west, feet to the east. The centurion had placed a coin in her hand, with a bronze brooch – her favourite piece of jewellery – by her head, and a dagger by her side, just in case she ever met the shades of her Saxon killers in the otherworld.

Bellicus spoke the words of the blessing – words he had heard his mentor, Qunavo, speak, after a young boy was killed by a falling rock while out playing almost twenty years ago, far to the north, in Pictish Dunnottar.

"A butterfly alights beside us like a sunbeam," he said, softly. "And, for a fleeting moment its glory and beauty belong to our world. But then it flies again. And, although we wish it could have stayed by our side forever, we feel blessed to have seen it."

Thoughts of that child from Dunnottar came to Bel's mind as he recited the blessing and, for a moment, he wondered why they were there at all. What was the point of living? He looked down at Catia who stood next to Duro and noticed she was crying silently, sobs wracking her small frame, and his own doubts seemed unimportant then.

He stepped down from the dais and went to her, kneeling on the grass to draw her into his strong embrace, tears in his own eyes as he once again cursed the Saxon vermin for ruining this little girl's previously happy childhood. Catia didn't grieve for any of the dead here in Luguvalium, even if she did feel sad for Duro. No, Catia mourned the loss of her own previous, innocent existence. Her world had changed forever Bellicus knew, and that seemed almost as sad as any death.

CHAPTER SIX

Gavo had been captain of Coroticus's guard for years and served Alt Clota faithfully his whole life. A bear of a man with long hair and an unkempt beard which was starting to show silver streaks through the brown, he was a good warrior to have at your side in a fight.

He had never known the king to behave as irrationally as he'd done in recent months but put it down to the little princess's abduction. As a father of four himself the guard captain could almost understand his ruler's actions in bringing war to their very door. Almost. Aye, it was natural to feel like you should have protected your child better, and to want to punish those who were to blame. But taking out your anger on the neighbouring tribes was only ever going to end in trouble.

No wonder the other kings had banded together and laid siege to the capital of Alt Clota. Gavo had no doubt at least one of the three enemy kings was ambitious enough to want Dun Breatann for himself. Drest was likeliest, being the most powerful of their besiegers, but it was Loarn Mac Eirc of the Dalriadans who Coroticus was making preparations to destroy at that moment.

"I knew they were bluffing," the king had grunted when, just a few days after the meeting with the enemy delegation, and a few more ineffectual attacks, the obvious signs of the armies making ready to leave could be seen from the eastern peak of Dun Breatann. "They're not even going to attempt to scale our walls." He snorted in disdain and looked at Gavo with a triumphant look on his face. "Get the men ready. We're going after the Dalriadans."

Gavo didn't question the wisdom of such a course of action. Once, he had been ever ready to speak up if he felt the king was acting rashly but recently Coroticus hadn't taken kindly to his orders being questioned, instead preferring to listen to men like Senecio who agreed with whatever he said. So Gavo, like everyone else in Dun Breatann lately, simply did as he was told.

"How many men should we take, my lord? Our spies suggested Loarn's warband numbered close to forty." The Dalriadans had the smallest contingent in the would-be invading army, with

Cunneda's Votadini bringing sixty spears, while Drest commanded nearly a hundred men. Still, forty warriors formed a larger assemblage than most of the Alt Clotan men had ever stood against, and needed to be met with a similarly-sized force. That could be a problem though.

"Fifty," Coroticus replied, eyes once again focused on the tiny figures on the plain far below making ready to depart for their own lands.

Gavo frowned but this time he knew he had to voice his concerns, despite the fact Senecio was nodding hearty agreement with the king's command.

"That's almost our full garrison, my lord," the captain noted. "It'll leave the place as good as undefended. What if this is a ploy to draw us out, so Drest can come back and take Dun Breatann while we're gone?"

Coroticus gave him an irritated, sidelong look, plainly unhappy at this suggestion his orders were a mistake. His sour look faded somewhat after a moment however, presumably as he accepted the truth of Gavo's words, and then he shrugged.

"Fine, we'll take thirty. That leaves more than enough to defend this place in our absence. We'll leave by way of the river to make sure we can get back should Drest indeed return and lay siege again. We can sail north and make landfall in the Dalriadans' own lands; they won't expect that, and we can choose the best spot for an ambuscade."

Gavo mulled it over. They would be outnumbered but, assuming they could find some favourable terrain to mount an ambush, the numbers wouldn't be so much of a concern.

Realising the strength of his own plan, and possibly rattled by Gavo's suggestion of Drest returning, Coroticus shook his head. "No, thirty still leaves our walls a little short on defenders. I don't want to come home and find Narina in Cunneda's bed and Drest the lord of my fortress." He spun and walked back, away from the wall, towards his own quarters to gather his weapons and armour. "Choose twenty of our best men, and have the ships made ready to depart in the morning."

Gavo's mouth dropped open as he realised the king was suggesting they meet the Dalriadans outnumbered two-to-one. The success or failure of this mission would now rest entirely on their being able to find some perfect killing ground from which to attack Loarn Mac Eirc's warband. But he had already questioned the king's orders and knew it would be ill-advised to do so again, especially with Senecio there to pounce on any opportunity to weaken Gavo's position and strengthen his own.

The captain sucked in a breath and followed Coroticus's departing figure down the shallow steps that curved around the peak back towards the centre of the fortress. If they succeeded in beating Loarn's men, this would go down as one of the greatest Damnonii triumphs in history.

If they lost, the people of Alt Clota, already muttering about their king's state of mind, might very well rise up against him.

Gavo wished Bellicus would return to them soon. The druid was the one man who might be able to get through to the king, but the captain had a horrible feeling they'd not see Bel, or Catia, ever again, and the likes of Senecio would goad Coroticus into a situation they would never recover from.

They left the next morning, once the two ships were loaded with provisions, the war-gear safely stowed, and all made ready for the short journey. Queen Narina was tasked with keeping things running smoothly in their absence, and Coroticus told her to heed the advice of old Senecio. Gavo could tell from the sour look on her face that she held no more love for the southern advisor than he did, however.

"Have a care, my queen," the guard captain murmured as they made their farewells. "I would suggest you don't need to look for advice from anyone. You've proven yourself more than capable of ruling Alt Clota in the past, when the king's been away at war or whatever."

Narina smiled graciously and replied in a similarly low tone. "Thank you, old friend. Have no fears, I can take care of myself. Just you make sure Coroticus comes back safely."

"He will," Gavo vowed, smiling. "Or neither of us will."

Dun Breatann, as well as being a fortress for the Britons of Alt Clota, was a busy port. Trade had come here from all across the world since the earliest days of Roman occupation and it continued to this day. As a result, the king maintained a small fleet of ships to defend the River Clota from pirates, and to move his warband around if there was ever any trouble in his settlements. So, there would usually be boats of various sizes and designs, from seafaring ships with forty oars, to tiny, animal-skin covered currachs, which Coroticus might have used for this mission. The majority had sailed away to nearby ports, however, to make sure the besieging Pictish army didn't steal them.

Five medium-sized vessels remained close to Dun Breatann though, two of which had been signalled to dock and take on supplies the night before. The boats selected were of the birlinn type. Built of oak planks, with a square sail and ten oars apiece, they had no space for cargo, being used mainly as troop transports. They could move quickly, but were small enough to be dragged on wooden rollers across land if need be.

Coroticus's plan was to sail west until they reached Loch Fada, then follow that north until they came to the settlement at Arachar. Loarn Mac Eirc's warband would need to pass through the tiny village on their way back to Dunadd, but Coroticus knew his ships could make the journey in half the time the Dalriadans would on foot.

Arachar was surrounded by massive, brooding hills which were stunningly beautiful no matter the season. That inhospitable terrain would undoubtedly provide a suitable place for the Alt Clotan's to lay an ambush for their enemy.

Gavo didn't know the area they were heading to particularly well, though. The Dalriadan's had made those lands their own over the past few years and there was no real reason for any Briton to travel there these days, other than trade. But he knew this stretch of the River Clota they were sailing along now like the back of his hand, having fished here as a child and patrolled it countless time as a man.

Cistumucus, captain of the small ship, called for the rowers to take up their oars on the port side and five of the men scrambled to comply, their powerful efforts enough to turn the vessel right, into the entrance to Loch Fada. Gavo looked back over his shoulder and saw their second ship follow suit.

It was a sunny day although there was little wind, so the journey was comfortable but not particularly fast. They didn't have much further to sail now though – a couple of more hours traversing the loch would see them making landfall near Arachar before night descended upon them. They would then have a little time to find a campsite, and a place to prepare their ambush, before it became too dark to see what they were doing.

The Dalriadan army would, assuming they travelled at an average walking speed, reach them sometime the following morning. And then Loarn would pay with his life for what he'd said about Princess Catia.

The Damnonii guard captain grasped the hilt of his sword and smiled grimly. There was little reason to suspect this mission would end in anything other than great success, he had to admit. Coroticus had come up with a good plan that should minimise their own losses while wiping out Loarn Mac Eirc and his followers.

What would the king do then? Gavo wondered. The Dalriadan stronghold at Dunadd would be without its king and warband – ripe for the taking. Yet Coroticus didn't have enough men for such a task, not on these two small ships. Dunadd, like Dun Breatann, was built on a steep hill, and even the small garrison Loarn mac Eirc would have left behind to man the walls would be enough to defend the place for weeks.

Gavo leaned back against the mast and raised his face to the sky, eyes closed, enjoying the warmth of the bright sun and the refreshing spray from the river. For now, they simply had to defeat Loarn. Coroticus would decide what should be done next, but Gavo expected they would simply loot the Dalriadan dead, harvest a few of their heads, and then return to Dun Breatann, victorious heroes.

Dunadd could wait.

The king had sent out mounted scouts that morning before they cast off, confirming Drest, Cunneda and Loarn had indeed departed Alt Clota to return to their homes, but the idea they might yet return played on Coroticus's mind. It was obvious from the way the king often glanced back homewards, an anxious frown on his face, until distance finally hid mighty Dun Breatann from view. Only then did Coroticus seem to relax.

That calm demeanour was now shattered however, as cries of alarm came to them from the ship behind.

"What in the name of Taranis is happening back there?" the king demanded, hurrying from the bow to the stern, trying not to step on any of the rowers blocking his passage.

From his position in the centre of the ship Gavo could see the men in the trailing vessel calling out in alarm, with Bri, their captain, gesticulating wildly to Coroticus.

"We've hit something!" Bri was shouting, dark features twisted in consternation. "The hull has a hole in it and we're taking on water."

"In the name of...How can you hit something this far away from the shore?" Coroticus cried, turning to Cistumucus who had made his way over to stand beside him. "Have the men row backwards – slow us down, so Bri can catch up. Will we be able to take the weight of them with all their supplies and gear?"

The captain mulled it over for a moment then nodded. "Aye, my lord, but it'll be a squeeze and we'll be low in the water. I'd suggest making for shore as soon as we've rescued them."

Again the king cursed, but there was nothing else for it. Most of the men couldn't swim, including Gavo, and, even if they could, the weight of their armour would draw them to the bottom of the loch.

By now Bri and Cistumucus had ordered their rowers to bring the oars in and ropes were tossed from one vessel to the other. Before long they were side-by-side and the men from the damaged ship began transferring their gear across.

When the hole had been discovered in their hull Bri's men hastily removed their armour and weapons, even the men who couldn't swim, terrified by the thought of being dragged to the bottom of the loch with no chance of survival. Now, they handed the war-gear to their comrades on Coroticus's ship or simply tossed it over to land on whatever free space of deck could be found.

Once the first of the warriors had transferred their arms and armour, they jumped across themselves, helped along the way by the king, Gavo and Cistumucus. It wasn't as easy a task as it should have been, as one boat rose in the water while the other dropped beneath its increasing weight, both vessels tossing and heaving all the while and the nervous men, no sailors, stumbled around as if drunk.

Eventually, only two warriors remained on the holed ship; they were brothers, Gavo knew. He recognised them easily enough as, although one was much younger than the other, they shared similar narrow features and large ears which stuck out like the handles on an amphora. They hailed from the settlement of Cardden Ros and had come to Dun Breatann when Coroticus commanded his nobles to send reinforcements for the fortress's garrison.

Gavo wondered what use the younger lad might be, seeming no more than about thirteen years of age and slightly built, but even the guard captain had been an untried youth many years ago. They all had to learn the killing trade sometime, and presumably that's why the older brother had brought the younger along on this mission.

Gavo smiled across the water at the siblings, glad to be seeing the next generation of warriors learning what it was to be men of Damnonii side-by-side, and held out his hand to the elder, Troucisso, who was nearest.

The man jumped nimbly across, landing on the deck beside Gavo with a thump. They grinned at one another, in relief, and in the eternal brotherhood of warriors on the same side sharing a moment of danger.

As Gavo turned away to make sure all was well there was a pitiful scream from behind him and a splash as something entered the water.

"NO!"

Instinctively, his subconscious mind telling him what had happened before he truly understood it himself, Gavo grasped the older brother – whose cry it was that had split the air so terribly – by the arms, hauling him back from the edge of their ship before the anguished man could jump into the loch in a pointless attempt to rescue his sibling.

There was a white froth where the younger lad had fallen in but, although the sunlight illuminated the depths on the other side of the ship, here the shadows made the depths murky and there was no sign of the boy.

"He wouldn't take off his chainmail," the older brother cried, struggling to break free of Gavo's hold. "But he can't swim!"

"Can you?" Gavo demanded, forcing the warrior to meet his eyes.

"No," was the near-hysterical reply. "But I'll learn!"

He tried again to slip free from the guard captain's grip but Gavo expected it and pinned him easily enough as more of their comrades rushed over to help restrain him.

"He can't swim," the man repeated, tears streaking his face, teeth bared in pure frustration and horror.

"Neither can you, Troucisso!" Gavo shouted, their tussle making his words angrier than he meant them to be. "None of us can, except—"

From the corner of his eye the captain noticed a blur of motion, and then there was another splash as a second figure entered the water.

"—Coroticus," Gavo finished lamely, grip relaxing on the astonished warrior.

There was a strange, near-total silence for long moments, as the shocked men of Dun Breatann stared at the rippling waters that had swallowed up their king.

* * *

"Ah, there's the place I was telling you about earlier," Bellicus pointed to the horizon, where a plume of smoke could be seen, the pungent smell from it travelling to them even at this distance on the southerly wind. "The settlement where they make the pottery."

"Where your sword, Melltgwyn, was stolen," Catia said, her voice a little shaky.

"Aye," the druid agreed. "But there's nothing to worry about now. The people there are friendly, and they gave me aid once they realised their own neighbour was a bad lot. Besides, I was able to beat them all when they attacked me, so fear not lass, we're safe enough." He smiled encouragingly, reassuringly, then sighed. "I miss that sword. Hopefully they found it in the thief's belongings. This thing is no weapon for a druid to be carrying." He patted the hilt of the longsword one of the potters had allowed him to borrow, admitting to himself that it had, in truth, proved its worth in battle and not been found wanting.

Still, he prayed to Lug that Melltgwyn would be returned to him one day.

Their mounts ate up the distance between them and the settlement and soon they rode into the centre of the place, Bel leading them directly to the single storey building the people used as a beer hall. It was a little after midday and he smiled, seeing more smoke, this time undoubtedly from a cooking fire in the rear of the structure.

"Matugena is the cook's name," he told them. "She's a fine woman and she'll see us well fed, have no fear on that. You might not want to go home to Dun Breatann when you taste her stew." He smiled at Catia as they dismounted but the girl's look of apprehension hadn't left her. She was still plainly frightened of the men here who had tried to kill Bellicus on his previous visit, despite how that tale had turned out. Or perhaps she was simply fearful of anything, and anyone, she didn't know. It was a worry for him as she'd started to relax a little more on the road north, but any time they saw other travellers, or stopped for supplies in settlements, Catia would be nervous and withdrawn.

"The pottery stinks," Duro muttered, raising a hand to waft away the stench, but his face brightened as they entered the beer hall and the aroma of roasting meat filled the room. "Oh, now, *that* smells much nicer! Is that coriander?"

"Probably," the druid said, holding the door open for Cai who was emptying his bladder before following Bel inside. "I left Matugena some of my herbs in return for her hospitality. No doubt she's made excellent use of them. Take a seat princess - here." He pulled out one of the stools and the girl sat, eyeing the door at the back of the hall. "I'll go and tell Matugena she has three—no four, sorry Cai—hungry visitors to feed." He winked at Catia. "Matugena *loves* dogs. She makes wonderful cakes for them. I almost wanted to eat one myself, it looked so good."

The girl merely nodded without returning his smile and Bel gave Duro a worried glance as he wandered over to the rear doorway and rapped on it with his knuckles. "Hello? Matugena? Anyone around?"

"Who's that?" The voice was loud and the speaker sounded irritated. "If that's you again Judd, looking for more stew, I'll knock you out with this pot. Oh!" The diatribe halted and a ruddy-faced woman appeared in the doorway, grinning. "It's you again druid. I'm pleased to see you. The herbs and spices you left me on your last visit are almost finished and I could use some more." She took in the sight of Duro and Catia at the table and held up a hand, as if silencing any further conversation. "Sit, druid. I'm guessing you're all hungry and looking for a meal, eh? Sit, then, go on. I'll fetch something for you." She shooed him away and finally Catia managed a smile as Bellicus returned to sit with them.

"What's the joke?" he demanded, but his tone was light.

"It's just funny to see a woman ordering you about like that. It's not something I've ever seen before. Even my mother doesn't talk to you the way that woman did."

Bel smiled ruefully. "I knew you'd like her." He leaned in and peered at Duro and the princess, lowering his voice to a conspiratorial whisper. "Truth be told, I think she probably runs this village—the headman, her father, doesn't seem to have half the natural authority she commands." He sat back suddenly, guiltily, as Matugena bustled in from the kitchen, somehow balancing three bowls and a trencher of buttered bread in her arms which she set down before them.

"Dig in," she ordered, ruffling Catia's hair before she went off to fetch their drinks.

The princess made a little groan of delight as she bit into the bread, crumbs falling onto the table. "This is lovely," she said. "And still warm too."

Duro chewed and nodded agreement, eyeing the bread with professional curiosity. "Tastes like she's added something to it—"

"Oregano," Matugena said, reappearing from the kitchen. "My own secret recipe. Have you tried the stew yet, lass?"

Catia shook her head, lifting the half-sized cup and washing down the tasty bread with a mouthful of weak beer. "Waiting on it too cool," she said softly.

Matugena smiled. "I'll leave you to it then. I hope you enjoy it." She patted the girl on the arm and Bel was pleased to see the princess smile and relax a little as she leaned forward to blow on the steaming bowl of food.

The travellers set-to with gusto, for this was the best meal any of them had eaten in a long, long while. Cai hadn't been forgotten either – Matugena had tossed him one of her meat cakes and he'd wolfed it down in moments before curling up near the dormant fire in the middle of the little hall and falling contentedly asleep.

"That was superb," Duro announced at length, pushing his chair back and patting his belly. "Why can't you cook a stew like that, druid, if all you need are a few of those herbs you carry in your cloak?"

Bel opened his mouth but Matugena came in before he could frame a suitable retort and began clearing away the empty bowls.

"Thank you," Catia said, drawing a grin from the cook.

"You're very welcome, little miss. I'm glad you liked it. Have you had enough?"

Catia glanced at Bellicus, but Matugena saw the look and tutted. "You don't need to ask his permission, lass, I'll bring you another bowl. Anyone else?"

Duro shook his head as did Bel, and the woman went off, returning soon enough with another bowl of the aromatic stew for Catia.

"You finish that, I'll talk to your father about those spices."

Catia looked up. "My father?"

Matugena nodded. "The druid." She frowned, then turned to Bellicus. "You are her da, aren't you? You look so alike. Have the same eyes. I just assumed..."

Duro cleared his throat and turned away although the druid couldn't tell if the centurion was embarrassed or amused by the exchange.

"I'm her protector," Bellicus said. "Catia is a princess of the Damnonii. Those Saxons I was hunting the last time I was here had kidnapped her, remember? We're taking her home to her father, Coroticus. The king."

Matugena's face, ruddy from her lifetime of cooking, flushed even redder than usual and she stuttered an apology, wide-eyed to be in the presence of royalty, but the druid waved her to silence and bade her sit with them. He smiled and assured her she hadn't caused any offence but inwardly he wondered if anyone else, at home in Dun Breatann, had ever noted the similarities between himself and the girl. It would certainly make things awkward if they did. Maybe he should grow a beard...

"Spices you wanted, didn't you?" He opened his cloak and took out the small pouches he carried there, laying them out on the table just as he had the last time. "Take your pick."

Glancing furtively at Catia – who placed her hand on the cook's arm reassuringly, their roles now reversed – Matugena selected a handful of the precious herbs and spices and, as before, Bel allowed her to pour them into brightly-coloured little pots which she brought through from the kitchen along with a cup of beer, no doubt to steady her nerves.

"And I have something else for you, druid," the cook said, eyes sparkling as she carried her bounty away to the shelves in the kitchen. "Give me a moment."

"Melltgwyn!" Bellicus stood up, massive form seeming to fill the small beer hall as Matugena returned moments later, carrying a sword in an exquisite scabbard. "You found it." He grinned like a child receiving the greatest gift in the world and pulled the blade free, examining it for signs of damage or ill-use but finding only bright, clean steel.

"You need another drink?" Matugena asked, eyeing Duro's empty cup. "You too, druid? Let me refill those, and then I'll tell you all about it. Would you like anything else, my…er…?" She trailed off, unsure how to properly address a princess.

"Just call me Catia," said the girl. "That's fine. And no, thank you. I don't need anything, the meal you provided was quite exquisite."

Matugena flushed in pleasure and Bellicus stared at Catia, pleasantly surprised at how comfortable she appeared now, to the extent she was playing the young royal to perfection once again.

The cook brought three more beers and set them on the table, half-emptying her own in one long pull before belching and staring, mortified, at Catia, who laughed so hard tears came to her eyes, which only embarrassed the cook even more.

"Tell us how the sword came to be in your possession," Bellicus prompted, sitting but holding Melltgwyn on his lap, eyeing it every so often as if worried it would disappear. "Duro and the princess both know the story of how I came to lose it, so they're almost as curious as me, I'm sure."

Just then a boy walked into the hall and asked Matugena if she needed him to sweep the floor. Before she could reply he saw the druid, who looked up at him, eyes locking on one another, and then the boy sprinted outside as if a demon was after him.

"That's the little shit that stole Melltgwyn," Bellicus growled, half-rising, but Matugena waved him back down.

"His name is Ward," she said. "And you're right—you have a good memory, although I suppose that's be expected from a druid."

"He cleans for you now? What happened to his father?"

"Atto? We gave him a trial, as you ordered, and found him guilty of murdering the family that you found on the next farm over. He was hanged. We couldn't hang the boy though."

"No," Bel agreed softly. "Of course not."

"He was taken in by a childless family and he does odd jobs around the village to earn his keep." She smiled fondly and sipped her beer. "He's a good worker, and it's nice to have him around when the men are all at work and I'm here myself." Her face became grim again as she remembered Atto. "That father of his was always a useless good-for-nothing. The boy's better off without him."

There was silence as the woman contemplated the hanged man and his worthlessness, then Bellicus bade her continue.

"Ward told us where his father had hidden your sword. The bastard had a secret stash of things he'd stolen, out in the woods, hidden in the hollow of a tree. Mostly rubbish, apart from your sword." She shrugged. "Once he realised we weren't going to hang him too, the boy was happy enough to tell us all about it."

Bellicus stood again, taking off the old longsword he'd worn for the past few weeks and buckling on Melltgwyn before taking his seat again.

"Thank you," he said. "This blade has been with me for years. I felt its loss keenly."

She shrugged and smiled at Catia. "Men and their swords eh?"

The princess sniggered as Bel and Duro looked mortally offended.

"Think of it as if someone had stolen your favourite pot," the centurion said plaintively.

"I'd get another one and think nothing of it," Matugena replied. "They all do the same thing, and I don't give them silly names like 'White Lightning' or 'Brain Biter' either."

Duro shook his head as if she was moon-touched. "Women just don't understand the sacred bond between a warrior and his weapon."

"And they never will, my friend," Bellicus agreed with mock-sadness. "But I just remembered." He turned back to Matugena, face serious again. "I asked you to try and find out Atto's recipe, remember? For the draught he made that knocked me out and allowed him to steal my things. Were you able to get it from him?"

"Aye," she said, getting up from the table and hurrying through once again to the kitchen. The sound of a chest opening and various utensils being shifted about came to them, and then she came back out to the table with a scrap of pottery. She handed it to the druid and he looked down at it curiously.

"You can write?" he asked in surprise as he took in the letters and numbers scratched onto the sherd

"Aye," Matugena replied proudly. "I keep the records for our business here in the pottery, so I need to be able to read and write."

Bellicus shook his head with a rueful smile as he read the recipe Atto had given Matugena. It was simple – so simple he was surprised he'd never come across it before.

"This recipe will be very useful I'm sure," he grinned, shoving the piece of pottery into his pack, although he'd already committed the formula to memory.

"Oh, it does," the woman agreed, smirking. "It's very handy when you want to keep your man's wandering hands away from you of an evening." She laughed wickedly and Duro gaped at her. Catia, Bellicus was pleased to see, hadn't understood what Matugena meant, although she was smiling anyway.

"Well, my thanks again to you," the druid said, getting to his feet and pointing to his discarded longsword which lay on the table. "Would you see that's returned to its rightful owner, along with this?" He took off a silver ring worth four or five times the old sword's value and placed it down beside the blade. Matugena nodded, and he took off another ring, this time of gold, and handed it to her.

She took it in astonishment. "Are you sure?" she mumbled. "This must be worth, well, I don't know exactly, but a lot!"

Bellicus laughed at her direct way of speaking and closed her fingers around the ring. "Aye, I'm sure. You've more than earned it, even if you don't understand what Melltgwyn means to me. Besides, we're almost home now and the princess's father will doubtless reward me with many rings like that when I return Catia to him."

"Before you go," Matugena said, as if remembering something that had been forgotten in the shock of receiving the ring. "Wait there."

She disappeared once more into the kitchen, and when she came back she held a sack which she tossed to Duro.

"Provisions," she said. "For you three, and this lovely big lad here." She knelt on one knee and grasped Cai by the head, jerking back with a laugh, almost falling over when the muscular hound licked her nose.

"I told you she loved dogs," Bellicus murmured to Catia, who grinned up at him, all trace of her previous apprehension gone completely, and his own spirits soared.

Aye, that gold ring he'd given Matugena was worth a fortune, true enough, but it was worth it. Not only for the return of his beloved sword, and the recipe for the sleeping draught, but to see Catia back to her old, cheerful self again.

Now lay the final stretch of the road to Dun Breatann. They would be home within a few days, and the princess could finally put everything behind her and start life anew with her parents.

CHAPTER SEVEN

"Someone do something!"
"Can no-one else swim?"
"Captain, *help him!*"

The men in the boat shouted excitedly and looked to Gavo for leadership but he was as lost as they were, and the waters of Loch Fada remained deathly still for what felt like an eternity. A strange calm settled over the warriors, and even the birds and buzzing insects seemed to fall silent as it became clear there would be no rescue for the king.

For weeks now the guard captain had wondered if it would serve Damnonii better if Coroticus was supplanted – replaced by someone who wasn't going mad with anxiety for their missing daughter. Yet Gavo had never once wanted to see his lord and friend – for they had been friends of a sort for many years – dead. He knew what had driven the king to jump into the water, or at least he thought he did. The king had heard the anguish in Troucisso's voice as he'd contemplated the death of his brother and it had struck a raw nerve within Coroticus.

This was no cynical attempt to be lauded as a hero by the king, who was a powerful swimmer, Gavo mused. This was simply one man suffering the loss of a family member and trying his best to save another from the same painful fate, with no thought for the consequences.

It was a truly kingly act and the reverential silence of the men on board the ship assured Gavo the sacrifice would never be forgotten. If the druid, Bellicus, ever did return to Dun Breatann he would have no shortage of testimony to inspire a song about that day's events and Coroticus's brave, selfless part in it.

The guard captain sighed, gazing into the inky depths, wishing the holed ship would either sink or be carried away although the lack of wind or any real current in the loch meant the vessel remained floating stubbornly in place, its shadow rendering the waters completely opaque.

Troucisso had fallen onto his backside and sat, weeping in silence, muttering to himself about what he'd tell their mother, for he'd swore to protect his young brother and failed in that duty before a blow had even been struck.

Around them, the world returned to normal, the sounds of gulls and other sea-birds mingling with the almost-inaudible buzzing of the tiny, despised, biting flies known as midges.

"My lord?" Cistumucus must have decided they'd lingered long enough, tapping Gavo softly on the arm and clearing his throat self-consciously. "Should I order the men to row for shore?"

The guard captain drew in a long breath, staring into the impenetrable, murderous waters of the loch, then, with a sigh, nodded his head.

"Aye. Once we're safely on solid ground again we'll—"

Without warning, the water next to him broke in a terrific splash from below and the tortured sound of a man drawing in as much air as possible split the air.

"Coroticus! The king is alive – help me!"

Gavo reached down, grasping his lord's outstretched arm and hauling upwards as Cistumucus, Bri and Taranis-knew who else joined in and, in a heartbeat, the gasping, coughing king was prone on the ship's deck.

There was no sign of the boy he'd tried to save.

"Are you all right, my lord? Just lie there for now, gather your breath. Gods be praised, we thought you were surely dead!"

The guard captain's joy at Coroticus's survival contrasted greatly with the sad warrior lamenting his sibling's drowning, but Gavo was only interested now in his friend who was attempting to stand up, despite spluttering and coughing as what seemed like half of Loch Fada dripped from him onto the sodden deck.

"Get off me, Gavo," the king growled irritably, shoving his guard captain's fretful hands away as he stretched up to his full height and drew in another deep breath before, finally, looking down at Troucisso.

The young soldier was oblivious to the attention and continued to weep into his drawn-up knees before Gavo, guessing the king's intention, kicked the man's foot, making him peer up from sad, wet eyes.

"You said he wouldn't remove his mail," the king said, drawing a nod from the sad warrior. "He wore no sword that I could see though. Which is his?"

A confused expression crossed Troucisso's face but then he shoved himself to his feet and hurried across to the deck where a number of weapons still lay, unclaimed in the drama. Recognising his brother's sword instantly, the man bent down and retrieved it before passing it silently, almost reverentially to Coroticus.

"I'll take it to him," the king murmured, grasping the hilt in one hand and placing the other on the grieving warrior's shoulder before, to Gavo's dismay, jumping back into the water and disappearing once more from view.

More tense moments passed but it wasn't long before the king resurfaced and was hauled aboard again. He spoke quietly to Troucisso, so quietly Gavo couldn't make out the words, and then, dripping wet and clearly exhausted, Coroticus pointed back towards the damaged ship that was still tethered to their stern.

"What will we do about that?" the king demanded. "Can we tow it ashore and repair it later, on our way back from Arachar?"

Before Bri or Cistumucus could offer their expert opinion the answer to the king's question became obvious as, overloaded at the stern where they were standing, water spilled in around their feet. Clearly, towing a dead weight was out of the question.

"Spread out," Cistumucus commanded, shoving the rescued warriors here and there as he attempted to distribute the weight evenly. Eventually he was happy enough—no more water leaked over the sides although they were still riding uncomfortably low. The captain cast off the doomed, holed shell and pushed the steering oar hard around so their remaining heavily loaded ship made its way, rowers hauling hard, towards the eastern shore. Gavo had commanded they make for that side of the loch despite it being further away than the other because he knew a well-used track followed that shore all the way around. If they had to continue on foot they might as well make things as easy as possible for themselves.

As the boat made its slow way towards land the guard captain muttered a prayer beseeching Lug the Light-Bringer to guide them past any more hidden obstacles like the one that had wrecked their other ship. He wasn't the only one petitioning the gods for aid in the quest for land, as at least half a dozen other low voices could be heard murmuring over the rhythmic swish of the oars.

The previously pleasant trip had almost turned into a disaster for the Damnonii Gavo mused, calculating how much time this would add onto their journey. Not to mention the fact the men would now arrive in Arachar tired and footsore instead of rested and fresh as they should have been had the ships not failed them.

Still, they should have gained enough ground on Loarn Mac Eirc's warband to reach their destination before the Dalriadans, although finding suitable ground for the ambush would be a rushed job now.

A solitary rook sailed overhead, calling out as if laughing at their plight and the guard captain shuddered involuntarily, seeing the bird, along with the young warrior's death, as bad omens. From the looks the rest of the men gave one another as the ship finally bumped ashore, he wasn't the only one whose thoughts had turned sour.

Outnumbered two-to-one and apparently victim to a cruel jest of the gods, they would need to march as quickly as possible and locate a killing ground before their enemy overtook them or the mission would be, at best a failure but, at worst, a disaster.

As he jumped onto dry land with a glad sigh Gavo uttered another imprecation to Lug. They were going to need all the help they could get over the next day or two.

CHAPTER EIGHT

Coroticus ordered Cistumucus to stay with the boat and the second captain, Bri, would also remain behind. They would look after the surviving vessel and make sure no-one came along to steal it. The king had no intention of walking any further than he had to on the return trip to Dun Breatann.

The second ship, rather irritatingly, had failed to sink. Instead, it floated back downstream until something—perhaps the very thing that had holed it in the first place—snagged it, and held it bobbing in place almost mockingly. Gavo, the king having turned away in disgust, ordered the two sailors to try and bring it into shore if possible and as long as the task didn't threaten the safety of their surviving vessel. It would be a welcome sight if the warband were to return from Arachar to find Bri back on board his own boat, hull temporarily repaired with compacted plants and mulch, as unlikely as that seemed.

The king led them north, nineteen warriors, grim and downcast, particularly the shaven-headed lad who'd lost his brother beneath the calm yet deadly waters. Gavo walked with him, learning he was but eighteen-years of age. Of average height and yet to fill out despite his broad shoulders, the lad looked even younger thanks to a wispy beard.

"That was a truly honourable act he did," the youth said, nodding almost reverentially at Coroticus's back. "Jumping into the loch to try and rescue a lowly, untried warrior."

The guard captain was relieved to hear Troucisso exonerating the king from any blame in his brother's drowning.

"That's why I follow him," the lad went on proudly, as if he'd been part of Coroticus's warband for decades. "He's a real man, a real king. Not like that whoreson Loarn Mac Eirc." A hate-filled sneer twisted the soldier's face. "I heard what he said about the princess. Made me sick to my guts—my ma brought us up to be respectful of women and, for that foreign prick to say such a thing about a wee girl…No wonder the king wants to take his head!" He looked up at Gavo and his face fell as if he'd just remembered who he was talking to—a lord, captain of the king's guard, a man way above his own humble rank. "I mean to make sure Loarn and his men pay for my brother's death," he muttered self-consciously, kicking a stone which went flying into the brush at the side of the track.

Gavo expected Troucisso to be as good as his word in the coming battle, but he doubted many of the older, more experienced members of the warband shared the lad's gratitude toward Coroticus. The king's recent actions, along with such a dark omen as a drowning before battle had even been joined, placed him in a bad light among a growing number of the Damnonii.

A good victory against Loarn would go some way to rebuilding that rapidly eroding loyalty, Gavo knew, allowing his thoughts to turn to the approaching confrontation, trying to recall the topography of their destination. He could think of one section of the road, where it dropped downhill from the neighbouring, even smaller, settlement of Tairbert towards Arachar. There were many trees flanking that stretch of the road and at least one place where the Damnonii warriors would be able to find higher ground from which to launch their attack on Loarn's unsuspecting Dalriadans.

He patted Troucisso on the arm encouragingly then hurried ahead to catch up with Coroticus at the front of the party.

"Do you have any thoughts on where we should lay our ambush, my lord?"

The king glanced around and raised a small smile at the appearance of his trusted advisor.

"I have an idea of my own," Gavo continued, encouraged by the friendly expression on the other's face. "Once we reach the head of the loch we can follow the main track upwards, towards—"

"Tairbert," the king finished for him. "Aye, I know the place you mean. I think you're right, it's probably the best place we'll find given our hurry after that hold-up with the boats." He shook his head in frustration. "It's not ideal – the raised ground you're thinking of isn't as steep as I'd have liked, meaning we can't just drop great boulders down on the bastards, but it will have to do."

Gavo grunted agreement. "The men will at least be able to conceal themselves amongst the trees, and those with slings and hunting bows will be able to loose a volley of missiles before Loarn knows what's hit him. If our aim is true, that first attack will even the numbers."

Coroticus grinned, picturing the scene in his head. "And then they'll need to find cover or try to attack us in our raised position, allowing us time to get off another flurry of arrows and shot."

Without realising it, the pair picked up the pace even more, eager to prepare the ground they'd selected for the planned ambush. The men marching behind didn't grumble, knowing themselves they stood a better chance of survival if they could reach Arachar well in advance of their approaching enemy.

"You agree with my decision to wipe out the Dalriadan warband, Gavo?"

The captain glanced at his king but saw only honest curiosity in Coroticus's expression.

"I thought it was the queen's command to kill Loarn," he replied with a smile, before nodding. "But aye, this is the best course of action. Without even taking into account what that prick said about Princess Catia, the Dalriadan's will always be a threat to us in Alt Clota. They are constantly expanding their territory as more of their kin sail across here from Hibernia. If we can smash their king and, at some point, take Dunadd..." He trailed off and both men walked in thoughtful silence, simply taking in scenery before Coroticus spoke again.

"How far ahead of them do you think we are?"

Gavo pondered the question, his long stride eating up the ground as he tried to calculate distances, and terrain, and the Dalriadan's marching speed.

"No way to tell," he finally replied, wiping sweat from his forehead. The sun was still high overhead so it wasn't too late in the day and they were almost at Arachar. "We made good time this morning thanks to the tide, but the gods only know how much that damn boat sinking cost us." He shrugged. "Loarn won't be forcing their pace. I expect they'll camp somewhere along Loch Laomainn and reach our ambush tomorrow morning."

"That means we can let the men enjoy tonight," Coroticus said thoughtfully. "They can drink and have fires to cook a warm, hearty supper. A full belly and a mug of ale can chase away thoughts of a companion's death better than anything."

"Hear that lads?" Gavo grinned, turning back towards the trailing warband. "The king says we can have a feast tonight when we reach Arachar. How does that sound?"

The cheers that greeted his pronouncement were loud and long and heavy feet seemed to become lighter as the small gap between those at the front of the group and the stragglers at the rear closed up within moments. Even Troucisso seemed to brighten a little Gavo noted and the guard captain shook his head in wonder.

Truly men were easy to please. Himself included, he had to admit, as the idea of ale and roast pork set his mouth to watering and his feet near flying along the worn old shore road.

It was a measure of the warriors' raised spirits that, when one of them struck up a marching song, the others—to a man—joined in, king and captain included.

Before long, though, their destination came in sight. Smoke rose high up on the horizon proclaiming the existence of cooking fires, with the small round homes that were the source of that sweet-smelling wood-smoke coming into sight a short time later. Coroticus hushed the men to silence as they looked down on Tairbert.

"We might as well avoid the place," Gavo suggested, eyes scanning the handful of buildings they could see facing the head of the loch but seeing no-one watching their approach. "This is very close to Dalriadan territory—who knows how loyal the folk here might be to you? If they've been trading with Loarn's folk they might feel some bonds of friendship with them and seek to do us a mischief."

Coroticus frowned, clearly wondering what on earth one or two peasants might do against the might of his warband, but he accepted his captain's recommendation without argument. They had a good idea where they were now, and how to get to the chosen ambush-point, so he allowed Gavo to lead them off the main path, into the trees to the east with the intention of bypassing the village completely.

The going was tough with it being summer, as briars ripped at the men's exposed flesh, drawing curses along with blood, and, in places, their swords were required to hack a way through the undergrowth. Their destination was near however and they made good progress until, at last, the track from Tairbert to Arachar was visible through the trees a little way above them.

"I hope that hassle was worth it," Coroticus grumbled, picking a thorn from his forearm, a spot of blood taking its place. "We could have just walked along the path that leads to the abandoned Christian chapel, instead of forcing our way through all those bushes."

Gavo grinned. "Someone will have taken over that chapel. If they saw us they might have wondered if we were an enemy about to attack and gone for aid up in Tairbert. Word travels fast even out here, my lord, and the last thing we need now is for Loarn Mac Eirc to find out there's a warband on the road ahead of him."

Coroticus muttered darkly but raised no more objections at his captain's caution as they shoved their way past the final remaining trees that separated them from the road and their ultimate destination – the ambush point which was only a very short distance away now.

"Remember the beer and roast meat," Gavo called back over his shoulder to the tired, irritable men. "And bread and cheese, before—"

His words were cut off as the king, staring through the trees to the road above them, raised his fist and jerked it once angrily, dropping to one knee as he did so.

Thoughts of a feast and a good night's sleep were forgotten as the warband followed their king's example and crouched low, gazing at the shadowy road ahead. A road that was filled with marching warriors, chattering and laughing amongst themselves, completely oblivious to the presence of the hostile force watching their progress.

Loarn Mac Eirc had somehow beaten them to Arachar. They were outnumbered two-to-one and their only chance to lay an ambush was gone.

"Shit," Gavo growled, knowing the mission was over. There was no way they could win a battle against the Dalriadans now. "What do we do, my lord? Wait for them to pass then head back to Cistumucus and Bri at the boat?"

The king turned to stare at him as if he were mad.

"No, Gavo," he hissed, eyes flaring. "We attack them, now, when they don't expect it. Who's with me?"

Only young Troucisso raised his fist in salute, looking like he'd have happily attacked the Dalriadan force on his own, the rest of the warband turning instead to Gavo with grim expressions of disbelief on their faces.

"Good," the king growled, somehow reading the men's silence as a positive sign. "We might be outnumbered, but we are Damnonii! Draw your weapons, lads, and prepare to attack."

The guard captain raised his face to the sky and mouthed a prayer to Taranis, wishing, as he often found himself doing these days, that the giant druid Bellicus was with them, but there was no help for it.

"Move as silently as possible," Coroticus urged. "They don't have any idea we're here yet. Slings and bows at the ready, if you have one." He grinned ferociously and glanced back to his warband, a hungry gleam in his eyes. "Ready? Let's show these Hibernian mongrels what it means to face warriors of the Damnonii!"

* * *

Coroticus's plan to sneak up behind Loarn mac Eirc's marching warband and mount a devastating attack was always a hopeful one and Gavo wasn't the least bit surprised when they were quickly spotted. Moving as stealthily as possible through the undergrowth, which was sparser here close to the road, they did get close to the rear ranks of the marching Dalriadans but then, inevitably, someone trod on a dry branch.

An enemy soldier looked over his shoulder at the crack, which echoed off the hills rising to the north and opened his mouth to alert his companions. A stone whistled through the air as one of the slingers, obviously well prepared, let fly, his stone smashing the shocked enemy in the face and dropping him, senseless and bleeding, to the ground.

"Charge!"

Coroticus, always ready to lead from the very front of the battle, raced towards their prey, ignoring the fallen man with the smashed cheekbone, instead focusing his efforts on another panicked warrior who tried to parry the king's thrust but only managed to turn the tip of the sword into his own guts.

Gavo wasn't far behind his leader, using his shield to block a Dalriadan's axe and following up the movement with a thrust of his sword which mimicked the king's.

Their surprise attack had been fairly successful, with half-a-dozen of the enemy already down, but the Dalriadans had realised their danger and rallied, a giant warrior at the back ordering men to stand fast, shields up. As well as being physically imposing the huge swordsman was a natural leader, no doubt placed in the rearguard to deal with a sneak attack just like this one. He was certainly doing his job, as battle was really joined now and the Damnonii's first, easy kills turned into a proper fight.

One which they could not win, Gavo knew.

Already he could see the grey-fringed bald pate of Loarn mac Eirc pushing through the ranks of his men, directing them to flank the Alt Clotans. There was nothing Gavo could do to stop such a pincer movement and, once they got around the sides of Coroticus's force, it would all be over. Encircled, they'd be mere food for the crows which had already begun to chatter in the trees all around, their guttural cries mingling with those of the combatants and their wounded companions.

Movement in his peripheral vision broke the guard captain's momentary reverie and he instinctively ducked, just in time to avoid a wildly swung blade. He barged the attacker with his shield, smashing the pointed boss into the man's chest then swung his own sword around, feeling it bite deeply into the Dalriadan's forearm. There was a scream, and a shocking spray of blood, then the man fell onto one knee and Gavo kicked him brutally in the mouth.

"We must retreat," he gasped, then, realising the king, lost in the battle fever, hadn't heard, repeated himself much louder.

The road was mercifully narrow at this point and the enemy soldiers were unable to flank them on the north side which rose too sharply, so Gavo ordered a handful of men to block the south, in the hope it would buy them some time. That was running out fast though. The captain couldn't stop fighting long enough to count their losses, but he knew they were losing this battle, even if their crazed king was winning his own, personal duels.

"Coroticus, we must retreat," he shouted again, hacking his way closer to their leader. "We can't keep this up for long. They'll get around behind us soon and that'll be it." He batted an oncoming sword thrust aside but was unable to land his own return blow. "Do you hear me, my lord?"

Whether the king heard him or not Gavo couldn't tell. The king had spotted Loarn mac Eirc and was now intent on cutting a path through the Dalriadans to the man who had insulted the missing Princess Catia.

Gavo's head spun as he frantically tried to keep the enemy at bay while also planning their next move. Clearly the king was beyond offering any leadership in this battle but Gavo couldn't order the retreat and abandon the king to fight on alone. That would bring eternal shame on the captain and his entire family line; yet to continue this battle would mean doom for every one of the Damnonii warriors.

It would be a pointless death.

Gritting his teeth, knowing there was nothing else for it but to die like a good soldier, Gavo redoubled his efforts to slaughter as many of Loarn's men as possible. If he was going to the afterlife, he would do it bravely, beside these men who were somehow still holding their own against the invaders from across the western sea.

His dismay grew along with his anger, as yet more of their men fell with cries of pain or terror. One of them, Gavo couldn't see who and was glad of it, begged for mercy before a triumphant roar accompanied a sickening thud, probably as an axe or hammer caved in the terrified Damnonii warrior's skull.

They were finished, and all the king cared about was reaching Loarn, who was no nearer than he'd been when the battle commenced, having moved back behind his warband, too experienced to stand toe-to-toe with the young men of Dun Breatann, and quite content to watch proceedings with a grim smile.

Gavo again parried a killing blow and, again, was unable to land a clean attack of his own, merely grazing his blade off the Dalriadan soldier's leather armour, but, as he set his feet defensively once more, he looked on almost blankly as the giant Dalriadan who had been leading their defence got near to Coroticus and battered his shield against the king's head.

The enemy champion lunged forward with his bloody sword outstretched and Gavo thought, with a mixture of relief and guilt, that he could now order the retreat.

Before the Dalriadan's sword could skewer the collapsing king, though, young Troucisso, whose brother lay now at the bottom of

Loch Fada, threw himself at the giant who roared in frustration, the sound ending in a higher pitched note which suggested Troucisso had injured him in some way.

"Retreat!" Gavo screamed, kicking a Dalriadan's knee and smashing the pommel of his sword into the man's face. "Retreat!"

He looked to the side and ordered two of the men there to watch his back as he bent down and lumbered towards the fallen king, grasping him beneath the armpits and, with prodigious strength, throwing him over one shoulder.

"Retreat!" he repeated, although the weight of the king pressing down on him meant the command wasn't issued with as much force this time.

He noticed, with a near-sob of gratitude to Taranis, that the injury to their champion had stunned the Dalriadan warriors. They paused, allowing the surviving Damnonii, less than ten of them Gavo noted, to move away, back down into the undergrowth they had appeared from.

Only Troucisso remained, his sword clattering against the giant's as they fought for their lives.

"Keep moving," Gavo ordered, mentally saluting the young warrior who was giving his own life to allow the rest of them to disappear into the trees. Even Loarn mac Eirc seemed intent on the strange duel which the battle had come down to: a slim young man of medium height, seemingly no different to any other faceless warrior, standing against a bear of a man who wore a multitude of his slaughtered enemies' teeth on a necklace that rattled with every blow he landed or parried.

"Thank the gods the Dalriadan king isn't as bloodthirsty as our own," one man gasped as they hurried back to the south. "Or he'd have ordered his men to come after us."

They made good progress, putting a good distance between themselves and their victorious enemy before there was a loud cheer and Gavo knew Troucisso was dead.

"He will now," the captain grunted, trying to walk as fast as he could with his kingly burden, while staring at the ground for hidden roots or other obstacles. If he twisted an ankle…

Incredibly, they made it almost to the loch before the sounds of pursuit came to them and Gavo exhorted the men to keep moving. Perhaps the Dalriadans would lose interest, since a good deal of their own number had fallen in the battle. Maybe they'd lose their appetite to renew the fight with every step they had to pursue the Damnonii through the trees.

"We're not getting away," a warrior gasped, looking back over his shoulder. "They're almost upon us. We should form a shield wall and prepare to die like men, not stabbed in the back or cut down by their slingers."

Whoops of triumph reached Gavo's ears from close behind, lending credence to his comrade's words and, despairingly, wondering what in Lug's name had been the point of this doomed raid, he sucked in a breath and began to slow, looking for somewhere relatively sheltered to lay down the king.

Perhaps he'd be better slitting Coroticus's throat he mused, knowing the man was still alive, merely knocked out cold by the giant's shield. Loarn mac Eirc would, at best humiliate the Damnonii king, at worst...who knew what horrible tortures the Dalriadans might dream up?

"They're behind us!"

"We must form a shield wall!"

Gavo stopped, opening his mouth to give the order to form up into a line, furious that he would die here, far from home, for nothing.

And then he heard a familiar voice, raised in greeting not far in front of them. They had somehow reached the loch and there, framed by the setting sun, were two boats.

"In the name of the gods," Gavo exploded, an astonished grin lighting up his face and giving his exhausted legs a great jolt of extra energy. "Keep moving men, keep moving!"

It was Cistumucus and Bri. And the Damnonii were saved.

* * *

Queen Narina watched the people feasting in Dun Breatann's great hall. It was early evening and through the open doors she could see the huge orange sun setting over the Clota. She wished she could get up and leave the hall, alone, to watch the sight from the higher of the two peaks, knowing the water would reflect the light beautifully, as if the whole river was aflame.

But Coroticus had insisted she remain by his side for the duration of the evening and, dutiful as ever, she sat there, eating little, bored and feeling almost dead inside.

They were celebrating the king's safe return from his mission to kill the Dalriadan Loarn mac Eirc. Narina saw little to celebrate, given half the men who'd gone to Arachar had failed to return while the hated enemy still lived, but Coroticus insisted the Damnonii nobles would want to make merry, and thank the gods for their ruler's survival.

Narina admitted the former but not the latter. Any man would enjoy a feast when someone else was paying for it, but the local chieftains, despite their smiling faces here tonight, were unhappy at how Coroticus was leading them. The only one who didn't seem to have heard the mutterings of discontent was the king himself. He still believed, thanks mainly to the fawning of people like Senecio, that everyone in Alt Clota was behind his efforts to destroy the raiders plundering their livestock and grain, even if it meant all-out war.

But Narina had heard the grumbles, and the doubts people cast on Coroticus's leadership. When the defeated warband had returned on ships manned by half the crew they'd departed with she heard the angry murmurs of discontent. *Why had the king allowed so many of their young men to die? What was the point? Coroticus had been driven mad by his daughter's disappearance. Maybe it was time for a new leader. The Picts and Dalriadans would be back in the spring and next time they'd not give up so easily.*

The complaints, doubts and rumours circulated around the entire area and Narina's informants kept her apprised of the situation which was looking worse for her husband with every passing day. The one saving grace was the fact autumn was upon them and people would be too busy preparing for the coming harsh weather – gathering crops, butchering animals, salting the meat, gathering firewood and so on – to really do much about challenging Coroticus's kingship. At least until the spring.

Narina looked up from the table which she'd been staring at as if in a waking dream, noting every pore of its wood and the way a drink spilled earlier still pooled on its surface despite the warm air coming through the open doors. She scorned the musicians – a flautist and a singer with a small drum – wishing Bellicus was there to sing for them, remembering how his powerful voice could fill even the highest of halls, even though he always claimed not to enjoy singing.

Will I ever see you again, Bel? she wondered, eyes becoming moist as that question inevitably led to another: *Will you bring my daughter back to me like you promised? Oh Bel, I miss her so much!*

The tears streamed down her cheeks but Narina didn't care who saw her misery in this ludicrous 'celebration'. How could Coroticus celebrate being alive when their daughter was probably dead?

A lump formed in the queen's throat at that thought and she coughed, retching, unable to breathe as she finally admitted to herself for the first time that Catia would never come back to her. She dipped her head, absent-mindedly noting the presence of a hungry dog at her feet no doubt mooching for a titbit, and then, picturing Cai and Eolas, gave into her grief.

Her tears went unnoticed in the drunken gathering. The king was too drunk to focus on anything other than the singing, dancing people on the floor in front of him who were determined to make the most of his hospitality, even if they disdained his recent leadership.

Their singing had grown louder as the noblemen and women became more inebriated, but the strong drink also made it less tuneful and Narina felt like her head might burst, trapped as she was in the stifling heat of the noisy hall. Although the doors and windows were open there was precious little breeze and the atmosphere was almost suffocating. Eyeing the doorway longingly, wishing she might leave the gathering for a while to get some fresh air, Narina imagined she saw a giant, hooded shadow on the torchlit wall outside and, terrified, blinked away her tears.

Was she going mad too?

CHAPTER NINE

"Open the gates, man. Do you not recognise us?"

The guard peered down at the small party who had stepped out of the shadows to be revealed by the guttering torches set on the fortress walls. A giant, a child, a Roman centurion in full armour, and a massive dog. It was a bizarre sight and completely unexpected, especially at this time of the evening.

"Hurry up, fool," Bellicus commanded. "We haven't been gone that long have we, that the men of Dun Breatann have forgotten us? Let us in, in the name of Lug the Light-Bringer, for we are returned to chase away the darkness!"

"We've been given orders not to open the gates to anyone, my lord," replied the guard fretfully, recognising the druid at last. "Anyone at all, the king said. I'll send a messenger to him know you're back and he can—"

"You'll send no messenger," Bel said flatly. "I am Bellicus the Druid and I bring Catia, princess of the Damnonii back from her Saxon hell. Open the gates for us now, or I'll make your cock shrivel up and turn black like a prune. I will tell Coroticus of our return myself."

The guard hesitated again, straining to make out the strange centurion in the gloom. "Who's that with you, my lord?"

"A great warrior and friend: Duro of Luguvalium. He helped me rescue the princess. Now open the damn gates man, we're tired and thirsty!"

More of the soldiers manning the walls hissed their opinions to the leader who appeared unable to make up his mind but, finally, fearing for his manhood more than he did even the king's wrath, the guard clattered down the wooden steps and, with the help of two others, pulled away the great beams that held the iron-studded gates barred.

As they swung open Bellicus strode inside and grinned at the fearful guards who mumbled apologies, although they smiled when they saw Catia gazing up at the rock and the sounds of carousing that could be heard echoing against the dark waters of the Clota.

Cai, intent on reclaiming his territory, moved about in the shadows sniffing intently and emptying his bladder wherever he found some interloper's scent.

"What's the celebration?" Bellicus asked.

One of the guards, hidden in the shadows, snorted derisively but the leader glared at him in warning.

"The king was badly injured in a battle against the Dalriadans, but Gavo managed to get him back on board their ship and return him home safely. He's well now, so he decided to throw a feast to thank the gods for his good luck."

"The dozen or so men slaughtered by the Dalriadans weren't so bloody lucky," growled the hidden guardsman, his leader once again ordering him to shut his mouth if he knew what was good for him.

Bellicus nodded for he already knew of Coroticus's defeat to Loarn mac Eirc. The people they'd met on their journey back through Alt Clota had heard all about it and were eager to pass on the news, questioning the king's state of mind in low tones, much like these men manning the walls.

It was only a few years ago that Coroticus had led a successful, and now legendary, raid across the water to Hibernia and taken Dalriadan Christians as slaves. Afterwards, their loudmouthed bishop, Patricius, had sent a letter to the king, upbraiding him for his terrible behaviour. He and Bellicus had laughed together as they read it.

"The king has been under huge stress recently," the druid said. "Hopefully, now that the princess is home safely, things can get back to normal." He stared into the gloom and the man with the loose tongue wisely held his peace this time. "You haven't sent word of our arrival, as I asked?"

"No, lord," the guard replied. "I just hope the king doesn't have our heads for it." He lifted a torch from its bracket inside the gatehouse and gestured at the many new skulls, in various stages of decomposition, that had been nailed onto the very rock of the fortress.

Catia shuddered at the grotesque sight and Bel placed a comforting hand on her shoulder, reassuring the guards that he'd make sure the king didn't trouble them over his secretive entrance.

The guards' leader came with them to the next, inner gateway, and ordered the soldiers there to let them in, then he returned to his post as the druid led Catia, Duro and Cai up the stairs towards Coroticus's great hall. The pleasant, distant drone of merry making resolved less pleasingly into single, off-key voices and musical instruments as they neared their destination.

"Why the need for secrecy?" the centurion asked, gazing all around him, almost tripping over his own feet on the steep stairs as he looked back at the impressive sight of the river far below, lit now by a gibbous moon. "Why didn't you want them to send a messenger informing the king of our arrival?"

Bel looked at Catia, mock disbelief on his face, as if Duro was an idiot.

"I'm a druid, my friend, and I have a reputation to uphold and even enhance," came the reply, accompanied by a wink. "It's my business to make impressive sights and deeds which folk will turn into stories that grow with every re-telling. Where would be the spectacle in a messenger going on ahead to warn people of our coming, then us trudging breathlessly up these stairs to stand, gasping for air, before a drunken rabble? Where's the tale in that?"

Duro admired Bel's forethought for, although he was rather fitter than he'd been only a few weeks before, there *were* an awful lot of steps to climb and it wouldn't make much of a first impression to meet the king and queen panting for breath like a dog on a sunny day.

They reached the midway point, between the two peaks, and Bel raised a hand so they could stop to rest and prepare themselves. The gentle burbling sound of the ancient spring just a little way above them could be heard even over the sounds of revelry and Bel surmised, idly, that it must have been rainy in Alt Clota recently.

"Are you ready to see your parents again?" the druid asked once they were suitably rested, leaning down so he was at eye-level with Catia. "I would counsel you to behave in a way befitting a princess of the Damnonii but..." He smiled at her and rose once more. "This will be a great moment for you, and for them. Behave however you like, lass." He turned his attention to Duro. "When we reach the great hall, I'll go in first and get their attention. You bring Catia when I give the signal, all right?"

The centurion smiled, his own excitement seeming to match Bel's. In fact, the druid mused, looking at the princess, she seemed the least pleased of any of them, as if she were more nervous than happy. Instinctively, he placed an arm around her small shoulders and squeezed. It brought a smile to her lips and he wondered, for the hundredth time that day, how their relationship would develop in the future.

The smell of roasting meat filled the tiny valley and Bellicus felt his mouth watering. It had been too long since he'd enjoyed a real feast.

"Right, let's go."

With that, he strode forward with Cai, towards the great hall, Catia behind and Duro bringing up the rear.

The king's hall was a rectangular structure near the top of the eastern summit, with windows that offered fine views of both the river, with its busy port, and the village of Dun Buic, where this whole adventure had first begun months ago.

Two more guards were positioned at the doorway, which was open, allowing light and that delicious smell to filter out into the warm evening. They stood sharply to attention when they spotted Bellicus and his companions, but these men were well known to the druid, and they grinned when they realised who approached. One even knelt down to greet Cai, who responded by licking the laughing man's face.

"Shh," Bel hissed, placing a finger to his lips before locking forearms with each smiling warrior in turn. "Are the king and queen still inside?"

"Aye, but you'll need to relinquish your sword before you enter. You know the law, Bel. You too, my, er…" The guard trailed off as he struggled to come up with a suitable epithet for Duro who, to the man's relief, handed over his spatha as the druid gave his own blade, and his staff of office, to the second guard.

The druid winked to the soldiers and pulled his hood up, entirely concealing his face in shadow, then, ordering Cai to stay, he made his way up the few more steps to the open doorway and walked inside.

The hall was a welcome sight – a place where he'd enjoyed many feasts and happy times over the years. Its walls were hung with colourfully painted shields, decorative old swords, and tapestries weaved with golden thread that caught the light from the tallow candles and hearth-fire, while music and the smell of cooking filled the air.

Bellicus strode past a handful of men and women who were dancing in the centre of the room, his massive black form passing between them like smoke until, at last, he stood, head bowed, before the high table.

His eyes had taken in everything as he walked, seeing the king, clearly well in his cups, talking loudly to Gavo and the queen, the sight of whom shocked him the most. Her eyes were red from weeping and she looked pale and gaunt. His appearance seemed to terrify her as she shrank back into her chair, apparently seeing him as some spectre of doom.

The singing and dancing didn't stop instantly, but it was only a few heartbeats before a hush fell on the gathering, all eyes fixed on him in wonder. Or fear. Some of the men, Gavo included, grasped their daggers, eyes betraying their wish for more substantial weapons.

Bellicus spread his arms wide, head still bowed and hidden in the shadows of his cowl, appearing even bigger than normal since he'd chosen to stand next to two of the smaller nobles in the room.

"Is this the way the Damnonii welcome home one of their kin?"

Narina's eyes flared at his voice but still she, like the king, remained seated, perhaps not believing what they were seeing.

Bel pointed back to the door and crooked a finger. A moment later the sight of a Roman centurion's helmet could be seen ascending the stairs and Duro, a fine sight in his well-maintained armour, came into the hall, holding the hand of the princess.

The sight of Catia finally broke the spell over the queen who, regardless of her position, climbed right over the table, spilling food and drink all about the floor in a clatter. She flew to her daughter, tears again streaming down her face but now they were tears of the purest joy as she cried out Catia's name and fell to her knees, embracing the laughing girl as if she would never again let go.

Coroticus, drink-addled brain working slower than his wife's, and his unsteady legs also not allowing him to mirror her nimble manoeuvre, ran past the grinning Gavo and threw his arms around both the princess and Narina, eyes closed, savouring the moment.

At the druid's side once again, Cai barked and howled, apparently as excited by the reunion as anyone.

"You did it," the king whispered at last in disbelief, gazing up at the now unhooded, smiling form of Bellicus. "Lug be praised, you brought my daughter back home to me."

Despite his own joy at the long-awaited homecoming, the druid couldn't deny the pang he felt on hearing Coroticus call Catia that.

* * *

The king ordered three days of feasting to celebrate the miraculous return of the princess and the druid, overseeing the erection of the great tents which were stored within one of the nearby port's warehouses for occasions like this. Invites were sent out to all the noble families in the settlements of Alt Clota and food, drink and entertainment in the form of musicians, fools and story-tellers were gathered.

The events were surprisingly poorly attended, however. Bellicus had never known the offer of free meat, drink and merriment in royal company to be ignored the way this celebration was. The invites were returned with the messengers reporting illness or some other excuse for the chieftains' inability to visit Dun Breatann for the festivities.

Narina didn't appear offended but Coroticus was angered by the poor attendance, with much of the food going to waste, uneaten, while the musicians played to less than half-empty tents each evening while still expecting full payment for their talents.

"Why have the ungrateful bastards not come?" the king demanded of Gavo on the second night. "What could be more important than free food and ale? It seems to me my own subjects are thumbing their damn noses at me for some reason."

Bellicus sat by Coroticus's right hand, relegating Senecio—who sometimes took that position nowadays—to a different table, while the guard captain was on the left. Narina and Catia had retired to their chambers in the fortress by this time and the king was, again, quite drunk, his voice seeming much louder than normal without the sounds of a tent-full of revellers to mask it.

One of the cooks had let a joint of beef roast too long and the not-unpleasant smell of it burning wafted through the air, making the druid's mouth water as he watched the guard captain trying to frame a reply to Coroticus's question.

Gavo held his palms up and glanced towards the king, lips pursed, eyebrows raised. "Having spoken to the messengers we sent out, it seems there's some illness sweeping the land," he said. "Who knows, perhaps Drest's druid cast some dark spell on our folk before they returned north?"

The king spat in disgust, clearly not quite believing the excuse but genuinely baffled by the whole affair.

"So, are all my chiefs dying then? They'd bloody well better be, I wasted a fortune on meat for them and it's all going to the dogs. Not to mention those tuneless fools. Look, I gave that one a silver arm-ring yesterday!" He pointed at the three musicians who were, Bellicus thought, quite skilled in their craft, singing a melancholy tune about two lovers separated by an evil witch. "Play something faster you three," Coroticus roared, halting the music instantly as the bards stared at the red-faced monarch fearfully. "Something people can dance to," he went on, finishing in a growl. "If anyone cares to."

"Perhaps there will be more here tomorrow," Bellicus said, smiling reassuringly and sipping his ale, feeling it warm him to his toes. He'd spent a fair amount of time talking to Gavo since his return home, the guard captain filling him in on what had been happening and the mood of the Damnonii, so he wasn't surprised by the low turnout for this feast. It didn't particularly bother Bel though, he was so pleased to have completed his mission successfully, and to have found a new friend in the process, that he was quite happy sitting there enjoying the evening. Duro, to his right, also seemed quite content with a plate full of meat and as much ale as he could drink brought to him whenever he waved by the slave-girls.

Most of the army, gathered to defend the fortress from Drest's forces, had been sent home to bring in the crops and prepare for the coming winter. The weather had already begun to turn, the long, warm nights of August growing colder and darker. Indeed, a persistent rain pattered on the leather roof of their tent even now, dripping through in places where the material needed repaired. The lower status warriors and their wives would normally be beneath those holes getting dripped upon, but, with so few there, everyone was able to find a dry place to enjoy Coroticus's hospitality.

"The people are probably still wary of travelling with the Pictish invasion so fresh in their memories," Bellicus said, turning back to the king. "Don't judge them too harshly for wanting to remain in their homes. It's been a time of great fear for everyone in our lands."

"That's why they should all appreciate their good fortune now that I've seen off Drest and his lackeys," Coroticus retorted, gesturing for a refill irritably. "The gods have favoured us Bel, you know that." He sipped the fresh ale, serving girl hurrying off, eyes downcast, as another man in the corner of the big tent waved her over. "They brought you and Catia – and the centurion there – home, and saw the Pictish turds off without us having to engage them in open battle. They didn't even burn our crops, although Gavo seems to think that's a *bad* sign for some reason." He raised an eyebrow and shook his head as if the guard captain worried too much.

Bellicus opened his mouth to tell the king he agreed with Gavo's assessment – the invaders had clearly left the crops alone because they wanted the Damnonii farmers on their side when they returned, as they surely would, in the spring. But now wasn't the time for that; now was the time for merry making. He absent-mindedly fingered a gold arm ring, one of many valuable gifts the king had given him, and Duro, for bringing the princess home safely, although he wasn't really one for wearing such ostentatious jewellery.

"Why don't I tell the full tale of my adventures over the past few weeks?" he offered, knowing Coroticus always loved stories, but the king shook his head and drained the last of his ale.

"Not tonight, my friend," he said, getting to his feet a little unsteadily. "I've had enough. I'm going to bed. You can regale us all with your adventures tomorrow when, I hope, there will be rather more people to join in celebrating Alt Clota's good fortune."

Everyone in the tent got to their feet although Coroticus was oblivious to the respectful gesture and Gavo waved two of the guards out from the shadows to escort the king to the fortress. At least the man wasn't so drunk he'd need carried up the myriad steps to the royal quarters, although the two bodyguards Gavo had selected were burly enough they would have been able to lift the king if necessary.

"Good night, my lord." Bellicus bowed his head, Duro following suit as Coroticus sauntered out into the night, Gavo placing a fur-lined waterproof cloak around the king's shoulders to keep the rain off. The captain re-joined the druid and the centurion at the high table once their lord was safely off and inside the walls of Dun Breatann.

With the king's departure came a noticeable lightening of the mood. Half a dozen of the men even began to sing along with the musicians and the hooded, wary eyes of the people brightened in glad relief.

"You know Drest, Cunneda and Loarn mac Eirc will be back just as soon as the winter snows pass and the roads are passable once again?" Gavo said, eyeing the druid frankly.

"Of course. They didn't come here for nothing." Bel nodded thoughtfully, absent-mindedly watching a pair of slave girls who'd been commanded to dance in the centre of the room by one of the noblemen. "Why *didn't* they burn the crops? Or rape and pillage our settlements which were, mostly, undefended since many of the warriors had been called here to defend the fortress? Drest is no fool, and neither are the other two. They'll have sent out men to try and turn our people against Coroticus, hoping to return here in the spring to a land still wealthy and populated by people ready to join them." He met Gavo's eyes. "Why doesn't Coroticus understand this? Has he become an idiot since I've been away? Did Catia's abduction addle his wits?"

The guard captain frowned, taken aback by the bluntness of the question, but he thought about it for a long moment before replying. As he opened his mouth to speak one of the ale servers approached their table and he held his peace until she'd left again, wary of their conversation somehow getting back to the king.

"To an extent, aye, the girl's disappearance did addle his mind," Gavo said, leaning in closer to Bellicus so even Duro wouldn't be able to overhear him. "It was as if he was in mourning – not just for Catia, but for his own manhood. He seems unable to hear criticism of his plans or his leadership now, even from me or the queen. He believes the people still back him as they always have, even when things like this happen." He gestured with his hand at the half-empty tent. "Which is probably just as well, to be honest. Who knows what he'd do if he genuinely believed folk were snubbing his grand celebrations?"

"I assume your excuse, about an illness taking everyone, was just a way to placate him then?"

"Aye," Gavo agreed. "The people are angry. It's just as well the Picts decided to invaded at this time of year – if they'd not had to go and prepare for winter I fear we'd have faced open rebellion, and you'd have returned to find a new king of Alt Clota, Bel."

"What should we do then?"

"First, I send riders out in the morning to the nearest villages, ordering the chiefs to get their arses here to join the final night's feasting." Gavo upended his mug and wiped foam from his long beard. "Then…well, I thank Cernunnos you've returned to us, druid. Maybe you'll be able to get through to the king, especially since his daughter is safe again. Things can return to the way they were before, perhaps."

Bellicus shook his head in frustration. "I had planned on asking Coroticus to send men south, to join the warlord, Arthur. He's a good man, a good leader, and he is standing against the Saxons, which I believe we all must do, before it's too late. But now…" He sighed. "We're going to need every warrior we can muster to hold off Loarn and Drest. I'm sorry my friend," he turned to Duro. "I know you wanted us to go with Arthur to smash Horsa and the rest of them and avenge your wife, but it will have to wait."

Gavo nodded. "Hopefully we can get things back to normal quickly, now that you're home, druid." The captain got to his feet, draining the last of his ale in one final, long pull. Bellicus reached up and they grasped forearms, wishing one another a good night.

"One last thing, Bel," the captain said, turning back as he recalled something important. "Like I say, Coroticus has changed since you left. Try not to do anything to irritate him or make him suspicious, and watch what you're saying around Senecio. Don't turn to look at him, he's watching us. He's always watching."

"Senecio?" The druid's brow furrowed. He knew the man, had nodded a greeting to him at the start of the meal, but he had no recollection of him ever being close to the king. "You think he's a spy? For Drest, or Loarn mac Eirc or…?"

"No," the captain shook his head gently. "I believe he is loyal to the king. But he tells Coroticus what he wants to hear, whether it's good advice or not. And I have no doubt he would report back to him if he thought anyone was speaking against him." He patted Bellicus on the arm and got to his feet. "Just mind what you say in front of him – the queen has suspicions he's been trained by your brother druids..."

Gavo left, following the same route the king had taken not so long before and Bel gazed thoughtfully up at the tent roof. He knew the Merlin had someone within Dun Breatann who sent him news about the place – the High Druid had made it clear when they met during Bellicus's quest to rescue Catia. Was Senecio the Merlin's man? Did it matter?

His earlier enjoyment had gone by now, replaced by a cold feeling in the pit of his stomach. He didn't need to check the entrails of a sacrificial lamb, or stare into the flickering orange flames of a bonfire to foresee great troubles approaching from all sides with the coming of spring.

Perhaps even before then.

CHAPTER TEN

With the army disbanded and returned to their own homes there wasn't such a pressing need for large stores of food. But, like every year in Dun Breatann when summer drew to an end, winter supplies had to be collected. Every settlement under King Coroticus's rule sent, as tribute or tax, a portion of their crops and salted meat to the fortress, where it was stored safely within the walls. The men who lived there, such as Gavo and his guards, as well as carpenters and other workers, would contribute by fishing or hunting for deer, hares, birds and whatever else could be snared or shot with a bow.

Sometimes the king himself would go out hunting, enjoying the thrill of chasing down a wild boar or a stag, if one could be found. Today was such a day.

Bellicus had come to the great hall in the morning just after sunrise, alone, letting Duro, who was sharing his roundhouse with him for now, sleep a while longer. He helped himself to some bread and cold ham to quell the rumbling in his empty belly, watching the servants lay fresh straw on the floor, mixed with late-summer flowers to take away the ever-present stench of vomit, stale drink, and dog.

The king came in soon after and, with a nod of greeting, joined the druid at the table although he ate nothing, signalling for a serving girl to bring him only a mug of ale.

"What are you doing today?" Coroticus asked somewhat brusquely, wiping froth from his beard. "I'm going out hunting if you want to come."

Bellicus finished what he was chewing so he didn't spit crumbs all over the king, then put his bread down on the trencher before him. "I was planning on visiting a few of the nearby villages to see if they have need of my services. Healing, spiritual guidance, curses lifted, that sort of thing. Does the people good to see a druid every once in a while."

"That's a shame," Coroticus grunted. "Never mind."

For some reason Bel thought he looked pleased, as if the king had invited him along merely as a formality and was secretly glad he wasn't coming.

Coroticus finished his drink then smiled and got to his feet. Behind him, the small figure of Catia came into the hall, accompanied by Queen Narina. They both grinned when they saw Bellicus eating breakfast and hurried over to the table.

In contrast, the king's smile faded, replaced with a frown when the princess went directly to the seated druid and grasped his arm excitedly.

"Did he tell you? Isn't it exciting?"

Bellicus glanced up from the girl to Narina then on to Coroticus. "Did who tell me what? What's happening, girl?"

The king pursed his lips and looked like he was going to say something, some rebuke, but the queen laid a hand on his arm and the words died although he looked even more irritated by the whole meeting now.

"I'm going hunting! Father says I can come along. Look." She patted her hip and the druid saw a small dagger sheathed there. "If the Saxons ever come back here, I mean to be able to use this," she patted the weapon, the grim expression on her face making her seem older than her eight years. "I've to learn how to shoot a hunting bow too."

Bellicus wasn't sure what to say. He thought it was a mad idea to let the girl go along on a hunt with the men, when they might come up against anything, even a wolf or a bear. Six months ago he'd have asked the king if he thought it was wise – if perhaps Catia should grow for another year or two before joining the hunt. He knew better than to question Coroticus now however, especially when it came to the matter of the princess.

So he simply smiled encouragingly and raised a piece of ham to his lips. "That's good," he said. "Be careful and stay close to the king or Gavo, if he's about. Hunts are very dangerous."

He popped the meat into his mouth and began to chew, savouring its salty flavour, but it almost lodged in his throat as the girl hauled impatiently on his arm.

"What do you mean, Bel? You're coming along too aren't you? Father said he'd ask you."

"I did ask him," Coroticus said in a hard tone. "He's got druid duties to see to today, so you'll just have to make do with my company, if that's all right?"

Catia was oblivious to the king's annoyance and pulled again on the druid's great arm. "You have to come with us," she said petulantly.

"Why?"

"Because I command it, and I'm your princess."

She might have been unable to sense the tension in the air but Bellicus could read it well enough and wondered what he should say. Obviously, the king didn't want him along, perhaps wondering if the girl believed he couldn't protect her from danger, while Narina didn't want to say the wrong thing so said nothing at all.

"Hurry up and decide, druid, whatever it is you're doing." Coroticus turned and strode from the room without a backward glance. "I'm away to get my horse ready. Don't be long, girl. If you're not in the stables soon I'll leave without you."

"Please come, Bel," Catia said, grasping his hand now. "I'd like you to."

She let go of him and ran after Coroticus, shouting for him to slow down and wait on her, leaving the druid and the queen alone.

"In the name of Lug, what was that all about?" he hissed, brows drawn together. "What's wrong with Coroticus? I thought he was going to reprimand me for something at one point there."

"Keep your voice down," Narina said. "He doesn't like you calling Catia 'girl', or 'lass', or anything like that. He thinks you should be calling her 'princess' and being more respectful."

Bellicus was astonished and stared at the queen with his mouth open. He'd always called Catia those things and it had never been an issue before. He wasn't some lowly guardsman by the gods, he was druid of the Damnonii and, as such, could address people as he damn well pleased.

"He's jealous of you," Narina went on, looking back nervously over her shoulder at the door. "You rescued Catia from the Saxons and now she sees you as her protector. She wakes up in the night crying for you, Bel. You must understand how that makes Coroticus feel."

The giant druid digested this information in thoughtful silence then, with a sigh, reached out to pat the queen on the hand but she stepped back, agitated and nervous.

"In the name of Sulis," she muttered, "don't let him see you doing anything like that either. He'll have you cast out if he thinks there's anything between us."

Bellicus shook his head and got his feet, angry himself now. This was all insane – he'd never been anything but loyal to the king. Aye, he'd slept with the queen once, years ago on the night of Beltaine, but he didn't even know it was her.

And Coroticus knew nothing of that – Lug, even Bellicus hadn't known about it until Catia was abducted and the queen confessed to him!

Why was Coroticus acting so belligerently towards him? The man had no right, not after he'd placed his own life in danger to travel the full length of the island to rescue the princess.

"Where are you going?" Narina asked, her tone softer now, conciliatory.

"Hunting," Bel replied and stalked from the hall.

Coroticus's mouth had formed into a thin line when he realised Bellicus would be joining them on their trip, but he'd not complained, simply kicked his heels into his horse and led the party – nine of them including Bel, Duro, Catia and, of course, faithful Gavo – out through the gates of Dun Breatann and north, towards the hills beside the village of Dun Buic. There would be plenty of game there although little in the way of bears or wolves as they'd been mostly killed off by local hunters.

Catia would be relatively safe in the woods there, although even a boar could be deadly if angered and fighting for its life, so Bellicus planned to keep a close eye on the girl, whether Coroticus liked it or not. He carried a spear instead of his druid's staff, just in case they met anything more dangerous than a deer.

The king led the party with the princess beside him on her own small pony, Gavo flanking her other side and the rest of the men in a ragged line behind. Everyone except Bel and the kennel master, Esico, carried a bow with arrows tucked inside their sword belts. The dogs, six of them, tall and rangy, raced along beside them, an apparently undisciplined pack, but the druid knew Esico could control them with an iron fist when the time came. Cai ran with them, tail wagging, enjoying the excitement and new smells of the autumn morning. Bel had brought him along not only because he would benefit from the exercise, but because the powerfully built dog had an excellent nose for tracking.

As they made their way along the road leading up towards the high woods Bel looked east, at the form of Dun Buic Hill, contemplating its resemblance from this direction to a sleeping giant. From any other side the hill looked much like any other shapeless lump in the earth, but here the rock seemed to form the profile of a forehead, nose, mouth, neck and long flat body in repose – it was uncanny, and many tales were told about it by the locals.

When would the giant awaken? When the Damnonii were in dire need, it was said.

Bellicus wondered if they should start petitioning the gods to waken the sleeping titan in time for Drest's inevitable return next spring.

"What are you thinking about?"

The high voice broke his reverie and he turned to the front, seeing the princess eyeing him with a curious half-smile.

"The giant," Bel said, nodding eastwards. "I wish we could wake him up and send him after the Picts and the Saxons. It would save us a lot of trouble."

"Well," she replied, laughing, "you're the one with the magic. Go and tell him to stop lying around and help his people."

He returned her smile, pleased that she seemed to be getting over the traumatic experiences with Horsa and the rest of her sea-wolf abductors. He hadn't been sure if she'd ever be able to put it behind her when he and Duro first rescued her away back at the Giant's Dance, so lost was she in her fear.

The days and weeks since they'd been home though, with Narina's loving presence in particular, had seen Catia's smile return more often and Bel hoped the nightmares the queen had mentioned would soon be banished. Certainly, the girl had nothing to fear in these lands, with winter drawing in. No Saxons, or any other raiders, would come until the spring, and the king's guards had been ordered to keep a close eye on her at all times.

Not to mention Duro – the centurion had taken a shine to the princess and, with him and Bellicus around, there was nothing to threaten her, apart from her own bad memories.

"Did you know Dun Breatann and Dun Buic Hill are formed from the same volcanic rock?" he said, and she looked a little confused as she took this information in.

"You mean they're connected?"

Bellicus eyed her thoughtfully, as if she'd said something unexpectedly insightful. "Perhaps," he replied, and they began to walk again.

They soon reached the top of the hill and made their way into the woods, heading towards the burn which ran down, all the way through Nectovelius's village where Catia had been kidnapped all those months ago. That settlement, over a mile away, couldn't be seen from their position however, and Bel doubted the girl knew her geography well enough to understand exactly where they were.

There was a well-maintained wooden hut amongst a birch grove, which the local hunters and herdsmen used for shelter, and Coroticus led them directly to it. They stowed their packs of provisions, bedrolls and tents inside, knowing it would all be safe while they went about the day's hunt. Those buildings were inviolate, gods-protected sanctuaries only the most desperate of fugitives would dare interfere with on pain of death. The hunters would also spend the night there.

No wonder Catia was so excited, Bel thought, smiling as he recalled similar adventures from his own childhood. The time when, on Iova, he had gone with the island's guards, to hunt seabirds and, ostensibly, boar, although there were very few of them around at that time. The men had caught little, but they spent a wonderful night under the stars beside the sea, drinking by the campfire, singing and telling tales. It was a memory the druid treasured, and he wondered if Catia would remember this trip with similar fondness in years to come.

"We'll lay the snares first," Coroticus said, lifting one of the simple but cleverly designed traps from his pack as the others followed his lead, Catia included. These would hopefully catch hares, squirrels or wood pigeons while the men went off in search of bigger game.

"Let's go," he commanded. "Uven will stay here with the horses. If anyone gets separated or lost, make your way back here. Got that?" He eyed Catia who nodded as he led her outside and gestured about them at the trees. "See anything you can use as a marker if you need to find your way back?"

She looked around, intent on her task, then smiled, pointing at a single Scots pine. At this time of the year the birch trees which surrounded their cabin had lost many of their leaves, with the remainder being various shades of gold, orange or brown. The Scots pine, in stark contrast, was a different shape and retained its green leaves.

It stood like a beacon just a few feet away from the cabin.

"Well done," the king nodded, patting the princess's shoulder. "The original builders of the cabin chose this spot because of that tree. If anyone is lost, in a blizzard say, that tree will lead them here to safety. Mark it well, my girl."

Catia nodded, lips pursed in concentration as she took in the king's words, and Bellicus knew she was taking this all quite seriously. She had managed to escape from her Saxon captors before he rescued her, but, without any idea of where she was, or any real landmark to aim for, she'd become lost and soon recaptured by Horsa. Her expression told the druid she meant to be better prepared should, gods forbid, anything similar ever happen to her again.

"You know how to set a trap like this, don't you? No? In the name of Cernunnos, Gavo, what have you been teaching my daughter?"

The words were spoken lightly, and the guard captain spread his hands apologetically, winking at Catia, who smiled in return as the king wandered deeper into the trees, waving her to follow. He bent down the branch of a willow tree then knelt and showed her how to set up a twitch-up snare with the pre-cut sticks in his hand, letting her do it mostly by herself, finally baiting it with a piece of mouldy cheese. If a small animal wandered into the noose they'd left on the grass the wire would twitch and the branch would spring back, hanging the animal in the air and keeping its body there to be collected later. Bellicus watched fondly, hoping the trap would catch something, knowing it would bring Catia a great sense of achievement.

Perhaps this was a good idea, he thought. The usual way of things was to teach the boys to hunt and fight and other ways of war, while girls learned etiquette and how to receive guests and run the household and so on. Catia had a spirit in her though, that would allow her to excel at the traditional 'manly' pursuits if nurtured properly.

They left Uven, the friendly stablemaster with a pronounced limp whom Bellicus had always liked, tending to the horses while the rest of the party slipped quietly into the trees to lay the rest of their traps, eyes scanning all around for signs of prey to shoot with their bows.

It was a pleasant day, dry and bright if a little chilly, as the sun was obscured by a blanket of light grey clouds and a breeze blew from the east. That would help the dogs locate game but also warn any beasts downwind of their proximity. Still, at least it wasn't raining.

Bellicus turned to Duro who had by now lost all of the flab he'd carried when they first met in Luguvalium, pleased to see the middle-aged centurion with a bright, eager gleam in his eyes. The man seemed to have accepted his wife's death and moved on, even if he was prone to occasional bouts of melancholy.

"You any good with that?" the druid muttered, nodding at the short bow Duro carried.

"I'm better with a javelin, that's what we trained with in the legions, not these," he shrugged. "But I can use one well enough, although you never had a chance to see it when we rescued the princess from the Saxons."

They grinned at one another, remembering how Duro had carried a hunting bow that dark, horror-filled night, ready to shoot down any of the enemy soldiers who came after them. Bellicus and Catia had managed to mount Darac and make good their escape before the Saxons realised what was happening and, laughing in delight, the centurion had thrown the bow aside and climbed atop his own horse to join them, riding like the wind for the hidden sacred grove where they found safety.

"Hopefully we come across a stag and I'll show you how good my aim is," Duro finished, eyes searching the undergrowth and densely packed trees ahead.

Bellicus didn't answer but he could well imagine the folk of Dun Breatann's delighted chatter should his friend return to the fortress with meat to feed a host of warriors, and a fine set of antlers to be mounted proudly in the great hall. It seemed more likely that they would go back home with only a few hares and a fox or two, Bel thought, but perhaps the gods would look favourably on them that day.

As they went, the men laid their snares, some of them allowing Catia to do it with them so she could practice, but they saw little in the way of game. No-one seemed to mind – the girl's presence, her eagerness to learn, appeared to have enchanted the entire party. Whatever they caught that day would be gratefully received, but even if their snares remained empty the druid didn't think the hunters would be overly disappointed.

There was a snap from ahead, as one of the men let fly an arrow and Bel caught a glimpse of orange as a fox darted away into the undergrowth. The missile missed its target and clattered uselessly into a tree as the bowman cursed his poor aim. He went to retrieve it as the other warriors jeered at him good-naturedly, and made a rude gesture over his shoulder in return.

"Perhaps we should split up into smaller groups," Coroticus said, bringing them to a halt. "I'll take Catia to the left, with Gavo. The rest of you pair off and Esico will follow a little way behind with the hounds, just in case we come across anything big. Make sure at least one of each pair has a horn to sound in case of danger. We can meet up at the little waterfall near the marsh, to the north-east – there – at midday, and have something to eat." He pointed and there were nods of agreement as the waterfall was a landmark as well known as the Scots pine back at the hunter's cabin.

"I want Bel and Duro to come with us too," the princess said, looking up at the king, who shook his head.

"We'll have more success if we hunt in smaller parties," he said, somewhat irritably. "I'm sure me and Gavo can keep you entertained until midday."

The girl appeared put out by his hard tone and glanced back at the druid who nodded surreptitiously, not wanting to aggravate Coroticus any further.

They split into the groups suggested and moved off, the others soon becoming lost to Bel's sight within the thick trees which cast shadows on the ground and made it hard to see very far ahead. Soon, even the sounds of the rest of their party were lost and Bellicus and Duro were essentially on their own with Cai, whose passage made even less noise than his two human companions.

A tall chestnut tree loomed up at them, much higher than the birch and elms surrounding it, and Bel knelt to lay his snare, Duro having already set his not far from the cabin. The centurion sat on a mossy rock and pulled out his ale skin, taking a short draught before replacing the stopper and ruffling Cai's ears. The dog didn't look up, brown eyes fixed on something only he could see, and Duro hissed the druid's name.

Bellicus, snare set, straightened, noting Cai's fixed gaze, then, as hackles began to rise on the dog's back, the druid drew his sword and Duro fitted an arrow to his bowstring, tapping the horn that hung on a long leather strap around his neck.

Whatever Cai had sensed, it was no hare.

They moved slowly ahead, alert for danger, stepping nimbly, instinctively, across dried out twigs which would break with a loud crack if stood upon, giving away their position to the unseen prey.

As they walked, a grouse wandered onto the path not far in front of them, stopping in surprise when it saw them approaching, but not one of the three hunters bothered with it and it ran clumsily back into the foliage. Bellicus hoped they could find it again later for he greatly enjoyed roast grouse, but for now, they had to concentrate on the animal that had made Cai's hackles rise.

It wasn't often the big dog would become roused to nervousness or fear and the druid felt his palms become sweaty, and the battle fever begin to course through his blood as he contemplated what they were about to encounter. A boar? A wolf? Should they sound the horn and wait for Esico's hounds to join them, along with the other warriors? Bellicus discarded the idea, knowing the noise and bustle would chase their prey off and likely ruin any chance they had of bringing it down. Besides, it was unlikely to be anything very big, or dangerous, as these woods were hunted so often that the bigger game was mostly all gone.

Another thought struck him as they moved in near-silence towards a clearing, where the land sloped down into a small valley: perhaps it wasn't an animal they were tracking at all, perhaps it was men.

Raiders.

He paused, looking across at Duro but, before he could alert the centurion to his fears a shout broke the silence.

"Father! Father, help!"

It was Catia, and, spell broken, Bellicus began to run.

CHAPTER ELEVEN

At the bottom of the slope, a small figure lay on the grass, staring up at something that must have appeared from the trees fringing the clearing there. Bellicus swore, wishing it was raiders after all, for what faced them down there was even more deadly.

Towering over the scene, so huge it would even dwarf the druid, stood a brown bear. Coroticus was face-down and unmoving on the grass a dozen feet away from the princess. Gavo had drawn his sword and was attempting to keep the giant beast away from Catia who seemed frozen with terror.

Cai streaked ahead and Duro blasted the hunting horn as Bellicus roared the forest god's name, "Cernunnos!" like a battle cry, hoping to distract the bear before its massive paws killed Gavo and the princess.

From behind him the sounds of barking could be heard, and Cai, far in front of Bellicus, cannoned into the bear, his powerful jaws locking onto the bigger animal's leg. There was a deafening roar as the bear moved to strike the dog away but Gavo jumped forward and managed to stab the point of his sword into the beast's belly.

Cai somehow managed to avoid the giant paws, letting go and backing away, snarling and barking furiously while the bear, confused and wounded – if only slightly – stood still, unsure which enemy to face first. Before it could decide, Duro's arrow slammed into its torso, prompting another angry roar.

Cai came forward again, drawing the bear's attention, and another of the centurion's missiles hammered home in the thick, dark fur.

"This bow doesn't have the power to kill a beast of that size," Duro shouted desperately, but Bellicus already knew that and he raced towards Catia, who remained on the ground, still shouting for her father to help. Her cries once again brought the bear's attention onto her and it roared in fury, stepping forward and leaning down to silence the girl forever.

The druid, without thinking about what he was doing, charged down the hill, building momentum on its slope, and ran directly into the giant animal, rocking it back, but only slightly. The attack caught it by surprise, however and, as Bellicus bounced off it and fell to the ground, Cai locked his teeth on the bear's rump and yet another arrow lodged in its front.

"Get up!" the druid shouted, stumbling to his feet and, half-running, half-crawling, lifted Catia in his left arm and tried to move away from the enraged bear which had now decided Gavo was the best target. One huge paw, bigger than a man's torso, swung out, catching the guard captain in mid-sword-swing, lifting him into the air and sending him flying onto the grass, where he lay still, arm bent at a weird angle.

A fourth arrow sprouted from the bear's body now, stopping it as it began moving forward to finish Gavo off properly, and then Esico's dogs, barking in fear and excitement, sprinted down from the trees behind and set about the hapless bear. The sound of Duro's horn had also alerted the other two hunters who, shouting to confuse the massive, angry beast even further, ran into the fray. One of them carried a spear and he was able to get behind the target and plunge it with quite some force into its back.

The bear spun, tearing the polearm from the warrior's grasp, and now the bear was like a pin-cushion, with arrows and a spear stuck in its flesh, while Cai and the other dogs continued to harry it and the final huntsman tried to land a blow with his sword while keeping safely away from the deadly paws.

Bellicus placed Catia on the ground although she didn't want to let him go, fastening her arms around his neck, crying, "Father," repeatedly.

"Hush, girl," he said, prying her loose and staring into her red, teary eyes. "Your father is lying on the ground. I need to go and help the others defeat the beast."

When he finally turned back and ran towards the battle one of the warriors and three of the hunting dogs were dead – sprawled broken and bloody on the grass around the bear. The spearman had managed to retrieve his weapon and prodded it at the animal's back, creating numerous wounds, while Esico, Duro and the other swordsman shouted and aimed their blades in slashing strokes which occasionally drew blood.

Before the druid could join the fight, the bear decided it wanted no more and fell onto its four paws, lumbering off towards the trees. Cai stood, panting, exhausted but apparently uninjured, and Bellicus whistled, calling him back now that the fight was done.

As the dog trotted towards him the scene seemed to trigger something within the druid's memory—it was as if he'd seen this before. In a dream perhaps? Time slowed, and all became silent as, unbidden, a fog settled upon the druid's mind.

Merlin's face appeared in his head and he remembered what the older druid had called Arthur, the warlord who was sworn to halt the Saxon invasion: Bear of Britain.

The trance passed and, blinking, Bellicus returned to himself. He had no idea what it meant, but he knew it would bring bad luck if they killed the bear.

"Leave it," he cried, powerful voice filling the clearing. "Let it live!" He had to repeat his words more than once before, at last, the men got the message and allowed the retreating bear to go unmolested, until it was lost within the trees, leaving only dead, prone, or panting warriors and hounds in its wake.

Bel glanced back once more to make sure Catia remained safely where he'd left her, then he ran to the king who still wasn't moving. The druid knelt and felt Coroticus's neck, trying to find a pulse.

"He's alive," he murmured in relief, examining a bruise on the king's temple which had already begun to turn a sickly yellow-brown colour. He could see no other visible injuries and suspected the bear had knocked the king flying just as it had done to Gavo.

"Catia," he called. "Fetch water from your pack and pour a little – just a little, mind – onto the king's lips. If you have a blanket, or there's one in Coroticus's pack, spread it over him. Don't worry, he'll be fine. We just need to make him comfortable."

He stood and hurried across to the guard captain, pleased to see Gavo was conscious but disoriented. The man's arm was broken in half, with the bone sticking out through the skin. It was a horrific wound, but not one that should be fatal if cleaned and looked after properly.

"We'll need to set that, my friend," Bel said, lowering himself onto his haunches by the captain and nodding at his arm. "It won't be pleasant."

Gavo didn't look down, undoubtedly knowing, from the way the limb flopped sickeningly of its own accord, what had happened. Yet he appeared surprisingly unconcerned and the druid suspected the guard captain had gone into shock, trauma masking the pain one would expect to be associated with such a horrific injury.

"Esico, I have a skin with unwatered wine in my pack, fetch it for me. Hurry! Bring the strips of cloth in there as well. Duro, go and remove the fletchings and heads from a couple of arrows, I'll need them for a splint."

When they were alone, Gavo looked at the druid with a strange expression, opening his mouth more than once as if about to ask a question, but lacking the courage to do so.

"What is it, man," Bel finally demanded, watching as Gavo tried to pry the heads from his unused arrows. "Out with it."

The injured guard captain gritted his teeth, as if the shock of their battle was finally leaving him and pain was beginning to register, but this time he forced himself to speak.

"The princess was shouting for her father to help her," he said.

"What of it?" Bel replied, turning back and gazing at him, puzzled.

"Her father was lying, dead or unconscious, on the ground. She'd seen the bear strike him and she'd seen him, unmoving, over there, as he still is even now."

Bellicus narrowed his eyes, not understanding what Gavo was getting at. "So?"

"She was calling for you, druid."

A chill ran down Bel's back, but he held his expression immobile, knowing a wrong move could spell disaster.

Esico returned then, mercifully, with the wineskin, and the druid told Gavo to drink deeply from it, holding it up to the captain's dry lips. Duro brought the arrows over and Bellicus told them all what was going to happen next, as they attempted to reset the broken arm.

The operation went smoothly enough and Bellicus thanked Sulis, goddess of healing, for such a calm patient. There was nothing worse than working on someone who was hysterical and unhelpful. Gavo was nothing like that, being calm and gritting his teeth against any pain he might have felt when Bel realigned the snapped arm and bound the splint into place. It helped that the 'unwatered wine' Esico had retrieved from his pack was actually a draught the druid had mixed for its anaesthetic properties.

Bellicus had learned from experience to be prepared for anything when men walked abroad with the intent of using deadly weaponry.

The guard captain was soon sleeping and placed on one of the stretchers which were brought from where they were always stored back in the hunting cabin. The spearman who fetched the stretchers also returned with a horse, and his dead companion was placed on its back for the journey to Dun Breatann, where he would receive a hero's burial.

Bel wondered if Esico would demand the bodies of his fallen dogs were brought back in similar, honoured fashion, but thankfully the kennel-master held his peace and allowed the beasts to be carried away like any other animal that died on a hunt. They would be butchered for their meat and fed to their canine brethren over the winter. Meat was too precious to waste at this time of the year, even that of heroic dogs who had helped save a princess.

Coroticus couldn't be roused but Bellicus was content the king wasn't in any real danger. He was more worried how the man would take things when he finally came to and realised he'd taken no part in the battle, and, not for the first time in the past year, had to be rescued by those around him.

How long had the king been unconscious? Bellicus wondered. Had he, like Gavo, heard Catia shouting 'father' and suspected the girl was calling for the druid?

"You ready?" Duro demanded, disturbing his thoughts. "It looks like the weather's about to take a turn for the worse. We better get these lads back to the cabin as soon as possible."

Bel nodded and lifted his end of the king's stretcher, the centurion taking the other, and they began to walk, Cai at their side, Esico and the spearman carrying Gavo while little Catia walked, leading the horse with its grim burden.

Her first hunting trip hadn't turned out as they'd all hoped, Bel thought sadly. She would look back on this day for years to come, aye, but her memories wouldn't be as happy as his own fondly remembered night of song under the stars on Iova.

CHAPTER TWELVE

As it turned out, Gavo's injuries were less debilitating than those Coroticus suffered. The blow to the temple had made the king violently sick when he came to, but, with his return to consciousness came the realisation he had also suffered a broken leg. It wasn't as severe as the guard captain's snapped arm, but it meant the king was confined to his bed in Dun Breatann for days once Bel had fashioned a splint around it. Even when the druid allowed him to leave the bedchamber he could only move around on wooden crutches and spent most of his time in the great hall, in front of the fire.

Of course, with the king's injury came fresh rumours of unrest among the folk of Alt Clota. Coroticus had suffered much misfortune in recent months, and it was said that the gods had abandoned him and, by extension, all the people and lands he ruled. There was little anyone could do to combat such talk however, especially once the weather turned.

And turn it did, as winter set in with a vengeance, bringing ice and snow which effectively cut off the roads for miles around, although the fortress was still able to get supplies when needed via the trading and fishing ships that plied the Clota all year round. Despite the cold and the wind that battered the buildings on the high rock of Dun Breatann it was a pleasant time for Bellicus.

His skill as a storyteller was called on often, to entertain the king, his family, and the few guests who travelled through the snow and rain for reasons of their own. And, when Bel wasn't telling tales, he sat at the high table listening to Gavo regaling them all with his version of various adventures he'd been part of. The recent battle against Loarn Mac Eirc might have been lost, but the eventful journey to Arachar, and miraculous rescue from the rampant Dalriadans was a favourite story. Naturally, the guard captain barely mentioned Coroticus's monomania in the ill-fated battle and exaggerated the king's attempted rescue of the young warrior who fell into the loch.

Bellicus very much enjoyed the tale, although he'd had the full truth of it from Gavo and, like the captain, worried about the morale of the Damnonii warriors come the spring.

Duro also made the most of the days spent in the fortress, honing his skills with the spatha, sparring against the young soldiers of the garrison. Despite his forty-two-years, the centurion was still a match for even the best of the Damnonii warriors, now that he'd regained his muscular, lean physique, the flour-stained apron and beer-belly but a fading memory.

It wasn't just his martial talents that Duro wanted to refine though, as Bellicus found, quite to his surprise one afternoon when he went for a walk around Dun Breatann's southern wall with Cai. He had some old bread soaked in cooking fat and he left it on the grass next to him as he looked out across the shining waters of the Clota. The dog peered at the food but knew better than to take it. This tasty morsel was for someone else.

Within moments, the raven, Uchaf, appeared, enormous wings spread majestically as it swept down to land gracefully on the wall. It eyed the druid, and the dog, and the bread, but remained where it was.

"Hello," Bellicus said, smiling. Sometimes the bird would reply with the same word, a feat Bel had taught it, and something that had astonished Duro the first time he heard it. But today Uchaf merely looked at him.

Bellicus turned away to gaze over the river again and, eventually, the raven hopped down onto the grass and wandered across to the food, before swallowing it and returning to its perch on the wooden wall again. Bird and druid looked at one another for a time before the sound of approaching footsteps scared Uchaf away, great wings opening wide as it dived towards the water far below only to swoop upwards at the last moment, cawing its thanks for the bread.

Bellicus grinned and turned to see Duro coming towards him.

"Well met, Bel," said the former baker with a slightly sheepish look on his face before he got straight to the point. "You, ah, you make up your own stories, don't you? You know how to make them, well, rhyme and flow with…"

He trailed off, lost for the words to properly describe what he meant, and the druid came to his rescue, nodding encouragingly, as if he was talking to Catia, rather than the middle-aged, battle-hardened centurion.

"Aye, I craft stories and even, sometimes, songs. What about it?"

"Well, eh, I'd..." Duro's face flushed red and he turned away, gazing out across the dark waters of the river, biting his lip.

"Come, my friend!" Bellicus laughed, truly surprised by Duro's behaviour. "What's the matter? I've never seen you like this before – spit it out. What do you need from me? You know I'll help in any way I can."

Duro stared at the calm waters below for a moment longer then grimaced, as if making up his mind to do something deeply unpleasant and turned back to the druid towering over him.

"I'd like you to help me write a song for Alatucca."

Now it was Bel's turn to be silent, the request so completely unexpected that he wasn't sure what to say although, of course, there was only one way he could respond.

He nodded seriously, all trace of amusement gone from his demeanour.

"I'd be honoured, Duro," he said. "I think it's a great idea. We're always needing more songs, especially in the depths of such a grim winter as this. I must admit, though," he pursed his lips and frowned at the centurion, "I never thought you had this side to you."

Again, Duro flushed and turned away towards the Clota, shrugging his broad shoulders. "I never thought I had either, until I met you and realised just how powerful words could be. I never had a chance to say goodbye to her, Bel. This seems as good a way as any to honour what we had."

So, as the snow and drizzle swirled about the high rock each afternoon, the druid and the centurion locked themselves away in Bel's roundhouse, fire blazing, and started working on a song for Alatucca.

An old Roman three-stringed lute was found in a store-room, and Bel used it to interpret Duro's hummed musical ideas, which weren't at all what the druid expected when they'd started this. Instead of a sad lament, or a sweet melody, the centurion's song was dark and ominous, with only short sections where pleasant arpeggiated chords contrasted jarringly with the grim feelings the rest of the music inspired. It was quite unlike anything Bellicus would ever have written by himself but, as Duro explained, the dark sections were for his feelings about the Saxons who had murdered his wife, while the happier parts were for the good times they'd spent together.

The song really did open the druid's eyes to a hitherto unseen, more sensitive side of the centurion and reminded Bellicus never to take anyone at face value or make hasty judgements about, well, people in general. They would always surprise you.

By the time they'd managed to put the music into a structure that the centurion was happy with, Duro had even taught himself how to play a simple wooden flute that one of the guards gifted to him when he heard the singing drifting down from the high tower. The centurion wasn't proficient by any means, but he was able to follow Bel's direction and, after practising over many days, learned how to play the whole song without making any mistakes. That allowed them to double many parts, playing the same notes together, giving the song an intensity and expansiveness that it lacked when only one instrument was playing.

"What about lyrics?" Bellicus asked when they'd been sitting together one morning, playing the same parts over and over until Duro's hand cramped up. "It's always good to have words people can sing along with. And this is supposed to be about your wife after all."

Duro set down the flute and reached for the tall pot of ale that rested on a table by the wall, filling their cups for the third time already that day. He sipped the brew and reached into his tunic, bringing out a small wax tablet which he handed to the druid with an apologetic shrug.

"That's the best I've been able to come up with so far. You could take a look and change it around a bit?"

Bel took the proffered tablet in one hand, and the refilled ale mug in the other and read Duro's words thoughtfully, imagining how they would fit into the music they'd come up with. When he finished, he looked up at the centurion, who stared back at him like a puppy seeking its master's reassurance and nodded.

"These lyrics are very good," the druid said. "We will work on them and get ready to perform this piece for the king. I think all the folk of Dun Breatann will like it!"

* * *

When he wasn't spending time playing music with Duro, Bellicus found himself in the king's chamber. Coroticus was bored, even more so than everyone else stuck indoors during the harsh winter months, being unable to walk and having to rest his broken leg for most of the day so it would set properly. As a result, the king regularly sent for his druid to tell him stories – the old ones everyone knew about heroes like Peredur and Fionn, or the gods, Maponos, Lug, and Dis Pater – but Coroticus would often command Bellicus to tell him about his time hunting for the abducted Princess Catia.

The king would stare at him disconcertingly when he talked about those times, nodding his head grimly whenever it came to the parts where the druid and Duro fought the Saxons, a strange gleam in his eyes

Bellicus grew ever more convinced Coroticus was a different man from the friend he'd known before Catia's abduction, and he was always very careful not to speak too fondly of the girl when she came up in his recounting of their adventures.

Queen Narina kept her distance from Bellicus throughout those cold months, which shouldn't have bothered the druid but, for some reason, he found his eyes drawn toward her slim, pleasant figure any time their paths did cross. His eyes lingered on her attractive but hardly beautiful features, and he often found himself recalling that pale complexion when he closed his eyes in bed at night.

He may have been a druid with a lifetime of learning and training in a multitude of disciplines, but he was still a young man, and the hazy memory of that Beltaine he'd spent with Narina – when they'd conceived the princess – made his loins stir uncomfortably every time he thought of it.

Princess Catia was a problem too. Not the girl herself, who had, as far as Bellicus could see, become her old self once again, no, it was the rumours about her that worried the druid.

Gavo had told him about them a few weeks after their run-in with the bear.

"I don't know how," the guard captain told him as they ate a cold breakfast of meat and cheese in the great hall one morning, "but the rumours of what the princess called to you on our ill-fated hunting trip have spread all throughout the fortress. The servants and guards are all gossiping about it, despite my best efforts to stamp it out." He shrugged and shook his head in puzzled disgust. "I would swear to Taranis that I was the only one who heard her call you 'Father', but, somehow, word of it has got out. How can that be? I can't explain it."

Bellicus put down his spoon, porridge forgotten at this news. It wasn't just the rumours that had driven away his appetite, it was the fact he – Druid of Dun Breatann – hadn't heard about them before now. And the thought that maybe the king had.

"Why did she call you that, do you think?"

Bellicus shrugged and forced himself to begin eating again, shaking his head slightly as he chewed. "She was terrified out of her wits and it's no surprise is it? Just back here after weeks as a captive of the Saxon animals, and attacked by another in a place where she's supposed to feel safe. I wouldn't read anything into it Gavo."

The captain nodded as if accepting the druid's explanation, but his eyes lingered just a moment too long on Bellicus's face and it was obvious his suspicions hadn't been fully allayed. Again, the druid thought about growing a beard for, as Catia grew older, it seemed likely her face would change to match his even more.

Then the gossip would be impossible to silence, and the king would…well, who knew what Coroticus would do?

As if on cue, the king hobbled into the room, leaning heavily on his wooden crutch which he still needed to get about although every day saw more of his old strength and mobility returning. He saw Gavo and Bellicus at the table together and came over to join them, waving them back onto their stools as they made to rise respectfully.

"Sit down, lads, sit down. Finish your meal." He sniffed and pursed his lips appreciatively. "Smells good. Woman! Bring me some of this porridge and a mug of ale."

The servant Coroticus had addressed, a plain, middle-aged lady with a thick waist and chest to match, bowed her head and set about gathering the food and drink.

Bellicus was pleased to see the king clapping his hands in eager anticipation as the woman set his steaming bowl on the table in front of him, a full mug by his right hand. It seemed Coroticus was in a good mood this day.

"Sleep well, my lord?"

"Aye," Coroticus agreed, spooning some of the porridge into his mouth. A little dribbled down his bearded chin but he ignored it, continuing to eat with gusto. "Like a babe. The pain from my injuries has almost gone away now, thanks in no small measure to you and your strange-smelling potions. I'll soon be back to my usual self. At last!" Setting down his spoon he took a long drink of ale and stretched back on the stool, raising his head up to the ceiling and rolling it from side to side. Bellicus could hear the muscles popping and, as Coroticus began eating again the druid thought his friend had aged a great deal in the past few months.

At thirty-three the king was seven years older than Bellicus, but the lines on his face had deepened recently and it seemed to Bel that his king appeared closer to forty now. Truly the stress of ruling Alt Clota, along with Catia's abduction, was taking a great deal from Coroticus.

As if reading his thoughts, the king, breakfast now finished, grinned. "It's been a long, hard year," he said, "and the winter solstice has passed. Yet I feel like celebrating something—my return to rude health perhaps, eh? Aye, it's tempting fate to celebrate before I'm fully healed, I know that druid, but..." He looked out through one of the small open windows and gestured. "It's so dark and miserable all the time. A good feast always chases away the gloom for a time, doesn't it Gavo?"

The guard captain grunted non-committally but didn't voice the fears Bellicus read in his eyes – fears that the people of Alt Clota, already irritated by their king's carousing when times were so hard, would become even angrier at his rule.

"Oh, don't worry," Coroticus grumbled, also sensing the unspoken reproach in Gavo's stiff posture and downcast eyes. "I don't mean anything too lavish. Just a bit of meat and ale, a well-banked fire in the hearth, with music and storytelling. I'm not suggesting we empty the larder while I drink myself insensible."

A small smile creased the corners of Gavo's mouth and he nodded. "Aye, my lord, that sounds good. A song or two always lightens the mood around the fortress."

"That's settled then." Coroticus lifted his crutch and used it to get to his feet. "I'll have Narina arrange it. If you have any new stories or songs for us Bel, they'd be most welcome. Right, time for my walk around the fortress. I'll take a piece of that buttered bread for your raven on the summit Bel, and I will see you both later on, at the feast."

"Not me, lord," the captain replied, a look of regret on his large face. "I'm on guard duty tonight. I'll come in for a song or two, but I'll need to be at my post. Can't have the men slacking off when we're at war with so many of our neighbours."

"Don't be ridiculous man," the king said. "Drest and Loarn mac Eirc and that lot are all gone. No one would attempt to take Dun Breatann in the depths of winter, it would be madness. No, I insist you join us tonight. Have someone else take your place on the walls – the men can do without you for one evening."

Without waiting for a reply Coroticus shuffled off, out the door towards the stairs that led outside where he would take his daily exercise. Climbing the hundreds of stairs all around the giant rock Dun Breatann was situated upon was exactly the sort of thing needed to strengthen his injured leg.

Bellicus and Gavo watched him go and then, when he was out of sight, the captain shook his head and blew out a long breath, clearly unhappy.

"What's wrong?" the druid asked. "You've been given the night off to drink and make merry with your friends. Anyone else would be happy."

Gavo shook his head, and Bellicus saw the lines on his face too were more deeply ingrained than they had been before Catia's abduction.

"The king seems to forget we are at war. Whether the Picts or the Dalriadans *are* miles away in their own lands, an army needs discipline or, when the time comes to fight, orders aren't carried out and battles are lost. He'd never have allowed me to miss my turn on the watch a year ago." He waited on the serving girl to clear the table and move out of earshot before leaning in close and muttering, "I fear where we're heading, Bel. When you returned with the princess, I hoped Coroticus would go back to the way he used to be. Give up his warlike streak, make amends with the likes of Drest but…"

"His whole being was rocked to the core, Gavo," the druid said softly. "And from what you've told me about Loarn mac Eirc – what the sick bastard said about Catia…I don't think Coroticus will ever let that rest. There will be no peace between Alt Clota and Dalriada while Loarn is king there. So, for now…" He leaned back on the stool and rested his hands on his thighs. "We follow orders, as we always do. Coroticus is our liege lord and, although we should continue to advise him if we think he is making a mistake, we must do as he commands." Getting to his feet he smiled down at the fretting guardsman. "You have a feast to look forward to, man, straighten your face. We've all had worse commands to obey in the past!"

With that he rose to his feet, shaved head almost brushing the ceiling, and clapped Gavo on the shoulder reassuringly. "I'm away to find Duro – we have a song to perfect if we're going to play it tonight at the feast. Try not to worry. Things will sort themselves out, they always do."

With a last grin at the guard captain Bellicus strode from the room but, as he climbed the stairs to the house he shared with Duro the smile fell from his face and was replaced with a frown just as deep as Gavo's had been.

* * *

Apparently, Coroticus had forgotten his earlier promise to only have a small feast, for, when Bellicus and Duro made their way into the hall between the fortress's twin peaks they found the place packed. Despite the freezing rain that made the many stairs slick and seemed to seep right into one's very bones, about twenty of the local folk had accepted the invitations Narina had sent out to them mere hours before.

The druid was a little surprised – and although he wouldn't admit it, put out – that the feast had begun so early, without his presence. In earlier times Bellicus would have been the master of ceremonies at a gathering such as this within the fortress. Now, he suspected the king cared little for such traditions – Coroticus had started the celebration early so he could begin drinking as soon as possible. It was a vice the king had never really been prone to before, but it had taken hold of him during Catia's absence, as happened to so many people, and was now a habit that would prove difficult, if not impossible, to curtail.

"Well, they seem happy enough," Duro said, not quite understanding the druid's unhappy expression when they walked into the packed room.

"Of course they are. They're getting a free feast aren't they? It's the dozens, nay, hundreds of families living nearby that haven't been invited that I worry about. They'll hear about this and…ah, well, there's nothing I can do about it now, me and Gavo can only offer advice. The king will do as he pleases."

They took their seats at the high table, Bellicus in his accustomed place to the right hand of Coroticus who appeared already merry, face flushed, beads of sweat on his forehead for, despite the chill outside, the hall was warm. The druid nodded a greeting to the king and sat down, blinking to clear his eyes from the smoke that was a by-product of the banked hearth and cooking fires and Duro took a place beside his giant friend.

Gavo waved to them from the other end of the hall, for he had a seat nearer the door. By rights he, as captain of the guards, should also have enjoyed a place at the high table, but, since the Saxon's attack on Dun Buic that led to the abduction of Princess Catia, he'd taken to sitting by the entrance, ready to meet any threat to the king as soon as it appeared. Of course, there was no chance of a hostile force sneaking inside the fortress of Dun Breatann without an alarm being raised, but the guard captain insisted on his position and Coroticus had simply shrugged and gone along with it.

Queen Narina was seated to the king's left, but Bellicus was careful not to attract her attention other than to nod a polite greeting. Catia was nowhere to be seen – presumably she'd been tucked up safely in bed with two or three soldiers guarding her chamber door. Senecio sat to the queen's left, a smug look on his face.

Or perhaps that was just Bel's imagination.

A group of musicians were performing a tune, and some of the guests danced in the centre of the room. Two trenchers laden with roast beef and freshly baked bread were brought for the two newcomers by a serving girl who also carried a jug of beer which she used to fill their mugs before hurrying away into the smoky gloom again.

"The common folk of Alt Clota might frown on their king's habit of wasting valuable resources on lavish, unnecessary feasts," Duro chuckled, tearing off a chunk of beef and washing it down with a long pull from his mug, "but I'm not complaining. This is the way to live, eh?"

"Aye, perhaps," Bellicus agreed half-heartedly, and then a wicked smile tugged at the edges of his mouth. "But I wouldn't eat or drink too much, my friend. We've to perform your new song in a little while and I don't want nerves getting the better of you. It wouldn't be the first time I've seen a musician throwing up before a performance when he realises how many people are there to see it."

The centurion waved the druid's warning away, but a worried look came over his face that only deepened when Bellicus barked an unsympathetic laugh and crammed a chunk of bread into his mouth. From that point on, Duro took half his friend's advice, eating only a little of his bread and meat, but downing more beer than he normally would, presumably to give himself courage to face the audience who were, like him, growing steadily more inebriated.

"You know the words?"

"Aye, like the back of my own hand," Duro nodded, raising his voice to answer Bellicus's question as the noise inside the hall had grown steadily louder, as was always the way during a feast.

"And you remember we only play that section once? The second time around we go into the new, faster part, right?"

"Don't worry," the centurion said, watching as the queen strode around to the front of the table and gestured for Coroticus to join her in a dance. "I know the song. I won't make any mistakes." The king spread his hands incredulously and tapped his crutch. How was he supposed to dance with an injured leg? "Just you make sure you don't mess it up, Bel, because I'm not a good enough flute player to mask any mistakes."

On the floor, Narina shook her head playfully and turned away, finding a partner – Bellicus recognised him as an elderly cobbler – amongst the people already dancing, and the musicians played even louder. As he looked on, the druid sensed someone watching him and he glanced sidelong to see the king glaring at him.

Apparently even watching Narina dance was enough to irritate Coroticus these days. The druid turned back to Duro and asked the centurion some vague, inane question, feeling the king's drunken stare boring into him the whole time.

Dun Breatann certainly wasn't the welcoming home it had once been. Bellicus wondered if it ever would be again. He could only guess that Coroticus was feeling jealous because he'd heard the rumours about Catia's parentage and, if that was indeed the case, it would only be a matter of time before things came to a head.

Perhaps it would be better if Bellicus and Duro headed back down south, perhaps join up with Arthur and Merlin again for a time, in their fight against Hengist and his hordes…He couldn't stop another surreptitious glance at Coroticus but this time the king was watching the dancers, eyes glazed, staring straight ahead in the almost unseeing way someone who's drunk too much tends to do. Leaving Dun Breatann would feel like a wrench – this was Bellicus's home, and the people here were his people. He owed them a duty as their druid. And what about Catia, his daughter?

That idea brought him back to reality, hard, and a shiver ran down his neck. He could not think of the girl as being his own flesh and blood, there was no future for any of them in that direction.

It would be easier if Coroticus was a bad father to her – maybe then Bellicus could feel justified in wanting to play a part in her life, but the truth was, the king doted on her and she loved him dearly in return.

With a start, Bellicus realised the beer and the cosy warmth from the blazing hearth nearby had lulled him into a waking dream, where he barely knew what was going on around him, and he stretched back on his seat, taking a deep breath to bring himself back to reality.

He could never be a father to Catia, and the longer he was about Dun Breatann the more chance there was Coroticus would turn against him. He had to leave.

"What are you thinking about, Bel?"

To his shock, Narina had come up behind him and leaned down so their faces were next to one another. It took all his druid training to stop himself from turning to look at Coroticus.

He said, "Duro has written a song for us to perform. You should take your seat by the king again, my lady. Now." His voice was powerful, commanding despite being low enough that only Narina could hear him. She appeared to understand his look, the unspoken message in his request, and she nodded regally before stepping back towards her chair.

Duro peered along at Narina, who was on the receiving end of some irritable questioning from her husband, and then he met the gaze of the druid.

"What in the name of Mithras is going on?" he demanded in a low hiss. "Is the atmosphere in Dun Breatann always as tense? It feels like the fortress might erupt in civil war at any moment. How do you stand it?"

The musicians' playing came to a stop and Bellicus, eagerly grasping the opportunity to escape the high table, got to his feet and, lifting the old Roman lute from where he'd left it against the wall, beckoned the centurion to follow him. They approached the players and the druid held out a hand to the flute player.

"May I? The centurion has a song we'd like to perform for the hall and your instrument has a much nicer tone than the one he's been practising on."

The man, somewhat flustered at being addressed by the famous druid, quickly handed over the flute and half bowed, awkwardly, as if unsure how to behave. Bellicus, preoccupied, didn't attempt to put the musician at ease, and Duro took the flute from him. At a gesture from the druid two of the musicians gave up their stools and, soon enough, the hall looked on in expectant near-silence. Only the murmurs of one or two guests, too drunk to take in what was happening, could be heard as druid and centurion picked the strings of their instruments, checking the tuning, making fine adjustments with the pegs until both were happy with the sound.

"It's your song," Bellicus said quietly to his companion. "Would you like to introduce it or…?"

Duro glanced around the room and the anxiety on his face was plain for all to see. He might have been a soldier of Rome – an officer, a centurion – but the thought of addressing the audience of Britons staring expectantly at him plainly terrified him. The druid took pity on his friend.

"Duro wrote this song to honour the memory of his beloved wife, who was murdered by the same Saxon vermin that stole our own Princess Catia." He let his words sink in for a moment, knowing the watching crowd would forgive them almost any mistake in their performance of the music after an introduction as powerful as that.

"What's it called?"

Bellicus peered into the shadows irritably, barely able to see the dark features of the questioner. His annoyance was directed at himself as much as the shadowy Alt Clotan, for he realised now they'd never properly settled on a title for this song. Duro had been against calling it 'The Song of the Centurion', and the problem of a name had been forgotten by both of them. Until now.

Again, one look at Duro told Bellicus this was no time for a discussion and so he said the first thing that came into his head.

"This is 'Alatucca's Song'."

And he began to play.

CHAPTER THIRTEEN

Seventy miles to the east, in Dunadd Hillfort, King Loarn mac Eirc of Dalriada sat with his bishop and advisor, Dotha. Portly, and in his early sixties, the bishop remained straight-backed and clear-eyed, with a golden headband on his bald head and wooden cross around his neck. He was a Christian now, but, like Loarn mac Eirc, had once been a pagan.

It was colder here than in Dun Breatann and snow swirled about the peak of the high fortress but in his hall the king's servants had a fire going in the hearth, and the scent of roasting meat lent the atmosphere a cosy, homely feel that Loarn always revelled in. Still, every time the door opened a flurry of snow would be swept in by the swirling, freezing air, and he would rearrange his long, grey hair around his neck to stop the draught. Indeed, that was one reason he wore it in such a style, despite being completely bald on top.

"Are you sure this is wise, my lord?" Dotha said, in a tone of voice that suggested he thought Loarn's plans were anything but. "These people are not like us. They're not even as trustworthy as the Britons. They follow harsh, vengeful gods, and think nothing of breaking oaths if it means they gain from it."

"Don't we all?" Loarn shrugged, gesturing for a serving girl to bring him a mug of warmed ale. "It doesn't matter whether we can trust them or not. Just that they join with us until our task is completed. So write this down, bishop, and pray to Christ and His angels that my plan is a success."

In truth, Loarn had never really harboured any great hatred of Coroticus or the people of Alt Clota. He had been quite content to gain more lands simply by assimilating with the Britons already living near the eastern coast, with the occasional skirmish to put down any towns or villages which resisted the Dalriadan newcomers. Even when he'd made the crude remark about the missing child princess, it had simply been a ploy to enrage the Damnonii king, to try and draw him out from behind the walls of Dun Breatann. Although even Drest and Cunneda his comment found unpalatable, there had been no real malice behind the words.

That had changed, however, when Coroticus had tried to murder him on the road in a cowardly ambush. At that point, Loarn knew he must destroy the people of Alt Clota if the Dalriadans were to continue their growth westwards.

And so he had decided to send a messenger south, to the opposite coast, where he knew he might find allies. Where he would find men in a similar position to the Dalriadans, coming from across the sea to settle here, in the lands of the Britons.

The Saxons.

Although he had never even met one of the so-called 'sea wolves', Loarn had heard all about them. And he knew they would jump at the chance to win territory as rich as that belonging to the Alt Clotans.

He began to dictate the letter to Hengist, offering an alliance, and promising he would allow the Saxons to keep the lands west of Dun Breatann, while Loarn would take the ancient fortress on the rock and everything to the east. Of course, from such a position of strength, the Dalriadans could then destroy the Saxons and take control of the entire north-western side of the country.

"Drest won't like this," Dotha warned, but Loarn merely smiled for this was exactly what he'd meant earlier when the bishop had talked of breaking oaths. He had sworn an oath to help Drest and Cunneda take Dun Breatann when the next spring came, and he was certain the kings of the Picts and Votadini would see his proposed alliance with the Saxons as a breaking of such an oath.

But was it really? He had simply sworn to help take Dun Breatann – if the Saxons joined them, aye, it would mean complications in splitting things between them all, but that would sort itself out. The main thing was to smash the heathen Coroticus and take over his lands, which were much richer than any others north of the Roman walls.

Did Dotha truly believe either Drest or Cunneda would hold to *their* oaths if an opportunity arose to break it and, in the process, gain from it? No, the bishop was a shrewd man – he had started training to become a druid at one point after all. He knew how things worked.

They completed the letter and Loarn smiled.

"You're sure they will understand the language?"

"Latin, my lord? I doubt the Saxon warlords will be able to read it. They probably can't even read their own vulgar letters. But they will have someone, a Christian slave no doubt, captured from one of the churches on the east coast, who will be able to read this, and write a reply."

"God works in mysterious ways," muttered Loarn, parroting a phrase Dotha used continually to explain away some misfortune or injustice. He waved to a commoner who was sitting at one of the tables nursing a mug of ale and the man, a trader, hurried across to stand before king and bishop.

Dotha gave the sealed letter to the trader, who took it and tucked it inside his thick cloak. Loarn had not commanded him to travel to the Saxon Shore, the trader had gladly volunteered his services, hoping to sell his goods to Hengist's followers while earning a reward for this service.

"Do not lose that scroll," Loarn mac Eirc said, his tone leaving no doubt what kind of fate would befall the messenger should he not complete his task successfully. "I expect you back here as quickly as the weather allows. You'll be very well rewarded for your service."

The man nodded and left, leaving another billowing drift of snow in the doorway as he went.

"Coroticus wants to destroy me," Loarn said to Dotha as they relaxed on their chairs and tucked into a trencher of meats and fresh bread. "That will be difficult, when he finds himself trapped between my hammer and the Saxons' anvil."

* * *

Bellicus could see the faces in the audience around them changing from excited interest to surprise, and then to unease as they began playing. The people expected something uplifting like 'Rhydderch The Red' which, although in a minor key, was essentially a song of hope which everyone could sing along with. This, 'Song of the Centurion' as he'd dubbed it, was something else entirely.

The opening notes were harsh and dissonant, and picked out with a simmering anger born of Duro's grief and rage at his beloved wife's fate. And then, when that gave way to a softer section, it too was strange and unsettling instead of happy. It wasn't quite the bawdy drinking song the gathered audience expected.

However, there was something compelling about the melody and, when it did finally give way to a more pleasing series of arpeggiated notes, and the burly centurion began to sing over the top of it in a nervous, but sincere voice that was filled with emotion, every ear strained to catch every note.

"A flock of geese fly overhead,
And I see you.
The sun sets on the water,
And I feel you near.
The smell of roses fills the air,
And you're with me again,
My wife, please don't leave me."

Duro's voice almost cracked on the last line, and his eyes were heavy with tears, but, again, the song returned to the earlier angry, dissonant flurry of notes and the people looked on, rapt. Bellicus was concentrating hard on playing his lute perfectly, but he could feel the magic his friend was creating within the smoky hall. This performance would go down in legend he knew, *if* they could just make it to the end without hitting any wrong notes.

Returning one final time to the happier verse section, Duro sang once again, and the two musicians slowed as the words went along, as if they had reached the end.

"Don't go away,
Don't leave me alone,
Hold my hand,
Never let it go,
Please don't leave me,
Please, don't leave me…
Alone."

There was a hush in the hall, as the audience prepared to applaud what had been a stunning, if somewhat unsettling performance, but Bellicus and Duro weren't finished yet. They began another section, with Duro tapping out a beat on the floor with his foot, the tempo much faster than any before it, and, at a nod from the druid, one of the other musicians joined in on his drum. There was something visceral and triumphant in the music now. It was no longer a sad lament for a lost love – it was a battle hymn, a promise to avenge wrongs done to good people. Again, there were no words in this final part, but, in truth, none were needed for the music said it all.

At last, the song did come to an end, with a chord ringing out in the air like a challenge, and this time the gathering did erupt in cheers and whistles and loud applause. Duro, who had been in tears of grief while singing now grinned with relief and stood up, grabbing Bellicus in a bear hug.

"That was incredible, Bel," he said, "I've not felt such a release of pent-up emotion since my days in the legions!"

Bel replied, grinning madly himself, "Aye, that was pretty good. You did well. The people will be talking about that performance for years to come."

Duro handed back the flute he'd borrowed and they walked back to the king's table where their mugs had been refilled. Bellicus propped his lute safely against the wall again, and Coroticus looked pleased as they sat down.

"I enjoyed that, centurion. We don't hear many songs like it here in Dun Breatann. In fact, I think that's the first time I've ever heard anything quite like it, eh, Narina? What d'you think?"

The queen looked along the table at Duro and nodded, her green eyes sparkling from wine and the flickering torches lighting the hall. "It was a very strange song, but I think everyone appreciated it. It's good to hear something a little different occasionally, and you sang it very powerfully. You must have loved your wife a great deal."

Duro looked embarrassed and muttered in agreement but the queen never heard, as the musicians had just launched into a dancing tune, a well-known old favourite. The people, although they'd liked the song of the centurion, were ready for something lighter, and they filled the floor, jigging this way and that, laughing and hooting with the wild abandon only inebriation brings.

"I'm away for a piss," Coroticus announced, pushing his tall chair back from the table and getting up somewhat unsteadily. He made it out the door safely enough though and, as he went, Narina's earlier dancing partner, the elderly old gentleman, waved to her to join him on the floor again. Bellicus frowned at the man's familiarity, but the queen laughed and went to join in with the spinning bodies.

The dance had finished and another started, and still the queen remained on the floor, moving around from partner to partner, as did all the women. Still the king hadn't returned.

"That's a long piss Coroticus is doing," Duro said, eyeing Bellicus curiously, as if he wasn't sure if they should check on the king's safety or not.

The druid grunted, watching the dancers as he sipped on his ale. "He'll have gone to bed probably, he seemed pretty drunk." He turned then, as if he'd just realised his friend's words held an unspoken question. "Don't worry. I know the Saxons attacked us not far from here, in a hall similar to this one, but that was in an undefended settlement with no wall. No enemy will come in here without alarms being raised and their entire force being slaughtered." He raised an eyebrow and set down his mug. "I'd be more worried about Coroticus falling down the slope and injuring himself in the dark, but he's got his guards with him. They can take care of him."

Although the king wasn't as popular with the folk of Alt Clota as he'd been just a year ago, he was liked well enough by the people at the feast. Even so, as with any social gathering when an authority figure leaves, everyone becomes even more relaxed and uninhibited, and that's what happened now. The music grew louder, the dances more boisterous, people fell over, and some of the slave-women serving the meat and drink found themselves the focus of much unwanted attention from the men.

"Would you like to dance?"

A pretty young woman who Bellicus had seen before – in a relatively small place like Alt Clota that was often the case – looked shyly up at the high table and Duro grinned, nudging his friend in the ribs.

"Now that is an offer you cannot refuse, Bel. She's a beauty!"

The centurion made no effort to lower his voice and the girl blushed, although Bellicus could see she wasn't nearly as coy, or shy, as her lowered eyes and clasped hands suggested.

The giant druid wasn't much interested in dancing right then but, as Duro had noted, the girl was very pretty, and he could think of worse ways to spend his time.

"Of course," he smiled, coming around the table to take her hands, which were completely dwarfed by his. She was really quite a small thing, especially next to his towering bulk.

He looked back at Duro as she drew him into the dance and the centurion winked and made an obscene, suggestive face, as if they were young lads just coming of age and mingling with girls for the first time. It was quite ridiculous and highly amusing to Bellicus – it was good to see his friend in such a silly mood, as their crafting of the song over the past few days had opened wounds in Duro that were still very raw.

"Who are you here with?"

The girl shouted a reply, but he couldn't quite make it out over the music, so he simply nodded, smiling, spinning her from one hand to the other in time with the music. The tune changed soon enough though, to another one they all knew, but this dance entailed switching partners every few bars of the song.

"Change!" shouted the drummer, and the women all moved one place to the side, joining arms with the next man along the line who then swept them around and back and forward. It was one of the first dances everyone in Alt Clota learned which meant, despite the speed of the music and the relatively complexity of the moves, there were no mishaps in this first switch of partners, or the next.

The third time the drummer shouted "change!" Bellicus realised with a start that it was Queen Narina who took his hands. He had been lost in the dance and hadn't even noticed she was still on the floor but, as they looked at one another, the druid felt a thrill run through him. It felt like he was a child doing something naughty that, if found out, he would be scolded for.

It was ridiculous, and he pushed the sensation aside, smiling back at Narina who was flushing and obviously having a fine time.

The music was faster now than it had been at the start, building to a climax which was still some way off, so there was no time to have a shouted conversation as the dancers had to concentrate on where they put their feet or come to an embarrassing end in a heap on the floor.

And that is exactly what happened to Narina. She opened her mouth to ask Bellicus something, missed a step, got her foot tangled in his, and fell over.

Shrieking with laughter, she quickly got back up, using the druid's strong arm as leverage and, trying to catch up with the other dancers, she fell in against his chest, looking up into his eyes.

Bellicus felt a stirring within him as he met her gaze, taking in the sight of her slightly parted mouth, sparkling green eyes, and the chest that pressed against his torso, and time seemed to halt for just a moment.

The spell was broken when Narina, eyes flaring, drew back, away from him, and then something hit him, hard, in the side of the face.

Instinct took over and, even as his head rocked to the side, he threw out an elbow, feeling it glance off something, but his momentum brought him around and he unleashed a left hook that hammered into his attackers open mouth.

Bellicus felt the skin split on his fingers as they hit bared teeth, but the stinging pain from that was nothing compared to the feeling, as if ice-water had been thrown over him, when he recognised whom he'd just punched unconscious.

King Coroticus.

CHAPTER FOURTEEN

Confused shouts went up from the revellers who had no real idea of what was going on – all they knew was Coroticus lay, unmoving on the floor of the hall after a brief, but rather violent, altercation.

"Guards!"

"The king has been attacked!"

"By the gods, what happened?"

"Did Bel just punch the king?"

Gavo pushed through the crowd, roaring for silence at the top of his considerable lungs, but it wasn't enough to stop the king's personal guard, stationed outside the hall, from charging inside at the commotion, swords drawn. Like their captain, the garrison of Dun Breatann wanted no repeat of the terrible Saxon raid on Dun Buic just a few months earlier.

"What's happening, lord?" the first of the soldiers to reach the centre of the room demanded and Gavo, who had seen the whole thing unfolding before him, waved the question away. The man knelt by the king though, outrage on his face. He wasn't to be put off so easily. "Who's done this? I'll throw them over the wall myself!" He looked around at the encircled, wide-eyed guests, not suspecting it was the giant druid who had assaulted the king.

"Get back to your post, Beda," Gavo commanded in a tone that warned the guard not to argue. "All of you. Go. I'll deal with this myself."

"Am I invisible?" Queen Narina suddenly interjected herself into the conversation. "A mere woman, to be ignored while the men put things to rights? You—" Her eyes fastened on the guard, Beda, who shrank under her gaze, "—get back to your post outside, there's nothing for you to do here." The man looked down at the king who was, mercifully, coming-to at last, and gave a nod of salute before leading his companions from the hall. "Gavo, help the king to his seat and get him a drink, no, not more beer damn it. Water. The rest of you," she addressed the silent revellers, smiling and spreading her arms wide. "Stop standing there, open-mouthed, like fish! This feast isn't over yet. Eat! Drink! Servers – fill those mugs, quickly now. And you musicians – play for us again, something we can sing along with!"

Bellicus could see the strain on her face, the fear in her eyes, but her words and forced jocularity were enough to divert the people's attention back to their merry-making. None of them wanted to leave now, not until they found out how this would all end.

The king was notoriously short-tempered and bloodthirsty these days – would he order his druid to be executed? Attacking a king was, surely, punishable by death? But Bellicus wasn't just some ordinary man. He was a druid, and to be judged by different standards, was he not?

All this chatter, and more, could be heard circulating around the hall as the drunken guests moved back to their tables, pretending not to be interested in what was about to transpire at the king's high table.

In truth, Bellicus himself had no idea what would happen. Why had Coroticus attacked him? And what would he do if the king ordered his arrest, or even execution? The king was so drunk, and behaved so erratically these days, that it was impossible to foresee his actions and plan ahead for them.

The druid turned to the side and a look passed between himself and Duro – at least the faithful centurion was on his side, no matter what, although even they couldn't hope to win a fight against the fortress's entire garrison.

"What in the name of Taranis was that?" Gavo hissed, returning from Coroticus's side and grasping Bellicus's arm roughly. "How are we going to mollify the king now? What are we going to do, oh druid – 'wise one'?"

Bellicus didn't reply for there was nothing else to do other than approach the high table where their lord watched them with a somewhat shocked look on his face, which still had blood trickling down it. His faculties soon returned though and his eyes narrowed as he gazed at the druid. The feasting locals tried to hide their interest, but the forced laughs and hushed conversations simply made the atmosphere more tense.

"Lord King," Gavo began, but he was silenced with a gesture and Coroticus continued to glare blearily at Bellicus who, knowing he couldn't appear frightened or unsure of himself, gazed stonily back.

In such a contest there could only be one winner – only the druid had spent hours perfecting his unblinking, piercing stare, and soon enough the king closed his eyes and turned away.

"Leave me."

Gavo opened his mouth, as the command wasn't clear. Who was to leave?

Coroticus spoke again though. "Leave me, druid. And take your Roman with you. I'll have nothing more to do with you. In the morning, you will leave Dun Breatann and never return."

There were shocked gasps all around the hall, the loudest being from the king's left where Narina sat.

"He is our druid, Coroticus," she muttered, stunned by his pronouncement. "We need him. We need his connection with the gods—"

"Be silent, woman!" the king thundered, then appeared to regret it as a spasm of nausea passed over his pale face and he closed his eyes until the sensation passed and he could speak to his wife once more. "I know what you need the druid for. I am not blind."

Hardly a sound could be heard in the hall after that obvious accusation. If Coroticus's words weren't plain enough, the expression of disgust on his face made everything clear. Bellicus knew the tale would be all over Alt Clota, and beyond, by this time tomorrow.

"Have you heard?" the gossips would say. "The druid is bedding the queen, right under the king's nose!"

And, although it wasn't true, Bellicus, glancing at Narina now – even now, at this tense, danger-filled moment – realised he would like to bed her again.

Exile would be the best thing for him, he thought, before there was more upset, more violence.

He said, "As you command, my lord," bowed at the waist, and, with a slight nod to Duro, turned and walked through the staring, stunned, crowd, out into the chill air. As they went, Coroticus could be heard calling for more ale, before the heavy door closed at their backs and the night fell about them like a cloak.

Bellicus placed a finger to his lips, warning Duro to remain silent as listening guards were stationed in the shadows beside the hall's entrance, then he led the way down the path to his own dwelling. Only when they were inside, a tallow candle lit, shutters bolted and door on the latch, did the tension ease a little and both collapsed onto their sleeping pallets, exhausted, and not from the short walk.

"What should we do?"

Bellicus lay in the gloom, trying desperately to marshal his thoughts. Even the many years of training he'd been given by his druid tutors couldn't quite prepare him for a scenario like this.

"The king could do anything – command the guards to do anything – in the condition he's in." Duro muttered, sitting up and pulling his sword out from the side of his pallet, eyeing it critically in the near-dark and finding it satisfactory. "Perhaps we should get out of here, now, before it's too late."

"I fear that would seem to Coroticus like an admission of my guilt." Bellicus shook his head. "We – I – need to see this out. I have faith in Gavo, he'll calm the king down and make sure we're left in peace for the night. By morning, everyone will be sober, and things will seem different."

"We just lie here then?" Duro persisted. "Praying to Mithras that the door isn't kicked in and we're not hacked to pieces by the soldiers? What about that little prick Senecio? What if he tells the King's Guard to attack us when we're resting? Maybe we should take turns on watch."

Again, Bel shook his head. "You're allowing your imagination to run wild, Duro, calm down. I'm a druid, that still counts for something with everyone in this fortress, no matter what the king believes I've been up to. We won't be murdered in our sleep, I promise you." He sighed, sensing the centurion's cynicism, and stood up, searching inside the pockets sewn into his dark cloak for some herbs.

He went outside but left the door open so Duro could see him, or his silhouette at least, and walked back and forward over the threshold, sprinkling the herbs on the ground while muttering some incantation. And then he came back inside and bolted the door before lying down again.

"There. We're safe. No one will come through there without my leave."

Duro blew out a relieved sigh, accepting the potency of his friend's magic. But, as he breathed in again, his face screwed up and he looked across at his giant companion suspiciously.

"Enchanted herbs eh? Smells like dried coriander to me."

Bellicus turned away to hide his smile. Caught! He should have chosen something less fragrant for his protective 'spell'.

"Doesn't matter what it is," he growled. "Could be dried pig shit. All that matters is the power that's put into it. Now go to sleep – Cai is here, and my magical coriander barrier will keep all foes at bay."

And so it did.

* * *

Coroticus woke up and felt good…for a few seconds, and then he remembered – some of – the previous night's events, and a cold chill ran through him. He realised his head ached, and his mouth was sore, and who was that next to him?

The servant girl, Enica, lay sleeping in the bed at his side, and a small snore issued from her open mouth which, for some reason, made the king feel queasy.

What had he done last night at the feast? He knew bad things had happened, but he'd been so drunk he couldn't for the life of him remember what they all were. Slowly, things came back to him.

He knew he'd tried to attack Bellicus, although what exactly had transpired was shrouded in a black fog. Then he remembered *why* he'd gone for the druid: the giant had been dancing with Narina and it enraged him because…well, he couldn't admit to himself, not in this fragile state, why that had made him so upset.

He knew though. Deep down, he knew well enough.

What else had happened? Everything else was a blur and he felt another icy chill pass through him as he wondered if he'd ordered Bellicus to be jailed or…worse.

He got up from the bed and saw a mug of ale on the old wooden chest against the wall. It was still half full and, without hesitation, he downed it, closed his eyes and breathed deeply, willing the drink to work its magic quickly.

"Guard!"

The door opened and a tall young man poked his head inside, eyes flickering to the sleeping, naked girl in the bed before returning to the king. "My lord?"

"Get me a jug of ale, quickly."

Mumbling something Coroticus couldn't hear the guard disappeared and returned just moments later with a brimming jug. Clearly it had been kept nearby – the guards knew his vices well by now.

"Here you are, lord."

Coroticus took it and walked back to the chest, refilling the mug with shaking hands, spilling more than a few drops, as the door closed behind him again, leaving him alone with Enica. He looked at her and drank down the entire mug of ale in just a few heartbeats, retching as he swallowed it so fast, almost desperately, as if his life depended on it.

And it did now, he knew that. Like so many weak fools he'd known over the years, he'd allowed the ale to become his master. Self-pity threatened to overcome him then – it was no wonder he'd needed something to help him get through the past few months – desperate with fear, wondering where Catia was and what was happening to her. It had consumed him and, with Narina facing the same fears, he had felt so alone that the numbing release ale brought him was welcome. Too welcome.

Now that Catia was home and that crushing, terrible fear was gone, he should go back to his old ways, his old happy self.

He refilled the mug and sat down on the bed, sipping it slower now, feeling the effects of the drink coming over him again like a warm, comforting blanket.

All would be well. He hadn't done anything to Bellicus, who was a good friend to him, loyal and true.

Or was he? Those rumours about the druid being Catia's real father had reached his ears and, although he knew they were no more than harmful gossip, put about by the Pict, Drest, and his bastard followers no doubt, it still played on his mind. As did the way he saw Narina and Bel looking at one another. Was he imagining it? Or was there really a barely-concealed attraction for one another in those surreptitious glances? He would always have thought both were true to him but, recently, his mind had been all over the place, with the lingering stress of Catia's abduction and the ale he relied upon doing his state of mind no favours.

Today was another low point, for he'd never before needed a couple of mugs of ale to help him get dressed and face up to the previous night's events.

He felt much better now though – the shaking in his hands had stopped, the pounding headache had become a gentle, even, warmth throughout his skull that wasn't entirely unpleasant, and no-one was dead. As far as he could recall anyway.

He would go out now and see what must be done.

He headed for the door, and then the memory of Bellicus's punch hit him, almost as if had happened again. He touched his mouth gingerly, surprised to find all his teeth still intact.

Coroticus knew he'd started the fight, if it could even be called that, but he also understood what the rumours would do to his reputation if he didn't do anything to address the fact that he'd been knocked out cold by the druid.

Theoretically, he was Bellicus's superior, but, in reality, the people of Alt Clota, and many other Britons, revered the druids, seeing them as the gods' representatives, and above all other mortal men.

But, even with that understanding, the simple fact was, someone in his court had punched Coroticus and laid him out flat in his own hall. If he let it go without any kind of reply, he would be the laughing stock of the entire country, and that would not do.

He would have to do *something* to punish Bellicus and regain some modicum of respect, there was nothing else for it.

He turned back to the bed as the girl in it started to awaken, turning over on her side, bare breasts making his loins tingle, and he wondered if he should linger there a little while longer. Before he could return to her though, the door opened, and his ardour vanished when he saw Narina standing there.

She glanced past him and her face flushed at the sight of the naked servant—her own maid! There was no anger in the queen's eyes though, merely resignation, as she sighed softly.

"We need to talk, Coroticus."

If she'd come in a little while earlier, before he'd downed the two mugs of ale, their conversation would have gone quite differently. As it was, he had a warm glow in him that gave him confidence—he wasn't drunk though, and he knew the previous night's events must be put to rights somehow. Narina would be vital for that.

He met her gaze and nodded. He still loved her, by Taranis! If she'd just show him some warmth when they were in bed together, he'd not have to lie with slaves. The look on her face suggested she would be more inclined to lie with him if he was not taking mistresses to this chamber every other night. Their relationship was caught in a vicious circle, just like he was with his reliance on ale, and now he was at odds with his old friend Bellicus too.

He would need the queen's help to set things back on an even keel in Alt Clota for she had proven herself to be much stronger than he was over the past few months.

"All right," Coroticus agreed and turned to the servant girl who had covered herself with a blanket by now but seemed unsure what to do next. "Get out, Enica. Dress and be about your duties, quickly."

"Aye, lord king." Throwing her tunic over her head, the girl took up her worn old shoes in her hand and hurried out of the room, keeping her eyes on the ground at all times, as if she could feel the queen's hard stare boring into her.

"Tell the guard to send in more ale as you go," Coroticus commanded her, but Narina broke in.

"Don't bother, girl," she said, even though, at twenty-eight, she was only a year older than Enica. "The king will need his wits about him if we're to have a worthwhile discussion."

The servant bit her lip and looked from one to the other, nervous and uncertain. "My lord?" she mumbled apologetically. Relief washed over face as he waved her away, giving in to the queen's wishes.

"You shouldn't countermand my orders," the king grumbled once the door was firmly shut and they were alone. "The servants will lose respect for me."

"You shouldn't spend your nights rutting with them," Narina returned, eyes flashing now with anger. "*I* will lose respect for you."

"Oh, you've made your lack of respect for me quite clear enough already," he said, but neither of them were in the mood for an argument and he pulled the blankets up neatly, making a clear space for them to sit down and talk properly. "Was it Enica you wanted to talk to me about?"

"Don't be obtuse, Coroticus, I've suspected that was going on for weeks, ever since she started talking about politics. No, we have more pressing matters to discuss. You must remember what happened in the hall last night."

"Aye. You and the druid were gazing into one another's eyes like lovestruck youngsters, and I snapped." He shrugged. "Perhaps I acted rashly, attacking him in front of so many of our people but…Bel knocked me out. He must be punished for it."

"Punished for defending himself against an unknown assailant?" Narina demanded. "You came at him from behind, he simply lashed out instinctively. You must know yourself how rash your actions were. Bel…"

The king's jaw clenched. "*'Bel is the greatest warrior in Dun Breatann. No-one can best him.'* Is that what you were about to say before you stopped yourself? Perhaps he is, but the fact remains, everyone in my hall saw him knock me to the ground. We will be the talk of the whole land this morning! You mentioned the slaves losing respect for me – how do you think the gossips will receive this tasty morsel of information? How will Drest, or Loarn mac Eirc, spin it when it reaches their ears? Do you suggest I do nothing about this, simply because Bellicus is your favourite?"

"Oh, grow up, Coroticus," Narina said irritably. "Your jealousy is unfounded – there's nothing between me and the druid. Before you started acting so irrationally our marriage was perfectly happy. You are allowing your emotions to be twisted, and losing yourself in an ale mug all the time isn't helping us any."

They sat in silence for a long time, both lost in their thoughts, trying to make sense of all that had happened to them over the past year.

"Bellicus is your friend, and our druid. He also travelled to the farthest reaches of the land to rescue your daughter and bring her home. You owe him more than the jewels and trinkets you rewarded him with for that. You owe him your gratitude, Coroticus, not punishment."

The king stared at the floor and then, as if it took him a great effort, muttered, "I don't know what the point is any more, Narina. Why are we here? Any of us, I mean?" He looked at her and his expression was that of a bemused child. "When I started to believe Catia was dead, it made me ask questions I'd never asked before and...I just don't know if there's any reason for this." He shook his head. "For living."

This was the first time Coroticus had really opened up to the queen and at least provided her with a motive for his drinking and recent behaviour but, before she could say anything the door was thrown open again and the moment passed. They saw the princess Catia striding into the room, a concerned look on her face.

"Are you all right, Father? The servants are saying you were attacked. Oh! Your mouth!" She spoke too fast for Coroticus to get a word in and, before he knew it, she was standing right before him, peering intently at his injured face. "Is it true Bel did it? Why? Why would Bel hit you?"

"Sometimes men have disagreements, Catia," the queen said in a tone of voice that suggested no more questions should be asked. The princess was too curious to stop now though.

"What about? Where is Bel anyway? Did you have him thrown in the prison?"

"No, girl!" the king shouted, halting the torrent of questions at last. "I have no idea where he is. We had a minor disagreement, aye, that's true. But he could have killed me, he hit me so hard. I must punish him – that's just how things work. I'm a king, not some slave to be beaten on a whim."

Catia's eyes narrowed before she looked to Narina, then back to Coroticus.

"You can't punish Bel. He—"

"I know, I know!" The king threw his hands up in the air and got to his feet to pace up and down the room in exasperation as Catia took his place beside the queen on the bed. "Bel is wonderful. Bel is so tall and strong. Everyone loves Bel." He stopped walking in front of a window and pushed open the wooden shutters to reveal a grey, yet beautiful, view of the River Clota. His eye followed a small fishing coracle as it drifted past on the shimmering grey waters, the peaceful scene calming his temper but doing little to provide him with answers on how to solve this dilemma.

As the boat sailed out of view an idea did come to him though, as if the gods had seen his turmoil and offered their counsel.

"Exile."

"What?" Narina's voice was sharp, disbelieving, as her husband came back across to stand over them.

"I could order him executed but, obviously, none of us want that. Exile seems the best way to punish him, and show the people I have acted against my attacker."

Catia stared at her father for a heartbeat and then her face screwed up and she jumped down from the bed and out of the room, sandaled feet slapping on the hard stone floor, tears filling her eyes as she cried, "I hate you. I hate you!"

Coroticus watched her go, more than a little irritated by her loyalty to the druid who had, after all, punched him in the face and knocked him out cold mere hours before.

"You can't do this," Narina said softly, shaking her head in the silence left by their daughter's hurried escape. "Bellicus does not deserve it. Dun Breatann is his home, as much as it is ours, and he's only just returned from the Saxon Shore."

But Coroticus was like a dog with a bone now and he sat on the bed, taking his wife's hand in his. He was smiling grimly, staring at – through – the wall, as he pondered the possibilities of this perfect solution he'd just devised for their problem. The chill, fresh air from the open window seemed to give him strength and he knew everything would be all right.

"Listen to me, Narina. This is my plan – it's a good one, and it *will* be carried out as I command, whatever Catia thinks. *I* am king – *I* rule here – and my word will be obeyed. Aye, even by a druid."

When he'd spoken to his daughter just now, Coroticus had realised that she really did look rather like Bellicus. The eyes, the shape of the face, those long, nimble fingers…He could quite understand why rumours had sprung up about who the girl's father really was. Besides, how many women like Enica had he slept with in his life? Quite a few, yet none, as far as he knew, had ever fallen pregnant with his child.

Apart from Narina, and even that had taken a few years and many, many attempts…

He might have just asked his wife straight out who Catia's real father was but, in truth, Coroticus feared the answer. What would he do if Narina said it was Bellicus who had fathered the girl?

Coroticus had gone half mad when his daughter was abducted by the Saxons – learning he wasn't even her real father would truly send him over the edge.

He was quite content to continue believing Catia was his flesh and blood – his heir. But the rumours about Bellicus, and his actions the previous night, had to be dealt with if Coroticus was to continue as Alt Clota's king.

Bellicus had to go.

CHAPTER FIFTEEN

"My lord." The guard addressed Bellicus somewhat sheepishly when the druid opened the door of his roundhouse and stared at the soldier who, dressed in full armour, had come for him. "The king commands your presence in the great hall."

There was only the one guard which, Bellicus thought, was a good sign. At least Coroticus didn't expect a fight at this stage in proceedings.

"Give me a moment," he replied, closing the door and turning to look at Duro who stood, grim-faced and ready for whatever was to come. The loyal centurion had wanted to wear his complete legionary uniform – crested helmet, cuirass and all – but the druid didn't want to come across as overtly confrontational or defensive at this meeting which they'd been expecting since they woke with the sunrise.

Neither did they want to appear frightened or contrite either though – Bellicus had acted in self-defence after all and, while it was regrettable what had happened, no-one could say it was the druid's fault. If you poke a sleeping bear with a stick, you should be prepared for the consequences, as Qunavo, his old tutor on the island of Iova, had often told him.

"This is all bloody stupid," Duro grumbled as Bellicus rinsed his mouth out with some clean water, freshly fetched from the spring between the fortress's two peaks that morning. "I thought you men were friends. This isn't how friends behave."

Bellicus spat the water out the window onto the grass at the back of the building and bent to stroke Cai's back as the dog lapped at its own bowl of water. "Think of it this way," he said. "You are a centurion in your old legion, and Coroticus is your commanding officer – a legate, say. Now, you may have been quite friendly with them over the years – fought beside one another, been drinking companions, and so on. Would any of that matter if you, centurion, had punched the legate in the face in front of the rank and file legionaries?"

"That's different, Bel, and you know it."

"How is it any different?"

Duro shook his head and peered out the window, exasperated. "The legions were built on rigid discipline. The scenario you describe might have ended in me being executed, depending on what the legate was like. Many of them, most really, were wealthy sorts who looked down on those below them."

"Not all of them, surely. That doesn't sound like a good way to inspire loyalty."

"No, some of them were all right," Duro conceded. "But this isn't the same at all. You and Coroticus have been genuine friends, and you...Well, you're a druid, which counts for much more than any rank I might have held in the Roman army."

"The simple fact is," Bellicus said, pulling his cloak on and putting the hood up both for warmth, and also for the impressive effect it had on his overall appearance, "I am his subordinate and he is the king. No matter who is right or wrong, the king cannot be seen to lose face."

"What's he going to do to you then?" Duro eyed his spatha in its sheath beside his sleeping pallet, wishing he could strap it on and go to this audience with the king properly armed. It was, of course, out of the question.

"I don't know," the druid admitted. "My fabled foresight has failed me in this." He lifted his staff – it was as much a weapon as the centurion's sword, but no soldier in Dun Breatann would seek to remove it from his hands by force. "Let's go and we shall see. You stay here lad, we'll be back soon." He stroked Cai's head and muzzle and there was another knock on the door, this one a little louder than before, suggesting their escort was growing impatient outside. Bellicus pulled it quickly open, sending the man back a step, an apologetic look on his face.

"Sorry, my lord, I hate to rush you, but we best not keep the king waiting."

"No, of course not, Butu. Lead the way."

The soldier seemed pleased that the druid had remembered his name, but he hesitated, eyeing Duro.

"Forgive me, lord, but the king only asked for you. He didn't mention your Roman friend there."

Duro's face darkened and he opened his mouth as if ready to issue a parade-ground style dressing down for the guard, but Bellicus placed a warning hand on his arm.

"He didn't say Duro shouldn't come though, did he?" the druid asked. "Well then, lead on. If Coroticus wants to see me alone, I'm sure he'll say so when we reach the hall."

The guard was pleased with that solution for he had no desire to argue with the giant druid, so he nodded agreement and walked up the path towards the long wooden building which had been the scene of the previous night's fracas just a few hours earlier. Smoke issued from the chimney hole in the roof and Bellicus was glad, for it was a chilly morning and he was a little hungover himself which always made him feel colder than usual.

He wondered how Coroticus must be feeling – sick, anxious, leaden-headed, shivery? All these were the usual side-products of a night spent drinking oneself into oblivion, and they might, just might, make the king easier to deal with. He would be in less of a mood to argue if he was as fragile as his consumption of ale at the feast would suggest.

Then they reached the hall and went inside and, once Bellicus's eyes adjusted to the gloom he felt disappointment. There sat the king at his long table and before him was a jug, and in his hand a wooden cup filled, undoubtedly with the very liquid that had caused all this trouble in the first place.

He heard Duro mutter an oath but managed to refrain from sighing or shaking his own head at the depressing sight as they approached, Bellicus slightly ahead of his companion, towards the centre of the room. He knew better than to try and take his usual place beside Coroticus.

Narina was at the table, and Gavo stood a little way behind them, fully armed and armoured as was usual in an audience like this, and Bellicus wondered who the guard captain would side with if it came to another fight, this time a true, unrestrained battle to the death. It was a silly thought that crossed unbidden through the druid's mind and he knew immediately there would only be one winner in such a loyalty contest: Gavo was the king's man and always would be.

To the right of the king sat Senecio, and Bellicus couldn't help feeling a little stab of irritation at the sight. That was *his* seat, his place – he was the king's trusted advisor, or at least he used to be. It seemed the druid had been supplanted by a man who only ever told Coroticus what he wanted to hear.

Things were changing in Alt Clota, and not for the better, as far as the druid could tell.

He stared at Senecio who met his gaze and held it for a moment before smirking and looking away.

The little prick was confident in his newfound position and Bellicus wondered what Coroticus had planned for him as punishment for the previous night's 'attack'.

He willed his mind to calm, then bowed and said respectfully, "Lord King. You summoned me."

"You," Coroticus agreed. "I summoned you, not your friend. No matter," he waved a hand as if dismissing his own objection and the room was uncomfortably silent for a time until, at last, the king shook his head sadly. "What have we come to, Bel? We've always been close."

"We still are, aren't we?"

Coroticus tilted his head uncertainly. "Perhaps. The pain in my mouth would suggest otherwise though."

Bellicus wondered if he should defend his actions, explain the situation, but he knew everyone in the room, including Coroticus, understood what had happened and why. He had no need to protest his innocence for he had acted as any warrior would have. He remained silent.

"Whatever the reasons for last night's…unpleasantness," the king went on, "you will accept that I must be seen to act. To punish you in some way for what you did?"

Bellicus could sense Duro at his back straining to keep silent. Thankfully the centurion's military discipline kept him in check and the king continued.

"You do understand that, Bel?" He took the druid's slight shrug as agreement. "Good. Well, what would you suggest we do in order to show the people I've acted?"

"Tell them you've sent me into exile, lord," Bellicus replied and was rewarded with a look of surprise from the king. Apparently he had read Coroticus's thoughts, judging by that stunned, somewhat fearful expression. He was pleased to know the story of this would get out and his magical powers confirmed once again.

He wasn't quite so happy to realise his friend was planning on exiling him.

"That seems like a good solution," Coroticus agreed warily, glancing at Senecio who remained expressionless beside him. "Where would you go in that case? And for how long? Obviously, this would only be a temporary thing, to show the people I did *something* to punish you for your behaviour at the feast – you could return after a time, perhaps after performing some service in reparation?"

Bellicus had thought about this all night and, without hesitation replied, "South, lord. To join the warlord Arthur, and the Merlin. They are all that stands between us and Hengist's forces and they need every man they can get. I would ask you to send as many men as you can to join me – I will command them as part of Arthur's army." He saw anger flash across the king's face and held up a hand. "Of course, you can wait a week or so before sending the men, so no-one connects them to me. We will simply tell the people I have been sent into exile for attacking you, and then, after a time, the men will travel south to join me. And Duro, of course."

To Bellicus this was the ideal solution to everyone's problems. Coroticus would save face, and not have to feel that ludicrous jealousy any time he and Narina – or Catia – were in a room together, and the Saxon threat would be met head on. The anger still hadn't left the king's face though and Bellicus could see he must be more persuasive.

"This will allow you to send a message to every king and petty warlord in the land, Coroticus. Hengist ordered his brother, Horsa, to abduct your daughter. They planned to slaughter her as a blood sacrifice to their twisted gods. Sending a portion of your army to stand against them will show everyone you won't sit idly by and accept what they've done."

Senecio leaned in and muttered something in Coroticus's ear and the king nodded. The anger never left his face – if anything he became even redder and took a long pull from his cup as if trying to steady himself.

This wasn't going as well as Bellicus had hoped. What was the problem with this idea of his?

"So, you punch me in the face," the king growled and, beside him, Narina flinched at his tone. "Then, as your punishment, you demand I give you command of an army? To travel away down south where you'll help your new friends?"

"Aye," Bellicus agreed somewhat testily. "I'd help the friends that helped me find Catia. I'd help them defeat the bastards that *took* Catia! Why wouldn't you see that as a good thing?" He looked to the queen, and Gavo in the shadows behind the high table but neither of them would speak up, undoubtedly knowing it would make them seem disloyal. Somehow, Coroticus saw this plan of Bellicus's as an abandonment, a defection even, leaving his service to join another would-be king – and he even had the temerity to ask if he could take some of Alt Clota's soldiers with him!

Truly, Coroticus's paranoia had taken over his senses so he could now only see the druid as an enemy, or at least a disruptive force, within his own camp.

"I have a better idea."

Senecio nodded grimly, obviously knowing in advance what the king's plan was, and Bellicus wished Taranis would send a bolt of lightning to strike the man's irritating face.

"Loarn Mac Eirc said some disgusting things to me when they had us under siege. I presume you've heard about it? Good, I'd rather not repeat them. I want you to kill him for me, Bellicus."

At this the queen sat up and looked pleasantly surprised, before her face fell again.

"How would he do that?" she wondered. "I want that piece of filth dead as much as you, of course, but he'll be safely inside his fortress at Dunadd, surrounded by his guards. It would be like someone trying to come in here to assassinate you, Coroticus."

"He's a druid," the king said, as if that explained everything. Who needed a plan, when one was a tool of the gods? "Besides, he has Cai, and Duro there will no doubt go with him. Well, what do you say to that, Bel?"

It seemed there was no choice. Coroticus was king after all and these were his orders. Bellicus bowed and murmured assent, noting the small, self-satisfied smile on Senecio's face. The advisor did not expect to see Bellicus again, and it was understandable, for if he failed in killing Loarn mac Eirc the druid would not be wise to return to Alt Clota.

Yet assassinating the Dalriadan king in his own fortress – set high on a hill and surrounded by natural and man-made defences, much like Dun Breatann – would be nigh on impossible.

Bellicus had done the impossible before though. He did not fear putting himself in such situations.

"I bow to your wishes, as always, lord king," he said, rapping the butt of his staff on the hard floor of the hall to mark his acceptance of the quest. "I urge you to heed my counsel though, Coroticus: the Saxons must be stopped before they are too strong, otherwise they will sweep us all away, eventually. Aye, even us in the north. Arthur seems a noble enough man to me and one we should be looking to aid." The king frowned but Bellicus didn't hold his tongue this time. "End your war with the Picts and Votadini and Dalriadans, my king. The Saxons are a much bigger threat to the future of our lands."

With that he bowed once more, pointed the eagle-topped head of his staff at Senecio in a gesture that made the advisor's face turn pale and Gavo grin in the shadows, then turned and led Duro out into the morning sunshine.

Overhead, the raven, Uchaf sailed past, its enormous wings spread wide, majestic and awe-inspiring, then it suddenly swooped down on a cat slinking between two of the buildings, sending the innocent tabby diving for safety. Bellicus took it as a good omen, a friend showing him how to chase away the annoyances of life.

"Shit," Duro muttered, looking up in dismay at the huge bird wheeling away towards the higher peak of the rock. "That has to be a bad sign, right?"

The druid couldn't help laughing.

"That depends, my friend, on whether you see yourself as the raven, or the cat. Come on, let's get our gear ready. The gods will see us right, they always do."

* * *

The first decision they had to make was how to reach Dunadd. Should they take a boat to Arachar, and then walk the rest of the way? It was tempting, especially since the weather was still cold and miserable, but Bellicus thought it might be good for them to make the whole journey on foot. They'd spent the winter mostly sitting around in Dun Breatann, playing music and drinking ale, so the walking would help them lose the extra weight they'd gained since returning with Catia. Duro, when the options were laid out, declared he'd rather take the boat.

"It's bloody freezing up here, Bel," he groaned. "And, since we're going even further north, it'll only get worse. We won't be able to kill a sheep once we reach Dunadd, never mind a king, if our toes and fingers have dropped off from frostbite."

"That's a bit dramatic," the druid smiled, throwing provisions for himself and Cai into his pack. "The worst of the winter is probably over. I'm sure I saw some buttercups growing by the well this morning."

Duro's reply was merely a grunt. The centurion would follow whatever path Bellicus chose, but he grinned when the druid decided they'd sail after all.

"It'll be faster than trying to walk, or even ride, since the roads – where there are any – will be in poor condition with the weather. Some might even be damaged or impassable." He stood up, tightening the leather cord around his pack. "Besides, we'll still have a few days walk to Dunadd once we disembark in Arachar. That will help us get back in condition, eh?"

"Some of us are already toned and strong," Duro said, drawing himself up and sucking in his belly which, to be fair, was nowhere near as large as it had been when the two men had first met in Luguvalium.

"You're a fat bastard," the druid growled, averting his face so Duro wouldn't see the smirk there. "Too much of Coroticus's meat and ale for you, centurion, you're a disgrace to your rank."

Duro knew his friend well enough by now to know the jibe wasn't meant to hurt, but his expression was sad nonetheless. "Maybe I am," he replied, following Bellicus out the room and down the stairs towards the docks. "But by the time we reach Dunadd I'll be half this size and damn sight colder!"

They finished packing provisions which Duro collected from the fortress's quartermaster, made sure they had whatever weapons, light armour and warm clothing they could carry and, finally, packed a small leather tent, knowing it would be absolutely vital for survival at this time of year. Then, hoping they hadn't forgotten anything, they headed for the docks.

Cai was the only one of the companions who seemed genuinely happy to be going on a journey. He ran down the steps ahead of them, tail wagging, eyes bright, nose sniffing the chill air for the rabbits that were always around in the undergrowth. The sight of the daft hound always brought a smile to Bellicus's face although he wished Eolas – the dog that had been killed in the fight with Horsa when they were tracking Catia – was also coming on this trip.

He ruffled Cai's ears as the powerfully built animal bounded up to them as if urging his master to hurry. "At least I still have you, boy," he muttered, and followed the eager beast down towards the boat that lay at anchor, awaiting their boarding.

Bri, captain of the vessel that would take them along the River Clota to Arachar, sat looking out across the water, ostensibly supervising his crew as they loaded barrels and crates on board. This was to be a trading voyage, with Bellicus and Duro slipping away along the western road once they docked, hopefully without attracting any attention.

As they stepped onto the wooden platform Bellicus noticed Gavo waiting for them, a somewhat regretful look on his hard face. The druid headed straight for him and held out his hand, which the guard captain took in the warriors' grasp and they embraced, both perhaps wondering if they'd ever see the other again.

"Come to say farewell, eh?" Duro smiled, but the expression wasn't returned.

"Come to make sure you leave, more like," Gavo grumbled, looking upwards as if checking no-one was watching. "Coroticus told me to see you were on board when the boat sails. He sends his best wishes for your journey, and bade me remind you that this is the best thing for everyone."

Bellicus raised an eyebrow then shrugged and called Cai back from a nearby bush which he was relieving himself against. "Get on board, lad," he commanded, before turning again to Gavo. "We'd best not hang around then, since the king wishes us gone as soon as possible."

The guard captain laid a hand on the druid's arm, gripping firmly, and they looked at one another awkwardly.

"Don't think too badly of him, Bel. I can understand why he's acting like this, with all the rumours going about...And the queen *was* furious at what Loarn mac Eirc said to her, so, if you can bring him back, or his head at least, you'll be held in high esteem again, and things will go back to normal."

"Will they?" Bellicus shook his head sadly. "I think Drest and Cunneda might not agree. As soon as the spring is here properly, their armies will be on the march and this time they might not be so kind to the people of Alt Clota. We should be going on a peace mission, not some wild assassination attempt that has no chance of succeeding."

Gavo raised an eyebrow and a small smile formed on his lips. "No chance of succeeding? Isn't that what everyone thought about you rescuing Catia from the Saxons? Yet you managed it." He looked at Duro, and then back to the giant druid, and his grin wasn't mocking, it was confident. As if he believed the pair of them really could kill the Dalriadan king. "You're a druid," he said, as if that was all that mattered. "If anyone can do this, it's you and that centurion. And, like I say, when you come back, everyone will rejoice and there'll be feasting, and all will be forgotten."

"That's what was supposed to happen when he brought the princess back," Duro muttered sourly. "So much for the returning hero."

Bellicus spoke before Gavo could reply. "How quickly do you think we'll be able to do this? The trip to Dunadd is a long one, and it'll be hard with the weather at this time of year. Do you really think we'll be back before Drest and Cunneda return with their armies?"

"Don't you worry about Dun Breatann," said the captain, pushing back a long strand of hair the breeze had blown across his eyes. "I'll take care of the place – just you complete your own mission and come home as soon as possible. It would be best to have you with us if there is another invasion."

"Not if," Bellicus said firmly. "When."

"Well you'd better be off then, hadn't you? The sooner you leave the sooner you'll be back."

They clasped hands once more, and Bellicus followed Duro aboard the boat which was lying heavily in the water now, fully laden with men and goods.

"You ready, my lord?"

"Aye, you can cast off, Bri. It doesn't look like anyone else is coming to wave farewell."

As the boat was pushed out into the current and the crew set about their duties Duro found a bench and Cai lay down next to him. They both had their heads raised up, eyes slightly hooded against the morning sun, breathing in the fresh, damp air. All the centurion had to do was open his mouth and let his tongue loll out and they might have been twins Bellicus thought in amusement. His happy mood was somewhat tempered though, as he looked back and waved at Gavo, alone on the dock.

"Take care of my horse, Darac," he shouted across the water to the guard captain. "Only the best oats for him!"

Gavo grinned and waved once more before turning and heading back towards the stairs as the druid watched him go a little sadly.

It would have been nice if Catia or Narina had come to see them off although, given the circumstances of their departure, it was always unlikely to happen.

His eyes travelled up the great, imposing rock of Dun Breatann as the boat picked up speed and then he saw a flash of white and focused on the small figure at one of the windows in the fortress. It was the princess, watching as her rescuers sailed away to the west. She must have noticed him looking up for her arm lifted in a wave and, smiling, he returned the gesture before the sail was hoisted and she grew too small to see any more.

"Goodbye, Catia," the druid whispered, gripping his eagle-topped staff tightly and looking skywards, beseeching the gods to protect her from the fruits of Coroticus's warmongering.

Gavo was right: he had to complete his mission to Dalriada as quickly as possible, for within just a few short weeks there would be an army, more likely two, converging on Alt Clota, and this time Drest and Cunneda would have the entire summer to complete their goal of taking Dun Breatann.

Bellicus walked to the prow of the boat and held up a hand to shade his eyes as he gazed into the distance, then he turned impatiently to Bri.

"Can't this thing go any faster?"

CHAPTER SIXTEEN

"We should try to keep to ourselves as much as possible," Bellicus said as the boat drew against the dock in Arachar. "We don't want Loarn finding out enemies are in his lands."

Duro raised an eyebrow and laughed incredulously. "Okay, let's keep our heads down, good idea. Although, even with *your* head down, you're still bigger than anyone I can see in that village we're about to walk through. Not to mention that giant dog that follows you everywhere." He slapped the druid on the arm and shook his head. "Sometimes I wonder if you realise just how you appear to other people."

The boat nudged the wooden jetty and the pair grasped the bow to keep from falling. "Sorry, my friend," Bellicus grumbled. "I can't make myself any smaller. The gods chose to make me a great, strapping young warrior."

Duro nodded agreement and smiled. "That they did, lad. Even if a fat baker had to rescue you from those Saxon fools not so long ago."

The ship's captain approached and bowed his head deferentially to the druid. "That's us here, lord," he said unnecessarily, as if the sight of land might have somehow escaped his passengers' notice. "Will you need any help to disembark?" He scratched Cai under the chin as Bellicus shook his head.

"No, thank you, Bri. We don't have much to carry." He grasped the captain by the forearm and thanked him again, this time for making their journey fast and smooth. Then the two men, along with the dog – excited to be on land with all its new sights and smells – made their way down the gangplank onto the dock.

"Got everything? The tent?"

Duro patted the rolled-up tent stowed over his shoulder, checked all his weapons were in place, including a hunting bow, and nodded. "Aye. You got our provisions?"

"I have. Let's go then. We'll follow the road until we're out of sight of the village, so we don't attract any attention. Just two normal travellers heading northwest, right? Then we'll do our best to keep off the well-travelled paths until we reach Dunadd."

He whistled for Cai to come to heel and they began to walk.

"You know where we're going?" Duro wondered, looking around at the snow-topped hills, brown fields, and leafless trees everywhere. "I mean, you've been here before?"

"Aye, more than once," the druid said. "When I was younger, I visited all the important sites across these northern lands. There weren't many settlements this far west, although things might have changed since then, with the new settlers coming all the time. Bri will return for us in two weeks, although Taranis knows how long it'll take us to complete our mission."

"Assuming it's even possible," Duro said. "If the fortress is impenetrable, how does Coroticus expect us to get in, kill the king, and escape again?"

"Maybe he doesn't," Bellicus replied ominously.

"You think he wants us to fail? To be captured or killed by Loarn?"

The druid shook his head. "I doubt he wants us dead, just out of the way for a bit." His face was troubled though, as this really was a fool's errand the king had sent them on.

"Hail, strangers!"

They halted, and Bellicus muttered an oath under his breath. So much for not drawing any attention to themselves. They hadn't even left the village yet, and here was someone already wanting to talk.

They turned to see an older man hurrying towards them. His hair and beard were neatly trimmed, and his long woollen cloak was clean and in good condition. Bellicus marked him as a person of good standing within the community, and his thoughts were confirmed when the man reached them, eyeing Cai somewhat warily.

"Forgive me," he said, eyes drawn to Bellicus and, in particular, his eagle-topped staff. "I'm Conall mac Gabrain, headman of this settlement. I saw you come off the boat and, well, are you a druid?"

Again, Bellicus cursed silently to himself – not only had they drawn attention to themselves but word of who he was would undoubtedly precede them now. He had thought of leaving his staff behind in Dun Breatann but rejected the idea – it was more than just a length of wood, it was his badge of office and came in useful much more often than it caused problems. Besides, being a druid was a sacred calling, and if the people here needed his help, he was bound to give it, if possible.

"I am, Conall," he replied, and the man sagged a little, as if a great weight had been lifted from his shoulders. The gesture didn't bode well. "My name is Bellicus. These are my friends, Duro and Cai."

"Praise be, you can help us sort this out then! Taranis knows it's too much for me alone." He looked at the ground as if in a daydream then shook his head and looked back to Bellicus and the perplexed Duro. "Forgive me," he said once again, "I will explain everything if you will follow me to the hall? We should hurry, it's starting to rain."

The headman walked northwards, towards the largest building in the village, but Duro grasped his companion by the arm, holding him in place.

"We have a mission to complete. Whatever's happening here is none of our business."

The druid patted the centurion's hand but shook his head and smiled almost apologetically. "You are thinking like a soldier again, my friend. We are not members of your old legion – I am a representative of the gods and I must do what I can for the people of this settlement."

Duro cursed under his breath as they followed the headman. "You know word will reach Loarn mac Eirc that a giant druid is in his lands? He'll figure out straight away who you are."

"That was always a possibility. It matters little. Loarn has no idea what our plans are, and he certainly won't see us as a threat. Besides, if we sort this out quickly, we'll be on our way before word can travel anywhere."

The rain was falling steadily now and Duro was still muttering to himself as they passed into the hall, although he cheered up at the sight of a cask of ale, and even managed a smile when Conall threw some kindling onto the fire in the centre of the room and poked the embers, bringing the welcoming flames to life. Cai padded silently across to it and lay down, eyes, as always, fixed on his master.

The downpour could be heard drumming on the thatched roof as the headman filled three mugs and set them down on the table the two companions had chosen to sit at.

"Your hall is comfortable, and well made," the druid noted, looking up at the roof. Not a drop of rain could be seen leaking through.

Conall mac Gabrain smiled proudly at the compliment. "We're a community of sailors, fishermen, boat-builders – we know how to keep the water out where it's not needed. Would you like something to eat?"

"Aye," Duro grinned, rubbing his stomach, but Bellicus shook his head.

"Later. First, Conall, you better tell us what troubles you."

The headman looked at Duro. "Is he a druid too? He doesn't look like one, although, no offence, neither do you, my lord."

"No, he's not a druid," Bellicus smiled. "He's my…servant." The smile on his face only widened at the outraged glare he received from the centurion. "You can talk freely, Conall. Duro is trustworthy. And, rather like Cai, once you feed him, he'll be your friend for life."

The headman laughed but, as he began telling them his tale the frivolity quickly evaporated.

"One of our people was murdered, just two days ago."

Bellicus said nothing. Such a crime wasn't particularly common, but it was hardly unheard of. Men fought over anything, from women to money to land. Gods, if drink was involved, someone might even be murdered over a misheard word! This was no simple drunken brawl gone wrong though, and a chill ran down the druid's back as Conall went on.

"It was a little girl."

Bellicus and Duro listened as the headman explained everything to them and, by the end of it, both men were filled with anger, for the child's death had been neither quick nor painless. Bellicus couldn't help thinking of Catia, and a sense of outrage, such as he'd never felt before, threatened to consume him.

"Do you know who did it?" he demanded, and the headman shrank back at the power in the druid's voice.

"No. There were only five men around that part of the island on the day the body was discovered, so it must have been one of them. All deny it, though, and I see no way to find the truth." He looked hopefully at Bellicus. "Perhaps the gods will shine their light on the perpetrator? Our community will never be able to move past this horrible time until justice is served."

"You've questioned all the suspects?"

"Of course. Some of them are not particularly well liked and their treatment hasn't been altogether pleasant. Yet, all continue to protest their innocence."

"Where are they now?"

Conall mac Gabrain shrugged. "At work I assume."

"You aren't worried the guilty man will simply flee?" Duro asked.

"What else can I do? I can't simply imprison five men. This is only a small village and they are needed at their work. Besides, four of them are innocent, and all have ties here – family and so on – so they're unlikely to go anywhere." He spread his hands wide. "You see why I was so glad when you appeared here today? I have no experience of dealing with something like this. It is a terribly heavy burden. That little girl…"

"Gather ten of your men and arrest the suspects," Bellicus said, staring thoughtfully into the fire. "Have them taken to the place where the girl was found. I will question them there. Tonight."

* * *

"Did you know the girl named Fedelmid?"

The man seated on the ground before Bellicus looked up at him with wide, frightened eyes.

"I did," he replied hoarsely.

Night had fallen and the rain had mercifully stopped, although clouds still covered the moon and only a couple of rushlights illuminated the site where the child's body had been discovered. Bellicus wore his hood up, and Cai lay by his side, a malevolent, silent shadow.

The man before him was the third of the five suspects, and, like the previous two, he was terrified by the giant druid and the spirits that undoubtedly haunted this place of ill-portent.

"Did you kill her?"

"No, I swear by Taranis, I did not! She was a nice wee thing, reminded me of my own daughter. No-one in their right mind could have done…that…" He trailed off and the dim light caught tears streaking his face. "Do you have children, druid?"

Bellicus, caught completely off guard by the question, stared at him, unsure how to reply. At last, he nodded.

"Then you'll understand," said the villager. "No father could have committed that crime."

The druid knew that statement was incorrect – many parents had been known to commit such crimes in the past – but it was obvious this fellow was innocent. As the other two had been.

"You may go," the druid said, and leaned down to help the man to his feet. When he was gone, Bellicus shouted back towards the village, where Duro, Conall mac Gabrain and some of the villagers held the two remaining suspects. "Send the next one," he shouted, and watched as the centurion's shadowy outline approached with a rather smaller figure in front of him.

"Sit," the druid commanded.

"Where? On the grass? No – it's wet." The voice was that of a youngster, sullen and uncooperative.

"I said, 'sit'!" Bellicus's massive palm lashed out, striking the lad on the side of the face, sending him flying. The druid, eyes well-adjusted to the gloom by now, took in the sight of this fourth suspect.

Aeron Cynbel, about seventeen years old, slim, strangely confident eyes and a defiant curl to his upper lip. This one, Conall had told him, was the least likely to have committed the crime.

"Quiet lad," the headman had attested. "Keeps himself to himself, does his work without much complaint and, although he's not exactly popular, he's never had a cross word with anyone as far as I know. Not the violent type."

Bellicus glared at the young man and compared his demeanour to that of the previous three suspects. The others had appeared terrified from the moment they were brought here to this secluded spot, next to the loch and overlooked by a small grove of yew and birch trees.

This young man didn't seem scared, just sullen and irritated after spending the day locked in a room with the other accused.

"Have you been here before?"

Aeron Cynbel nodded. "Of course. This is a small village. I've been to every part of it."

"Did you kill the girl here?"

A smile tugged at the man's mouth. "I'm not stupid, you won't trick me into confessing," he said. "Because I didn't do anything wrong."

"Do you find this amusing?" Bellicus growled, crouching down and staring into the other's face. "A child was raped and murdered here. Her spirit still haunts the place, tied to the land until justice is done and her killer pays the price for his crime. Yet you sit there, smiling."

The young man simply shrugged and stared back at the druid. "Why shouldn't I? You don't frighten me; I did nothing wrong."

"I may not frighten you, but what about the gods?"

No reply.

"The gods know what you did," Bellicus said softly, standing up once again, wondering how best to rattle this strangely confident youngster. Was he unmoved by the druid and this ill-fated place because he was innocent of the horrific crime, or was something else happening behind that sullen façade?

"Do you know what happened to the girl?"

Cynbel nodded. "Everyone does, it's all people have talked about for the past two days."

"How does it make you feel?"

"Sad."

Bellicus couldn't read the man at all. He seemed to have a natural gift of hiding his emotions, a talent that often took trainee-druids months or years of practice. His face betrayed no fear, remorse, guilt, or, for that matter, sadness.

The druid sighed loudly and shook his head. "So you're innocent? All right, I'm done." He sat down on the damp grass, next to the suspect who watched him blankly. "I'm sure it was the second man I questioned anyway. He nearly shit himself when we brought him here, like he was terrified the child's vengeful shade would come for him. Ha! Poor fool. It won't be a ghost he needs to fear in the morning, it'll be the wrath of the villagers." He pulled the stopper from his ale-skin and tipped it back. Wiping his mouth with the back of his hand he handed it to the young man who took it gladly.

Bellicus had ordered the five suspects be given no food or drink all day to make them more pliable, and less alert for his questioning. The young man greedily sucked at the ale-skin like a newborn at its mother's breast, then handed it back with a grin.

"Can I go then, druid? Are we finished?"

"Not yet," Bellicus replied after a few moments, and he too grinned. "First I would have the truth from you."

"I already told you the truth," Cynbel replied irritably, getting to his feet although somewhat unsteadily.

"I didn't say you could go, boy. Sit down!"

The young man instantly collapsed onto the grass as if his legs had become boneless, and fear was written all across his face for the druid hadn't even touched him.

"What have you done to me?"

"The gods have come," Bellicus whispered, looking around at the trees. "Do you see them? There is Taranis, borne over the sea on the north wind…And there –" he pointed at the shadows cast behind the birch trees by the weak rushlights. "Cernunnos."

Aeron Cynbel lay on the hard, frosty ground and now there was a change in him – his eyes bulged as he scanned the night sky, seeing things Bellicus could only guess at. The ale, which the druid had only pretended to drink, was laced with a concoction of hallucinogenic mushrooms and now the potent mixture was taking effect.

"Who is that rising up from beneath the earth?" the druid hissed, nudging Cai, who growled in response. "Ah, hear that? It is Dis, the god of dead."

"What's happening to me?" the man mumbled, staring at the dog which turned its head towards him, sending him scurrying backwards until he came up against a tree.

"What's happening?" Bellicus repeated, striding across the ground to stand, towering over the hallucinating suspect. "The gods have come for you Aeron Cynbel, and they will hear your confession."

* * *

The next morning dawned cold, grey and cloudy, and Bellicus didn't feel at all rested. The story the murderer had told him the previous night still lingered in his mind, and would do for a long time. He felt changed by what he'd heard – he'd always known men were capable of despicable acts of sadism and wickedness, but never before had he been so close to something such as this and he wished he was back in Dun Breatann, standing protectively over young Catia.

If the druid felt scarred by his experience so too did the man accused of the child's murder. Gone was the sullen confidence of the night before, replaced by a haunted look and darting eyes that swept fearfully about the room he'd been confined to by the headman and the villagers.

"What did you do to him?" Duro asked, noting the change in the young man. "He seemed unshakeable yesterday."

"So he was," Bellicus replied as they watched two tall villagers bind the murderer's hands behind his back, then drag him out into the open where he was met with jeers and hisses and screams of rage from the family of the defiled girl. "Because he did not believe in the gods. You must have met men in the legions who cared nothing for other people's suffering. Men who enjoy hurting others." He ruffled Cai's ears, letting the dog know there was no danger to them from the angry, shouting mob.

"Of course," Duro agreed. "They make fine soldiers, but poor friends."

"Indeed. Without a natural sense of compassion though, why don't they all become murderers or rapists?"

Duro thought about it a moment. "Fear of the law?"

"Exactly." The dead child's mother ran to the prisoner and attacked him with her bare hands, clawing at his face and screaming in fury. The two guards allowed her to draw blood and then she was held back by the crowd who wanted to see the rest of the spectacle play out. "Men usually fear retribution from other men, or from the gods. That's what stops our entire culture disintegrating into chaos and killing."

The prisoner, face a mass of bloody claw marks, stumbled and was dragged roughly to his feet by the guards who led him inexorably towards a wagon.

"That young man did not believe in the gods and did not fear the men of the village here. Or me, for that matter."

"How did you get him to confess then?" Duro demanded, somewhat exasperated now.

"I showed him the gods. And then, probably for the first time ever, he knew real fear."

A man, probably another relative of the murder victim, was kicking the prisoner now and, again, he was allowed to land several savage blows before being restrained. Small flakes of snow started to fall but few in the crowd noticed.

"What will they do to him?" the centurion asked, peering at the wagon which had a large cauldron sitting beside it. Conall mac Gabrain stood there, lips drawn into a thin line as he glared at the killer, who was unceremoniously helped up onto the wagon by his guards.

"Drown him," Bellicus replied.

Duro grunted. "Shouldn't we be on our way then, now that you've done your duty? We still have a king to kill and if this snow gets heavier it'll make our journey even harder."

The druid shook his head slowly and looked on as the murderer was dragged, crying and begging for mercy now, up, onto the bed of the wagon. "Not yet. I want to see the bastard die. Besides, my duty isn't done just yet. Stay, Cai."

He strode forward, past Conall and the other angry villagers and climbed onto the wagon, raising his staff high into the air. The crowd fell silent, respecting the druid's office and feeling suddenly that the gods were in attendance – come to receive this sacrifice and see justice done.

"You all know what this man is accused of," Bellicus said, powerful voice carrying out across the gathering. There were nods and shouts of agreement, and vengeful cries from the dead girl's family. "He killed the child, Fedelmid, and confessed his actions to me last night, in the presence of Dis, God of the Dead." More cries of outrage, and he turned to the condemned man. "Do you have anything to say?"

"It wasn't me. You're making a mistake." The prisoner's features contorted with anger and he struggled to get down from the wagon but one of the guards punched him hard in the face, then again, and Bellicus, to his shame, enjoyed seeing the blows strike home. There should be no pleasure in these proceedings, he thought, but by all the gods, that young man deserved to suffer for what he'd done.

"In accordance with the law of this settlement, I pronounce you guilty of murder," the druid announced, raising his staff again and nodding towards the two guards. "The sentence is death. Lift him up."

One man swept the prisoner's legs away, so he fell awkwardly and struggled to rise again, but, with his hands tied behind his back he merely flopped like a landed fish until the guards grasped his ankles and lifted him up.

"No! Please, don't! Please!" It was as if the condemned man only now realised what was about to happen and he screamed, pleading for mercy, for his life, for forgiveness, beseeching the murdered girl's mother, oddly, to help him.

His words were cut off as Bel nodded and the guards lowered the victim headfirst into the freezing water in the cauldron.

"Dis take him, and make him the servant of Fedelmid in the underworld."

There was no clap of thunder or other sign from the gods as the Aeron Cynbel was slowly suffocated. The guards were strong, and the hatred for the prisoner so deep, that they prolonged the ritual killing for as long as possible and, by the time they were finished a thin shaft of sunlight had broken through the clouds, casting the scene in a dull, yellow hue.

"Justice is done," said the druid into the silence, and then he jumped down from the wagon and walked to Duro.

"What now?" the centurion asked.

"Now we go and find Loarn mac Eirc."

CHAPTER SEVENTEEN

In many places the terrain was hard from the winter frosts, but, in others, the rain and general dampness of the country made it soft and muddy. Bellicus and Duro had wanted to avoid the well-worn paths and roads as they made their way deeper into Dalriadan lands, but there seemed little need for there were few other travellers.

"No-one else is stupid enough to go wandering about the place in the depths of winter," Duro grumbled, fatigued by the uniformity of the landscape. "We should be back in Dun Breatann playing music and drinking ale in front of that fire."

The druid laughed, well used to his friend's moaning by now. "Depths of winter? It's almost spring. You just feel the cold worse in those old joints of yours."

"We must be nearly there," Duro said, not rising to the bait this time.

Bellicus agreed with his assessment of their position. "Aye, we'll be able to see Dunadd by tomorrow morning I'd say, if we keep up this pace."

"Why don't we stop for the night then?" The centurion pointed at a grove of yew trees. "No one will see us if we camp there."

"Looks like it's surrounded by marsh," Bellicus said, eyes scanning the ground. "There must be a path leading in, for a sacred grove like this would have been well-tended before Loarn made his people convert to Christianity."

"That's good then," Duro said. "Should prevent anyone sneaking up on us if there's only one way in."

The druid liked the idea and there seemed no better place for them to spend the night, so he led the way towards the yew grove, keeping Cai close by his side in case the dog became bogged down in the marsh.

"Should we chance a fire?"

Bellicus shrugged. "Why not? We're just a couple of travellers trying to keep warm. There's no reason anyone should come and check us out, even if they see our smoke."

"What if word's reached Loarn mac Eirc that you're in his lands?"

"I don't think we're in any danger yet."

Despite the druid's earlier claim that it was nearly spring, he knew they might freeze to death without a fire to keep the chill at bay, especially if it snowed during the night.

So they looked for dry kindling and also two long, straight branches which they used to erect their simple two-man leather tent, then Duro set about igniting the dried mushrooms he kept in his pack as tinder. While he did this, the druid took out some fresh cuts of meat the headman in Arachar had gifted him and poked a couple of the sticks through them, ready to cook.

"You keep your nose away, boy," he said sternly to Cai, who looked sheepishly away, out across the marshes, although his eyes came back often to the raw pork. Bellicus smiled, knowing exactly how the dog felt, for he was just as hungry after their day's march.

It didn't take Duro long to get the fire going and the pair found logs to sit on as they waited for their meal to heat, ale-skins in hand and a shallow bowl of water for Cai who made short work of it before returning to his previous task of guarding the roasting pork.

"So," Duro said. "You don't think Loarn mac Eirc will think anything of it if he hears you, the druid of Dun Breatann, is in his lands? Bearing in mind your king is at war with these people and swore to kill Loarn in a quite brutal manner?"

Bellicus stretched out his legs and rolled his shoulders, trying to work out the stiffness brought on by their recent travelling as he pondered the question.

"He might wonder what we're doing here," he conceded. "And send soldiers to question us. But I doubt he'll see the two of us as any threat – how could we be?"

"We might be scouts, going ahead of a bigger force of Coroticus's men," Duro replied, although he didn't really believe that was a realistic suggestion himself, and Bellicus shook his head.

"Who would send such conspicuous scouts? No," the druid leaned forward and turned his chunks of pork to save one side from charring. "I've been thinking about this all the way here. We need to capture, or kill, Loarn mac Eirc, right? That seems like an impossible task, but we'll visit some of the settlements and find out what the local gossips have to say—maybe we'll hear something useful. If not…"

Duro took lifted one of his own skewers and blew on the glistening, smoke-darkened meat before biting a small piece and, inevitably, burning his mouth. He cursed and reached for his aleskin as Bellicus shook his head in amusement.

"By Lug, you're worse than the dog."

Cai's head jerked around at this and the druid lifted off a piece of his own meat, one with rather more gristle than he'd like, and set it aside to cool for his canine friend.

"If not?"

Bellicus looked puzzled. "If not, what?"

Duro sighed and took another bite of his pork, this time finding it just about cool enough to chew. "You said, 'if not'. What did you mean? What are we going to do if the settlements hereabouts don't offer any clue as to how we should proceed? Which," he noted with a raised eyebrow, "they probably won't, let's be honest."

"Well," the druid said, setting about his own meal with gusto, "it's possible that news of my fight with Coroticus has reached Loarn by now. Probable, in fact. So, we have the perfect reason for being here, and, if we're taken by his soldiers, well…At least it will get us inside the fort."

Duro chewed that over along with his roast meat. "Shouldn't be too hard to kill the king then. Getting out alive afterwards is another matter though."

Bellicus tossed the fatty pieces of pork to Cai who wolfed them down in moments then lay watching his master finish the rest of the food as the sun went down and the temperature dropped even further.

"What's that?" Bellicus suddenly demanded, gesturing at something protruding from the centurion's pack.

Duro smiled and drew out the rest of the item, firelight glinting off its smooth surface. "My flute," he replied. "Thought a bit of music might do us good on this adventure."

"Music?" Bellicus frowned and looked around at the darkness before shrugging. "I suppose no-one will come to investigate the sound of a flute any more than the smoke from our fire." He grinned. "Actually, if anyone hears it, out here in the middle of nowhere, they'll probably think fairies or demons are abroad and make sure to keep away. I rather wish I'd brought my lute now!"

The centurion began to play – just little flurries of notes at first as he warmed up, and then the simple, well-known melodies that he'd used to learn the instrument back in Dun Breatann. Bellicus drank his ale and enjoyed his friend's music until, at last, Duro handed the flute to him.

"You play now. 'Alatucca's Song'. I'll sing."

The druid took the instrument and they performed the song that meant so much to the centurion, although without the rousing end section which really required more musicians to work properly. When it was over they stared into the campfire, both lost in their thoughts, remembering times and people now gone forever.

Eventually, Duro placed more wood into the dying fire and poked it back to life. The flames licked higher and the two men sat in companionable silence, comfortable, warm and relaxed, as a barn owl called out from somewhere across the marshes.

"Do you think there is any possible way we can succeed in this insane quest?" Duro murmured at last, and Bellicus's teeth flashed white in the gloom as he smiled confidently.

"Of course. Loarn is only a man, and the gods will guide us, as always. You get some sleep now. I'll take first watch."

The centurion offered no argument and was soon snoring softly within the tent. Bellicus was still smiling as he got up and walked silently away from the camp to empty his bladder.

He didn't really believe they would kill Loarn mac Eirc – he didn't think they would even get close enough to try, and he had no intention of being captured by the Dalriadan king who had a reputation for being cruel to captured enemies.

There were worse places to be in life though, than on the road with two friends, a campfire, music, and plentiful meat and ale. Tomorrow would bring what it may, but Bellicus was content with his lot at that moment.

* * *

The next morning brought rain again, which made the trip back over the marshes to the road even more treacherous than the previous day, but the downpour also meant many of the inhabitants of the nearest settlement were indoors. This allowed the giant druid and his companions to walk around the place without drawing too much attention to themselves.

The village only consisted of a handful of houses and workshops and appeared to be, rather to Duro's surprise, populated by skilled craftsmen – artisans who made carved wooden or cast metal ornaments and jewellery.

"I didn't realise they did such fine work this far north," the centurion admitted after speaking for a few moments to the man in the first building.

"Did you think everyone further up than the old Roman wall was a dirty savage?" Bellicus asked, only half in jest. "I must admit I don't know much about the Dalriadan culture, compared to, say, the Picts. But everyone, no matter where they're from, appreciates nice things, whether it be the eagle on my staff, or the amulet you carry showing Mithras slaying the bull, or Queen Narina's gem-encrusted brooches. They have to be made somewhere and, in my experience, artists like to spend a lot of time on their own. It doesn't surprise me that a few of them have come here to live and work."

"I suppose so," Duro said. "And we're not far from Dunadd anyway, you say, so, if there was trouble – an invasion or something like that – the folk here would just retreat to the fort. Not a bad way to live actually. Peaceful if nothing else."

"Boring more like," Bellicus said. "Fine for a while but I'd like to see something of the world, rather than shutting myself off from it."

"You're young though," Duro noted. "By the time you're my age you might feel different."

"By the Dagda, you're a big lad." The companions stopped walking through the rain to see a wizened face peering out at them from an open doorway. "Come in, strangers, out of this terrible weather, before you drown!"

The man's accent was, at first, completely impenetrable to Duro who was only just getting used to the language of the Alt Clotans', but Bellicus shepherded both the centurion and Cai, who looked quite dejected, coat sopping with rain, into the low house gladly.

"Sit down, before you knock yourself out on my rafters," the old man commanded, gesturing to an ancient wooden chest carved, quite exquisitely, with strange markings. "Mochan's my name, and it's not often we see visitors here in Carngheal."

"You use this as a seat?" Duro asked, eyeing the workmanship in wonder. "It's incredible."

"Aye," the man smiled. "Made it myself, before my sight faded and my hands grew too shaky for such work. Don't worry, it'll take the weight of the two of you." He stroked Cai's muzzle happily then raised a finger in the air thoughtfully. "I've got just the thing for you, boy. Terrible weather this, eh? I'll be glad when summer comes – feel it worse in my joints the older I get."

Chatting away, to himself more than anyone else it seemed, the man went to the far end of the small house and returned carrying a piece of dried meat that was so shrivelled Bellicus couldn't tell what animal it had come from.

"Not much use to me," Mochan gurned, revealing a mouth almost completely bereft of teeth. "But this one will enjoy it, if I'm any judge." He held the unappetising stick of meat out to Cai, who sniffed it curiously for a moment, and then gently pulled it out of the man's hand and disappeared into a corner.

"Powerful beast. Quite the handsome fellow too."

"Are you talking about me or my dog?" Bellicus replied, grinning.

"You're a man?" the old craftsman asked in mock surprise, eyebrows raised as he peered at the druid. "You're so big, I thought you must be one of the kelpies folk around here tell tales of."

Duro laughed, having heard about kelpies, the mythical, often malevolent, sea-horses that could transform themselves into human form, from Bellicus himself.

"No, I'm just a man." The druid shook his head, enjoying this wizened character's company. "And a thankful one at that, for your hospitality. Cai seems to be enjoying that treat you gave him."

"Is that a hint?" Mochan demanded fiercely, although not seriously. "That you want something to eat too? Where are my manners? Feeding the dog before the men. My wife would give me a clip about the ear if she hadn't died ten years ago."

He filled wooden mugs with clear water and placed a loaf of black bread on Duro's lap.

"I'm afraid your dog is the only one with meat, for this is all I have to offer until one of my neighbours is good enough to gift me some."

"This is fine," Bellicus assured him, sipping the water, noting again the wonderful carvings on the mug he'd been given. Truly, this man had been a master of his trade in his younger days if these were examples of his work. "And we have meat, here." He fished in his pack and brought out the rest of the meat Connall had given him in Arachar. "We can share this. What we don't eat, you can keep."

Mochan smiled and helped himself to some of the pork. Bellicus could see Cai still worrying the hard, dried out meat in the corner, and it was gratifying to see the toothless old man doing much the same to the salted pork.

"What brings you two here, to our little village?"

"I'm a druid," Bellicus replied and, for the first time, the old man looked slightly flustered, although his composure soon returned as he waited for his guest to continue. "I'm travelling the lands, gathering tales – folklore – from people like you."

"Why?" The look on Mochan's face suggested he thought such an occupation unfathomable.

"We druids like to know things," Bellicus shrugged. "It helps us understand the world and allows us to mould it to our purposes."

"What sort of things?" Still, the old man wasn't convinced and Duro could understand why, for his nature was much the same.

"Well, the kelpies you mentioned, for example. We gather stories about them and pass the knowledge on through our songs and stories, building a picture of the world so that we might better serve the people."

"Stories, eh?" Mochan swallowed what must have been a large chunk of pork given his lack of molars and eyed Bellicus thoughtfully. "You want a story?"

"Always," the druid said, covering his mouth with a hand to stifle a belch. "Any local folklore is of interest to me."

"Have you heard about the huge stag that's been seen around here for…" He paused and thought for a moment before continuing, rather unhelpfully. "Years?"

Bellicus shook his head. There was nothing special about a stag, even a big one. The beasts were seen all over the lands after all, and had provided much sport for kings and warlords since time immemorial. It was quite likely a stag's head adorned at least one wall in a building within a half-a-day's walking distance of this hovel. He was too tactful to say any of that though, so he just watched Mochan, waiting for the man to tell his story.

"It's white," said the Dalriadan, and both Bellicus and Duro stopped, mid-chew, wondering if they'd heard him correctly.

"White?"

"Aye," Mochan grinned at the centurion's question. "And bigger than any normal stag."

"You've seen it?" Bellicus asked, returning to his meal now that the initial surprise had passed. "Here in Carngheal?"

"Only once, and, well, as you know already, my eyesight isn't very good anymore. But I saw it alright, and I'd swear to the Dagda it was real." He gazed at the wall of his small house, as if reliving that experience, mouth working furiously as he tried to masticate his dinner. "Beautiful creature, to be sure." His gaze returned to Bellicus at last and he smiled again. "There's all sorts of tales been spun about that stag, as you can imagine. I don't believe the more outlandish ones, but you could ask the other folk hereabouts what they've heard. You'll pick up just the sort of story you're looking for, I'd wager."

The druid finished off his food and washed it down with a final long pull of the water Mochan had furnished them with as Duro leaned back against the wall and let out a contented sigh. The house might be small, but, with the rain battering the roof outside and the fire crackling nicely in the hearth, it was certainly cosy.

"Why hasn't anyone managed to bring down this great white stag?" Bellicus asked, making their old host jerk upright as if he'd been about to doze off where he sat. "If it's as magnificent as you say – and I don't doubt you – why hasn't the king killed it yet?"

"Oh he's tried!" Mochan said, spreading his hands as he went on. "But these lands are vast and it's not so easy to find one animal, no matter how big it is. King Loarn is a fine warrior though, and he's vowed to kill the beast one day, and mount its great antlered head over the entrance to the hill fort at Dunadd, like young Cormac the metalworker has done at his workshop, albeit with a smaller trophy. I don't doubt the king, for he's a man of his word. Aye, that he is, eh, boy? Did you see Cormac's stag on the way here? No? Oh well."

The warmth of the room seemed to be making the old storyteller ramble and Bellicus decided it was time they took their leave.

He got to his feet, stooping from habit so his shaved head didn't clatter against the rafters, and held out his hand to Mochan who grasped it firmly.

"Thank you for your hospitality," the druid said, and gestured to the pack of dried meat on the table. "I hope that goes some way to repaying our debt to you. We'll take our leave now, for it sounds as if the rain's stopped hammering on your roof."

"It's been a pleasure, lads," Mochan said, following them towards the door. "Any time you're in Carngheal, make sure and come visit me, eh? I hardly ever get visitors these days." He grabbed Cai's head and stroked the massive dog almost roughly, as if he didn't want the hound to leave. Cai took the old man's fussing without complaint and then wandered off to leave his scent on the next house along the track.

"We'll do that," Bellicus said, but his mind was already moving on to other things, making plans from what they'd learned from the Dalriadan. "Farewell, friend, and may the gods bless your house."

"They already have," Mochan smiled. "It's not every day I enjoy the company of a druid and his travelling companions."

The old man watched as they walked away, back towards their campsite of the previous night and then, looking over his shoulder and seeing Mochan disappear inside his house, Duro shook his head. "I could hardly understand a damn word he was saying."

Bellicus laughed and lengthened his stride. "His accent was thick, I'll grant you that, for he must have been one of the earliest settlers. The younger folk are more intelligible. Come on, we have one more thing to do today before it gets dark."

"The fort?" Duro asked, to a nod from the druid.

"Aye. We should get a look at it – see what we're up against." He led the way to the north, eyes searching the land for signs of scouts marking their approach.

"I thought you'd been there before."

"I have," Bellicus agreed, relaxing into his stride, seeing no spies ahead of them. "It was a long time ago though, when I was just a young student. And I wasn't marking things like entrances, wall heights, garrison numbers or any of that."

"I can answer any questions on those three points," the centurion muttered darkly. "Too well defended, too high to climb up, and too many men to fight."

"Undoubtedly," Bellicus agreed. "But there might be a weak spot that we can exploit."

Duro held his peace this time, merely raising his eyebrows as if he thought the druid mad, but he knew himself they had to get a look at the hillfort and the terrain around it. Besides, it was possible the gods would give them some sign, some hint of how to kill the Dalriadan king. Stranger things had happened since he'd been in the company of Bellicus after all.

It wasn't that long before the imposing bulk of Dunadd appeared on the grey horizon and Bellicus called Cai back close to him. Both men hunched instinctively, hoping to make themselves harder to spot.

"It does look similar to Dun Breatann," Duro noted as they left the main road and headed for a neighbouring hill, upon which stood a distinctive rock, or tree – it was impossible to tell which it was from this distance.

"Similar, aye," Bellicus said. "It's a big hill with some walls and buildings on it. Nothing gets by you, eh?"

"You know what I mean, you cheeky bastard," Duro retorted. "I've seen other hill forts, but none looked more like Dun Breatann than that." He nodded towards Dunadd, proud in its position amongst the low marshes and fields, appreciating its rather bleak majesty.

They reached the strange feature upon the low hill they were climbing, finding it to be a rock which drew Bellicus's attention immediately when he noticed strange symbols carved into it and recognised it as some kind of religious artefact or marker.

"You get a good look at the fort," he said. "I want to examine these markings for a moment."

Both men settled down to their tasks, Duro scanning the approach road towards Dunadd, his eyes tracing the route through the imposing gatehouse and up, past the few workshops and dwellings, taking in the thick walls of wood and stone, and at last fixing on the great hall at the summit.

The druid muttered to himself as he tried to make sense of the images and inscriptions carved into the enigmatic rock which was about the same height as he was. Eventually, only able to decipher some of the message the thing had been left to impart, and finding it irrelevant to their task, he joined the centurion in mentally mapping Loarn mac Eirc's seat of power.

There was a citadel on the summit, not large, but sturdy and impressive even at this distance. Beneath that were two, maybe even three other levels with buildings of various design – houses, workshops, and defensive structures. The main entrance was cut from the solid rock, forming a passageway that led to the gatehouse. This was obviously a killing ground, where any attacking force would be penned in as they attempted to break through, pelted by arrows, javelins, rocks and whatever else the Dalriadans had to hand.

The entire fortress was a succession of steps, narrow walkways, and natural defensive features cleverly supplemented and enhanced by stone walls. No wonder it had never been taken by force as far as Bellicus was aware.

Yet, despite its obvious strength as a fortress, the smells carried on the afternoon breeze suggested pottery was being made within some of the workshops on the hill. This wasn't merely a place for the king to spend the winter in safety, feasting and drinking the cold months away, it was also a centre of industry, administration, and Dalriadan culture as a whole.

"See any 'weak spots' then, druid?" Duro asked with a sidelong glance at his companion, who shook his head.

"None. Even if we could fly like those buzzards circling overhead, we'd still struggle to get in and out without one of the soldiers spearing us."

"What are we going to do then?"

Bellicus rose up again, jerking his head for Cai to follow suit. "For now, we'll return to camp and have a think." He began making his way gingerly back down the hill, using the trees and bushes growing there to stop himself sliding, and also to mask him from any watching sentries in Dunadd. "Don't lose hope yet, my friend – something will come up. It always does."

Duro didn't reply and Bellicus could see why. The centurion was lost in thought, picturing the hillfort, trying to come up with some way of striking at its ruler without him and his companions being killed in the process. Ropes? Climbing equipment? Perhaps the far, hitherto unseen, side of the hill offered a better chance of ingress?

Both men knew, realistically, that it would be impossible to enter the fortress by stealth, however. If they were going to capture or kill the Dalriadan king they would have to either gain entry to Dunadd by some clever subterfuge, perhaps acting the part of travelling musicians seeking shelter, or by forgetting the hillfort completely and finding another way to complete their mission.

The sun was beginning to set, even though it wasn't particularly late, so the three travellers picked up their pace once the fort was well behind them and made for their temporary home back amongst the marshes near Carngheal.

The gods would offer some hope, or they would not, just as they did in every aspect of every man's life. There was nothing to be gained by worrying about it.

CHAPTER EIGHTEEN

There was a full moon that night, hanging like a great ripe apple in a clear sky that revealed the full majesty of the heavens. Constellations and the strangely beautiful smudges that seemed to play in the periphery of one's vision were all visible and Bellicus felt drawn to simply walk. Not to any particular destination, just to wander, taking in the glory of the night and the world around them.

"Are you insane?" Duro demanded, when the druid informed him of his desire to go for a stroll. "We're in a marsh! One wrong step could see you drowned, man. Even in the daylight this place is treacherous."

"I'll pick my way slowly," Bellicus promised, brandishing his staff. "This will probe ahead and show me where to step. Besides, the gods will guide me." He gazed up at the silver face of the moon and knew he spoke the truth. "They are calling to me, and I've found it always pays to listen when that happens. You wait here with the centurion, all right, Cai? I don't want you slipping into a bog."

Duro stroked the big dog's head, noting the sad expression, wondering, not for the first time, if Cai could understand his master's words. "Don't worry about us," he said. "We'll not move from here. Just you take care – maybe some god *is* calling to you, but it might be Lug in one of his trickster guises..."

"I'll be careful," Bellicus grinned, teeth flashing in the moonlight. "If I meet a bent old man, I'll know it's the god trying to trick me."

"Or a beautiful nymph," Duro replied, then returned his friend's grin. "Although I'm not sure that would be such a bad thing – it's a while since..."

His face fell again as he realised what he was about to say, and thoughts of his murdered wife filled his head.

"You rest," Bellicus said, squeezing Duro's shoulder and pulling his dark cloak around himself so he appeared nothing more than a shadow. "Have some more of that ale, but leave a drop for me. It's a cold night without any clouds and I'll need warming up when I return."

He pondered which direction to take for a moment, then decided to stick to the path they already knew. Taking any other way would surely lead to disaster so, although he truly felt like he was doing the right thing, there was no point in tempting fate and blundering off into the darkness like an inexperienced youngster.

Still, even though they'd passed this way a number of times in the past two days, he stepped carefully, using the end of his staff to make sure he didn't inadvertently blunder into a patch of standing water. He didn't really expect it to be fatal even if he did, but it always paid to respect nature, especially on a night such as this, when the veil between the worlds felt like it might be pulled aside, revealing strange, wondrous secrets.

With no clear idea of where he was going, the druid walked slowly, enjoying the crisp air and the near silence of the Dalriadan lands. A tawny owl cried, three times, not too far away and it brought back memories of his childhood on the island of Iova, learning to be a druid. For some reason Iova seemed to have more owls than anywhere else he'd ever lived, and it had always been a great pleasure to spot one in the branches of a tree, so big it would weigh down the branch it was using as a perch. He guessed there must be plenty of prey for such nocturnal hunters out here, relatively far away from the disruptive influence of humanity.

The ground here was firmer and he found himself relaxing as he walked, feeling the stress of his recent confrontation with Coroticus ebbing away, and the prospect of somehow killing Loarn mac Eirc didn't seem so pressing any more. This often happened when he took himself off alone, away from civilisation – the petty squabbles and transitory lives of his fellow humans seemed utterly inconsequential in the grand scheme of things. When Coroticus was nothing but dust – when Bellicus himself was not even a memory – these marshes would still be here, with the yew grove and the owls hunting mice and hares.

A stream burbled a little way to the east and he headed for it, pulling his hood up over his head as he went for a chill wind had begun to blow. The gently flowing water reflected the moon and Bellicus found a large, dry stone to sit on, stretching his feet out and moving his head from side to side, feeling freer than he had in many long weeks. The night, and his surroundings, brought to mind the time when he'd just set off from Dun Buic to rescue the abducted Princess Catia and he stopped in the settlement known as Litana. There, he'd sacrificed a fowl in a spot very similar to this, and the gift had worked, for the gods sent him news, via the medium of a local shepherd, of the girl's position. He'd been lost and close to despair when that happened, and he wished he had something to sacrifice right now.

His mind turned to the problem of Loarn mac Eirc. Aye, it was true that petty human problems were ultimately insignificant, but Bellicus was a man, and he was driven to make the most of the time allotted to him here by the gods. If he could – somehow! – assassinate the Dalriadan king it would surely save Damnonii lives, for, without Loarn mac Eirc to lead their army, they would not travel in the spring to lay siege to Dun Breatann. Besides, Narina had told the druid what Loarn said about Catia and he understood her desire to see the foul-tongued warlord dead. Men had been killed for far less after all.

If only he'd thought to bring a chicken, or a dove, or even a rat, from one of the settlements they'd passed on the way here. He could have slaughtered it as an offering to the gods, in return for aid. For some sign or indication how he might go about bringing down the Dalriadan ruler.

He closed his eyes and allowed himself to fall into a trance, shutting out the sound of the stream and the cold breeze that was blowing on the back of his neck. For a long time he sat, clearing his mind of all thoughts, opening himself up like an empty chalice, hoping the gods might see fit to provide him with a sign despite his lack of a sacrificial offering. At one point he even thought he could hear the faint sound of Duro's flute, carried across the marshes on the wind.

That made him think of the centurion, who had never once asked Bellicus if he was really Catia's father. Duro was his friend, and it didn't matter—

Bellicus realised his thoughts were wandering again and forced himself to relax.

To empty his mind completely…

When he opened his eyes, he thought he must have crossed through the barrier to the otherworld, for standing before him was a great white stag, utterly magnificent in the silver moonshine.

Too stunned to move, and groggy from his meditations, the druid stared at the glorious animal, wondering if he'd perhaps fallen asleep and was dreaming this whole thing. The beast was completely unaware of his presence, presumably because the wind was blowing any tell-tale scent in the opposite direction, and he'd been sitting as still as a rock for a very long time.

It bent its great antlered head to the ground and chewed something, twigs from the sound of it and undoubtedly poor fare, for with a last look around, its eyes even fixing directly on Bellicus before sweeping on, it wandered off, leaving the druid too amazed to move until it had been swallowed up by the darkness.

"Thank you, Cernunnos," he finally whispered, smiling at his good fortune to have witnessed such an incredible sight up close. "I swear I'll repay you with a suitable offering when I have the chance."

A freezing rain began to fall and he got to his feet, rubbing life and warmth back into his limbs before lifting his staff and heading once more to camp. Duro had not let the fire die, for he could smell the woodsmoke on the wind, offering a beacon for him to head towards until he grew near enough to see its orange glow amongst the yew grove.

"Did the gods send you any messages?" The centurion – whose flute was still tucked safely inside his pack Bellicus noted – tossed his friend an ale-skin and skewered a piece of bread. This he held over the fire to toast, then smeared a little butter on it and gave that to the druid too. Bellicus took it gratefully and settled down next to Cai who had come to meet him as he returned through the marsh.

"They did," he replied and looked out into the darkness, hoping to catch just one more glimpse of the great white stag. "I saw it, and it's given me an idea."

They sat together until midnight, as Bellicus recounted his tale and, together, they worked out his idea and how best to proceed.

"It's a good plan," Duro admitted, smiling at the audacity – madness even – of the whole thing. "And you certainly seem to have the ear of the gods so…Let's do it. We can spend tomorrow spreading rumours of the white stag, but, for now...You want to take first watch?"

"Watch?" Bellicus shook his head with a grin. "Are you ready for sleep? We've got a job to do and what better time to do it than now?"

Duro put his head in one large hand and groaned. "Are you serious, druid? It's the middle of the bloody night, it's near pitch black and we don't even know where we're going."

Bellicus jumped to his feet and Cai, always ready to follow wherever his master led, did the same. "It won't be hard to find by Lug! A stag's head attached to a wall is easy to see. And everyone will be asleep, so it'll make our task much easier. Besides, it's hardly pitch black – the moon will guide us, and we'll be back here with our prize before you know it."

The centurion knew when he was beaten and got up, buckling on his sword belt, muttering the whole time although, in truth, the thought of this night-time raid was exciting. Life as this giant druid's companion was never dull.

* * *

Bellicus led the way through the marshes to the road and the trio began walking at a fair pace towards old Mochan's village of Carngheal.

"What makes you think we'll be able to find what we're looking for?" Duro asked, pulling his cloak up around his neck for the night had grown very cold by now, and he was missing their cosy campfire.

"Well, Mochan asked if we'd seen it on the way to his house," Bellicus replied. "That suggests it's fairly visible, and mounted on one of the buildings between here and Mochan's place." He shrugged, a gesture that was lost in the darkness. "It's only a small settlement so I'd say it won't be too hard to find what we want. Getting the thing down might be a different matter, admittedly, but—"

"The gods will guide us, I know," Duro said, shaking his head ruefully. "What if someone challenges us though? Raises the alarm?"

The druid didn't answer for the space of a few footsteps then he said, "We are at war with these people. Well, you may not be, but I'm a man of Alt Clota regardless of what its king thinks of me, and the Damnonii are my people." He looked at Duro and their eyes met in the gloom, Catia's parentage to the front of both their minds. "I – we – have been sent on a mission to stop the Dalriadans invading Alt Clota and, if that means someone must die here, so be it. Better them than some innocent family living in the protective shadow of Dun Breatann."

Duro didn't reply. He was a soldier and he was used to following orders and, despite the fact he had been a centurion in the Roman legions and was the senior of Bellicus in years, he had gladly accepted the charismatic druid as his commanding officer. He would do what he had to, although he hoped they would be find themselves back at camp in a few hours without any shedding of blood.

The village loomed in the darkness ahead, a collection of angular shapes easily visible against the rounded outlines of hills and sharper black edges of trees. The scent of meat roasting suggested not everyone in the village was asleep, despite the lateness of the hour.

"Keep your eyes peeled for our goal, and don't talk unless you have to," Bellicus murmured as they entered the main street of the settlement. "Whoever's cooking that meat will doubtless have a large cleaver to chop it apart..."

Behind him, Duro rolled his eyes. "I was a soldier of Rome, lad, I know how to conduct myself."

The druid slipped through the darkness like a shadow, a half-smile on his lips. They passed a handful of dwellings and workshops and, for the first time, Bellicus noticed they were all secured with sturdy locks. Of course, in a settlement like this, populated by skilled craftsmen and metalworkers, things like that were bound to be of good quality.

"There," Duro mouthed, pointing at the small house belonging to Mochan, their host from earlier that day.

"Shit," Bellicus spat. "We must have passed it." He turned back and the pair started to make their way along again, this time even slower, eyes straining for some sign of the trophy Mochan had said was attached to the wall of a workshop.

He knew they couldn't just start breaking into these houses and places of work for that would certainly bring unwanted attention and lead to a bloody fight. No, if they couldn't locate the stag's head they would just have to return in the morning, when folk were awake and about their work.

There was a loud sniffing noise and both warriors spun to see what had made it. Cai had his nose pressed to the bottom of a door and it was obvious why as the scent of cooking was much stronger here.

"Here!" Bellicus hissed angrily, drawing the sheepish-looking dog back to his side and dragging him into the shadows beneath an overhanging roof. Duro followed suit, and just in time, for the cook threw his door open and peered outside, brow furrowed, wicked-looking knife in his hand. The man glanced about, his gaze passing right over the hidden druid without noticing his massive bulk in the darkness.

"Damn wolves must be about again," the cook growled before taking another long look up and down the street then, satisfied he had chased away the nocturnal visitor, he went back inside and the sound of a heavy bolt slotting into place was heard.

Bellicus let out his breath and silently wagged a finger of reproach at his dog's face, then they came back out of the shadow and began walking once more, praying the gods would guide them. A cat, startled by their passing, peered at them, green eyes reflected in the moonlight before it disappeared.

"Cats, cooks and wolves," the druid muttered softly in irritation. "But no stag's head."

As he spoke, he noticed something on a building set a little way back from the road and gestured for Duro to follow as he, with Cai close by his side, went to investigate. On the door of the workshop was a stylised image of a bearded old man with a hammer. Bellicus looked at Duro who simply shrugged, a confused look on his face.

"Blacksmith's forge," said the centurion softly. "So what?"

"This is no smithy," Bellicus disagreed. "Too small." He gestured at the walls which were surely not long enough to house the furnace, anvil, bellows and other accoutrements needed to fashion things like ploughs and firedogs.

Duro said again, "So what?" and it was clear he was becoming impatient.

"That image," Bellicus replied, nodding towards the depiction of the hammer-wielding old man on the workshop door, "is of Goibniu. To the Dalriadans he is the god of, aye, blacksmiths, but also metalworking in general." He looked pleased and bent to examine the lock on the door. "I'd wager this is the building we're looking for, although I'm not sure how we get in without making a lot of noise."

"I'm not sure we *want* to get in," Duro hissed, eyeing the Dalriadan god with trepidation. "When we were chasing after the Saxons you said their gods held little power in these lands because they were interlopers or whatever. You said your gods would defeat them, and, on that occasion, so they did. But here? We're in Dalriadan lands, Bel."

The druid shook his head. "The Dalriadans are also newcomers. They've been allowed to settle here because there is room enough and they're too damn troublesome to keep out. But make no mistake, this," he spread his giant arms to encompass everything around them, "all belongs to my gods. Besides," he bent again to the lock, pulling at it in hopes it might simply snap apart, "we share many gods with the Dalriadans so don't fear the wrath of Goibniu."

His efforts to open the lock were futile and he muttered a curse before making a circuit of the building, searching the walls for another way in. As he suspected though, the workshop was in excellent repair and sealed up as tight as the skin on a bard's drum.

"Hide!" Duro suddenly lunged past, hauling on the druid's robe and crouching in the deepest shadows beside the metalworker's shop as the druid and Cai followed suit.

They peered around the side of the building as a light approached, each holding his breath, wondering who – or what – might be abroad at this time.

A man carrying an oil lamp appeared on the street, walking briskly, purposefully, as if he knew exactly where he was going and why. Bellicus and Duro watched until he had passed, and then the sound of a door opening and closing could be heard and, after that, muffled thuds and even soft singing could be heard.

"By Mithras, what's going on down there?" Duro muttered, shaking his head at the strange ways of the northern folk. "Is he murdering someone?"

Bellicus stifled a laugh and got back to his feet. "This is a community of artisans," he said. "Craftsmen and women – artists! Such folk are prone to find inspiration at strange hours. I suspect that's someone who had a dream, woke up, and couldn't wait until first light to get to work on whatever creation his dream inspired." He walked back around to the front door of the metalworker's shop. "Did you never wake up in the night when you were writing your song for Alatucca? Inspired to play some new part on your flute?"

The centurion looked back at him as if he was insane. "No."

"Ha!" Bellicus laughed again at his bluff friend's manner and gestured to the door. "How are we going to get in there?"

"We could just kick it in, grab the skull and run as fast as we can back to camp."

"What if this is the wrong place?" Bellicus demanded. "Or it's the right place but the stag's head isn't here?"

"Isn't here?" Duro asked, face screwed up in confusion. "What do you mean? I doubt the man takes the damn thing home with him every night. Do you think he cuddles up to it in bed?"

Bellicus shook his head, then frowned. "Where's Cai?"

Wordlessly, the two warriors walked to the rear of the workshop again, hands on sword-hilts, fearing the great hound had been lured away by some enemy.

They found him emptying his bowels outside the house directly behind the workshop, bringing a smile of relief from Bellicus which quickly turned into a massive grin.

"What are you so happy about?" Duro demanded. "I thought only children laughed at the sight of a shitting dog."

In reply Bellicus pointed, and the centurion glanced up, squinting for, despite the moonlight, it was very dark.

There, above the door of the house, was a mounted stag's head.

They'd found their trophy.

Bellicus crept forward and pressed his ear against the door, listening for signs of life. There was only silence and he gestured to Duro, cupping his hands, silently ordering the centurion to give him a boost up.

The stag's head was attached to the wall of the metalworker's house by a pair of rusty iron nails. Bellicus drew his dagger and used the point to lever them out which took longer, and required more effort, than he would have liked. His blade was not the right tool for such a job but, after much fumbling and silent cursing, he removed both nails and held the stag's head in his hands.

Duro watched from below, looking surprisingly comfortable given his heavy load, and, when he saw the prize was in the druid's possession, he lowered himself down, allowing Bellicus to step softly back onto the ground.

They grinned at one another like naughty children, but then the sound of movement inside the house brought them back to reality and they started to run towards the main road.

Behind them, the door opened, and the metalworker stared out into the night, eyes searching for some sign of what had disturbed his slumber. The sounds of the artisan who couldn't sleep filled the night air and the metalworker shook his head irritably.

"Third night in a row that crazy bastard's woke me with his thumping about," was all he said before slamming his door and heading back to bed.

CHAPTER NINETEEN

"I saw it last night. It was the most magnificent animal I've ever seen in my life." Bellicus placed a hand on Cai's side and stroked him apologetically as Mochan grinned.

"I told you, didn't I, druid?" The old man's eyes gleamed at the memory of his own previous sighting of the white stag. "It's a trophy worthy of champions isn't it? Did you take a shot at it?"

"No," Bellicus admitted.

"He was rooted to the spot in amazement," Duro smirked, enjoying an opportunity to poke fun at his giant companion. "Some champion."

"Aye, well, you'd have been struck dumb too, if you'd been there to see it," the druid shot back. "I think anyone with any appreciation of the gods' creations would be. It was incredible."

"That it is," Mochan agreed. "Where did you see it?"

Bellicus recounted his sighting, although he told the old Dalriadan a different location to where he'd actually spotted the stag, not wanting to give away any hints as to the general location of their campsite in case Loarn mac Eirc's men came looking for them.

"I can't wait to tell the other folk in the village," Mochan said, smiling at the prospect of sharing the druid's tale with his compatriots and, perhaps, earning a few free ales in return.

Bellicus grinned, for this is exactly what he wanted, but he placed a hand on the Dalriadan's shoulder and leaned in confidentially.

"By all means," he said. "Share the tale with your kinsfolk, but…" He paused, then shrugged regretfully. "Please don't tell them it was a druid who saw the beast, or that we've shared a meal with you these last two days." He noted the suspicious look in Mochan's eyes at his words and carried on hastily. "I'd rather no-one knew about my presence here. From past experience, when folk in small settlements such as this find out there's a druid nearby they come looking for me, wanting miracle cures for all sorts of ailments, or demanding some justice for a neighbour's slight, or…well," he winked conspiratorially at Mochan. "Let's just keep it a secret between us, eh? Just tell your friends a traveller told you about the stag – it'll save me a lot of trouble. You know what people are like. Besides, your king is a Christian and he might not want me around…"

The pre-prepared statement appealed to Mochan's sense of adventure and he tapped the side of his nose, happy to join in with Bellicus's subterfuge. "Your secret is safe with me, druid," he promised and, job done, the druid rose to his feet, Duro and Cai following his lead. They bid the old man farewell and, as they left his house, Bellicus casually asked Mochan if there were any fishmongers in the village.

"No, that's one thing we don't have here," the artisan replied. "Once a week or so a trader from Creonan, that's the village to the west," he pointed, "brings us fish, along with other things. Creonan is on the coast you see, so it takes in much trade, and then we have a market every Wednesday. I've got a nice bit of trout in my larder if you're really—"

Bellicus shook his head. "It's shellfish I want."

Mochan made a face. "I don't have any of those, I'm afraid," he replied. "Just looking at the things make me feel sick. You'll find plenty in Creonan though, and it's not far."

Bellicus did not lead them towards Creonan however, for they had other places to visit before gathering the needed shellfish, so they headed north, following the road until they came to another village.

The usual smells reached them long before they saw the thatched roofs of the low dwellings and Bellicus sat down on a rock, peering ahead at the settlement which was even smaller than Carngheal

"I'll only draw attention if I go down there," the druid said. "You go into the village, share an ale with one or two of the younger locals, so you can understand them, and spread the word about the amazing white stag you saw. Be sure to let them know you spoke to a druid and he told you the beast only appears to lone travellers. We don't want Loarn's soldiers coming to Mochan's village looking for me, it's too close to our camp, but everywhere else is fine."

"If you insist," Duro smiled. "I can think of worse ways to spend an afternoon. What will you do?"

Bellicus glanced about the land but his expression was glum. "I'll have a look for herbs and ingredients I can use for various things, but, at this time of year, I expect my harvest will be a poor one. Don't be spending all day in that village downing ale though," he cautioned. "We've got more villages to visit before its dark, and you need to be somewhat sober if we're going to spread the news of the white stag to as many people as possible."

"Don't worry about me, druid," Duro retorted in mock outrage. "I know my limits. Before the end of the day the seed will be planted and, before we know it, the whole of Dalriada will know about the magnificent white stag roaming about these lands just begging for its great head to be hung over someone's door."

And so the next four days went, the trio moving from one settlement to the next, Duro recounting his ever-expanding tale in the alehouses while Bellicus and Cai waited, hidden in the trees half-a-mile or so away. They camped at night, risking a fire since it was still bitterly cold, and enjoying meat and drink the centurion procured on his daytime visits to the Dalriadan villages. That meant their travels were never too arduous and, by the time they had circled back to their original campsite not far from Carngheal, Bellicus knew the entire countryside would be aflame with the tale of the white stag.

Their final destination that day had been the fishing village of Creonan, where Duro, after detailed instructions from the druid, had managed to buy a battered old wooden bucket filled with the particular kind of shellfish known as piddocks, although the centurion hadn't noticed the druid eating a single one of the slimy things.

"What now?" Duro asked as they relaxed in the yew grove, fire blazing merrily. "Just wait for King Loarn to hear the stag rumours and come looking for it?"

"Of course not," Bellicus replied. "Why do you think we went to so much trouble to get this?" He lifted the stag's head they'd stolen from the metalworker in Carngheal and Duro gaped at it in the darkness.

It was glowing in the moonlight, almost as if lit from within somehow.

"How did you...?"

The druid grinned and, mirroring Mochan's gesture from days earlier, tapped the side of his nose secretively, offering no clue as to how he had worked such magic on the stag's head although Duro, having some idea by now of how Bellicus worked, had his suspicions. A concoction of powders and herbs, or some other natural substance, were most likely the key to the luminescence, rather than any magical spell. Although, as the druid often told him, there was little difference, as magic was simply the art of causing a change in accordance with one's will, no matter how that change was achieved.

"That's impressive," Duro admitted, nodding slowly in appreciation of the stag's head. "No doubt you want to carry the thing about the countryside in the dead of night. I'm getting blisters on my feet here, druid. I'm not used to all this marching anymore."

Bellicus laughed at his friend's perceptiveness. "You know me too well my friend, that's exactly what we're going to do. Every time some villager spots this in the dark the legend will only grow."

Duro shook his head as if utterly disgusted although, in truth, he'd expected something like this since the moment Bellicus had decided they had to procure a stag's head. What else could it be for after all? He had to admit though, glowing that whitish green colour in the moonshine…it would amaze any Dalriadan who saw it – assuming the local didn't spot the perfectly normal human carrying the antlered head about the place.

"You can wear it," the centurion said firmly. "Aye, most of the folk about here will stand gaping, open-mouthed like idiots when they see this appearing out of the mist. But, sooner or later, one of them will loose an arrow, or a sling shot, or whatever else they might have to hand." He shook his head and turned back to the merrily blazing campfire. "This is your idea, druid – you can be the one to see it through. I'll be ready at your back with my spatha honed and oiled, ready to strike, but I'm not wearing that thing around the marshes."

Bellicus smiled but, perhaps wisely, didn't reply.

Tomorrow would bring what it may.

"And when are you going to eat one of those damn shellfish?" the centurion demanded. "I went to a lot of trouble to get them.

Had to visit more than one fishmonger in the village to gather that many."

Once again, Duro's only reply was that enigmatic smile.

CHAPTER TWENTY

For their first foray into the countryside with the stag's head Bellicus and Duro decided to pick an easy target – one where they were unlikely to face armed, trained soldiers. A village not too far from their campsite was chosen as the place, and they huddled now behind a rocky outcropping at the top of a low hill close to the main road. They had spotted two men repairing a bridge used to transfer cattle from one field to another during the day and hoped the job would last until night began to fall.

It had, and now the workers were returning to their homes in the village. Their voices carried, although the conversation appeared to be mostly about the weather and some woman one of the men wanted to bed.

"Perfect," Duro whispered, eyes flashing in the gloom as he smiled in expectation of what was to come. "When they see you on the horizon though, they'll have something more exciting to talk about."

Bellicus grunted a reply but he wasn't too pleased with his night's work. The stag's head had proved difficult to modify so it could be worn as a costume and, furthermore, since he was the biggest and therefore the easiest for people to spot in the dark, the druid was given the job of wearing the resultant headdress.

They had sewn and stuck – using birch tar obtained from one of the villages – pieces of fabric braced with wooden strips around the stag's head, so it could be worn like some great helmet. It was heavy and uncomfortable to wear and looked ridiculous in the daylight, but that mattered little for, at a distance, and at night, the effect should be spectacular. Unless someone came too close, of course, but the companions doubted that would be a problem this night.

"Tell me when they're near," Bellicus said, and made sure, for the hundredth time, that his headdress was firmly in place. Their scheme wouldn't last long if the antlered head fell off when the villagers were gazing up at him.

Duro allowed the workmen to come closer, and then he said softly, "Now".

Bellicus pushed himself up on his knees, so only the stag's head showed above the rocks they were hiding behind, and then he let out an enormous roar. It sounded similar to the moo of a cow, but harsher, more guttural, and Duro blinked in surprise, staring at his friend in amazement for he'd never heard such a noise emanating from a human before.

On the road below, the workmen looked up, and already fear was written plainly on their faces before they'd even spotted the antlered head glowing softly on the starlit horizon. When the first of them saw the apparition, he cried out in alarm and was soon joined by the other man.

"What in the name of the Dagda is that?"

"It's a demon!"

"Don't be stupid, it's just a stag. Look, it has big horns. Besides, what kind of demon moos like an angry cow?"

"What kind of stag glows in the bloody dark?"

Bellicus decided that was enough and he slowly lowered the head down, as if the stag was bending its head towards the grass or perhaps to drink from a puddle behind the rock. He removed the costume and shoved it into a sack, grinning at Duro as the two villagers on the road below continued to discuss what they'd seen.

"Did you see the size of it?" one was shouting. "It was enormous!"

"It must be that one everyone's talking about," the other said. "The white one."

"Was it white?"

"Aye, I think so. It glowed didn't it? How many giant white stags do you think are wandering about the place? It has to be that same one."

Then Bellicus and Duro glanced at one another and dropped their hands to their sword hilts as the workmen went on discussing the sighting.

"We should go up and kill it. Can you imagine the looks on everyone's faces when we walk into the village carrying that thing? We'll be heroes!"

But the companions on the hill relaxed as the other villager proved more realistic and less excitable.

"Kill it?" he demanded. "With what? We don't have spears, just these hammers. Have you ever seen an angry stag? That thing would make short work of us you idiot. Come on, let's get home before the beast charges down here. Our story will be enough to win us a few drinks this night, I'm thinking."

It seemed the suggestion to hunt the stag had been little more than bravado and the excited voices slowly receded into the distance until Bel and Duro knew they were gone.

"Ha, that was perfect." Bellicus laughed and ruffled Cai's ears, the dog gazing at him with what looked like a smile of his own.

"Couldn't really have gone any better," Duro agreed and stood up, stretching his tired legs. "A few more nights like this and the king will soon hear about it. Then, hopefully, he'll come out hunting."

They headed back to camp, which was an hour or so to the southwest, happy at the success of their night's work, and already planning how to improve on things for the next time the white stag appeared to Dalriadans.

Over the next week they were careful to only ever show the stag's head to single, or paired, travellers. Then, sometimes, Duro would go into the villages and speak to the locals, always playing that fact up. The last thing they wanted was a large force of soldiers riding around the land hunting them.

Each time Bellicus donned the glowing headdress in the dark he was viewed with awe by the Dalriadans they'd chosen to be the witnesses on that occasion and, from Duro's chats with the people he knew the legend of the white stag was growing with every telling. Guided by his own comments, often suggested by the druid, a narrative soon formed around the beast.

It was said the stag was huge, bigger than any such animal ever seen before, with muscular limbs and a sleek, glossy coat which glowed white in the dark. Sometimes it was claimed the beast had glowing red eyes, occasionally it roared so loud that one witness was deaf for three days after hearing it. And, always, it only showed itself to one or two people at a time.

Finally, when the seed had been planted and the tales were growing, Duro mentioned the fact that a druid told him the stag could only be killed by a king.

Then, fearing their luck would run out sooner or later, they stopped showing the stag's head to the villagers and waited for the rumours to do their work.

* * *

The chief of the Dalriadan settlement of Balmeanoc was a man called Lóegaire, and he had travelled to Dunadd that day, hoping to be the first to tell his king about the magnificent white stag stalking the countryside.

Balmeanoc was only a small village with less than sixty inhabitants, but Lóegaire was a proud man, a veteran warrior originally from Clonmacnois in Hibernia, and King Loarn mac Eirc valued him, and the cattle his settlement reared, greatly.

The king already knew about the stag of course, for travellers had been bringing news of it for days, but Loarn was greatly intrigued by the sightings and eagerly listened to what people had to say, hoping to learn something new every time. He stood on the summit of Dunadd, watching Lóegaire ascending the hill, a walk which was never too easy, especially on a winter's day like this with frost making the ground slippery.

The land here was harsh, but it had a stark beauty that touched Loarn's soul and, although his line came from another country across the western sea, he felt a deep connection with this place. Dunadd belonged to him now, and one day—with the help of the Saxons, hopefully—so would the even mightier fortress of Dun Breatann.

The gate guards had seen Lóegaire approaching and opened the massive doors to let him pass inside the hillfort, one of their number running ahead to announce the chief's arrival and the purpose of his visit. He was accompanied that day by his two sons who wandered away, presumably to buy provisions from the market at the foot of the hill while their father headed up to meet with the king.

Loarn waited, breath steaming in the cold air, until Lóegaire reached the summit.

"Well met, old friend," the king smiled, stepping forward and clasping forearms with the breathless chief of Balmeanoc. "I would offer you some warmed ale, but I think your walk has heated you enough, eh?"

"Aye," the chief admitted ruefully, wiping sweat from his forehead. "I remember I could run up here in the space of a few heartbeats."

"You and me both, my friend. It gets harder every day." Loarn waited until the chief got his wind back and then moved towards the doors of the great hall. "Come, I have bread and meat inside. You can rest—eat and drink your fill—before telling me your news."

Lóegaire began to follow, then noticed a grim, hollow-faced man slouched against the wall of the building.

"What's his problem?"

"He's fasting," the king muttered, throwing the man a dark look which was returned venomously.

"Fasting? You mean against you?"

"Aye." Loarn replied irritably. "He's a farmer from a little village to the north. Some of his sheep were stolen by raiders and he's come here to protest. Says I should have protected him against the thieves."

"Ah." Lóegaire knew this custom which had come across with the settlers from the old country. The farmer was too insignificant, too far beneath the king, to have any legal recourse against him in court. But the law did allow the farmer to fast which, it was said, would sully the king's reputation and leave him vulnerable to magical attacks.

Apparently Loarn cared little for such superstitions.

"Why don't you just give him a few sheep and send him on his way then?" Lóegaire asked, eyeing the filthy, gaunt farmer who looked like he'd been camping outside the great hall for weeks, making a nuisance of himself.

"That would set a dangerous precedent. Folk would expect me to pay them off any time something went wrong," the king said. "It's not my fault his animals were taken – I can't be everywhere. Sometimes raiders manage to steal a few sheep. That's the way of things and there's not much I can do about it. The mad old bastard can lie out here until he rots - he'll get nothing from me."

He shrugged and pushed open the hall door, bored with the farmer's plight, and Lóegaire followed him inside. They were immediately assailed by the gloom and its accompanying sounds and smells.

Meat was roasting and a smoky, pungent haze permeated the atmosphere while the heat, after the crisp morning air outside, was welcomed by Loarn and his guest. A number of men were already in the hall – warriors, spending winter with their king and wishing for the swift return of spring that they might return to their adventures battling Picts, Britons and even fellow Scots from back over the sea in Hibernia.

"Here," the king nodded, thrusting a mug of ale into Lóegaire's hand and beckoning for the man seated next to him to move so the newcomer could take his ease. "Eat. Drink. Then tell me what brings you here to Dunadd, other than the market."

The chief took a long drink and sighed happily. This was good ale, much better than the stuff brewed in his village and he savoured the woody taste before replying.

"The market, aye. My boys are down there now getting supplies. But I wanted to tell you about the white stag some of my kinfolk have seen recently."

"Ah, the stag," Loarn said, tilting his head backwards thoughtfully as the other men in the hall, sensing a tale in the offing, fell silent.

"You've heard about it already, I believe," Lóegaire said. "Your guards told me a few people had visited with similar tales in recent days."

"That's right," the king agreed. "Of course, we've known for years that a white stag occasionally visited these lands. It's been seen a handful of times before this. I was lucky enough to see it myself once." He sat in silence for a few heartbeats, lost in the memory of the day when he'd crossed paths with the giant stag. "A magnificent beast, for sure," he said at last. "And, judging by the recent tales, it's even more impressive now. 'The biggest stag anyone's ever seen'. 'It glows white in the moonlight'. 'It has fiery red eyes'. 'It only shows itself to lone travellers.' Like I say," Loarn smiled, "I've seen a white stag myself, but it was just a normal beast. Whatever people are seeing now is apparently some kind of magical thing. An angel come down to walk amongst us in stag form perhaps." He made the sign of the cross for he, like many of the Dalriadans, had converted to the new Christian religion while still following the old ways in some things.

Lóegaire, along with the gathered, listening warriors, mimicked his king's gesture and sipped his ale. "Could be," he admitted. "Three people from my village have seen the beast, on two separate occasions. All the witnesses swear the stag did, indeed, glow with some unearthly, ethereal light. One of them said it made a great bellowing noise, like a cow which," he raised an eyebrow at one soldier's chuckle, "sounds amusing unless you've ever heard a stag roaring yourself." He looked back to the king who nodded emphatic agreement.

"Nothing funny about it," Loarn mac Eirc said. "And I expect that sound, in the dark, might make a lone traveller shit his breeches in fright."

"Indeed, lord king," Lóegaire smiled. "And that's not the only weird sound folk have reported. Some of the people in my village swear they can hear a flute playing during the night, out in the darkness, far off." He shivered and so did many of the gathered warriors.

"Ghostly music?" someone muttered fearfully. "That doesn't bode well."

The king frowned, sharing his men's uneasiness at this new information. "Well," he said, "apart from the nocturnal music, your tale is much the same as the others we've heard so far. Whatever this animal is, whoever hunts it down will win great renown."

The listening warriors, expecting this was now the end of the chief's story turned away to continue their earlier conversations and games of dice, but Lóegaire regained their attention when he spoke once more.

"That's another thing you might not have heard yet, though, my lord." He waited until there was silence again before continuing. "Apparently the stag – which is essentially a king amongst its own kind – can only be killed by another monarch." He gazed at Loarn mac Eirc who narrowed his eyes for this was indeed a new element to the story. "That means, of all the men in Dalriada, only you, my lord, can hunt down this beast."

There were rumbles from the audience at this proclamation. Some of them thought it an interesting addition to the legend, while others were angry because they had looked forward to claiming the white stag's head for their own.

"Who says?" Loarn mac Eirc demanded, turning away from the chief dismissively.

"A druid."

That brought Loarn's head back around immediately, and it also brought another man out of the shadows behind them: Dotha, Bishop of Dunadd.

"What's this?" demanded the clergyman.

"A traveller told us so, two days ago," Lóegaire confirmed, shrinking back slightly beneath Dotha's piercing stare. "Said he'd met a druid on the road, and they'd shared meat together. The druid, on hearing about the white stag, told the traveller only the king would be able to hunt it successfully. Everyone else would be wasting their time for a normal man's weapons would be ineffective against it."

"Interesting," Loarn mac Eirc said, pursing his lips, but Bishop Dotha wasn't finished with the chief of Balmeanoc.

"Who was this traveller? What did he look like?"

Lóegaire shrugged. "Quite tall, middle-aged, muscular. Like a warrior I suppose. He was warned not to go wandering about the place on his own, but he seemed confident enough so, either he was stupid, or well-skilled with the sword he carried."

"Where did he come from?" Dotha demanded. "And where was he going?"

Again, Lóegaire raised his shoulders in a shrug, irritated now by the bishop's fierce gaze and harsh tone. "He came from somewhere down south. One of the old Roman towns. Said his wife had been killed and he didn't have much to live for anymore, so he'd decided to just start walking and see where his feet took him."

Dotha looked at the chief as if he was an imbecile. "And you believed him? Come on, man, does that sound realistic?"

Lóegaire bridled and half-stood up, but Loarn held his arm, bidding him to remain seated.

"I never thought to question whether he spoke the truth or not, bishop," the chief spat. "It didn't seem important. He was just a single man, a lone traveller, and, when he spoke about his wife's death anyone could tell he was being honest. It was written all over his face. What's so damn important about him anyway?"

"What did he say about the druid?"

"Only that he met him on the road, and they shared a meal together before parting and going their separate ways. Why?"

"There are no Dalriadan druids in these parts," Dotha retorted. "Or I'd have been informed of their presence and we'd have run them off. So, if there's genuinely one of the old religion's representatives travelling in our lands, he must be either a Pict or a Briton, and that means he's most likely a spy!" Dotha waved a hand and glanced at the king. "You've heard the rumours about Coroticus arguing with the giant, Bellicus, in Dun Breatann. I think this is more than a little worrying." He shook his head thoughtfully. "We will talk of this later, Loarn, I have to pray just now. I suggest you send out riders to find this druid, and bring him here." With that, he lost himself once more in the shadows to the rear of the hall.

The king rolled his eyes and some of the warriors sniggered for the bishop was not popular in Dunadd, always telling the folk how to behave and upbraiding them for indulging their vices too much. That sort of talk was never greatly appreciated by fighting men, especially ones like those cooped up here in the hillfort for the entire winter, with little else to do *but* drink and fight and harass the women.

"He's got a point about the druid, though," Loarn said. "Why would such a person be in my lands? It might be completely innocent – perhaps he's gathering herbs, or some other magical items only found around here. And, if he knows we're Christians, as he must do, it would seem sensible to not come here in case we treat him badly. Which we would." He gazed into his ale mug and Lóegaire promised to arrest the traveller from the Roman town if he should come to Balmeanoc again.

Dotha could question the man himself then, instead of moaning at the chief.

The doors opened, framing two tall young men in the pale sunlight. "Come ahead, lads," the king grinned, recognising Lóegaire's sons. They had taken part in the recent siege of Dun Breatann and fought bravely when Coroticus had ambushed their warband on the road home. "Pull up a stool and help yourself to ale," Loarn commanded. "There's beef and bread on the trenchers there as well."

Lóegaire and his sons spent a pleasant afternoon in the great hall then, before remembering they should make the trip back to Balmeanoc while the light held. They got up, unsteadily, for they were considerably drunk by that point, and said farewell to their host.

"What will you do, my lord?" Lóegaire asked. "About the stag I mean? Will you hunt it?"

The king nodded and clapped the chief on the arm, laughing. "Of course! Look," he pointed to a spot on the wall near the fire. "I can imagine that white, antlered head mounted just there, between the weapons. It would look mightily impressive, wouldn't it?"

He wished the three men a safe journey and, as they opened the doors, shouted, "Give that old farmer out there a kick on your way past! With any luck it'll snow in the night and the bastard will freeze so I don't have to worry about him anymore."

"It's already started my lord," Lóegaire replied, showing the flakes gently settling on the mud at his feet and, as the door closed behind him, Loarn and his warriors cheered and refilled their ale mugs as a servant placed another log on the fire.

CHAPTER TWENTY-ONE

Bellicus and Duro agreed that it would be safer if the druid stopped leaving their camp during the day. It was more than likely that word of a druid's presence in the area would have reached the king since they'd started that very rumour themselves. They knew it was probable that Bellicus wouldn't be welcomed with open arms by the Dalriadan king or his advisors, and Loarn mac Eirc might even ask the locals to capture or kill Bellicus if he should be seen.

They needed to keep abreast of the latest rumours circulating amongst the Dalriadans though, so it was decided Duro would visit Mochan and find out what news, if any, he might be able to impart regarding the white stag and the king's possible interest in it. The centurion would take Cai with him, just as an extra layer of protection. If word had been spread about that travellers should be held for questioning, the villagers would be less likely to try and take Duro by force with the giant wardog by his side.

"You take care of him," Bellicus commanded the centurion. "He's been my loyal companion for years, and he smells better than you. So, if it comes to a fight, I'd rather he came back to me than you."

Duro knew the druid was joking, or at least he hoped so, but he nodded in agreement nonetheless. "I'll be cautious, don't worry about that. I won't put the hound in any unnecessary danger."

Off he went then, canine shadow by his side, to visit Mochan in the nearby settlement. Bellicus settled down to wait, spending the time alone praying and sharpening his weapons, knowing, or at least hoping, he would need them soon, should their carefully-planned scheme bear fruit.

Winter was drawing to a close, as evidenced by the buttercups sprouting on the outskirts of the marshes, and the druid wanted to complete his mission as soon as possible so they might return to Dun Breatann and face Drest and his returning army.

Duro's return a few hours later gave Bellicus hope.

"I saw men – warriors – leaving the village just as I was approaching," the centurion recounted as he settled himself by the fire with a drink and some well-earned meat and cheese. "I hid in the bushes until they were gone, then went straight to old Mochan's place."

Bellicus pulled a gristly piece of roast beef from a skewer over the fire and blew on it before tossing it to Cai who swallowed it without even chewing. "What did the soldiers want?"

"Two things," Duro said, and the druid could tell from the twinkle in his eyes that he'd heard good news in the village that day. "One: the white stag is the property of the king, since it's on his lands, so only he can hunt it. Sightings should be reported and passed to Dunadd. Anyone caught trying to bring down the beast will be punished."

"That's good," Bellicus smiled, tossing another chunk of meat to the salivating dog. "Whatever Loarn mac Eirc believes about the rumours, this edict will stop people trying to kill me any time I wear the head-dress."

Duro nodded. "Aye, that's true. But," he grinned and carried on. "Two: a foreign druid has been reported within Dalriadan lands and should be taken into custody if sighted. A reward will be paid for his capture."

Bellicus popped a piece of beef into his own mouth this time, much to Cai's disappointment. "That's not a huge surprise. We knew Loarn would be suspicious when he heard a possible spy was near Dunadd. I think the white stag should begin appearing again."

The pair knew the lands around them quite well by now, thanks to their travels, and they'd already chosen a suitable place to lay the final trap: a wooded area not far from Dunadd itself. Although most trees at this time of year were dormant and leafless, there was enough evergreen foliage in the spot they'd chosen – holly, ivy, yew and juniper – to provide cover, especially in the dark.

So, that night Bellicus appeared, glowing stag's head atop his shoulders, to a single, astonished traveller passing by the woods.

He did the same two nights later. And again the night after that.

It was the first time the white stag had appeared in the same place more than once and that, the druid hoped, would draw Loarn mac Eirc straight to them, seeking glory and fame and a trophy for his wall.

Their time in Dalriada was coming to an end, one way or another. Either the king would come to them and there would be a fight, or he would not take the bait and they would go home empty handed.

Bellicus wasn't at all sure how King Coroticus would take such a failure.

* * *

They watched the road to Dunadd that night, praying to the gods that King Loarn would ride out to hunt the now-legendary white stag. For the first few hours only hedgehogs and owls kept them company, the former silent, the latter invisible in the darkness as they made their eerie cries.

Now, at last, it looked like their prayers had been answered.

On the road below, two riders, accompanied by a pair of dogs, were visible in the wan moonlight, long spears held ready as they cantered towards Bellicus and his friend's hiding place. At that distance, and in the gloom, it was impossible to tell who the riders were – kings didn't usually go about the place wearing a golden crown after all. But the presence of the dogs, smaller beasts bred for tracking rather than fighting, and the spears, told the druid that these Dalriadans had come to hunt something.

"There it is!"

Bellicus heard the cry, just, through the material of the antlered headdress, and he knew he'd been spotted. Quickly, he lowered himself down behind the juniper bush and hurried away, through the trees a short distance to where Duro and Cai waited for him.

"They saw you?"

Bellicus nodded and shoved the stag's head into its sack. The luminescence had faded over time but it still gave off a faint glow and the last thing he wanted was for their pursuers to notice it bobbing about in his hands, destroying the illusion. He lifted his staff of office from the ground where he'd left it and strapped it onto his back – it was Melltgwyn, he would need for what was to come next.

"Get ready," he said, drawing the sword from its sheath. "They'll be along soon. The dogs will head straight for us. Cai – stay." The great mastiff lay down amongst the leaves while Bellicus led Duro a few strides east to a clearing. He crouched behind a massive oak tree, while the centurion went to hide by a bush a few feet away from him.

Earlier in the day Bellicus had managed to catch a dove in a trap and, before butchering it, the druid offered its lifeblood in the centre of this clearing, as a sacrifice to Cernunnos, that the forest lord might bring them success in their night's endeavours. The edible parts were then quickly cut away, salted, wrapped in leaves and placed in the druid's pack, while the rest of the remains were left on the ground with the drying blood.

"Two against two," Duro murmured as they crouched in the trees awaiting their victims. "And we have the element of surprise."

Bellicus nodded wordlessly. The odds were good, and the hunting dogs would be no threat – Cai would see them off without any problems, that was a certainty.

They waited, senses straining, for what seemed like hours before, at last, soft footsteps could be heard converging on their position. The hunters were almost silent, but it was impossible not to step on a twig or catch a foot on hidden undergrowth and Bellicus was easily able to gauge their approach.

From what little he had been able to see of the Dalriadan riders on the road both men were large and well-armed. It was possible a fight could go badly if the plan didn't work as well as Bellicus hoped, but he trusted the gods. They had led him this far after all, and now the end of what once seemed an impossible mission was in sight.

The dense woods had forced the hunters to dismount and they came in sight at last, dark shapes that moved slowly, stealthily, heads turning from side to side as they tried to catch sight of the elusive white stag. The foliage hid their dogs from view, but Bellicus could hear their questing noses, sniffing the air and the leaf-strewn floor.

The beasts had brought their masters directly towards the ambush, but now they sensed the danger lurking nearby, possibly from the scent of Cai who lay ahead of them, silent and unmoving, in the shadows at the edge of the clearing. They pulled up, despite the blood and remains of the sacrificed dove just a few paces ahead of them.

"What is it, lad?" There was a hint of uncertainty, of anxiety, in the Dalriadan's voice as he bent down to reassure his skittish dog. When he straightened again the moonlight reflected off his bald pate and revealed his face clearly. Bellicus had seen this man before, when he was training to become a druid in Iova.

Loarn mac Eirc had sometimes visited the little island back then, as it wasn't far from the Dalriadan King's homeland, and widely renowned as a great centre of learning and healing. Although the hair was now gone, or turned to grey, Loarn's light blue eyes and pinched features were unmistakeable in the gloom, as was his strange accent as he spoke again in clipped tones, this time to his human companion.

"The dogs can sense something. Something they fear. Might be a bear or a wolf. We should be on our guard, Faelan."

"Always," came the reply, and the second Dalriadan's voice was strong and confident.

They began to move again, although it seemed like the king had to drag on his dog's leash to get it to move forward.

The king was so close to Bellicus it would have been a simple matter to thrust his sword into the man's back. That was what he should have done, but he was loath to send a warrior to the afterlife in such a cowardly, dishonourable way and besides, Coroticus and Narina both wanted the whoreson to know why he was dying – to regret the loathsome words he'd spoken about Princess Catia.

"King Loarn."

The Dalriadans' spun around, and their hunting dogs yelped in fear, straining at their leashes, although neither hound seemed to know whether to run towards this new person or away in the other direction.

"Who the hell are you?" demanded the king, gazing up at the hooded apparition that had appeared from nowhere to stand here, in the moonlit woods, like something from a fireside tale.

"I am Bellicus, Druid of Alt Clota. I believe my king, Coroticus, vowed to cut out your tongue and shove your balls in your mouth? Well, he couldn't make it, so I'm here to do it for him. May Dis Pater take you, Loarn mac Eirc!"

CHAPTER TWENTY-TWO

"Get him!"

King Loarn's bodyguard, Faelan, was an experienced warrior – no superstitious fool to cower before the giant druid – and he reacted instantly to his king's command. He let go of his dog's leash, exhorting it to attack, and grasped his spear with both hands. The dog ran towards Bellicus, snarling, and Loarn set his animal loose too.

The hounds weren't the only problem though.

"Shit. Stop him, Duro!" the druid shouted, swinging his sword in an arc to hold off the Dalriadan dogs which, thankfully, hadn't been trained to bring down such large prey and were too frightened to really try anyway.

Loarn mac Eirc raised a horn to his lips and, before the centurion – unnoticed in the gloom by the Dalriadans until now – could do anything, a loud, brash tone filled the night air.

Bellicus stepped forward, but the terrified hunting dogs bared their teeth at him and, although they would be unlikely to injure him too badly, the last thing he wanted was to try and escape these lands while leaving an easily followed trail of fresh blood.

"Cai! Here!"

Loarn mac Eirc turned at the sound of the massive wardog bursting out from the undergrowth behind him, but before he knew what was happening, Cai had torn into the Dalriadan dogs like a battering ram, sending them flying, yelping in fright.

Bellicus attempted to strike down the king but Faelan, sidestepping an attack from Duro, lunged at the druid, thrusting his spear forward and forcing Bel to parry it away desperately. Loarn blew another blast on his horn and the druid knew their chance to kill the king was slipping rapidly away. How had it all gone so wrong?

"You bastards," Faelan cried in anguish, as Cai silenced one of the hunting dogs for good and sent the other haring off into the night, tail between its legs. "That hound served me well over the years."

He attacked again, moving with lightning speed despite his powerful build, and Bellicus was lucky to escape injury again.

Over the years he had trained himself to go into a trance during battles, but that was out of the question here, in the dark, with so much going on around him.

"We need to end this, quickly," Duro shouted. "Before more of his soldiers turn up."

"Why would we need more soldiers?" Loarn laughed, glorying in the joy of his enemy's failed ambush. "Faelan is the greatest swordsman in my retinue—"

"He's not wielding a sword," Bellicus broke in, parrying another lunge from the bodyguard's spear and stepping forward to grab the weapon's shaft beneath his arm. Then, using all his considerable strength, he twisted his body around. The speed, and power, of his unexpected movement caught Faelan by surprise and the spear was wrenched from his hands and he was thrown to the ground.

Before the Dalriadan could get up, Cai's crimson maw clamped down on his forearm. Faelan was wearing leather bracers which took some of the force out of the bite, stopping the teeth from fully penetrating his skin, but the dog's jaws were so powerful that Faelan roared in pain.

His cry broke off as Bellicus's sword tore through his breastplate and out through his back in a spray of blood.

"Leave him, Cai!" the druid commanded, turning to see how the centurion fared.

Duro had engaged the Dalriadan king, but he was finding it impossible to get inside the spear's reach for the moon was now hidden by clouds, making it almost impossible to see anything. Both combatants were warily dodging backwards and forwards, side to side, feinting, beginning an attack, only to draw back again for fear they would be caught off guard.

Bellicus moved forward to help his friend but the sound of drumming hooves could be heard, or, more accurately perhaps, felt, heading in their direction.

"Dotha warned me this might be some trap," Loarn mac Eirc growled, answering the question in the druid's mind. "You might remember him. He was once a druid himself, although he's converted and now follows the One True God."

"He was no druid," Bellicus spat, desperately trying to avoid the deadly spear-point that suddenly came at him in the near-impenetrable gloom. "He never completed his training – it was too difficult for him. He's a weak fool, and always has been."

"What's more important to you, boy?" Loarn grinned, batting aside Duro's sword before turning back to Bel. "Killing me, or escaping these lands alive? You see, I wanted badly to bring down the mythical white stag so I followed the advice of the stories we were hearing, and came hunting with only one companion, but—" He jumped backwards, out of the swords' range, and then swung his spear in an arc, the shaft catching Duro on the side of the head. As the centurion stumbled back and fell onto his knees, Loarn went on.

"I commanded ten of my warband to follow us at a distance and listen for my hunting horn. Dotha's idea. He was suspicious when we heard a druid was abroad in our lands. He's a cantankerous old sot, but very clever at times, despite what you might think."

Bellicus eyed the Dalriadan king bitterly. He was loath to order Cai to attack, for fear the faithful dog would be caught like Duro, by the spear which Loarn wielded surprisingly well. Yet the longer they tarried here, trying to get inside the king's defences, the closer his warriors came. Aye, the reinforcements would have to leave their horses and come through the night-shrouded woods on foot, but it wouldn't be long before they arrived, and then…

"You know Dun Breatann will soon be mine?" Loarn spoke again, plainly buying time for his soldiers to arrive. "Drest and Cunneda will march soon enough, but I've also been in contact with the Saxon warlord, Hengist. Coroticus will be nothing more than a memory come the spring, and your lands will all belong to me."

Bellicus was stunned by the Dalriadan's news. The Saxons were coming to help Loarn invade Alt Clota? He shook his head – he had more pressing matters to deal with right now. "Are you all right, Duro?"

"Aye, I'm fine," the centurion grunted. Thankfully he was on his feet again, but a large bruise was forming on his face, to go with the angry expression at their inability to kill the king they'd come all this way to find.

Bellicus nodded in relief and, as the moon broke through the rolling clouds, launched another attack, and this time he did manage to get inside the spear's reach, raking the edge of his blade down Loarn's hand, leaving a line of crimson and drawing a curse from the injured king before they broke apart again.

"Let's go, Duro."

"Go?"

"Aye," Bellicus said, backing away from Loarn who grinned, not bothering to come after the giant druid. Why should he, when his warband could hunt these interlopers down at their leisure? "Come on, Centurion. We can't take on all those approaching warriors, it would be suicide."

"But…we're so close to completing our mission…!"

"We are," Bellicus agreed unhappily. "But the gods have chosen to thwart us tonight, and it's time to retreat while we still can. Come on, we should put as much distance between ourselves and his men as we can. Cai! To me."

"That's right," the king laughed. "Make your escape now, my lads. Quick, run! I'm sure I'll see you again soon enough." His voice faded away as Bellicus and Duro began to run, but righteous fury filled every word that came behind them.

"You'll never leave my lands alive, druid. I swear it by Christ!"

* * *

"That didn't go very well," said Duro, glancing back towards the hill they'd left behind at last.

"It went terribly," Bellicus replied, a mixture of emotions plain in his voice: exhaustion, excitement, fear, but, most of all, anger. Anger at himself for the failure of their mission. "I should have just stabbed Loarn mac Eirc in the back. It would have been so easy."

Duro nodded, wishing that was exactly what his friend had done. He knew better than to say so though. "That's not the way of a true warrior," he said. "I fear the gods would frown on anyone, even a druid, killing a king in such a cowardly manner. Besides, I might have used my hunting bow to do the same thing – we're both much too honourable."

Bellicus spat on the frost-rimed ground and glanced to his side, making sure Cai still kept pace with them. "Loarn is a Christian now," he said. "He deserves no respect from me, or you, or the gods. I should have gutted him. All our preparations…wasted."

"That's enough of the self-pity," Duro barked, using his parade-ground voice, as if he were back in the legions and disciplining some unruly young recruit. "What's done is done – we move on and try to get out of these lands before Loarn makes good on his promise to hunt us down. This whole thing was a fool's errand from the start – it's testament to your talents that we came so close to pulling it off."

Bellicus didn't reply for a long time, taking the rebuke in the manner it was intended, his long strides eating up the miles back towards their campsite near Carngheal.

"Their dogs won't be able to follow our scent thanks to the marshes," he said eventually. Like Duro, he would periodically look back over his shoulder, fearing pursuit. Thus far, there was no sign, although it was now the deepest part of the night and, for all they knew, the Dalriadan king's men had ridden past them on another path, unknown to the druid.

Neither man would fully relax until they were back in Alt Clota, and that seemed a long way off just then.

"What's our next move?" Duro asked and Bellicus, shrugged, unsure of himself for once.

"Our priority is to reach the camp, catch our breath, and tend to any wounds we have. Then…" He shrugged. "What would you suggest, my friend? Without horses I don't really know how we stay ahead of Loarn's riders, and the whole land will be aflame with news of us. We're marked men, and the marshes will only hide us for a day or two, if even that."

Duro thought about their predicament for a long time, until Bellicus started to think the centurion hadn't heard his question, but then the reply came, and it was quite unexpected.

"What's the point in going back to the camp? The dogs might not be able to track us through the marshes, but they'll lead Loarn's men to the general area. And then it'll just be a matter of time before they close in on us." He looked at Bellicus and, although he was obviously fatigued, and possibly still groggy from the blow to the head, a fire lit his eyes – a determination that had seen him rise so high within the Roman ranks as a young man. "I say we must get out of Dalriadan lands as soon as possible. We must find horses and keep moving all through the night. Our injuries are minor anyway – they'll keep until we're on safer ground."

The very idea of travelling when they'd already spent so much energy over the past few hours wasn't a pleasing one for Bellicus, whose first thought was to reject the plan. Most of their provisions were back at the camp, along with their tent, their extra clothes, even Duro's flute. Thinking about it seriously though, he could see the merits in Duro's suggestion.

Returning to the marshes would only buy time until the final battle, and the druid knew they could not win against the warband, and entire population, of Dalriada.

A flute could be replaced.

"Surely some of the people in these lands – most perhaps – are still loyal to the old gods," Duro mused. "Isn't that how it usually goes? The king converts to a new religion and everyone else follows suit, but it takes time for it to reach those at the bottom of the social scale." He rubbed at his side, as if a stitch was developing. His pace didn't slacken though, as he continued. "Mochan and some of the others referred to Taranis or the Dagda, not Christ."

"You think they might help us, on account of me being a druid?"

"Aye," Duro said. "I've seen you in action. You can tell them the gods will punish them if they don't help us, and I know they'll believe it."

Bellicus thought about it but shook his head. "I suspect the threat of their own king's retribution will outweigh any fear of the gods for the likes of Mochan. Besides, you know what Loarn mac Eirc would do to anyone helping us."

Duro frowned. Did he value his own life over that of the kindly old craftsman in Carngheal? Loarn would certainly kill anyone helping the fugitives escape his wrath. At best he might spare Mochan, but the sentence for his crimes would likely be banishment – cast out from his kith and kin, to wander alone for the rest of his days. It was as good as a death sentence for a man of that age anyway.

"What, then?" the centurion demanded. "It's not even as if we could rig up traps and fortifications at the camp. Even if we could, there's only two—" He paused and smiled at Cai. "Three of us.

We can't fight this time, Bel. We have to run. Or sail. Or ride, or whatever!"

The druid stopped jogging and Duro pulled up as well, eyeing his friend inquisitively.

"You're right," Bellicus conceded, looking around at the land, trying to get his bearings. "We've had a head start because Loarn's men had no idea where we came from, or where we were heading. But it's time we changed course. If my knowledge of the area is accurate, I believe there's a settlement not too far to the south." He shrugged and met Duro's eyes. "We'll head there and hope there's a couple of horses we can steal without getting into another fight."

The centurion smiled. "Oh, I 'm not too bothered about that. I wouldn't mind a fight – didn't get to do much in the last one, and I'm still pretty angry."

The druid laughed at that, and they began running again, this time towards the village in the south, rather than to their camp near Carngheal.

"Be careful what you wish for," Bellicus said. "I have a feeling we'll see more than our fair share of battle soon enough."

They covered the miles in silence after that, conserving their breath and wishing the settlement Bellicus had spoken of would soon appear. They were close to dropping now, particularly Duro who, although much fitter than he'd been at any time in the past ten years, was not as young as the druid, and their night's exertions had taken a lot out of him.

Bellicus prayed silently to Cernunnos to let them find horses soon. If Loarn mac Eirc's men were to catch up with them there wouldn't be much of a fight, despite Duro's earlier suggestion.

He watched Cai as they ran, relieved to see the huge dog still moving freely. He felt guilty at the thought of riding throughout the night to escape their pursuers, while Cai would have to remain on his own four paws.

What would they do if the dog's stamina gave out? It wasn't even a question: Bellicus would never leave Cai behind, even if Loarn's spearmen were almost upon them. The dog had been a loyal companion to him for years and, besides, Bellicus valued Cai's life over most humans.

He turned away and noticed Duro also looking at the dog. He too was questioning Cai's ability to keep going until they'd left their pursuers safely behind.

All they could do for now was find mounts and try to steal them without the alarm being raised.

The fragility of their existence struck the druid at that moment. All it would take was for one of them to turn their ankle in a pothole and that would be it for all of them. Yet they couldn't afford to slow their pace, despite the blackness of the night and the uneven terrain, for that would certainly mean capture and death.

"Praise be to Mithras," Duro huffed in relief, as the whitewashed silhouettes of low buildings finally appeared in the gloom. They had reached the settlement.

They slowed their pace to a walk, fearing the sound of their footsteps would be heard by any guards or light sleepers within the Dalriadan roundhouses.

"You were here the other day," Bellicus said very softly. "Do you remember? Did you take note of any of the buildings?"

Duro looked at the black shapes in the darkness, trying to think back. In truth, he hadn't even recognised the place yet. It was just a jumble of shadows to him thus far, and he peered around, trying to find a landmark that might jog his memory.

"Four days ago," Bellicus murmured. "You said there was a very pretty red-haired serving girl in the alehouse."

"Ah!" A light flickered then within Duro's memory and he nodded. The girl had indeed been beautiful, much more so than any of the settlement's other inhabitants, although she was young enough to be his daughter, if he'd ever had one… "Aye, I remember now." He turned his thoughts to the main street he'd walked down, nodding a greeting to the inhabitants who had, mostly, returned it pleasantly enough.

There was a smithy on the right, a dilapidated old hovel two middle-aged men appeared to be renovating next to it, the alehouse itself, which was barely bigger than the other buildings, and…

"There's a field behind the smithy," Duro said, a smile splitting his face. "I remember – there were three or four horses in it. Unimpressive animals, small, but they'll serve us well enough I' d say."

"Stables?"

Duro shook his head. "Not that I remember. I mean, I suppose there is one, somewhere. But I don't remember noticing it." He moved forward silently, head turning left and right, alert for danger. "Come on. We'll check the field. It's Dalriadans we're dealing with, not Roman cavalry. I doubt the horses sleep in the same building as their rider."

Bellicus watched his friend walk ahead and a bemused frown appeared on his face. Roman horsemen slept beside their mounts? That was a little fact his tutors had never imparted to him and his naturally inquisitive mind was fascinated by it. Seeing Duro disappear into the dark street ahead brought him back to himself though, and he hurried after the centurion, Cai by his side.

"Who's that?"

A muffled shout came from the house Bellicus was passing and he stopped dead in his tracks.

"Who's out there?" The voice came again, a man's voice, deep and strong and irritated, although the druid detected a hint of fear too.

"It's Connall," he replied, trying his best to imitate the Dalriadans' accent. "My dog ran off. I'm trying to catch the bastard. Go back to sleep, friend."

There was a grunt from the other side of the wall and Bellicus breathed a sigh of relief. Mimicking other peoples' ways of speech had been something his tutors *did* teach him.

Apparently not well enough, though, for the door of the roundhouse was suddenly thrown open and a red-bearded, half-naked Dalriadan glared out at him. The two men looked at one another for a moment, and then the villager's eyes grew wide as he realised the giant standing before him was a stranger.

Cai growled and the Dalriadan turned his gaze on the massive wardog, who pulled back his muzzle and bared his teeth. Blanching in fear, the man looked back to Bellicus who had silently drawn Melltgwyn, its flawless steel blade reflecting the pale moonlight. The villager raised his hands to show he was unarmed and not a threat, and backed into his house again.

"That's right," Bellicus nodded, staring at the man. "Close the door and forget you saw me. I'm just passing through."

"Who…who are you?"

The man's voice was low now, matching Bellicus's soft tones, and the earlier anger was gone, replaced by amazement and more than a hint of fear.

The druid thought for a moment, trying to come up with a name the Dalriadan would find impressive.

"Bel," he replied, giving the short form of not only his own name, but, more relevantly to this villager, of Belenus, the sun god. Known as 'the Shining One', Belenus was venerated by Dalriadans and Alt Clotans alike. Even the Romans worshipped him, in the guise of Apollo.

"Forgive me, lord," the man mumbled, eyes growing wider again, apparently not wondering why a god of light was wandering about in the shadows outside his house. "Forgive me," he repeated, and closed his door, leaving the village shrouded in silence once more.

Bellicus shook his head, amazed at how superstitious some people could be, and hurried after Duro for the moon was beginning to dip beneath the treeline and the land was even darker than it had been earlier. The frightened villager might feel foolish when the sun was up and his kinfolk told him horses had been stolen in the night, but, when word got around that he'd given his name as Bel, he knew Loarn mac Eirc, or at least Dotha, the king's pet bishop, would understand all too well what had happened.

"I've found the horses," Duro said when Bellicus caught up with him. "There might be some in the field, but it's too bloody dark to see, never mind try and catch them if they decide not to co-operate. Thankfully, there is a stable."

Bellicus frowned. "So why are you standing here, instead of readying two of them for us to ride?"

Duro nodded in the direction of the stable. "There's two guards. One asleep, the other awake."

"Ah," Bellicus said. "Well, there's nothing else for it. We need those horses if we're to escape. Come on, you know what to do."

He turned to Cai and placed a finger to his lips, which Duro found amusing, given the dog moved as silently as a wraith anyway, without needing the druid's sign-language commands, then they headed for the stable.

The centurion led the way to the door, which stood ajar, letting the dim glow of a rushlight spill out into the street. Duro pointed to the left and held his hands up against his head like a pillow, telling his companion that the resting guard was on that side of the building. Bellicus nodded and pointed to himself, then to the right – he would take on the guard who was awake. After their earlier disaster with Loarn mac Eirc, he knew Duro would not hesitate to dispatch the sleeping Dalriadan, no matter how dishonourable such a killing might be.

Bellicus crouched low and gently squeezed Cai's neck between thumb and forefinger. The dog growled, as he'd been trained to do, and Bel rose up to his full height again, pressing himself against the stable wall.

"What the hell was that?"

The sound of a man getting to his feet came from inside the building, and then silence. Bellicus could picture the scene as the guard listened, trying to figure out what the low growl had been, not wanting to appear a coward by waking his companion, but wary of looking outside in case some monster waited for him there.

Finally, hearing nothing, the guard must have gathered his courage, for soft footsteps came towards the door, and a soft muttering, as if the man was trying to convince himself he hadn't really heard anything at all.

"Must have been my guts rumbling. I'm bloody starving…"

The light was blocked as the Dalriadan's form filled the doorway, then a questing head appeared, eyeing the village for signs of wild beasts. He locked gazes with Bellicus for an instant, before the druid's hand reached out and grasped him around the throat, squeezing with impossible strength, stifling any cry. With his other hand Bellicus rammed the tip of his sword into the man's stomach, drew it out, thrust it in again.

He held the man against the wall as the light faded from his eyes and Duro slipped past, into the stable to deal with the second guard.

"Bad business, this," the centurion muttered as he wiped the blood from his spatha on the victim's cloak.

"Come on," Bellicus muttered as he dragged the man he'd killed into the stable. "Remember we're at war with these people. Get the horses ready."

"Aye," the centurion said, wiping the blade of his spatha again until the blood was all gone. "Sorry, I'm not used to murdering men like that." He hurried into the back of the stable and quickly selected a horse for himself as Bellicus followed.

"It's not exactly my idea of a glorious night's work either," the druid admitted, choosing the largest beast in the stalls and placing the crude saddle on the wall on its back. "If only we'd cut Loarn mac Eirc down when we had the chance, these men wouldn't have had to die."

Duro shook his head sadly and opened the rear, double doors, before leading his mount out into the night. "War is never glamourous, is it, my friend," he muttered. "I'll pray for those two's souls when we get a chance to rest."

"That's a long way off yet," Bellicus cautioned, bringing his stolen horse out from the stable, glad to see it didn't appear nervous or skittish. Another benefit of killing the guards quickly, he thought – the horses hadn't been frightened by the violence and now they stood calmly, ready to carry their new masters to freedom.

The men quickly mounted and looked at one another.

"Which way now, druid?"

Bellicus stared up at the sky, noting the positions of the stars, and pointed. "South. That way."

They kicked their heels in and began to move, slowly so as not to make too much noise and draw attention from the sleeping villagers. Cai came at the side of Bellicus, but the druid could tell from the set of the dog's shoulders that he was very tired. They would have to get away from the village and find somewhere to rest before the sun came up. With any luck Loarn's men would have completely lost their trail and they'd be safe enough to sleep and gather their strength again.

It had been a long night. But it wasn't over yet.

"Murderers! Murderers! Wake up, wake up you lazy bastards!"

"Ride!"

Bellicus kicked his mount into a canter and they raced away, as more shouts came from the village behind them. Perhaps the man he'd frightened had been more curious than afraid, and come to investigate what the tall stranger had been up to, finding the dead guards in the stables. Whatever had happened, the alarm was raised now, and pursuit was being organised. The men of the village would know the terrain well, unlike Bellicus and Duro who were racing into the unknown and forced to travel at a slower pace as a result. They might be heading straight for the side of a cliff for all they knew, and that meant there was a chance they might be caught.

"Are we going back to Dun Breatann the same way we came?" Duro shouted as the wind whipped past their charging forms.

"No," Bellicus cried. "Even if we could reach Arachar, Bri's boat is hardly likely to be there waiting for us now. We'll head for the docks, south, at a village called Ard Drisaig, and hope we get there before Loarn mac Eirc does."

If they could just find passage on a boat, no matter its destination – as long as it was away from Dalriada – they would have a chance of survival. Dogs couldn't track them when they were sailing, and riders carrying orders for their capture on land would be bypassed completely.

"Shit, we've stirred up a wasps' nest back there," Duro noted, turning to see riders bearing flaming torches already chasing after them. "How did they manage to mount up and come after us so quickly? Bastards were all fast asleep not long ago!"

"They're farmers, many of them," Bellicus replied. "Sunrise isn't that far off – they were probably about ready to get up and be about their business anyway."

"Farmers or no," Duro said. "We need to shake them off."

Bellicus tried to conjure a mental image of the topography of their location but, even if he could remember exactly where he was and what the terrain was like, the locals coming after them would know it better.

And then he looked at Cai and saw the dog was limping.

Glancing back over his shoulder, he counted their pursuers. Four horsemen, with others coming on foot, although those were a fair distance off.

"We can't outrun them," he shouted, slowing his pace and pulling Melltgwyn from its sheath once more. "We have to take the riders out at least. Do you have your bow ready?"

They were moving at a walk now, and Duro cursed, but pulled the short hunting bow from his back as requested. "Aye, I've got it," he growled, taking an arrow from his belt and turning his horse to face the approaching enemy.

Bellicus nodded grimly.

"Let's get this over with then."

CHAPTER TWENTY-THREE

"Cai. Stay here." Bellicus looked from the dog to Duro and forced a smile. "Follow me, centurion. When we get within range try and hit the ones on the right of their line. I'll take the left."

"This is madness," Duro grumbled but began riding after the druid nonetheless. "We're exhausted and outnumbered deep in enemy territory."

"And yet," Bellicus turned and his smile was gone, replaced by a determined glare. "We will win this fight, and escape."

"Just like we did against Loarn mac Eirc," Duro muttered, raising his bow up and using his knees to bring the horse to a halt so he could aim properly.

Bellicus waited by his side, the four enemy horsemen coming towards them at a gallop, sure of themselves, or perhaps just enraged by what had been done to their kinsmen.

"Remember, they're farmers, not warriors like us," the druid said. "Once they realise what they're up against they'll panic, and their battle-fever will die."

"So you'd think," Duro said, unconvinced. "But I've stood amongst the legions, facing men just like this. They're crazy bastards, and might not fold as quickly as you suggest."

The Dalriadans were close now, and the centurion loosed his first arrow. It went wide of its target, but he'd already drawn and let fly another. This one hit a rider in the chest – not hard enough to send him flying off his horse, but enough to slow him and, given the lack of armour on any of the Dalriadans, might even be a killing strike.

Bellicus kicked his mount into a charge and headed directly for their pursuers as another of the centurion's arrows whistled close by him, again missing its target.

"Sorry! I'm not used to shooting from the back of a horse!"

The druid waved his sword in the air in response to the shouted apology and bore down on his target, a blonde-bearded young rider holding a hay-fork. It wasn't the sleekest weapon Bellicus had ever seen, but he knew it would kill him just as quickly as any spear if it should hit him at speed.

His opponent's eyes blazed, and he angled his mount to head directly for the druid. Time seemed to slow for Bellicus as the distance between them closed and the Dalriadan drew back his arm, preparing to thrust his fork ahead. The druid kicked his horse to the right though, and switched his sword to his left hand. Confusion filled the Dalriadan's eyes and he tried to change his own weapon to the other side, to counter the druid's movement, but it was too late. Bellicus's sword had already swung round and hammered into the man's neck.

Duro had managed to loose yet another arrow, hitting one of the enemy horses in the side, but now he'd been forced to draw his sword and trade blows with a farmer wielding a long knife.

Bellicus switched Melltgwyn back to his right hand and charged at the man fighting Duro, slicing a wide gash in the man's bald head as he rode past. The Dalriadan screamed and fell to the ground as the druid turned his horse and walked it over to stand beside his friend's.

"For cart-horses," he noted, "these are surprisingly biddable."

Duro merely grunted and watched as the two remaining riders faced off against them.

They didn't have time to wait though, for each moment allowed the footmen to catch up and sheer force of numbers would see the end of the fight. Bellicus looked at Duro and they nodded in unison, then kicked their mounts ahead and attacked.

The Dalriadans were brave, but they were unskilled in battle and, no matter how crazy Duro thought them, they were no match for the druid and the centurion, both of whom were well-versed in the art of swordplay, even from horseback.

"Let's go," Bellicus cried when the last of the enemy riders had fallen. He could see that at least one of the men – the bald one – still lived, but he was no threat. The villagers running towards them were screaming in rage as they watched the slaughter of more of their kin, but they were too far away to do anything other than shout.

The druid urged his horse into a gallop in the opposite direction, back towards Cai who lay on the grass, patiently awaiting his master's return. Duro thundered along behind him and, when they reached the dog it stood up and ran by their side, still limping, but moving quickly enough.

Unless it pulled up, or one of their mounts stepped in a pothole, they would easily outrun their pursuers now.

The first part of their escape was complete, and they were all still alive. Bellicus prayed the gods would continue to look favourably on them until they could rest, for he was close to collapse.

They all were.

* * *

"We have to stop."

It was a measure of their exhaustion that Duro didn't even bother to answer his friend's pronouncement, simply reined in his stolen mount and slipped down, onto the grass.

They had been riding for close to an hour, Bellicus judged, since the fight at the village. Ideally, of course, they should have kept going, putting as much distance between themselves and the Dalriadan's chasing them as they could, but it simply wasn't possible.

If they didn't rest now, they would be unable to move when the sun came up in a few hours.

"Here. Eat this." Duro tossed some bread to the druid and they slumped onto the grass, chewing hurriedly. They had stopped by a copse of beech trees which, although leafless at this time of year, offered some concealment from searching eyes. There were some evergreen bushes and Scots pine trees with low-growing foliage that at least hid them should Loarn mac Eirc's subjects come close.

The horses' bridles were, helpfully, equipped with pegs on ropes so they could be tethered to the ground and not wander off home. At least that was one less thing to worry about.

Bellicus poured some water into his hand for Cai to drink and shared some fatty meat from his pack with the dog. "Sleep, my friend," he said softly, stroking the animal's sleek brown coat. "You've earned it."

The dog seemed only too happy to follow his master's orders and lay down on his side, eyes closing almost immediately after, muscles jerking as he experienced some dream.

"You too."

Duro shook his head. "No. You sleep while I take first watch. I'd say you've exerted yourself more than me this night."

"And I'd agree with you," Bellicus replied with a glint in his eye and a grin the centurion knew all too well now. "I did do most of the work back there, but, well, you're older than me. You need to rest more than I do."

Duro nodded and managed a smile but, again, it was a measure of how drained he was that he didn't offer a retort. He simply found a space on the grass beside Cai, placed his pack beneath his head as a makeshift pillow, and was snoring within moments.

As their exertions wore off, so did the heat that had filled their tired bodies, and Bellicus pulled his own blanket from his pack and covered the two sleeping travellers with it. It was far too risky to light a fire, so he had to hope their combined warmth would be enough to not only keep them alive, but to afford them a sleep deep enough to regenerate them.

As he sat on the grass, his head suddenly dropped and he jumped, mortified to have almost fallen asleep. There were few worse crimes a warrior could commit than slumbering while he was supposed to be watching for danger and he got to his feet, despite his body's protestations, and walked slowly, silently, away from the camp. He didn't go far, just a few paces, so he could wander and keep warm without the sound of his feet crunching in the frost-rimed leaves disturbing Duro and Cai.

What would the next day bring? he wondered. It was likely the villagers they'd stolen the horses from would give up and return home. Without dogs to help them track, and given how hard the ground was, it would be very difficult for farmers to follow them. Besides, they would be wary of another fight, given how easily Bellicus and Duro had dispatched their fellows.

So, the most probable scenario was that word would reach Loarn of their flight, and the direction it had taken, and the Dalriadan king, who did have hunting dogs in his retinue, would come after them as quickly as possible. Would the druid and his companions be able to reach the docks at Ard Drisaig before them? What if Loarn had guessed their intentions already, and sent messengers ahead to all the nearby ports, warning them not to grant passage to any strangers?

He shook his head and stared up at the cloudy sky, searching for some hint of stars or moon but seeing nothing. There was no point worrying about fate – it was inexorable, and tomorrow would bring what it would, as it always did. Whatever that might be, he would be ready, Melltgwyn in hand, to face it.

* * *

Bellicus groaned and pulled his blanket up over his head, but Duro was used to such a reaction when trying to wake someone after much too short a rest period.

"Wake up, soldier!" the centurion barked, and Bellicus found himself jerking upright, wide-eyed.

"I've still got it," Duro smiled, turning away to continue preparing his horse to travel.

"It can't be time to go already," the druid muttered, rubbing sleep from his eyes. "Feels like I only just put my head down."

"Sorry, lad," Duro said, handing him a skin of water. "That's as long as we can afford. Sun's coming up and we've been lucky no-one's found us yet."

Cursing the Dalriadans, Bellicus got to his feet, rolling his head and shoulders, stretching his great arms above his head and yawning as if he might draw in all the air in the world. The pair were soon ready to move though, and Cai too, once he'd wolfed down a chunk of salted meat and some bread. The men would eat their own meagre breakfast on horseback.

The sun came up as they rode, casting a bright light across the land but little warmth, and the breath steamed from the travellers' mouths as they made their way steadily south. Every so often one of them would glance backwards, eyeing the horizon for signs of pursuit, but, by mid-morning, they'd still seen no-one. They skirted any dwellings they came across, which were few and far between out here, but they didn't want anyone to report their movements once Loarn mac Eirc or the pursuing villagers finally reached this point.

"They will, you know," Duro said after yet another look back. "Find us I mean. They'll be on proper horses, not these farm beasts. No offence, lad." He patted his mount's neck, but it resolutely ignored him and continued to plod steadily onwards.

Bellicus nodded glumly. "At least we've had a rest and some food," he said. "And it's done Cai a power of good. He's not limping anymore – must have just been tired muscles, and he had double the sleep we did."

"Aye, we're in better shape if it comes to a battle," Duro conceded. "But still not enough to fight off a king's warband."

"What are you getting at?" the druid asked, hearing something beneath the surface of his friend's words.

Duro looked up at the sky and gestured vaguely. "Well, can't you magic up a bit of fog or a thunderstorm or something?"

"Perhaps," Bellicus said, peering at the land before them from beneath a hand shading the sunlight. "But the time it would take to prepare – to find a sacrifice, and to enter the magical trance – would give our pursuers time to catch up. If the ritual worked, it might not matter, because Loarn would be close enough to catch us anyway, fog or no."

Duro looked at him and his face was deadly serious for once. "They're going to catch us anyway, Bel. Unless something happens to divert them, or to hide our movements from them. The moment they appear on the horizon," he couldn't help turning for another look, "they'll have us. We can't win a race against experienced riders, not on these docile cart horses."

Bellicus looked down at Cai and fancied he could see the dog beginning to limp again. Perhaps it was his imagination, but it once again hammered home just how vulnerable they were out there in the Dalriadan countryside. "You think it's worth taking the chance?" he asked. "What if the magic fails? We'll have given the bastards time to catch us up, for no return."

"I do. Look around us – there's precious little variation in the topography here, and the winter's killed off most of the foliage we might have used as cover on our way. We came on this mission knowing it was unlikely to be successful, and so it's proved. But we always thought there was a chance we could pull it off because," another glance over the shoulder, "we have certain talents."

"Aye?" Bellicus smiled wryly. "What's yours?"

"I can bake a great loaf," Duro retorted. "And I don't attract attention the way you do, walking about the countryside like a giant turd."

The druid laughed. "That's true," he admitted. "You do bake a nice loaf."

"And you can, so you say, commune with the gods," Duro went on, serious again. "Which I believe to be true. Look," he reined in his mount and they stared at one another, all humour gone now as they faced up to the reality of the threat facing them. "You should do this. Seek aid from Cernunnos, or Lug, or Belenus the Sun God, or…whoever."

"What about you?" Bellicus asked.

Duro's smile returned and he dismounted. "I'll have a word with Mithras, but I've never thought he listened much to me."

"All right," the druid agreed, peering inside his robe for the pouches of ingredients he stored there. "I'll do it. But get back in your saddle – we need to find running water. I always have more success when I perform a ritual next to a burn or a river."

On they rode until they came to a stream. It was narrow and, in the summer, would be almost invisible, but now, it burbled pleasantly across the stones of its bed and Bellicus knew it would be ideal for his purpose.

"Right," he said, tethering his horse to the ground a short distance away, fearing what he was about to do would frighten the beast. "I'll get things sorted. You go and find me something to sacrifice."

Duro's face fell – clearly he'd been hoping to sit and rest while the druid conducted his business with the gods. "Sacrifice? Like what? I haven't noticed any bulls or sheep roaming about the place, Bel."

"A pigeon will do. Or a squirrel. Anything. Even a field mouse if that's what you manage to snare. Whatever it is should still be alive though. You can't just shoot something with your bow."

Duro went off, muttering to himself, but this had been his idea, and this was his part to play in it. Bellicus watched him go, confident in his friend's hunting ability, then he led his own horse to graze next to Duro's, and bade Cai stand guard beside them.

Moving back to the stream he sat down cross-legged on his pack and slowed his breathing, calming his whirling thoughts, gazing out at the land they'd just travelled from as he waited for Duro's return.

It was quite a long time before the centurion reappeared, but when he did he was smiling, and carried something within his blanket, the thick wool no doubt protecting Duro from the captured animal's teeth and claws.

Bellicus could tell it was no field mouse his friend had snared, and, pleased, he pulled out the mugwort leaves from his pockets and began to chew slowly. The bitter taste flooded his mouth and he rinsed it away, a little, with a drink from his ale-skin.

"What have you brought me?"

Duro arched an eyebrow at the druid's speech, which was already slower than normal, but he held out the struggling bundle almost reverently.

"Pigeon."

Bellicus took this in, and then frowned at the blanket. "Why have you wrapped it up like that? I thought you'd snared a wildcat or something. Were you afraid the bird might peck you to death?"

Duro reddened, as much from the mocking accusation as his own lack of knowledge of the druid's magic. "I didn't know if it was supposed to see…this…" He gestured towards the ground, but his voice trailed off. "I thought you'd be building an altar or something."

"No time. No need," the druid replied dreamily. He held out his hands for the bundle and took it carefully, pulling down the material to reveal the grey head of a wood pigeon. It blinked at him. He unwrapped it from the blanket which he handed to Duro. "Go."

Duro dutifully wandered off to check on the dog and the horses.

Bellicus held the bird, and they stared at one another, the only sounds the wind bending the branches of the nearby trees and the stream flowing towards what he hoped was the nearby loch and the port that would provide them with passage back to Dun Breatann.

With his free hand he took out his sword and used the tip of the blade to mark a circle around himself, to hold in any magical power and keep out any malevolent forces. He sheathed the sword then lifted the ale-skin and took another long pull, stoppered it, and put it on the ground before reaching inside his robe again. This time he didn't bring forth a herb, or leaf, or other magical ingredient – now he drew out a short, stone-bladed dagger and sat down once more.

The pigeon watched him, but even the druid couldn't tell what it might be thinking, the expressionless, blank face unreadable. The dagger did its job quickly and efficiently, and the bird did not suffer, Bellicus made sure of that. He held it tightly as, even though its head was detached, the body and wings thrashed within his grasp for a time until, at last, it stilled.

The blood drained down, onto the hard grass, the crimson contrasting starkly with the white frost as it seeped in. The druid looked on, practically feeling the earth absorbing the bird's lifeforce and drawing its power up, into himself, through his legs, into his torso and up, until it filled his whole body and being. Then he closed his eyes.

For what seemed like an eternity he sat there motionless, thoughts temporarily stilled, before a spark, like a glowing ember thrown out by a campfire, seemed to grow in the darkness of his mind's eye. Slowly, the light took on the familiar shape of a man – a tall, lean warrior of indeterminate age, wearing a golden torc with snarling dragons at either end.

"Peredur," he murmured in greeting, and the warrior in the otherworld smiled.

"You again?"

"Aye," Bellicus agreed and, although he was already sitting on the grass of Dalriada, in his mind he lowered himself down and sat on a seat he couldn't see. All he could see was Peredur, a man, or a being at least, who often 'spoke' to the druid when he entered a trance like this.

"Made an arse of killing Loarn mac Eirc, didn't you?"

Bellicus smiled and nodded. "I did. Came so close too."

"Maybe you came closer than you think," the lean warrior replied, sitting down himself on some other unseen chair or stool. "What can I do for you today, Bel?"

"We need the weather to change, my friend," Bellicus said, looking up at the sky, but here, in this place, only Peredur was visible in the darkness. "A heavy fog would conceal us from our pursuers. We can't be too far away from the docks where we can take a ship back to Dun Breatann, but, travelling in the open, as we must, we're too easy to spot."

"Loarn mac Eirc isn't the only one hunting you," Peredur replied, confirming the druid's fears.

"The villagers are still coming after us then."

"They are," Peredur said. "And they did not come this far without a great, murderous anger burning within them." The warrior stopped talking and furrowed his brow, head tilted as if listening for something.

"What is it?" Bellicus asked, perplexed at this unusual reaction.

Peredur looked at him and his face was grim, almost fearful as he replied.

"They have come for you."

CHAPTER TWENTY-FOUR

Duro sat on a tree root next to Cai and the horses and watched as Bellicus dispatched the wood pigeon then appeared to fall asleep holding the dead bird in his blood-soaked hands.

The centurion looked at the dog, wondering how the animal would react, but it was obviously used to its master's unusual behaviour, for it never moved during the whole ritual. The horses, on the other hand, became a little skittish, feet stamping, nostrils flaring, and Duro wondered idly if they could smell the spilt blood. Did horses have sensitive noses, the way dogs did?

Whatever the truth, Bellicus didn't move a muscle despite the noises from their nervous mounts, so deeply was he lost in his trance. Duro stared at him, searching for a twitch of an eyelid, or a finger, or a sniff, or anything else to suggest the druid was still alive and not departed forever to some magical otherworld.

Then Bellicus's eyes snapped open and Duro felt a shiver run down his spine. Instinctively, the centurion got up, drawing his sword from its sheath although he feared no earthly blade could harm whatever the druid was seeing.

He realised his mistake when the sound of a dry twig snapping came from behind him. He turned, as Cai also stood up, growling, hackles forming a ridge along his muscular back.

"Shit." Duro counted four enemies, but he suspected they were merely the vanguard of a larger force belonging to Loarn mac Eirc. The horses' skittishness had masked the sound of their approach, and, since Cai and Duro had been so engrossed in watching the druid's ritual, the Dalriadans had managed to get right up beside them before being discovered.

The time for thinking was past though. The four warriors coming at them looked grim and determined, although the centurion's experience told him they were, like the villagers they had fought the previous night, not well-versed in the ways of combat.

"You two get that prick," one of them said, his voice heavily accented but all-too clear to Duro, who spread his feet and prepared to defend himself from the sword and spear that were now aiming directly at him.

The other two circled past him, heading for the druid. Before anyone could launch an attack, Bellicus drew his sword and raised it to the sky. His hands and face were now stained with blood, making him such a terrible sight that even the enraged Dalriadans blanched momentarily, before their pride encouraged them onwards again.

"Taranis!" the druid called, staring at the clouds overhead. "You have your sacrifice. Now I offer you two more souls." He lowered his sword and pointed it at the warriors coming towards him. "May their blood please you."

Duro's opponents were also watching the druid's performance, looks of horror on their faces, and he took advantage of their hesitation. He pulled an arrow from his belt and threw it, whipping his arm down so it flew point-first, straight at the closest Dalriadan. Without the power of a bow behind it, it was never going to do much damage, and indeed, it spun slightly in flight, so it merely bounced off the enemy soldier's arm, which he threw up to protect his face.

The distraction allowed Duro to charge forward though, covering the ground between them, and his sword slipped between the man's ribs before he had a chance to parry.

"Cai!" he shouted, turning to point towards the men striding towards Bellicus who still stood as if rooted to the spot. "Get them!"

"You bastard!"

Duro spun, raising his sword just in time to bat aside the spear heading for his guts. The sharp blade missed its target, but caught him in the side, with enough force to tear a hole in his mail shirt. He felt the tell-tale burning that often accompanied a wound and cursed his clumsiness.

"You killed my brother," the Dalriadan cried, swinging his spear over his head, slamming it into the ground where Duro had just been standing, as if he was an axeman chopping firewood. "And now we're going to kill you and your damn dog!"

Duro shook his head, surprised by the wild ferocity of the man's attacks as the spear whistled past his face in an arc. The Dalriadan was no skilled warrior, but he was making up for it with sheer crazed savagery at that moment.

Duro had faced many such warriors in the past however, and, the next time his opponent made a lunge, the centurion stepped inside the spear's reach and chopped his sword down into the man's hand. Blood spurted and at least one finger dropped onto the grass along with the spear as the warrior screamed in a mixture of rage and disbelief.

The sound was cut short though, Duro spinning around the shocked Dalriadan and slamming the edge of his blade into the nape of the man's neck. It wasn't a clean enough blow to decapitate the warrior, but it was enough to kill him instantly and, without stopping, the centurion ran towards the stream.

He slowed his pace to a walk though, when he saw what was happening. Bellicus needed no aid – not even from Cai, whose order to attack by Duro had been countermanded.

The druid wanted to face his opponents within the protective circle his blade had carved in the frost-rimed grass.

Duro raised his eyebrows and whistled softly as he approached for both Dalriadan warriors were already dead. The druid had dispatched them in an astonishing display of martial prowess and now they lay on the grass, lifeblood emptying out of their bodies to mingle with that of the sacrificed pigeon.

Bellicus wasn't even out of breath. He was a shocking sight to behold though, his eyes wide with battle fury, face spattered with their enemies' blood.

"We should be on our way," he growled as Duro strode up to stand before him. "The ritual is complete."

Without another word, they hurried back to the horses, pleased to see them still tethered to the ground by the pegs attached to their reins. Bellicus placed the dead pigeon inside his pack to be butchered and cooked later, then they mounted.

Cai padded along at their backs like a shadow as they rode past the site of the druid's ritual and Duro looked from the corpses of the Dalriadans to the man who had dispatched them. The sheer power that emanated from Bellicus astonished Duro, who had never met anyone quite like him in all his forty-odd years of life. The druid was truly a frightening individual and Duro had never been happier to be fighting on the same side, for the thought of facing the shaven-headed giant in battle was deeply unsettling.

They kicked their horses into a canter and a chill swept over Duro as he looked back to make sure Loarn mac Eirc's men weren't in sight. They weren't, but a freezing fog was already beginning to settle over the land around them.

* * *

"What are you mumbling about?"

Bellicus was in a fine mood as they rode through the mist, heading, hopefully, southwards. He knew they must be very close to their destination, where they would find passage on a ship one way or another. Cai's limp was still in evidence, but it hadn't grown worse and the dog appeared content enough, loping along at the horses' rear or side as the fancy took him. Yet, on his left, the druid could hear Duro's low voice as he muttered away to himself.

"I was just saying," the centurion replied, pulling his thick cloak – now damp and heavy from the moisture conjured by Bellicus's ritual – up around his neck. "You might have made a warmer fog. It's bloody freezing."

Bellicus shook his head in mock disbelief. "Fear not, my cold friend," he said. "Soon enough we'll be on board a fast boat, a brazier warming us and roasting the meat of our pigeon."

Duro grinned at the thought and replied in a serious voice. "I'll be glad to get dry and warm – I'm sick of sleeping in that tent, cuddling Cai for warmth. What do you think we'll find when we get back to Dun Breatann? Will Coroticus have forgiven you by now?"

Bellicus waggled a hand, the way a pair of scales moved from side to side, weighing the chances of things being back to normal in Alt Clota. "Who can say? Hopefully he'll just be glad to have two warriors back with him in time for spring, and the coming hostilities with the Picts and Saxons and Lug knows who else. Ah…" He fell silent, and cocked his head, listening.

The thick fog muffled any sounds but, as the riders strained their ears, the unmistakeable high-pitched barking of hunting dogs came to them.

"Shit. They're right behind us." Duro said angrily, and Bellicus nodded, urging his horse to a faster pace.

"The know the terrain better than us, even with the fog. We must be almost on top of Ard Drisaig by now though, keep your eyes open."

"We won't have time to negotiate with the sailors, Bel," the centurion warned. "You can hear how close Loarn is, assuming those are his dogs – and it's hard to imagine who else they might belong to."

Bellicus frowned, knowing his friend was right. Had the gods brought down their magical fog, giving the fugitives hope, only to allow the pursuing king to claim their heads after all? He refused to believe the gods had forsaken him, not after the powerful blood sacrifices of two Dalriadan men.

"What are you thinking now?" Duro demanded, tearing his eyes away from the mist-shrouded ground they were cantering blindly into and seeing a familiar, not entirely welcome, expression on the druid's face. "I don't like it when you get that look in your eyes."

Bellicus simply laughed and pressed his knees into his horse's flanks so it would reach the settlement faster.

* * *

Loarn mac Eirc's captain, Aedan, riding hard at his king's side, pointed into the fog on the left as they passed the ruined trunk of a once-proud oak tree. "Look there, my lord! It's the tree the lightning shattered last autumn."

The king nodded, and drew his sword, wincing at the wound on his hand that the assassin sent from Dun Breatann had inflicted on him mere hours before. "Then we're almost at Ard Drisaig," he said. "I was right about their destination – they're heading for the docks to try and get away on a ship." Then he raised his voice so the rest of the men riding with him could hear. "Ready your weapons, lads! The dogs still have their scent so we know we're on the right track, and there's no way the sailors will cast off in this fog. That means the Damnonii arseholes are somewhere up ahead. Be ready – they're no fools, and I don't want to lose any more of my people to them this day."

"Close formation," Aedan commanded, bringing his galloping horse to a walk, the rest of their party following his lead. "Stay in sight of the warriors to each side of you so the druid and his mate can't pick us off in the fog without being seen. Although…" He looked up to the sky and, for the first time in hours, noticed the wan yellow light of the sun, attempting weakly to penetrate the mist.

"The fog is lifting," Loarn mac Eirc said, finishing his captain's sentence with a grim smile. "Perfect timing. There'll be nowhere for them to hide soon enough."

The Dalriadan warband stared ahead, searching for any sign of their quarry. They had been well briefed before they started the hunt so they knew they faced two dangerous men and a wardog that would kill them just as surely as any blade, but these were the best warriors in Loarn's service. When the fighting started there could only be one possible outcome – even a druid could not fend off the spears of a dozen of Dalriada's finest sons.

"Coroticus must be insane, right enough," Loarn said to Aedan as they reached the outskirts of the fishing settlement. "Sending just two men and a dog to kill me." He shook his head in amazement. "The disappearance of his daughter last year truly addled the man's brains. I'd love to be there when I send the heads of these three back to Dun Breatann in a sack and he opens it up. It'll send him right over the edge."

Aedan laughed. "Aye, I expect so, lord. That'll only make it even easier for us to take his fortress when we return with Drest and Cunneda."

The fog had lifted enough now to reveal the first few buildings in the settlement of Ard Drisaig, but there was no-one in sight, unsurprisingly – anyone with any sense would be indoors with their family, a cheery fire blazing in the hearth.

"Come on, lads," Loarn said, urging his mount to a faster pace. "We're here."

Ard Drisaig wasn't the biggest village in Dalriada, but it was an important port, serving trading vessels bringing things from places like Gaul and Rome. That meant the place was quite heavily populated as men were needed to work the docks, but also to guard the warehouses where the goods were stored before being transferred to their next destination, be that abroad, or to the markets of Britain.

The dogs were straining at their leashes and Aedan ordered their handlers to halt, while the rest of the riders moved past. These hounds were perfect for tracking prey, but they'd not be much use in a fight against two men and a wardog which, from King Loarn's description, was something of a monster.

"We should dismount. Can't really fight from horseback when your opponent is hiding behind, or in, a building."

The Dalriadan warriors followed their ruler's lead and quickly tethered their horses to covered staging posts outside a stable, handily placed for visitors such as them.

"No sign of the fugitives' mounts," Aedan noted, but he knew that meant little. The druid would not be coming back for his stolen horses, so he probably just set them free when they'd reached the settlement, allowing them to run off into the fog-shrouded fields nearby. Loarn's men would recover the animals soon enough, now that the sky was clearing, but the priority was to find the Alt Clotan spies. "You think they'll hide if they've heard us on their tail?" Aedan asked the king, who shook his head emphatically.

"They will know we're coming for them, and what their fate will be when we catch them," Loarn said as he strode into the village, head moving from left to right as he searched for signs of their quarry. "So they'll head directly to the docks and try to find a sailor who'll take them home immediately." He eyed the rapidly clearing fog and waved his men forward into a run. "Come on, hurry. The docks are just ahead, we have them now!"

The sounds of their mail jangling, and booted feet thumping on the path, brought men and women out of the workshops and warehouses that lined the road leading to the docks, curious faces watching them pass – another strange event to follow the freak fog that had provided them with a welcome break for a while that morning.

Their approach also drew out the captains and crew of the vessels that were docked there at that time. There weren't many – the numerous fishing boats simply pulled their catches out on the nearby beach, as they'd done since time immemorial, so the docks were populated that day by only three medium-sized boats and a larger ship, all of which were used for trading.

"You!" Loarn mac Eirc shouted to the most important looking man on the first boat they came to, beckoning him forward. "Have any vessels sailed in the past hour or two? No? You're sure? Oh, in the name of Christ..." The king moved on, irritated by the boat captain's uncertainty, and roared to the next in line.

By the time he and Aedan had questioned the men in charge of all four vessels, learning that no-one had asked them for passage that day, and no other ship had, as far as they knew, left the port, Loarn was furious.

"The bastards didn't just disappear into the air along with the fog," he growled, gazing up at the now clear sky before turning to Aedan. "Search the holds of each of these vessels," he commanded. "Look in every crate or barrel you find – the druid is around somewhere, or the dogs wouldn't have led us here."

Such a thorough search took quite a while but, by the end of it, there was still no sign of their quarry. The Dalriadan warriors were beginning to murmur amongst themselves, irritated by Loarn mac Eirc's impatient, angry commands, and fearful of the Damnonii druid's powers. They had all seen the bloodied corpses of the warriors left behind in the magic circle drawn in the frost and it frightened them more than they could admit, since they were all supposed to be Christians. In reality, of course, the Dalriadan soldiers were as superstitious as any man, and they knew the followers of the old ways had strange and terrifying abilities. Perhaps the druid *had* somehow flown away, carried back to Alt Clota by some weird power they couldn't even begin to comprehend.

King Loarn walked to the end of the pier and gazed out across the loch's waters, sparkling in the sun that had finally burned away the last of the mist, and shook his injured fist at the horizon.

"I'll find you, Bellicus of Dun Breatann!" he roared, voice seeming to carry for miles around, fuelled by his impotent rage. "I'll find you, and I'll kill you, you filthy heathen scum. May God strike me dead if I don't!"

CHAPTER TWENTY-FIVE

It had been easy, even in the fog, to find a boat big enough to take all three of them. The beach was littered with coracles, from one-man currachs to larger vessels that could take a much bigger crew.

Neither Bellicus nor Duro knew much about boats – sailing wasn't part of either a druid's or a centurion's training – so they simply chose something that looked in good repair, had oars stowed inside, and wouldn't sink under their weight. It had a sail, but, since Cai knew as much as the men about how to work the thing, they weren't very confident about its use, and had simply taken turns with the single pair of oars to get as far from land as possible before the fog burned away.

"I hope you have some idea of where we're going," Duro said, staring out into the middle distance, dry land still on the left but only rippling water ahead of them. "Mithras knows where we might end up."

The druid hauled on the oars, sending the boat sliding forward in a continuous smooth motion, staring back towards the port they'd just come from but, although the fog was lifting, they'd covered enough distance that Ard Drisaig wasn't visible even to his sharp eyes.

"I'm sure the land curves around to the left about here," he said. "But following it will just bring us back into Dalriadan lands and take us north again – the wrong direction altogether." He pulled on the oars and glanced up at the mast, wondering how hard it could be to use. "We need to keep moving south until the land disappears. When we see it again on the east, we should be able to head for it and leave the boat. We're ahead of Loarn mac Eirc, and he doesn't know where we've gone so we should be safe enough to find passage on a ship to Alt Clota somewhere. It's either that or walk all the way, and, if I remember correctly, the land about here is dotted with lochs and hills. There's no Roman roads to make passage easier." He dragged the oars backwards again with a low grunt. "But a ship, with a captain who knows his business, will have us home in no time."

They took turns rowing and put in at a small settlement just as the sun was beginning to set. The druid was fairly confident the

Dalriadan king, or his messengers, could not have reached this place before them since, even if Loarn guessed where they were, the journey by land was at least a hundred miles longer than by boat.

There were a few fishing boats on the beach, one or two of them very similar to the vessel they'd stolen, so they knew someone here must have the sailing skills to take them home. Their arrival caused a stir, for the place saw very few visitors, and none as interesting as the giant druid and his two hard-looking companions.

"How are ye, strangers?" said the first, smiling local as they left behind their stolen boat and walked up the beach towards the village. A crowd of about thirty or forty men, women and children, probably the entire population of the place, had turned out to greet them and, although some carried crude weapons, they seemed friendly enough. "What brings ye here? Ye don't look like fishermen."

The spokesman grinned, eyeing the druid's eagle-topped staff knowingly, and Bellicus couldn't help liking the fellow who was broad of shoulder and clearly no fool.

"No," he admitted. "We're not fishermen. We were attacked," he gestured vaguely back towards the water, as if he had no idea where they'd come from, "and took this boat to get away from the men that tried to rob us."

Duro nodded and all eyes turned to him. "My friend is a druid. We were travelling in the lands over yonder," he mimicked Bellicus's gesture, waving a hand to the west, "gathering myths and legends from the people."

"Apparently the folk there aren't as welcoming as you," Bellicus finished, striding forward to grasp the still-smiling headman's wrist. "We thank you for your hospitality." His grin was mirrored on the villager's face who shook his head in consternation.

"They're a bunch of arseholes over there," he said, to murmurs of agreement from his people. "Think they're above the rest of us because they're closer to King Loarn's fortress. Well, you'll spend the night with us here in Auchalic, and we'll show you proper Dalriadan hospitality."

"Hey, some of us still call ourselves Britons, Galchobhar!" someone piped up among the gathered villagers, but the comment was met only with smiles and shakes of the head and the three visitors followed their hosts towards the centre of the settlement. Bellicus merely raised his shoulders in a slight shrug at Duro's questioning glance, planning to find out what the cryptic comment meant for himself once a few ales had loosened the folks' tongues later on.

Their destination proved to be a roundhouse, rather larger than the rest of the buildings here although it wasn't even as big as the hall of Nectovelius back in Dun Buic. It might be used as a hall, but it was far from 'great'. Still, as they went inside Bellicus glanced around, eyes quickly adjusting to the gloom, pleased to see the structure was in good repair and built with good, thick timber. Only the headman, and a couple of middle-aged women came into the building with them, the rest of the villagers going back about their own business, promising to return when the sun went down and their day's work was finished.

"Light the fire, Luigsech," the headman said to one of the women who had already been moving in that direction of her own accord. He grinned at the two travellers. "Now, lads – take a seat close to the hearth. We'll soon have this place cosy." He turned serious then, almost apologetic as he asked, "Ye don't have any food of yer own we can use do ye? I know it's not very hospitable to ask a guest to feed himself but…"

The druid raised a hand and shook his head to assuage the headman's embarrassment. "It's fine," he said, lifting his pack from the rush-strewn floor and reaching in to find the headless pigeon. "Food is scarce at this time of year and we'll be glad to share what we have with you in return for a roof over our heads and a warm fire. Here." He tossed the bird to the headman who took it gladly. "There'll be enough there for the three of us to share, if we add some bread and oats, eh?"

Galchobhar looked down at Cai with a slightly disappointed look and Bellicus laughed. "I meant you could share it, man, not the dog. I've got other food for him."

Galchobhar's grin returned at the druid's promise and he passed the bird off to the same woman who'd just got the fire going, ordering her to pluck and cook it in a soup, before he went to a barrel in the corner and drew three mugs of ale.

By the time the bird had been prepared and set before the three men the sun had set outside and a few of the people began to filter in, rubbing numb hands by the hearty fire and stamping their feet on the floor to try and get the blood flowing again.

Then the inevitable request came from Galchobhar: would Bellicus sing for them?

Normally the druid would refuse, for he wasn't particularly fond of singing, preferring instead to tell stories in return for his hosts' hospitality, but he wanted these people in a good mood, for he had questions to ask them, and they would answer better if they were pleased.

"Aye, all right," he agreed, to whoops and cheers of delight. "I'll sing a few songs. My friend Duro might even join me for one, eh? Good."

Some of the folk had simple things like skin drums and bone flutes and, as Bellicus expected, they all knew "Rhydderch The Red" and various other old songs of Hibernian origin. Everyone joined in as he sang the better-known ones, and then he hushed them to silence and Duro took out his flute and handed it to Bellicus. As they performed "Alatucca's Song" the people remained quiet, appreciating their skill for they had become rather good performing at this tune by now. When they finished there was a round of applause and calls for another, but Galchobhar told the people to leave their guests alone, for they had more than earned their keep for the night.

The musicians in the hall continued where Bellicus and Duro left off, entertaining those who wanted music, but things had reached a stage where many of the villagers were content to simply enjoy their ale or wine and chat to one another. The druid from Dun Breatann felt the same, and he settled comfortably on his stool next to Galchobhar and conversed with the headman, telling him the news from the wider world. From rumours of a wonderful white stag in the north, to the massing Saxon armies in the south, Galchobhar was soon lost within Bellicus's words, charmed by the giant druid and the strong drink.

"It's not often we have one like you here in our village," the headman of Auchalic smiled, glad to change the subject after hearing about Horsa and Hengist's plans to subdue all the people dwelling in these lands, be they Briton, Pict or Dalriadan. "Well, never actually," he corrected himself. "This is the first time I've ever met a real druid."

"What about Dotha," Bellicus asked, thinking of King Loarn's Christian Bishop. "You might have met him. He was training to be a druid originally, before he converted."

"Pah." Galchobhar's obscene hand gesture made it clear what he thought of the old bishop. "He doesn't count. The man's an arse."

Bellicus heard the venom in the headman's voice and knew something must lie behind it.

"You don't like him?"

Galchobhar shook his head with a scowl. "You're right, I've met him. I've known him for years, even before we came over from the old country to settle here. Back then he wasn't any trouble but…" He glanced about, finally realising his words might find their way back to either Dotha or Loarn, and then he'd be in trouble. No-one was listening though, not even Duro, who was watching the musicians entertain the handful of villagers who still wanted to sing and dance. "Since he became bishop, Dotha has been the scourge of the hard-working people in these lands."

"In what way?"

Leaning in close to make certain he couldn't be overheard, Galchobhar began setting out his issues with the bishop. "He made us all convert to his new religion, whether we wanted to or not."

"Did you not want to then?"

"Of course not, druid!" the headman retorted. "I've followed the old gods all my life and they've always taken care of me. Why should I forget them all, and worship just one? Are we Dalriadans free? Or are we slaves, to be told what to do and how to think? No," he went on, looking into Bellicus's eyes, and there was a sadness there, hidden behind the angry mask. "I fear this new religion will be the end of our people – it makes us weak, and it's made Loarn weak. If these sea wolves – Saxons – ye speak of, do come here, they'll find us an easy target."

The headman turned away to watch the dancers, and Bellicus took in his words before drawing Galchobhar's attention back to him.

"Do you think the folk in the other settlements about here feel the same way?" He knew well enough how those living further away from a king's seat of power would always feel less inclined to support them – far from the protection of Loarn's warband, probably losing sheep and cattle to raiders from the islands to the south-west or his own Alt Clotan compatriots, the people of Auchalic would understandably be put out at having to pay fealty to a king that, through no real fault of his own it had to be said, couldn't offer them protection the way he could to those living closer to Dunadd.

"The headmen of the surrounding settlements do, aye. We meet at the markets and it's always the same tales of woe." He gazed at the druid, impotent anger burning in his eyes. "We send our wealth as taxes to King Loarn, leaving our people hungry during hard winters like this one. We even renounced our old gods to placate that fool Dotha. But what do we get in return?"

He left the question hanging in the air – it needed no answer.

"These lands once belonged to the Britons of Alt Clota," Bellicus said at last, once Galchobhar had calmed down again. "Before you came from over the sea."

Galchobhar looked sidelong at the druid, warily, unsure where this was going. "Some of the men and women you see here," he gestured to the gathered villagers enjoying the celebration as if they hadn't a care in the world, "have lived in this settlement since before we came. We didn't just turn up and start killing everyone." He shook his head emphatically. "This village was dying before we came. Not enough people to support it. Most of the people were happy to let us join them."

Bellicus didn't ask what happened to those who didn't want the Dalriadans to settle here. The fact was, things were changing all across the country. Newcomers were arriving all the time now that the Romans were gone. Sometimes they killed everyone in an existing settlement and just took over their dwellings and belongings and often even their wives.

From what the druid could see, that hadn't happened in Auchalic. He could hear the different accents, and even pick out differences in skin tone or facial structure that he imagined separated the Dalriadans from the Britons. It appeared the two peoples had found a way to live together in harmony, content to continue their lives as fishermen and simple farmers, without killing one another simply because they came from a different place.

Bellicus wondered if there was a lesson here for him. Should he, once they got back to Dun Breatann, advise Coroticus to try and make peace with the Saxons, offering them lands, or even taking some of them in to live and work in Alt Clotan settlements?

He discarded the idea at once, knowing such a policy would be naïve and foolishly idealistic. The Dalriadans, much like the Picts, shared many similarities with Bellicus's people – the Saxons were another matter. Horsa, for one, would need to be defeated in battle before he gave up his notions of conquest.

Bellicus's thoughts moved away from the Saxons, returning to matters closer at hand as he addressed Galchobhar once more.

"You say many of your people are Britons," he noted. "Yet this is a Dalriadan settlement: your king is Loarn mac Eirc and, if he calls your men to his armies, they will go."

"A man needs a king," Galchobhar countered, and Bellicus dipped his head in agreement.

"But you, and the others of this settlement, and those nearby," he said, sipping from his ale, "feel no great loyalty, or love, for Loarn mac Eirc?"

The enormity of what was being said – of what he had said already – suddenly seemed to penetrate the ale-induced fog shrouding Galchobhar's mind and his hand dropped to the knife at his belt as he stared into the druid's eyes, wondering if he was a spy.

Time seemed to slow then, as Bellicus gazed back, unblinking, ready to defend himself should Galchobhar decide this guest was more dangerous than he'd first thought. Treason was a crime punishable by death after all.

Galchobhar, unnerved by the druid's stony visage, dropped his eyes only to see the massive wardog, Cai, watching him intently beneath the table, and a shiver ran down his spine as he realised how close to death he'd just come. He lifted his cup and took a long pull.

"You have nothing to fear from me," Bellicus said and his tone was warm, reassuring – the result of many long hours spent learning how to control his voice under the tutelage of Qunavo and the other elder druids in Iova. "I am no spy, sent here from Loarn mac Eirc. In truth, I hate Dotha even more than you, and I despise the king for being led like a fool by the Christians. Your words here tonight will not be held against you, Galchobhar, I swear it, and may Taranis strike me down if I lie."

The headman, fortified by his swig of ale, managed a smile then noticed Duro also sitting watching him. "By the Tuatha De," he said, with a wry shake of his head. "I wouldn't like to meet you three on a dark night. I'm glad you're my friends!"

Bellicus sensed the change in tone of the conversation and, rather than forcing it back to talk of allegiances and misplaced loyalty, he remained silent, allowing Galchobhar to enjoy the rest of the night.

After another song or two, toasts to new friends and gods, old and new, those who were sober enough went to their homes. The rest, including the three visitors, bedded down in the hall.

Before he fell asleep, Bellicus saw a young woman, quite attractive, lie next to Duro. The centurion looked surprised, and then embarrassed, and the druid could hear their conversation.

"Do ye not find me desirable?"

Duro shook his head. "It's not that...I just...My wife was..." He looked down and Bel could see the tears glistening in his friend's eyes. "I'm flattered, but not tonight, girl."

She apparently understood his pain and touched his arm as he laid his head back down and turned away, facing the wall so no-one else could see his anguish.

The girl, apparently finding outsiders extremely alluring, looked towards Bellicus but he too shook his head and she wandered off. The druid wasn't sure if she was disappointed or angered by their rejection of her charms, but it didn't matter – he had made it a rule never to sleep with women in a situation like this. It only led to trouble, as jealous men would start a fight even when sober, never mind after a heavy drinking session like they'd all enjoyed this night.

Bellicus didn't want to battle with the good folk of Auchalic. Quite the opposite in fact, as their unplanned visit here had set several wheels in motion within his head...

"What's our plans for tomorrow?" Duro asked eventually, turning back towards Bel, face composed once more. The fire was now almost burned out, offering only a little heat and orange light.

"Leave as soon as possible," Bellicus replied drowsily. "Did you find someone to take us home? I noticed you talking to one of the men, with some of your Roman coins changing hands."

Duro snorted. "Nothing gets past you, does it, druid? Aye." Laughing now. "You're half right. The lad will indeed take us back to Dun Breatann, but the only payment I offered was the boat we sailed here in. We won't need it, but he can make use of it and we'll be back in front of the jovial Coroticus in no time."

"What about the coins? I definitely saw you passing some to the villager."

The centurion grinned, pleased to know something his friend didn't. "Can't you guess? No? The wise druid, Bellicus, scourge of the Saxons and—"

"Get on with it, by Dis. I want to get to sleep before the sun comes up again!"

"The boy had never seen Roman money before," Duro said, still smiling. "I was simply showing it to him. It's basically worthless here anyway."

"Good night, Duro," said the druid and within seconds, both the druid and his dog were snoring as if they were safely tucked up in a comfortable bed in the fortress of Dun Breatann. Duro lay awake, planning on keeping watch for although the headman and the rest of the villagers seemed friendly enough, you could never tell what people would do when night fell. A full moon, like the one that hung overhead outside tonight, often made folk act a little strangely.

Soon enough though, the centurion's eyelids became heavy, and he too felt the comforting blanket of sleep draw over him.

* * *

The next day proved stormy, and so did the one after that. Despite Bellicus's desire to be away from Dalriada, it would have been folly to sail in such weather and they were forced to remain in Auchalic for a little longer. There was a chance Loarn mac Eirc would still be on their trail but even dogs couldn't follow a scent across the water so it would only be chance that brought the pursuing king to the very settlement the druid and Duro were staying in.

The pair earned their keep though, for although the wind and rain weren't ideal for travelling, it didn't stop them wandering about the land near the village, cloaks pulled tightly around themselves, hunting for game. Hares were plentiful in this part of the country, and their meat was a welcome addition to the table in Auchalic. Bellicus further endeared himself to the locals by gifting the cook, Luigsech, some of the herbs and spices he carried in his cloak pockets, which she used to make a wonderful, aromatic stew. Duro too, became a favourite amongst the women in the village, showing them a recipe for simple sweet cakes he'd come up with himself back in his days as a baker.

The nights, while not as raucous as that first occasion when they'd washed ashore, were still pleasant affairs spent in the hall, chatting to people, learning their ways, their hopes and dreams, which were, of course, much the same as anyone in any other part of the world. Bellicus spent hours in Galchobhar's company, becoming fast friends with the clever headman.

At last the weather changed and, on the third morning, the sun rose above the settlement, making the rippling waves on the loch sparkle in its brilliance.

"I'm sorry to see ye go, lads," Galchobhar said to both men, grasping their forearms tightly before pulling Cai in tight against his legs and rubbing the dog's muscular body affectionately. "I don't suppose we'll ever see ye again, but it's been good having ye around. We'll miss yer tales, and yer recipes!"

"Maybe you will see us again," Bellicus said, turning back from looking at their boat being readied to leave. "Perhaps Loarn's time as king will come to an end and the loyalties of Auchalic will move to another. One better placed to offer you the protection from raids you require, while taking less in tribute every month?"

The headman shrugged. "Perhaps. But, for now, Loarn is our king and Dotha our spiritual leader." His mouth twisted in distaste before he continued in a more upbeat voice. "Who knows how long that will last though? Kings come and go and it's possible the people in the lands around here will look favourably on one who still follows the old ways."

"You will speak to them?" the druid asked, and received a nod in response.

"I will, my friend. If ye come this way again, accompanied by yer king or just with Duro and Cai, ye will always be welcome. Now go – Maedoc is ready to sail. Make the most of this fine weather, for it might change at any time."

The three travellers made their way down the beach to the boat and the two men tossed their packs on board before Bellicus lifted Cai into the vessel and Duro followed. It was cramped with the three of them plus their Dalriadan pilot, Maedoc, but the journey should, all being well, be over by the evening. If the wind was against them, or the weather turned again, they should still make it back to Dun Breatann some time the next day.

Duro and Maedoc pushed the boat from the beach into the water, grunting with the effort, but Bellicus insisted he remain on board to steady Cai who was understandably nervous of being in such a small boat without even a proper flat deck to sit or lie on.

"At least we don't have to row all the way this time," the druid grinned, patting Duro, who was puffing hard as he jumped into the boat and it floated forward at little more than a walking pace. "Maedoc will have the sail up and we can just relax and enjoy the view."

"Unless Loarn mac Eirc appears behind us," the centurion muttered. "We'll bloody need to row if that happens."

"What's that?" Maedoc asked, brows lowered. "Why would the king be coming after us?"

Bellicus threw Duro a dark look. The experienced soldier really should have known better than to let slip such an important – secret – piece of information.

"Never mind, lad," the centurion said, smiling reassuringly, but placing his hand on the hilt of his sword to remind the Dalriadan to do as he was told or there would be consequences. "Just get us back to Dun Breatann and you'll be well rewarded with this fine boat."

The young sailor turned his blue eyes on the druid who stared back at him stony-faced and the lad simply nodded and set about unfurling the sail. He was no fool and besides, Galchobhar had told Bellicus the men of Auchalic held no great love for their Christian king. Maedoc would not hinder their journey, even if he thought he might survive such a foolish course of action. Which he would not.

Of course, the Dalriadan sailor's views might change if a ship with Loarn mac Eirc on board did appear on the horizon behind them, but they would deal with that if it happened. Until then...The druid placed his back against the hull of the boat and gazed up at the blue sky, watching the clouds scud across it as the sail was raised and they began to pick up speed.

"This beats walking anyway," he murmured, before closing his eyes and basking in the sun and the gentle motion of the waves.

Around midday Bellicus asked their pilot how far they'd travelled and was pleased to hear they were almost in Damnonii lands, and halfway to Dun Breatann itself. They shared a meal of bread and smoked fish and the druid asked Maedoc how the sail worked, just in case he ever needed to steal a boat again in the future.

The day passed pleasantly, although the temperature dropped around mid-afternoon as clouds covered the sun. They weren't the heavy, dark thunderheads of the previous two days though, and it seemed they would reach their destination without being drenched.

When the great bulk of Dun Breatann at last appeared on the horizon Bellicus couldn't help a smile tugging at his lips. They would soon be home, and safe within the impenetrable fortress – Loarn mac Eirc had been thwarted.

Still, their own mission to kill the Dalriadan king hadn't been completed successfully either, and Coroticus, well...The druid would not worry about their reception. They had nowhere else to go and they would just have to trust in the gods to take care of them.

The gloomy thoughts turned then to little Catia and the druid's smile returned. They had been away only a matter of weeks, but children grew and changed so quickly he wondered what the princess would be like now. She at least would be pleased to see him, he was sure of that.

Yet, as he gazed into the distance at the giant rock, towering above the river around it, a sudden fear gripped Bellicus and he bit his lip in consternation.

"What's up? Sea sick?"

The sailor had noticed the druid's change in expression, and Duro glanced across at his friend curiously.

"We're nearly home," the centurion said, nodding ahead, towards Dun Breatann. "And you're only just feeling sick now?"

"Not sick," Bellicus replied softly, but his face had turned ashen and he had no idea what had come over him. "Put in at Cardden Ros," he commanded their pilot, pointing at a small settlement near a peninsula that jutted out from the land into the river.

"What?" Duro demanded. "We're almost home. All we have to do is sit here in the boat and we'll be dropped right off at Dun Breatann. What in Hades has come over you?"

Bellicus wasn't sure how to answer his friend's perfectly reasonable question. By disembarking at Cardden Ros they would need to walk the rest of the way – around five miles – and they would not reach home before sunset.

"I'm sorry," he said, turning to meet Duro's irritated gaze. "I can't say why, but I feel it would be a terrible mistake to just turn up at Dun Breatann." The centurion's expression softened, and Bellicus was pleased at the trust his friend had in him, even if it meant an extra walk he hadn't been expecting. "Don't worry, I have friends in Cardden Ros, they'll take good care of us."

"What about me?" the sailor asked. It was one thing docking at a major port like Dun Breatann, where traders could expect to be safe, protected by custom and a code of honour set down for generations, quite another to simply put in at a random town or village. "You know Dalriada is at war with these people?"

"You're with me," Bellicus said. "I'm the druid of these lands so you have nothing to fear. Make the most of the hospitality in Cardden Ros tonight, and you'll be safely on your way home tomorrow morning."

The Dalriadan didn't look entirely convinced but he had little choice in the matter so he trimmed the sail, setting the boat on a course that would bring them straight to the druid's chosen destination. Bellicus could hear him muttering though, wondering what made him think he'd be safe in Cardden Ros, if he thought there was danger in Dun Breatann.

It was a fair question, the druid had to concede, but they couldn't spend the rest of their lives on this little boat in the middle of the River Clota and, as he said, there were friends in the village they were sailing towards. Men and women Bellicus had known for years and, more importantly, men and women he'd helped with various problems in that time.

The people of Cardden Ros would not turn them away.

And yet, as the boat struck the stony beach and Maedoc jumped out with Duro to drag its hull right out of the foaming water, Bellicus checked his weapons were in place and ready for use. Something had caused him to be fearful of Dun Breatann, it was only common sense to be wary of what they might find here in Cardden Ros since this was also part of King Coroticus's lands.

He lifted Cai out onto the beach and the dog rather incongruously shook his body as if he had swum there instead of coming by boat. Then, as the men shook their heads at the strange behaviour, sharing bemused smiles, Cai ran to the long grass a little way ahead, sniffing excitedly and emptying his bladder.

"Come on," Bellicus said, leading the way towards the village, the others falling in behind him. "We'll get a warmer welcome if we arrive while it's still light."

CHAPTER TWENTY-SIX

Cardden Ros was a small, quiet village, that, although situated on the banks of the Clota, was well insulated from the threat of invaders by the bigger settlements along the river. A large fleet would not reach their tiny village without being spotted and attacked further west.

A solitary three-man boat was not seen as a threat though, and, as a result, Bellicus's party made it into the village without being challenged. There were no gates, no palisade walls, and no sentries but, as the druid knew, the men here were as hardy as any he'd come across from Drumcrew to Soriodunum. Farmers and fishermen, as they were back in Auchalic, the people of Cardden Ros needed no walls to protect them – their sheepdogs and legendary tempers were enough to deal with any who caused trouble within their sparsely populated lands.

As they walked towards the centre of the village Bellicus had a sudden thought. "I'd been going to head for the roundhouse the folk use as their meeting hall," he said softly to his companions, raising an arm to halt their steps. "Many of them will be in there on a cold night like this, enjoying the communal hearth and one another's company." He started walking again but this time he headed for the left, away from the main paths, towards the fields, and he pulled his hood up over his head as he went.

"Well, if they're in there, where are we going?" Duro hissed in confusion. "You said yourself we'd get a better welcome if the people see us now, when there's still some light. Creeping about in the fields won't look suspicious at all, will it?"

"Don't worry, my sarcastic friend," Bellicus smiled over his shoulder as they reached a stone wall and he raised a long leg over it. "There's no livestock in this field so I doubt there'll be any sheep or cattle-herders around to see us. I know one of the farmers not far from here who'll be glad to see us. Or me at any rate. You two? He might let you sleep in his stable I suppose. You can huddle together for warmth when the frost begins to settle."

The Dalriadan didn't seem to know whether the druid was joking or not but Duro didn't bother reassuring him – the look on the man's face was too comical. And the centurion had to stifle a laugh when Cai vaulted the wall, claws momentarily scrabbling on the stone, and the fretful sailor looked like he might shit his breeches so bemused was he by the whole strange situation he found himself in.

They walked for a little while and, by the time a farmhouse came into view the sun had dipped beneath the horizon. The building was merely a black spot against a dark background until they grew nearer, and a weak light could be seen emanating from the gaps in a shuttered window.

"Someone's not out drinking in the village hall," Duro muttered, eyes scanning the gloomy fields around them, ever alert for danger. "You sure they'll be glad to find three strangers on their threshold? I don't want some mad farmer attacking me with his hoe."

As he spoke, there came a sudden barking, and, already wary, the centurion drew his spatha, while the Dalriadan sailor pulled out his long knife. The dogs, which must have been bedded down in an outhouse or barn, charged towards them, invisible in the night, but given away by their excited, aggressive barking.

A man's voice came from inside the dwelling, asking, as dog-owners are wont to do, "What's the matter?" even though he must have known his only reply would be yet more yammering.

The sheepdogs came up to the travellers and their rangy forms were visible now that they were closer. Cai barked too, his deeper tones mixing with the others to form a cacophony that seemed to fill the entire field, all the way back down to the starlit Clota. The hounds did not set to fighting though, rather they seemed excited to meet and began sniffing and playing with one another as the door opened in the farmhouse and a tall figure loomed against the light within.

"Who's there?"

The farmer's voice was calm but Bellicus could make out the unmistakable shape of a hatchet in his hand and the druid called out, not wanting to cause any alarm to the man, whose supper had no doubt been rudely interrupted by their sudden appearance on his land.

"It's Bellicus the Druid, Cadeyrn. I'm sorry to arrive like this, as night is falling but—"

"Bel! By Cernunnos, what are you doing creeping about in the dark?" the farmer broke in, and gestured the three men to come inside, as he scolded his dogs and ordered them to quieten down. They failed to do so until Cai had followed his master into the farmhouse and the sheepdogs were left outside to return to their beds.

"What are you doing here?"

Bellicus hadn't even been offered a seat, never mind meat or drink, before the farmer's question, and the druid stared at him, surprised by the unexpected lack of hospitality.

"We've been travelling," he replied. "On a mission for King Coroticus."

Cadeyrn's eyes narrowed at the mention of the king and he seemed unsure how to proceed.

Duro and the sailor glanced at one another awkwardly, unsure what was happening. Hadn't the druid said this farmer was a friend?

"Out with it, man," the druid suddenly commanded, his voice taking on a powerful tone that Duro had heard before. As he expected, the farmer began to speak.

"Have you not heard? No, I suppose not, or you wouldn't be looking at me like that." Suddenly, it seemed as if Cadeyrn remembered his duties as a host, and he muttered, showing the three newcomers to a table in the corner of the room. It was by another window and Bellicus knew, from a previous visit one past summer, that it offered a wonderful view of the Clota and the fields on the far shore that the farmer could enjoy while eating his meals. Now, though, it was shuttered like the other windows, and Bellicus felt glad of it, as if there might be someone or something out there waiting to do them harm if given the chance.

He sat in silence, letting the vague feeling pass as the farmer placed a jug of ale and two cups on the table. "They're the only ones I've got," he said apologetically. "We'll have to share." Also for sharing was the remains of a black loaf and some butter, which he set down before on a trencher with a knife and bid them dig in.

Like the cups, there were only two stools, one for the host, and the other taken by Bellicus while Duro and the sailor sat on a bench attached to the wall by hinges so it could be folded down when not in use. The farmhouse wasn't particularly small, but, with four men inside it was a little cramped, although the crackling fire in the hearth meant it was also wonderfully cosy after the cold boat trip.

Without preamble, the farmer spoke again once everyone was seated and furnished with food and drink. "The king has put word out, Bel, that, when you return to Alt Clota you've to be arrested."

Bellicus stopped mid-chew and stared at the farmer, while Duro muttered an oath, crumbs flying from his mouth. The sailor, perhaps unconsciously, seemed to move away from his two travelling companions, as if distancing himself from their company.

Time seemed to grind to a halt just for an instant, as Cadeyrn's words sank in, but then Bellicus began to masticate his buttered bread again and the moment passed. "What for?" he asked. "I mean, what am I accused of?"

Cadeyrn shook his head and looked as bewildered as anyone else around the table. "No idea. The word was just put about that you were to be taken into custody when you returned. Everyone's been talking about it – seemed a strange thing to ask people. I mean…you're Coroticus's closest advisor. A druid!"

They sat again in silence, finishing the simple meal and allowing the warmth to penetrate their tired muscles. Cai whined by the door but Bellicus took no notice, lost in his thoughts, wondering what had happened in his absence from Dun Breatann to bring about this royal edict.

"Why *are* you here – at my place – anyway?" Cadeyrn asked, repeating his earlier, as-yet unanswered question, and the druid heard the trepidation in the farmer's voice this time.

"I had a foreshadowing of trouble when Dun Breatann came into sight when we were on the river, although I did not expect…this. I'm sorry," he said, meeting the farmer's gaze. "I wouldn't have come here if I'd known it might bring trouble to you. You can rest assured though, no-one saw us coming to your house, and we will be gone before sun-up tomorrow. Coroticus will have no knowledge of our presence here, or the hospitality you've provided us."

The farmer flinched almost imperceptibly at that last statement, and Bellicus felt a little guilty at having thrown it in, but he wanted Cadeyrn to know the king might very well punish him. If

Coroticus found out he'd given Bellicus food and drink and a place to sleep, without immediately hurrying to raise the alarm in Carden Ros, Cadeyrn might be seen as a traitor to the crown.

It was ridiculous, the druid mused. The whole thing – from the fight with Coroticus, to their enforced mission to Dalriada, to this latest nonsense calling for his arrest.

What had prompted the king to act in this manner? He had no idea, and his fabled, if mostly mythical, powers of clairvoyance offered no clues.

"What are we going to do?" Duro asked.

Bellicus shook his head. "I'll sleep on it, but, right now, I don't know. Sail back to Auchalic with our friend here, perhaps."

The Dalriadan shrugged. "I'm going there anyway," he said. "You're welcome to return with me if you like. I'm sure the people will be glad to hear more of your songs and tales, druid." He took the cup he was sharing with Duro and refilled it. "I still get to keep the boat though, right?"

Bellicus smiled almost sadly, not relishing the thought of heading back to the little fishing village but knowing it might be their best option for now, until they could find out what was happening in Dun Breatann. "Aye, you get the boat no matter what, my friend."

Again, the four men fell into a maudlin silence, with only the crackling fire to brighten the atmosphere. Bellicus found his head nodding as sleep threatened to claim him and he sucked in a deep breath, planning to find a spot on the floor where he might find some rest, but then the farmer spoke again.

"Please don't tell anyone I said this," Cadeyrn muttered, leaning in over the table so he could keep his voice low but still be heard by those around the table. "But I think King Coroticus might have gone mad."

"Why do you say that?" the druid asked, keeping his own voice low, wondering what new information the farmer might impart. When it came, the druid was shocked to his very core.

"You're not the only person that's pissed him off, Bellicus," Cadeyrn said. "He's arrested the queen as well."

CHAPTER TWENTY-SEVEN

"He's lost his mind," Bellicus muttered, staring into the fire as if it might offer some hint as to how he should proceed after Cadeyrn's shocking news. He didn't want to say too much in front of their Dalriadan companion, just in case the man passed on his words to those back at home and it reached the ears of Loarn mac Eirc. Alt Clota was still the druid's home after all, and the last thing he wanted was to let their enemies know they were weak and labouring under the rule of a madman. But the sailor had fallen fast asleep and so had the farmer, leaving Bellicus and Duro to chat quietly between themselves.

"We don't know that," the centurion said. "Perhaps the queen tried to overthrow Coroticus or something..." He trailed off, knowing himself how ludicrous that idea sounded.

"You're probably closer to the truth than you realise," Bellicus replied, so softly that his companion didn't hear him. He had a feeling Coroticus had begun to see enemies at every turn – he was paranoid when he forced Bellicus and Duro into what was essentially exile after all, so it would be no surprise if he also suspected Narina was plotting against him.

Yet that theory didn't explain why Coroticus had ordered the druid's arrest should he be seen in Alt Clota.

Despite the warmth from the fire a chill ran down the back of Bellicus's neck and he suddenly saw everything with great clarity: Coroticus had been given confirmation of Catia's true conception.

The king knew he was not the princess's father. He had found out, somehow, about Narina and Bellicus's liaison in the sacred grove all those years ago. Or, he suspected it at least, and it had been enough for him to throw the queen in prison and seek to hunt the druid down.

"This is just perfect," he growled, shaking his head in disgust. "Now we have two kings trying to kill us."

"And all the people in Dalriada and Alt Clota," Duro agreed.

They looked at one another and both burst out laughing at the absurdity of it all.

"You should be a hero to Coroticus," the centurion said when their mirth had passed and reality returned. "You went into an impossible situation, hunting a Saxon warband the length of the country just to rescue his daughter. Which you did, by Mithras!"

"Which *we* did," Bellicus corrected him.

"And he rewarded you by sending you on yet another impossible fool's errand, to kill a king, during winter, when the bastard's safely tucked up in his impenetrable fortress all day." He sighed, then put his hand out, gesturing for Bellicus to pass the cup of ale that sat on the table beside him. "So, I'll ask you again, and don't give me that 'I'll sleep on it' bollocks: What are we going to do?"

The druid waited until the cup was returned to him, refilled it, drained it, then wiped his mouth with the back of his hand and smiled.

"It seems to me the gods are amused by sending us on fool's errands."

Duro raised an eyebrow and used his tongue to try and displace a piece of bread that had become lodged between his teeth. "I don't like the sound of that," he replied, before repeating his question for what felt like the tenth time that night. "What are we going to do?"

Bellicus set the empty cup down on the table and stretched his great body out on the floor next to Cai, who was already asleep, back leg jerking as if he was dreaming of chasing hares in a summer meadow.

"Coroticus will leave Narina to rot in Dun Breatann's prison," he said, bunching up his pack and placing it beneath his head as a pillow. "Unless someone gets her out."

"Someone?" Duro's tone was despairing, but his eyes were sparkling, and the druid knew his friend's loyalty, or readiness for adventure, would never be in question.

"Us," he replied with a grim nod. "Obviously."

* * *

The next morning was cold and overcast, but dry, and there was a hint of spring returning to the land which gave Bellicus hope for their coming 'fool's errand' as Duro had called it.

They said their farewells to Maedoc, and he went on his way, smiling with relief that his own adventure was over, and he was the proud owner of a new boat to sail back to Auchalic. The farmer was also glad to see his visitors off, fearing the wrath of Coroticus should word get out of him providing hospitality to the fugitives.

"Where will you go now, Bel? My advice would be to get out of Alt Clota and seek refuge with one of your brother druids. You'd have been better going with your Dalriadan friend and having him take you off in his boat."

Bellicus nodded at the farmer's advice and murmured noises of agreement. Of course, it would be sensible to travel somewhere, perhaps south to join up with the Merlin and Arthur – they would be more than happy to take him in after all, and he believed in their cause completely.

But he knew he had to try and rescue Narina from whatever fate Coroticus had planned for her. If the king had discovered the truth of Catia's parentage, well, Bellicus was almost as much to blame as the queen. She hadn't become pregnant with the girl on her own, even if she had concealed her identity so he didn't know who he was sleeping with.

"I have one more favour to ask of you," the druid said, and the farmer looked apprehensive. "Nothing dangerous," Bellicus laughed, clapping a hand on the man's bicep reassuringly. "I'd just like some candles, if you have any. If we're going to be travelling again, I'd like to have a little light during the dark hours. Rushlights would also do."

Cadeyrn smiled, apparently relieved at the simple request. "Wait a moment," he said, before disappearing into the barn where his dogs had been the night before. When he returned, followed by his excitable hounds, he was grinning.

"I'm sorry I couldn't offer you better hospitality, Bel," he said, holding out a lantern to the druid. "Hopefully this will make up for it."

Bellicus took the proffered item gratefully. It was of a simple design, with a handle at one end, a linen wick at the other, and a hole for olive oil to be added in the middle, but it would be much better than flickering candles or smoky rushlights. He took it with profuse thanks, stowing it in his pack along with a little jar of oil, promising to repay the farmer's kindness one day.

The sun's light was just beginning to force its way through the heavy clouds as Bellicus and Duro thanked their host one more time and then started off, Cai trotting at the druid's side, into the trees that grew close to the farmhouse and stretched for miles to the north and east.

"This really is stupidity," Duro said as they trudged through the trees, glad for once that it was winter, and the undergrowth wasn't as full, or as jagged, as it would be in just a few weeks. "Everyone in Dun Breatann knows you and can recognise you on sight. Many of them will know me too. And the fortress is even harder to get inside than Dunadd. Are you going to magic us inside the walls or something?"

Bellicus chewed a piece of bread and glanced at his friend as they walked. "It will seem like that, I expect, to those living there."

The enigmatic reply didn't satisfy the centurion, who opened his mouth to demand more from the druid, but then, exasperated, shook his head and continued walking in silence, as if accepting his fate, no matter what it was going to be.

They travelled for a while and Duro was surprised not to see the massive bulk of Dun Breatann until they were almost there, for the land they were walking through appeared to be in a little valley that only opened out around a mile or so away from it. They passed a couple of small villages, but no-one noticed them and, when they came to a river, they walked along the bank until they found a coracle.

"Isn't there a bridge?" Duro asked, realising his friend planned to cross the fast-flowing river in the small boat. "This is stealing. How will the owner get this back?"

Bellicus raised his eyebrows and climbed into the tiny vessel, coaxing Cai to follow him. The dog was reluctant to leave dry land after their recent voyage from Dalriada, but his master's command was obeyed soon enough.

"We're going to save the life of the queen," Bellicus said, as Duro shoved the coracle into the current and jumped on board, rocking the thing alarmingly. It soon righted itself though, and the centurion used the oars stowed within to propel them across to the opposite bank. "Does it really matter if some fisherman has to find a way to get his boat back?"

"Well, no," Duro replied sourly. "I'd just rather have walked, since it's always me that has to do the hard work while you just sit there holding the dog, watching the scenery go by."

Bellicus grinned and pressed his face affectionately against Cai's. "Well, you're much better at rowing than me," he said. "And we'd be seen if we used the bridge. Think about it – there'll be traders and other travellers crossing the river all day. That bridge is one of the busiest in Alt Clota."

It wasn't a wide river and soon enough they were at the other side, although a fair distance downstream from where they'd started.

"It's a shame we're not heading straight for the fortress," Bellicus said as they climbed out and dragged the coracle up onto the grass so its owner could retrieve it later. "This flows straight to Dun Breatann, so we'd have been at the docks in just a few moments."

"If we're not going straight there," Duro puffed, stretching his back and catching his breath after rowing so hard, "where are we going?"

"This way," Bellicus replied and, rather to the centurion's surprise, headed in the direction of the other great volcanic rock in the area – Dun Buic Hill.

It took less than half an hour to reach the foot of the hill, and Duro nodded in recognition. "This is where we came hunting that time," he said. "Remember? The king was nearly killed by that bear."

"That's right," the druid said. "It was also just a little further along the road that the Saxons abducted Catia and I set out on the journey that would eventually lead me to you."

"Lucky me," Duro grunted, shaking his head in amusement. "My life has been so much fun since that day." His face fell then, as he remembered his wife, and they continued on in silence, Bellicus leading the way up the southern face of the slope.

"Where are we going anyway, by Hades?" the centurion grumbled as they moved upwards. "We're nowhere near the fortress. Are we hiding out here until nightfall or something?"

Bellicus didn't reply but after a short time they reached a level section of ground and he led the way ahead. There were animal skulls set atop some rocks here, and strange runes carved into the stones jutting out from the grass.

"What are they there for?" Duro demanded, eyeing his friend warily for it was obvious this area was not supposed to be strayed into.

"To guard against intruders, and nosey locals," Bellicus confirmed, striding past the magical wards without a care, and why would he? He'd placed them there himself, and he returned there at least once a year, usually more, to make sure they were still there, undisturbed and in good condition. "Don't worry, you're safe as long as you're with me."

To Duro's further bemusement, Bellicus stopped and placed his pack on the ground.

"We'll spend the rest of the day here," he said. "I'll go and fetch some firewood, while you start preparing some food for us, eh?" Without waiting for a reply, the druid wandered off, eyes on the ground, searching for dry twigs and branches. Cai lay on the grass beside Duro and watched his master moving about.

Rolling his eyes, the centurion set down his own pack and looked inside it for ingredients. If they were going to be there for the rest of the day – which was a good few hours – he might as well spend some time making the tastiest meal the contents of his pack, and the druid's pockets of spices, would allow.

Eventually, the two men had a fire going and some hare meat they'd procured back in Auchalic was roasting over it, while Duro was boiling carrots and a little turnip, lightly seasoned with salt and coriander. The smell was delicious, and so was the taste when it was all finally ready to eat without burning their fingers. Cai was given the leftovers, and some bread which was used to soak up the remaining juices in the pan.

Then they sat, backs against smooth boulders, sipping ale happily.

"I suppose I owe you an explanation," Bellicus finally said, and Duro, quite content after his meal, shrugged.

"If you like," he replied. "I expect I'll be finding out your plans soon enough anyway."

Bellicus looked up at the sky, watching a white cloud, out of place amongst the almost uniform grey of the rest, as it floated past. "What I'm about to tell you must never be repeated to anyone," he said at last, and his voice held no trace of amusement or jocularity. The druid was deadly serious now, and the centurion nodded agreement, sitting up to concentrate on his friend's words.

"You can trust me. I know how to keep a secret. Who would I tell anyway – everyone about here wants to arrest us!"

"There," Bellicus said, pointing to where the hill behind them began to slope again, "is where we will be going."

Duro frowned.

"Not up the hill," the druid clarified, seeing the confusion on his companion's face. "*Into* the hill."

A sudden memory of being underground flooded Duro's mind and he felt a momentary stab of fear. His initiation into the mysteries of Mithras had taken place in a subterranean temple beneath the streets of a Gaulish town, and it had been a frightening experience. Few followed the cult by that point, its exalted status amongst the middle-ranking members of Rome's legions no longer as pervasive as it had been in previous centuries, but one of Duro's brother officers was a member and invited him to join.

With an effort, the centurion brought himself back to reality, but the memories of that earlier life made him suddenly feel quite old. "What do you mean, *into* the hill?" he asked, and his voice was gruff.

"Again, I repeat: You must never speak of what I'm about to tell you, to anyone, other than me. And I mean anyone. Not even another druid, do you understand?"

Duro was quite bemused by his friend's warnings and the apprehension showed on his face, but he nodded again. "I swear it, Bellicus. By Mithras, you have my word."

The druid accepted the oath and pointed at the hill again. "There's a secret tunnel, possibly even more than one, that runs beneath Dun Buic," he turned and swept his arm towards Dun Breatann in the middle-distance. "It leads right to the fortress." He held up a hand to forestall the centurion's disbelief. "Trust me – I've walked, or crawled, through it more than once over the years. This is no mere folk tale. The tunnel exists and it will gain us entry to very centre of the Rock, between the two peaks."

Duro's eyes traced the land from where they sat enjoying meat and ale, to the west, and the great volcanic plug that was Dun Breatann, and then he grinned.

"That's incredible," he said, eyes twinkling like a small boy who'd just been given a new toy. Clearly this fantastical new route into the fortress spoke to the centurion's sense of adventure. "And it explains why you wanted that lantern." The excitement faded slightly as he once again traced the route with his eyes and dropped a hand to the hilt of his spatha without noticing he'd done it. "That's a long way to go in a tunnel though. Crawling, you say?"

"Only in some places," the druid said reassuringly. "It looks like the roof has almost caved in at some points, and the rubble only partially cleared, so it can get a little tight." He smiled and patted his stomach. "You've lost most of your baker's fat now though, you'll be fine."

"Gods below," Duro muttered, eyes moving now to the lantern which Bellicus was removing from his pack. "This won't even make a good tale, since I'm not allowed to tell anyone about it. Why is that anyway? And won't the opening be guarded within Dun Breatann?"

"No," Bellicus replied, pouring a small measure of olive oil into the lantern. "You and me are the only two people in Alt Clota, perhaps the whole world, who know of the tunnel's existence, hence my request that you keep it to yourself. Are you ready to go? Or would you like a few moments to prepare yourself? I know some people get frightened within enclosed spaces…No? Good, come on then."

He had used a smouldering twig to set alight to the lantern and it was giving off a good yellow flame now. Even to one that didn't fear the dark, or enclosed spaces, Bellicus knew from past experience that it was a nerve-shredding journey and it might send a man mad if their light died halfway through. "Light one of the candles from our pack," he ordered Duro, and waited for the centurion to comply. Then they headed for the tunnel, Cai at their backs as ever.

"Will he be alright?"

Bellicus nodded. "Cai has been in with me before. I periodically come through the tunnel, to make sure it's still useable and to check the magical wards are in place to stop anyone stumbling upon it by accident. Eolas wasn't so keen," he said sadly, remembering the lean hound that had been killed the very night

Duro had joined him on his quest to rescue Catia. "But Cai...nothing frightens you, does it, lad?" The dog looked up, eyes shining, tongue lolling, and it was as if he was grinning, which made the druid smile in turn.

"If we get lost, I suppose he can lead us out," Duro said but Bellicus shook his head, bending down to lift a section of turf away from the ground.

"We can't really get lost – there's only two ways in or out. The one at Dun Breatann, and this." The grass peeled back easily, revealing a square flagstone about the length of Duro's sword, with a mass of woodlice on top, now scrambling for another hiding place. A rope was threaded through the block and the druid pulled it without much effort, raising the stone which was on a hinge of some sort.

A damp smell wafted out from within the darkness and both men turned away, sucking in one last deep breath of fresh air, before Bellicus led the way down the stairs that were carved into the tunnel wall.

"Mithras protect us," Duro prayed, following the druid and the dog and pulling the flagstone back into position.

"The turf will fall back as well," Bellicus said, face dim in the lantern's weak light. "It's a clever setup, as is the whole tunnel. I'd love to know who built it. Come on."

As the druid had said, the tunnel was a marvel. The lantern revealed stone walls and a ceiling that Duro thought rivalled any Roman constructions he'd seen on his travels in its engineering, although he didn't have time to stop and admire it as Bellicus led the way at a steady pace.

Every so often there would some damage to the structure, and Duro wondered aloud just how long ago the tunnel had been dug, and why.

"Questions we will probably never have answers for," the druid replied, a little gloomily, for he was just as curious as his friend. "But I know that even our best craftsmen could not do a better job, if they could manage it at all. It's remarkable."

"How did you find out about it, if it's such a secret?"

"My predecessor told me," Bellicus said. "Before I took over the position of Druid in Dun Breatann there was a wise-woman acting in a similar role. She was old though, and when I visited one day with my mentor, she must have been informed I would replace her when she passed onto the Otherlands. She showed me the entrance to the tunnel and made me swear an oath to tell my own successor about it."

"Why the secrecy though?" Duro wondered. "If the king knew about this, he might have used it to sally forth when the Picts laid the fortress to siege last summer. Taken them by surprise and crushed them."

Bellicus shook his head dismissively. "Kings come and go. The tunnel is only to be used in the direst emergencies. If everyone knew about it, it would be misused and, eventually, blocked off."

Duro wondered why rescuing Narina was such an emergency, but he held his tongue. The druid knew his business and the knowledge of the tunnel's existence was his to use as he saw fit. Even if he was leading them into a lion's den…

They continued along in silence then, both men imagining the weight of hundreds of tons of rock and earth pressing down on them, half-fearing the ancient tunnel would choose that day to give way and collapse on top of them. Indeed, in places, some of the stones forming the wall or ceiling had fallen, but they had been cleared by someone – Bellicus did not know who, since it had been before his time – and the shaft seemed to have settled into a steady balance that might last for another thousand years, or perhaps only another hour.

There was little point worrying about it, and the two men simply crawled where the rubble was piled too high, and walked, hunched over, when possible.

At last Bellicus placed a finger to his lips and closed the shutter on the lantern halfway. "We're almost there," he said. "I want you to remain at the tunnel entrance with Cai." He raised a hand, cutting off the centurion's angry retort. "It will be much easier for me to get into the prison by myself than with the two of you. To be honest, if we're discovered, that's the whole thing finished anyway, for I can't fight my own people."

Duro frowned but blew out a sigh and grunted agreement.

"Good," said the druid, grasping his friend by the shoulder. "You keep the lantern alight, but shuttered, and await my return. The entrance leads out into the well between the two peaks."

Duro noticed now that the floor around where they were standing was damp, with moisture trickling down from the wall at what appeared to be end of the tunnel, glistening in the weak light cast by the lantern.

"The water level in the well rarely comes up this high," Bellicus said, bending to remove the stone blocks in the wall. "In winter it comes through like this, but most of the time it's fine."

By the time he'd lifted out a dozen or so stones, leaving a hole wide enough for him to fit through, Duro could see the water had drained away, and, relieved, he knew they wouldn't be flooded by tons of water.

"If we're in the well," he asked, frowning, "how are you going to get out into the fortress without getting soaked?"

Bellicus smiled. "The tunnel-builders thought of that, don't worry. A ledge runs around the top of the well and leads to here. It's only a short distance to the entrance, so even at this time of year when the water table is highest, it'll just be my feet that get wet. Unless I slip and fall in."

Duro shuddered at the thought of being immersed in the icy, black water of the well. They would have to seek aid from Coroticus's men if that happened, for it would be a sure death sentence for the druid unless he could be dried and warmed up quickly.

"Don't worry, I won't fall," Bellicus said, reading the concern in the other's eyes. "There's handholds in the wall."

"This all seems very…convenient," the centurion said. "If it's so easy, how come no-one has ever discovered the tunnel by chance? There must be dozens of people using the well every week, every day. Over the course of decades, why hasn't anyone thought, 'I wonder where that ledge with the handholds in the wall leads to?'"

"Think about it," Bellicus replied, shaking his head as if the centurion was stupid. "The well sees no natural light, it's almost pitch black apart from at the very front of the doorway leading in, isn't it? And no-one ever comes snooping about – why would they? It's a well! The ledge is hidden either by the water level or the darkness, as are the handholds which aren't really obvious even if you know they're there." He shrugged and got down onto his stomach. "You ask too many questions for a centurion," he muttered. "Just keep an eye and an ear open for my return. If I'm chased the guards *will* be using their torches to try and figure out where I've disappeared to, so we'll want to get the stones back into the wall as quickly as possible."

"What if you're…caught?" Duro had been about to say 'killed', but they both knew what he meant.

"Put the stones back and take Cai through the tunnel again, to Dun Buic. Then…You should go home to Luguvalium I suppose."

The two friends stared at one another in the gloom and then grasped arms silently. No more needed to be said, and, with a final grin, Bellicus was gone, the sound of his footsteps splashing softly in the water of the well, fading away until there was only silence.

Cai lay on the tunnel floor, eyeing Duro quizzically, and the centurion sat down beside the dog to wait.

CHAPTER TWENTY-EIGHT

Bellicus waited at the entrance to the well for a long time, making sure no-one was nearby, then he opened the iron gate and crept up the short flight of stairs that led onto the level ground between the twin peaks of Dun Breatann. It was dark, with no moon to betray him, although there were of course flickering torches dotted around so the guards could patrol, and he knew he would have to tread carefully.

The prison was located by the north western wall, not far from where he stood now, but first he headed for his own small roundhouse in the opposite direction, making sure to make no sound as he went. The king's great hall was right next to him, but everyone must have been asleep for there were no lights shining through the shuttered windows and no sounds of talking or singing.

The space here between the peaks was not large, so the buildings were all relatively small, with some of them even built on the slope up to the lower summit.

Bellicus stopped outside the small building he had called home for the past nine or so years, wondering if anyone had taken ownership of it since his fall from grace. He could hear nothing though, and, taking a deep breath, he lifted the latch on the door and slipped inside. His eyes were accustomed to the gloom now and he felt the tension ease from his muscles a little as he saw the sleeping pallet was unoccupied. In fact, it looked as if his things were all untouched.

Hidden beneath the bed, in a depression on the ground, was a bunch of keys. They could open every door within the fortress, even the one to the king's own chamber. Coroticus knew they were there, indeed it had been his idea to have them made, in case of emergencies, but it surprised Bellicus that they had not been searched for in his absence. He could only assume the king, and the guards, feared the druid had placed magical wards over the house to stop anyone from defiling it.

"Lug, light my way," he muttered, and went back out into the night, moving like a wraith towards the north-western wall. A light in his peripheral vision stopped him in his tracks and he willed himself to blend into the shadows as the guard on the slope above checked all was well. The soldier stood for what felt like an eternity, and Bellicus expected a cry of alarm at any moment but, at last, the torchlight faded further up the hill and disappeared behind one of the buildings.

Hurrying on again, the druid reached the entrance to the prison. Like the well, it was protected by a door made of iron bars. Unlike the well, this door was locked.

Now came the hard part, for he knew there would be at least one man guarding the prisoners, possibly more, and he could not kill them. Not even to save the queen, or himself. It might be some poor farm boy from Dun Buic, or Cardden Ros, called up by Coroticus to serve in his warband and given this duty tonight.

Praying to Lug once again, he took out the ring of keys and peered at them, wondering which was the right one. The first he tried was too big, as was the second, then the third fitted but failed to turn and the druid had to calm himself for he knew the longer he took, the more chance he'd be spotted. The fourth key turned the lock, thank the gods, and he pushed inside the corridor, closing over the door at his back.

He could hear a man humming to himself in a room on the right, which was lit by, from the smell, a beeswax candle. Bellicus edged towards the light, and began to hum the same tune himself, for he knew it well.

"Is that you already, Sentica?" the guard said, loudly, and Bellicus heard him standing up. "Is it time for your watch already? Ha, it feels like I only just came on duty, I must have fallen asleep if it's near morning already."

Bellicus stepped into the room and faced the guard, a veteran of about forty-five years of age. The soldier's face fell as he realised that he had just admitted, however inaccurately, falling asleep at his post to the king's closest advisor. But then confusion filled his eyes as he remembered the druid was to be arrested on sight.

"My lord. Wait…How did you get in here? What's happening? You're supposed to be—"

Before the man could finally make his mind up about what to do, Bellicus's staff flicked out, the butt catching the guard beneath the chin. There was a clicking of teeth and the soldier fell backwards, tripping over the stool he'd been sitting on just moments before.

The druid took some rope from the wall, handily placed there for tying up prisoners, and used it to bind the dazed man's hands behind his back.

"Forgive me, my friend," the druid muttered, pulling off the guard's woollen sock and stuffing it into his mouth as a gag. "If it's any consolation, I won't tell Coroticus that you fell asleep on duty. Next time, be more alert." Then, as if the soldier was no more than a child, Bellicus bent his legs and lifted his captive with the intention of locking him safely in one of the cells. As he completed the move, though, the druid felt a searing pain in his left shoulder and almost screamed. For a moment he stood, breathing heavily, teeth gritted, cursing himself. All the way to Dunadd and back, fighting off enemies all the way, only to injure himself now.

The pain subsided eventually but Bellicus knew he would have to be careful not to place any more undue strain on that part of his body. He drew in a deep breath and walked along the corridor, peering into each cell as he went.

Narina was in the furthest away, hands gripping the bars of her cell door. She looked pale and thin and her filthy face was streaked with dried tears. Her mouth fell open when she saw the giant druid approaching.

"No questions, my lady," he urged. "Later. First," he pulled back the bolts on the door and threw it wide. As he laid the guard on the ground the man tried to shout something, but a furious glance from the druid – whose shoulder had flared painfully again with the effort – and a threat to curse his bollocks with foul, weeping sores, was enough to shut the man up.

"Can you walk?"

Narina nodded and the druid quickly ushered her out into the corridor. He closed the cell door and bolted it with a final warning glance at the guard who, realising he was thoroughly beaten, slumped onto the floor to await his relief coming in the morning to free him.

"Follow me," Bellicus said softly, leading the way to the prison entrance. "We don't have far to go, and then you'll be safe."

The queen grasped the sleeve of his robe and pulled him back. Even this fairly gentle pressure sent a jolt of pain lancing through his shoulder and he turned to look at her, biting off another pained cry. The last thing he wanted to show the queen was weakness; she needed him to be strong now.

"We can't leave without Catia."

Bellicus shook his head. "I'm sorry, my lady, but we'll be lucky to get out of here with just the two of us in one piece. We must get you to safety first, and then we'll think about what to do about the princess."

"No, Bel," the queen said firmly, refusing to follow him any further. "You've been away for weeks. You don't know what's been happening in your absence. Coroticus has, well, you know what he was like before – he essentially exiled you after all. But he found out about…the truth, about Catia." She looked up at him and the fear was written plainly across her face. "He's gone mad, Bel. So far, he's not done anything to her, but, if I escape, he'll be left with no-one to take out his anger upon."

"You think he would harm Catia? Surely not. He loves the girl, that's what started him down the path of madness in the first place!"

"Exactly! Put yourself in his place, Bel," Narina hissed. "How would you feel if you were him? And bear in mind he's drinking himself senseless most nights so he can't think clearly, and that slut of a serving girl, Enica, is in his ear constantly, turning him against me. Against everyone except herself."

It was too much information to take in properly, considering they might be discovered at any moment, and Bellicus was at a loss how to proceed. The pain in his shoulder was a constant irritation and, as he tried to take things in, he reached into one of his pockets and shook out some fine powder. Taken from the bark of the white willow tree, the druid knew it would mask the worst of his pain, so he swallowed it down with a swig from his ale-skin and wiped his mouth on his sleeve.

"Where is Catia now?" he demanded, but any thoughts of fetching her on their way out were dashed when Narina said the girl would be in the king's house.

"I can't get in there," he said. "Too many guards. Either we go now, the two of us, or…" They stood in silence, facing one another in the dim light from the candle in the guardroom, wishing a solution would present itself. "How did Coroticus find out about all this anyway?" Bellicus finally demanded.

Narina turned away and she wore an expression the druid had never seen on her pretty face before: shame.

"I told him," she admitted. "During an argument. He pushed me too far, I couldn't stop myself." She turned back to him and the old, familiar determination was back. "So you see, Bel, I can't just run away and leave Catia to her fate. This is all my fault."

There was no point in admonishing her for her lack of control, the damage was already done. What were they to do now, though? Should Bellicus simply head back to the tunnel and leave her to untie the guard, who could then lock her away again, as if nothing had ever happened? That was what she wanted, and it would certainly make life easier for the guard but…Maybe he could somehow get inside Catia's chamber and free her. There was still a little time before the sun would rise.

The sound of soft, cautious footsteps came to them then, and they froze, eyeing the doorway as a stocky figure, sword in hand, walked in. Bellicus recognised the man with long brown hair and a grizzled beard that seemed to have more grey in it than just a few weeks earlier.

It was the captain of the guards: Gavo.

"Sulis help us," Narina whispered, staring at the man in despair. "It's all over now."

CHAPTER TWENTY-NINE

"How did you get in here?" Gavo demanded, stepping into the corridor with a glance back over his shoulder. The astonishment was plain on his face, but it soon turned to anger as the thoughts whirled through his head. "Did the gate guards let you in? Those bastards, I'll have them—"

"No," Bellicus shook his head. "I let myself in." He tapped the bronze eagle on his staff. "With my magic."

Gavo shivered and accepted the explanation without question. He knew the guards at the gates, knew they wouldn't have let the druid in without seeking advice from their captain. He also knew it would be impossible for Bellicus to scale the walls without being spotted for the men tasked with keeping watch for invaders were on high alert. The suggestion that magic had been used to gain access to this inner section of the fortress was more realistic than any other to the guard captain.

"Can you magic yourself back outside then? It would save a lot of trouble."

Bellicus smiled grimly. "Sorry, my friend. It's not as easy as that. What will happen to Catia?" he finished, changing the subject.

Gavo didn't answer for a long time, the two warriors just stared at one another and Bellicus realised the captain had no idea what Coroticus might do with the princess. Probably the king himself didn't even know.

At last Gavo seemed to come to a decision and drew himself up, a hard look on his bearded face.

"Where's the guard that was in here? Did you kill him, Bel?"

"Of course not," the druid retorted. "He's in the cell at the back, with a sore face but otherwise unharmed. I came to rescue the queen, not to murder my own people."

Gavo gave a satisfied nod, pleased by the druid's response, and pushed past both Bellicus and Narina, apologising to the queen as he did so, but ordering them both to remain where they were for they were still prisoners.

He reached Narina's former cell and peered through the bars at the forlorn, gagged soldier within, then, shaking his head in disgust, unbolted the door and went inside to cut the man's bonds.

The queen watched Bellicus, hoping or expecting the giant would lock Gavo in and make good his escape, for there seemed only one end to this night now, and it would not be pleasant for any of them. The druid remained where he was though and the captain was soon back outside the cell, the guard at his back, rubbing life into his freed limbs, a purple and yellow bruise starting to appear on his chin.

"Go and rouse the men," Gavo commanded and the guard, still dazed, simply stared at the captain as if he hadn't understood the order. "Give yourself a shake, lad! Go and gather the men, apart from the king's guard and the men on the walls. Wake those who are asleep and tell them to line up outside. Move!"

Finally, the words penetrated the guard's sluggish mind and, with a final, fearful glance at Bellicus, the man hurried off to do as he was told.

"What now?" Narina said, eyes flashing angrily at the captain. "Your loyalty to my husband is commendable, Gavo, but also stupid. You do realise that Coroticus will destroy Alt Clota? The people are close to revolting already."

Gavo sighed but didn't offer a reply. He looked Bellicus up and down, then jerked his head towards the doorway. "Come on, I'm taking you to the king. You can come too, please, my lady."

There was something strange about Gavo's demeanour and, as they emerged from the prison into the cold night air Bellicus wondered if the guard captain's state of mind had been affected by the king's own descent into…what? Madness? Was the king mad, or simply unable to think clearly thanks to his constant drinking? It amounted to the same thing, the druid thought, and it could very well have started to change the way those surrounding Coroticus viewed the world themselves.

Why had Gavo summoned the soldiers after all? Some were already gathering, one or two carrying torches to light the space between the peaks. Was there really any need for an escort of such size? The druid gazed around at those guards, their faces pale and tense, perhaps even fearful—of him, or what might be about to happen, he couldn't say. There must be at least twenty-five soldiers here, practically the entire winter garrison.

Before Bellicus could ponder the matter further, Gavo pointed to the path that wound up the lower, eastern summit. "Lead the way, druid," said the guard captain, and the grim procession, Narina silent and frightened at Bellicus's side, began to walk, the flickering torchlight casting weird shadows all around them.

It was only a short distance, and they were soon standing on the ground outside the king's own dwelling. One man stood guard outside and he appeared confused by the sight of his captain approaching with the unexpected retinue.

"What's happening, my lord?"

Gavo gestured for Bellicus and the rest to stop while he moved forward.

"We've captured the druid," said the captain. "I'm here to give the king the good news."

The guard's confusion turned to embarrassment when he noticed Narina amongst the party gathered before him, and he placed a hand on Gavo's sleeve, restraining the captain from entering the house.

"Maybe we should just, you know…shout for him?" He eyed Narina surreptitiously and Gavo understood his meaning only too well.

But he shrugged off the guard's hand and, muttering to himself, shoved open the door and went inside. Everyone could hear the mumbled conversation as Gavo woke the king. The irritated, groggy tones of Coroticus combining with the captain's low, steady voice and the dancing shadows cast by the torches outside the house to create an atmosphere that was tense and laden with portent.

Eventually Gavo reappeared, and the king followed shortly after. He must have had the presence of mind to throw on his tunic and sword-belt so he would appear before the men with some semblance of dignity, yet, even so, his eyes were bloodshot, and he was still inebriated from the night's carousing.

When he saw Bellicus standing before him, his expression turned dark and he stepped out from the house, walking across to stop just before the druid, who noticed the white, naked body and face of a woman peering out from the shadows just inside the door.

"You came back," Coroticus spat, as Gavo took up a position behind him, hand on his sword hilt.

"Why would I not?" the druid replied. "This is my home."

"You have some nerve," the king said in a low voice. "All these years, acting like my friend and closest advisor, when, all along you—"

"Lord King," Gavo suddenly broke in and Coroticus turned to face him, features flushing red with anger at the interruption. Before he could reprimand him, the captain spoke again. "You told Bellicus he could return to Dun Breatann if he completed the mission you set him. He did so."

Bellicus frowned. What was happening here? What mission? The only task Coroticus had set him was to kill Loarn mac Eirc, and that had been an abject failure.

"Are you king here, or am I, Gavo? Hold your tongue, or—"

"My lord." Gavo spoke over the king again and some of the gathered soldiers began to murmur amongst themselves. Bellicus could detect a hint of excitement in their hushed tones and it saddened him. Did they really want to see their captain disciplined by Coroticus? It seemed poor entertainment to him, but Gavo was continuing to talk, and his words astonished the druid.

"Bellicus killed Loarn mac Eirc, as you commanded, Lord King. You must hold true to your word, and welcome him back within your household. That is the way of it – to do otherwise is to invite the wrath of the gods on us all."

Again, the mutterings of the men, but now Bellicus realised they were agreeing with their captain. What was the man talking about though? Why was he telling the king he'd managed to kill Loarn? Was this some ploy of Gavo's to save the druid and have things go back to normal? For now, he simply remained silent, hoping the gods would lead things to a satisfactory conclusion somehow.

"How dare you talk to me like that?" Coroticus demanded, and pointed to the open-mouthed guard still standing at the door of the royal house. "You. Arrest the captain and toss him in the prison along with the druid and the woman. I'll deal with them in the morning, when I've got my wits about me."

The king threw a final, angry glance at Gavo and the others gathered about, before turning and heading for his quarters again.

The door guard walked towards Gavo, but his step was slow and reluctant and, before he could reach the captain, three of the soldiers in the crowd moved to block his path. The guard halted and looked to the king who had noticed what was happening and appeared just as bemused as anyone else.

"Stand down, Sentica," one of the three soldiers growled and Gavo turned to face the men behind him, confident he wouldn't be arrested any time soon.

"You all know why we're here," he said and Bellicus finally understood that this had been planned in advance. Perhaps not this exact scenario, but some form of coup at least. It seemed Coroticus had finally pushed his people too far, yet Gavo, loyal Gavo, could not bring himself to simply stab the king in the back. He had to do things properly, and he faced the king once more now.

"My lord, we have all been loyal to you over the years, and none more than me. But your position has become untenable. The people see you as unfit to rule over us, and I call on you now to step down, and let Queen Narina take your place as monarch of Alt Clota."

Bellicus felt like he was in some waking dream for, of all the things he imagined might happen one day, faithful Gavo demanding King Coroticus give up his throne was not one of them. It was surreal, and, turning to look at Narina, he could see she was just as stunned by the captain's words. She opened her mouth to protest, no doubt to deny her suitability for the post, but the druid reached out and grasped her wrist, silencing her.

She might not want to rule Alt Clota, but this was their only way out of this situation, and it had to be followed through to the end. They could deal with the aftermath in the days to come.

Coroticus glared at the silent soldiers, but he knew they would not follow his orders if he once again demanded Gavo's arrest. Instead, he turned and walked back inside his house, a move which surprised everyone and saw more than one loosen the swords in their sheaths warily. The king returned a moment later though, and all he had in his hand was a wine skin, which he upended into his mouth as he stood facing them again.

"What will you do if I refuse?" he demanded, glaring at Gavo.

"Please don't," was the low reply and Coroticus drained his wine and threw the empty container at the guard captain.

"If you think I'll give up my throne without a fight, you can think again—"

Once more, Gavo broke in without letting the king finish and Bellicus was impressed with how the captain had guided this whole thing. It might have dragged on half the night and the men lost their early determination to see the thing through to the end if Coroticus had been allowed to talk and question their loyalty and sworn oaths to him. By taking charge, Gavo had steered them to this point, and now the captain had the king right where he wanted him.

"It is your right to fight for the throne, of course, my lord," Gavo said.

"Come on then, you treasonous bastard," Coroticus cried, drawing his sword and setting his feet defensively. The wine he'd downed had worked its magic, and confidence and vitality flowed through his veins now, if only temporarily. "Or is it my wife I'm to fight? I care little – you both fight like women anyway."

"The Queen has the right to choose her own champion," Gavo stated, to nods from the men at his back and a shrug from Coroticus.

Narina had, by now, understood what the captain was doing, and she looked up, meeting the gaze of the giant druid who towered over everyone else gathered there.

"I choose Bellicus as my champion."

The druid opened his mouth to protest. To tell her he had an injury, and suggest she choose Gavo for this fight instead, but, before he could speak, he realised that to refuse the challenge would destroy the moment, and possibly his own reputation. What would he say? "Sorry, my queen, but I've got a sore shoulder, get someone else to fight"?

He looked at the soldiers, all eyeing him grimly, and some of them nodded encouragingly, willing him to beat the king and restore the old normality back to their lands.

He handed his staff to Narina, and drew Melltgwyn.

"How fitting," Coroticus spat, rolling his head from side to side and swinging his sword around as they faced off, loosening his muscles in preparation for the biggest fight of his life. "The man who took my family from me, now wants to take my crown as well."

Bellicus heard confused murmurs from the watching guards and guessed the truth of Narina's imprisonment hadn't been publicly divulged. It made sense of course, the stories would make Coroticus seem like a fool, even if the reality of the situation hadn't been like that at all. How did they get to this place, the druid wondered, when they had all been relatively happy just a couple of years ago?

The king came at him though, and he had to focus on the task at hand. Swinging his sword up, he parried Coroticus's blow and moved to thrust Melltgwyn into his opponent's belly, but his shoulder flared and he had to halt, crying out in pain. The white willow powder had helped, but he was still vulnerable.

Teeth gritted, he saw the king's eyes narrow, then he smiled and came forward again and Bellicus knew his injury had been noted. He tried to call on the battle trance that had saved him so many times in the past but something, perhaps the willow powder, perhaps his own past friendship with the king, stopped it from taking over.

"Perhaps this won't be as easy as my wife assumed," Coroticus growled, raining blow after blow on the druid, who parried each one easily enough but found it impossible to mount any attacks of his own thanks to his reduced mobility.

"You have to beat him, Bel," Gavo called out from the side. Apparently, the guard captain had misread the way things were going and assumed the druid was holding back from a sense of loyalty or friendship. "If you don't, things will go badly for us all."

"He's right," Coroticus said, stepping back and circling around to Bel's left, injured side. "Once I've dealt with you, I'll have to find some suitably nasty punishment for Narina and Gavo, traitors that they are!" He came in again, blade smashing against the druid's with a clatter that echoed back from the walls and buildings of the fortress. The druid saw it coming and was able to bat each attack aside but, again, any time he moved to land a thrust or swing of his own, his shoulder protested, sending a line of fire along his arm and back, and now the soldiers began to mutter nervously.

They hadn't expected things to go like this. Some of them were young, fairly recent recruits brought in to bolster Damnonii forces when Coroticus became more warlike towards the neighbouring peoples, but many were older. They had seen Bellicus fight, and they knew what he was capable of.

They could tell something was wrong but there was nothing anyone could do about it. The fate of the kingdom was in the lap of the gods now.

At last, unable to spin out of the way quickly enough, Coroticus's blade caught the druid on the right bicep, neatly cutting through the dark robe and into the flesh. It was a deep wound and it hurt terribly, but Bellicus kept his sword up to ward off any further attacks. Injured on both sides of his body now, and losing blood, he knew he was in trouble and wondered if this was the gods way of punishing him for sleeping with Narina all those years ago.

No. They would not forsake him for something that was outside his control.

Coroticus grinned and mounted more attacks, but the urgency had gone from his swordplay as he sensed victory and didn't want to make a foolish error just to hasten the end of the fight. All he had to do was keep the druid at bay until he collapsed from blood loss.

"Gavo, help him!" Narina suddenly shouted, drawing the eyes of the soldiers to her. "In the name of Taranis, man, if Coroticus wins we might as well jump over the wall into the Clota below!"

Gavo frowned but shook his head stolidly. "Sorry my lady. No man can interfere in a battle such as this."

"No man?" Narina cried out in disbelief. "What about a woman then?"

Gavo shook his head and made a gesture to the guards behind the queen. They stepped forward and grasped her by the arms as her eyes widened in despair.

"I'm sorry," Gavo said again, eyes flicking from the queen to the mortal battle that was ending so unexpectedly before them. "But the druid knows the old ways – the old traditions – must be observed."

"Damn them," Narina screamed, struggling ineffectually against her captors. "Damn you, you bastard! He'll not stop with us, he'll kill Catia too!" The fight suddenly went out of her and she bent her head, racked with sobs, unable or unwilling to watch, as Bellicus dropped to one knee then forced himself back up as Coroticus came on again. "No man can interfere," she wept. "If only Cai or Eolas were here to help their master."

The king heard her words and they halted his attack. He looked thoughtfully around, as if expecting the druid's dogs to appear. "Where is Cai anyway?" he asked the druid.

There was no reply and, with a shrug, Coroticus attacked again, but this time his blows were faster and harder, spurred to end this once and for all by the thought of Cai perhaps magically appearing at Bel's side. If the druid could get into the fortress, why not his dog too?

Bellicus cried out as he failed once more to properly dodge the edge of his opponent's blade and this time it sliced along his hip, opening another bloody wound. This wasn't as deep as the one on his bicep but, with less muscle to absorb the damage, Bellicus felt it even more keenly.

His head was spinning now from fatigue and blood loss, and he fell again onto one knee, wishing Duro would hear the commotion and bring Cai to help him. The druid wanted to cry out, to call for the faithful hound, but pride kept his mouth shut.

He would rather die than beg for help.

Coroticus pointed his sword at him. "You were the best of friends, Bel," he said, and there was genuine sorrow in his voice as the battle-lust left him. "And that's what hurts the most. That you, and her," he nodded to the queen who had pulled herself together and glared back at her husband now, face streaked with tears but upright and proud, "could betray me as you did."

He looked around at the audience of guardsmen and shook his head bitterly. "I will overlook your part in this night's disgraceful work," he said, for he had no other choice. Threatening the men would only lead them to cut him down. Letting them live, after the gods had favoured him over Bellicus, would hopefully buy some loyalty which, he hadn't fully realised until today, was so lacking.

The druid sighed and fell onto the grass, a dazed look on his normally confident features.

"Have you nothing to say for yourself?" Coroticus demanded as he stepped forward to loom over Bellicus. "I wouldn't expect you to beg for your life, not you. I don't think I'd want you to either." He shrugged and placed his right leg behind him as he drew his sword up over his head. The strong drink was finally taking its toll and he wanted to get this over with. "I sentence you to death, Bellicus. Your gods have forsaken you and recognised my right to rule. May Taranis take you!"

His blade glinted in the torchlight as it reached the height of its swing.

CHAPTER THIRTY

Another voice broke the night air.

"Father!"

The small figure of the princess appeared from within the king's roundhouse, and, nimbly evading the grasping arms of the door guard, Catia sprinted towards the combatants.

The shock of her high voice startled Coroticus and he turned, fury on his face, to upbraid the girl for disturbing him during such a momentous event.

Bellicus saw the girl from the corner of his eye and he mouthed a prayer to Lug, to momentarily blind her so she didn't have to see what was about to happen.

There was no flash of light or other divine intervention though, as the shattered druid gathered what remained of his strength and thrust the tip of Melltgwyn up, forcing the blade deep into Coroticus's belly.

Screaming in agony, the king fell forward, on top of Bellicus who had no strength left to roll out of the way, and the pair collapsed in a heap on the ground as Catia was finally intercepted by one of the soldiers, her terrified cries mingling with those of the fallen men and the shocked queen to create an atmosphere of pure horror on the summit of Dun Breatann.

For a long time, no-one moved and the cries dropped in volume, and then another new voice broke the strange, momentary calm.

"Bel! What's going on? I heard fighting and knew you'd need help."

The guards looked on in confusion as Duro ran up the path, Cai at his side.

"In the name of Dis," one of the senior guards said as they watched the centurion approach his fallen companion. "Can *anyone* just wander in here? It's supposed to be impregnable."

"What have you done to him you bastards?" Duro was furious at the sight of the druid lying on the grass, and he drew his spatha as Cai ran to his master's side.

"Calm yourself," Gavo commanded, waving angrily at the centurion. "Bellicus sacrificed himself to save the queen and all of Alt Clota. He will be remembered as a hero for what he's done."

Duro turned to Narina, who had been released by her guards in order to deal with Catia, and she nodded silent confirmation, too upset to speak.

The centurion, not a native of Alt Clota, so less overawed than the others by the king's presence, bent down and dragged Coroticus's torn body off the unmoving, bloodstained druid. He knelt and placed a hand on Bellicus's shoulder, tears blurring his vision as he mumbled angrily, "Damn you, Bel, you can't die. I don't want to write a song about you too."

There was no response, not even a flicker to suggest his friend had heard him, and Catia began to cry again, hiding her face in Narina's clothes as they held one another for comfort. Then Cai licked a drop of blood from a cut on Bellicus's face and, to everyone's surprise, the druid's eyes fluttered open.

"What took you so long to come and rescue me?" he muttered to Duro. "Next time, don't wait so long."

And then his eyes closed again, and the sobbing grew louder and, as the centurion looked around at the gathered people of Dun Breatann, he realised it wasn't only the womenfolk with tears streaming down their cheeks.

* * *

"What do we do now then?"

It was midday and not a lot had been accomplished since the previous night's momentous events. First, Narina had taken control of the king's house again, throwing out his concubine, the serving girl Enica, and banishing her from Alt Clota. Then the queen had simply gone to bed with Catia by her side and they had slept as best they could while the men cleared up the mess left behind by the fight. When she woke up, word reached her that Senecio had also left Dun Breatann.

Now, Narina sat on a stool beside Gavo and Duro in Bellicus's small roundhouse between the peaks, looking for advice from a man who had almost died just hours before, and still wasn't out of danger given the severity of his injuries. *Look what happened to Loarn mac Eirc*, the druid had thought to himself as he lay on his bed during the night after the guards had carried him there and bound his wounds.

Duro had also listened with amazement as Gavo informed them of the news that had only preceded their appearance in Dun Breatann by a couple of days: the king of Dalriada was dead, the result of an infection from a wound in his hand that spread rapidly throughout his body and resisted all the healing prayers of Bishop Dotha.

A wound that had been delivered by Melltgwyn during the fight in the Dalriadan woods.

"Coroticus should have known better than to stand against you," Gavo said, shaking his head ruefully. "A druid, who somehow got the better of the Saxon *Bretwalda*, and then walked into Dalriada and killed their king before making good his escape."

"I had some help," Bellicus said weakly, just managing a smile in Duro's direction. "On both those adventures."

Gavo nodded and petted Cai, who was lying on the floor by his master's bedside, a post he'd never moved from all night. "Aye, the dog is a fine warrior alright." He grinned at Duro who made an obscene gesture in return.

Their pleasant mood evaporated though, as Narina broke in. "I'm happy everything has turned out well, but I hardly think what's gone on in the past few hours warrants such cheeriness."

"Apologies, my queen," Gavo muttered sheepishly, and Duro made similar sorrowful noises.

Bellicus didn't even attempt to hide his smile. Almost dying on the end of a sword gave a man a new outlook on life, even if only for a short time.

"I ask again," the queen said. "What do we do now?"

All eyes turned again to Bellicus and a small part of him felt irritation, that these people, two veteran soldiers of high rank, and a woman who had been queen for years, looked to him for leadership even as he lay in his sick-bed. Yet this was a druid's lot and, despite his mere twenty-seven years he had trained for situations just like this one.

He marshalled his thoughts and then reached down to stroke Cai's ears, wincing as pain lanced through his arm.

"When we were fighting Loarn mac Eirc, he implied the Saxons were coming to help him take Dun Breatann." Gavo and Narina exclaimed loudly at this bad news and he waved them irritably to silence. "I have no idea if he spoke the truth – he was stalling for time so his soldiers could reach us. Whether it's true or not doesn't really matter," he observed. "We have to make peace with the other kings north of Hadrian's Wall anyway, before they lay siege to Dun Breatann again."

Gavo looked out through the un-shuttered window, at the bluebell shoots that had begun to appear on the grass of the fortress in the past day or so. "Drest will be on his way here soon," he noted. "If he hasn't already started out."

Bellicus would have shrugged if he hadn't known it would be agony. "We will, of course, have to offer him something in return for peace, and as reparation for the men Coroticus killed in the recent skirmishes. But the Picts are not our enemies – the Saxons are the biggest threat to our way of life, and we must make Drest see that."

"And Cunneda?"

"Cunneda too," the druid replied to Narina's question. "We need peace with the Votadini just as much as with the Picts, if we are to defend our lands properly against the Saxons."

"What about the Dalriadans?" the queen asked. "They are without a king thanks to you and Duro."

Bellicus didn't reply immediately for he wasn't sure how to deal with the people on the western shores of the island. It was true they were leaderless, and he knew himself how many of the people in the small fishing villages felt little loyalty to the men wielding power in Dunadd. Would it be worthwhile invading Dalriada while the populace was in disarray, their nobles undoubtedly jockeying for position and possibly the kingship?

He felt too weak, too fuzzy headed, to make such a decision at that moment.

"If Loarn mac Eirc is truly dead," he said at last. "We have nothing to fear from Dalriada, for a while at least. Even if a new man takes the throne tomorrow, he will need to consolidate his position, rather than marching here to join up with Drest and Cunneda."

"So, we make peace with the Picts and Votadini our priority," Gavo said, and the others nodded, sensing the wisdom in Bellicus's words. "If they will listen. I can see such a peace costing us very dearly though, druid. They will want sheep, cattle, slaves, gold…Anything they can get!"

"Better that, than losing dozens – hundreds – of men, fighting meaningless battles brought on by Coroticus in a drunken madness, surely?"

Narina was fidgeting, poking at the dry skin on her fingertips, but she spoke now, lending her weight to the druid's words. "Enough of our people have died senselessly, Gavo. You know this yourself. If we can unite the kingdoms the Saxons will find us a more difficult enemy to defeat when they make their inevitable way north to these lands."

"You think they are coming?"

Bellicus grunted. "Aye. If not now, they will come eventually."

"I do not think Drest will accept peace with us," Narina sighed, standing and walking over to look out on her fortress, which looked beautiful to her in the bright morning sunshine. "He's been preparing for war all winter, and Alt Clota is a prize he covets greatly." She turned back to Bellicus. "I saw it in his eyes when they had us under siege the last time."

The druid met her gaze and pursed his lips. "Then we must prepare for the worst."

They sat in the little roundhouse in silence then, pondering the future, and the past, and finding more questions than answers on the banks of time's ever-flowing river.

What would the coming year bring? Only the gods could say, Bellicus thought, but, as he looked around the room – at Gavo, and Cai, and Duro, and Narina – he knew Dun Breatann was, for the first time in months, in good hands once again.

Their enemies would not find them wanting when spring came.

If you enjoyed *Song of the Centurion* **please** leave a review on Amazon and/or Goodreads.
Every single one really helps me out, and they are all HUGELY appreciated.

Also, if you'd like a **FREE** Forest Lord short story, sign up for my email list at https://stevenamckay.com/free-forest-lord-story/ and get "The Rescue" delivered straight to your inbox.
I regularly run competitions to win signed books and Audible downloads
and I promise not to spam you constantly.

Thank you so much for reading!
Steven

AUTHOR'S NOTE

Song of the Centurion has been a strange book for me to write. I started it not long after I completed *The Druid* but at that time I had an agent who was trying to find a big publisher for the series. So what should I do? I could start work on *Song of the Centurion* only for a publisher to come in and tell me they wanted *The Druid* completely changed, and then where would that leave the sequel? I might have written a full novel that would need reworked. It seemed pointless. But sitting on my hands doing nothing for months wasn't an option.

So I set aside the 30,000 words I had written for *Song* and spent 2018 writing a standalone novel, *Lucia*.

The Druid never was picked up by a publisher and I parted ways with my agent to self-publish the series. And then I managed to sell *Lucia* to Audible! Around the same time, I was hired to write some things for a secret project which is really exciting, but I'm forbidden to talk about it for now…

So, between working on *Lucia* with Audible and writing pieces for the Secret Project, I've also spent this year, 2019, completing *Song of the Centurion*. Hopefully it reads well despite all the other distractions. Incidentally, I recorded a demo version of the titular song which you can find on YouTube. One day I'll do it with flute and vocals and acoustic guitar, when I find time…

Although I like to make my novels historically 'accurate' or at least as realistic as possible, one thing I added here is the tunnel leading from Dun Buic to Dun Breatann. Is this a real thing? Maybe. Almost twenty years ago I worked in Dumbarton Castle as a steward, and my manager at the time liked to collect any gossip or folklore about the area from locals and visitors. Generally, I liked to hear ghost stories, but I remember her talking about this tunnel that led between the two great volcanic rocks that dominate Dumbarton – the castle and the modern-day quarry at Dumbuck. I have no idea where she heard the tale, but it really captured my imagination and it seemed like the perfect way for Bellicus to enter what is, otherwise, an impenetrable fortress. Could it be real? I don't know, but I do know there are caves in the area, one of which apparently hid William Wallace hundreds of years later, when the English were after him. If it was good enough for Braveheart, why not Bel?

My next book, as far as I know, will be part three in this Warrior Druid of Britain series. Bellicus, Duro and Narina will have to deal with the Dalriadans and Picts, but those pesky Saxons are, of course, growing in power in the south and Arthur and Merlin will need some help soon. I hope you will join them all in their continuing adventures. Who knows what will happen next? I certainly don't!

Steven A. McKay,
Old Kilpatrick,
August 2019

CONCEPT ART by Robert Travis

DURO

BELLICUS

Printed in Poland
by Amazon Fulfillment
Poland Sp. z o.o., Wrocław